Bargaining with a Rake

JULIE JOHNSTONE

Julie Johnstone

BARGAINING WITH A RAKE

Cover Design by Tammy Falkner

ISBN: 978-1482309423

By Julie Johnstone

Dedication

For my husband for putting up with the long hours.
For my children for putting up with my distraction.
And for the original historical critique group ~ Amy,
Gayle, Heather, Jerrica, Jodie, Michelle and Tammy.
Without your guidance, encouragement and help I would
have been lost.
~ Julie

One

London, England
The Year of Our Lord 1817

LADY GILLIAN RUTHERFORD WAS either going to faint or scream.

The chatter of the crowd roared in her ears. She blew out a frustrated breath and snapped her fan open. Whoever had been in charge of the guest list at this ball had been deep in their cups when they sent out the invitations. The guest list was too large by half.

A booted foot crushed her toes, proving her point. "Beg pardon, my lady."

Gillian smiled at the footman as she plucked a glass of lemonade from his tray. "Think nothing of it." Beads of sweat dripped from his forehead. *Poor fellow.* At least she could take refuge on the terrace in the cool breeze. Except, of course, not just yet.

As notes of music picked up in volume and somewhat drowned the hum of gossip, she glanced longingly at the open double doors. Four gazes met hers at once. She cursed herself for forgetting to avoid the stares of the pinch-faced matrons who'd been less than adept at hiding the fact that they were talking about her. Instantly, gloved hands covered whispering mouths.

She hid her snort behind her fan. If these were Society's finest, then she would rather consort with the poor any day of the week.

This would not do. Not at all. If she stuck to this tactic of finding her prey, the ball would be over before she knew it. Why was this so difficult? She craned her neck to see around a large man in need of a good lecture on the wisdom of not over indulging in sweet meats and pies. How hard could it be to locate an American who was supposed to be a good head taller than the average Englishman?

She turned to search through the crowd once again; her effort was rewarded with a new set of stuffy matrons giving her quizzical looks. *Hmm.* At least she seemed to be improving in Society's esteem since open disdain no longer lingered on their faces. She pasted on a fake smile as she scanned the lords and ladies.

Where was the blasted American? Maybe Mr. Sutherland was on the terrace. He was supposed to be brilliant, after all. Surely, a man smart enough to build a shipping empire would seek refuge from the oppressive heat in this over-stuffed room.

She didn't need any further excuse to get fresh air. Almost giddy with the thought of escape, she swiveled toward the terrace and cringed. *Blast.* Her father stood directly in her path to freedom. *How utterly typical.*

Yet, for once, his disapproving stare was not focused on her. She followed his line of vision past her Aunt Millicent to the champagne-laden tray passing just out of his reach. *Blessed be the ton and their need to display their wealth and frivolousness. Oh! And blessed be Father for being predictable,* even if the predictability did include drunkenness and coldness.

She was smart enough to know when retreat was in order. She whirled on her heel and headed in the direction of the card room. If the gossip sheets were correct, Mr. Sutherland could very well be in the gaming room. Three steps into her flight she stopped in her charge and ground her teeth on the terrible words she wanted to say.

Of all the ill luck. Harrison Mallorian lounged against the very statue she would have to pass to get to the card room. He brushed a lock of his white-blond hair out of his eyes and lifted his hawk-like nose as he spoke to the glazed-eyed gentleman who stood beside him. Luckily, he did not see her yet.

Mr. Mallorian, with his lecherous gaze and roaming hands, was the last person she wanted to encounter. She'd barely escaped being accosted by him the last time she encountered him in the village, and she'd overheard gossip by the maids that a tavern wench had not been so lucky.

Gillian's stomach rolled at the thought. She'd seen the wench just last week, heavy with child and no husband. But Mr. Mallorian roamed around without repercussions. The maids said there was no proof, but it was more than a lack of witnesses. The wench was lower than a commoner, so her word would never stand against Mr. Mallorian's.

Between her father and Mr. Mallorian she was trapped in this room with no escape. Except... She studied the dark corner where long red velvet curtains covered a window and formed a crimson puddle on the floor. It was the perfect place to hide until they moved to another room.

She shouldn't. It was scandalous. The very idea that she was worried about her name being associated with scandal made her giggle. Thank goodness, a young fop was now entertaining the staring matrons, so they had forgotten her for this moment. She'd hate to add suspicions of lunacy to the taint associated with murder on her first day back in Society.

She moved toward the shadowy alcove with a glance to see if anyone had observed her. For the moment, no one gawked. Taking a deep breath, she scurried into the dusty darkness.

Her heavy breathing filled the cramped space. How was it possible that it was hotter in here? What if she swooned and fell into the crowd? Father really wouldn't like that. The *ton* would be ablaze with talk about the Duke of Death's odd daughter who hid behind curtains at balls. She could picture the next ball. Gone would be the attempts at hushed whispers and sideways glances.

She and her sister would be laughed right out of the ballroom. Gillian cared little for herself, except it would make meeting Mr. Sutherland extremely hard. But to imagine Whitney being ostracized made Gillian ache. She gulped down her lemonade and groaned. Men had to have had a hand in the latest fashion. No woman would have designed so many layers. The silk suffocated her. Her chemise already clung to her damp skin. She rubbed her temples. Some escape plan this was. She glared at the corner that confined her.

Breathing seemed to be harder behind the curtains. She reached to part the heavy material, but the velvet suddenly opened, and light from the ballroom split the darkness. A man plunged into the alcove and yanked the curtain closed behind him. She drew in a sharp breath as a warm hand clamped over her mouth.

"No need to scream," a baritone that promised nothing but trouble ordered. "I assure you I mean you no harm."

She pushed his hand away. "I feel completely better now. I bet all murderers assure their victims the same thing before slitting their throats."

"Well, if I was going to kill you, which I'm not, I certainly wouldn't do it in the middle of a ball, and I would kill you with pleasure."

She frowned at the odd statement. "Fine. I won't scream, and you may go."

"I'm sorry," the man said in a voice that indicated he was anything but. "I didn't realize you owned this curtain."

"You're funny. Run along and display your wit for a debutante that cares."

"Interesting twist," he said with a laugh.

"I beg your pardon?" She tried to instill a frosty note of warning into her tone.

"Don't worry, kitten. I want to play. You're the innocent and I'm the pursuer, right?" He grasped her gloved hand. "I bet you get a hundred marriage proposals this season with that sweet disposition."

She jerked her hand away. "I don't need a hundred." *Insufferable* man. He'd irritated her into saying too much.

When his fingers gently glided over her waist, she jerked away and pressed as far against the window ledge as she could manage.

"I like your commitment to the ruse." Husky tones vibrated his voice. "Got one special fellow in mind, do you?"

Thank God, it was too dark in here for this man to see her face. Her cheeks burned from the blood gathering under her skin. "You're not very astute, sir."

"Is he meeting you in here?" His deep chuckle filled the space at the same moment he brushed her hair back from her face.

"Stop that!" She slapped at his fingers, but he didn't release his hold on her hair. The grind of the strands between his fingers grated in her ears.

"Good God," he whispered. "I'm sorry. I thought you were someone else."

"And my hair alerted you to your mistake?" Gillian allowed disbelief to color her words.

"She has short hair," he ground out. "It was an honest mistake. I must have the wrong curtain."

Likely story. Still, what was the point of arguing? Men of the *ton* were lecherous creatures, and this man had just proven what she had learned years ago. "I'm glad we've cleared things up. If you would be so kind as to quickly leave the way you came."

"I'll be gone as soon as I can. I can't just barge back out there."

"Worried about your reputation?"

Hands came on either side of her waist; his warm breath caressed her cheek. "No. I'm worried about the marriage noose."

With the shock of being so close to this man, it took a moment for her brain to register what he said. When she did, she tried to shove him away, but her hand met corded steel. He was certainly no dandy. And clearly trouble. Trouble, she already had plenty of. "You have no worries from me. I don't want to marry you any more than you want to marry me."

He chuckled, low and deep. "I'm relieved."

"Lovely. Now off you go."

His hands came to cup her face, shocking her with their warmth. Smooth fingertips touched her eyelids, her cheeks, and stopped on her lips. Her heart hammered in her ears. His fingers brushed over her mouth once before her senses crashed back into reality, and she smacked his hands away.

"What are you doing?"

"Making sure I don't know you. Are you *sure you* aren't following me?"

"How could I be following you? I was here first, you pompous—"

A finger pressed against her lips. "Ladies don't curse."

She brushed his fingers aside. "And gentleman take their leave when asked."

"Good point," he replied and split the curtain once again. Light washed over his back and head, revealing thick black hair and outlining broad shoulders. The curtain dropped back into place and covered him in darkness once again.

"My lady," he murmured, stepping toward her until his breath washed over her face once again. He smelled of whiskey and cigars. *That figured.* Strange it didn't repel her as it did when her father or one of his drunken friends forced her to endure conversation with them.

Before she could say anything, the stranger grasped her gloved hand and whisked the shield of material away. His mouth touched her skin, hot and searing. As his lips left a feathery kiss, her world tilted and her breath exhaled in a slow hiss. "It was a pleasure to meet you. I'd wish you luck in the marriage hunt, but—"

"You don't believe in luck," Gillian interrupted.

"Wrong. I don't believe you need it."

He was gone before she could reply. She pressed a hand to her pounding heart. *Typical English scoundrel.* She took a breath and focused on what she needed to do. A quick peek between the curtains let her know all was safe. She scurried out of the darkness with her lemonade glass still clutched in her hand.

As a butler passed, she stopped him and set the glass on the tray. She ran a self-conscious hand through her hair. She needed to regain her confidence and find Mr. Sutherland. She glanced around, searching for him. But her search stopped at the sight of a man who stood to the side of the terrace doors.

He had jet-black hair and broad shoulders. Something fluttered in her stomach. Was that the stranger from the curtains? His wink and smug smile left little doubt.

Dressed head to toe in black save his shirt and untied snowy white cravat that hung negligently from his neck, he appeared every bit as dangerous as he had sounded behind the curtain.

He possessed a rugged beauty with his bronze skin, untamed curls, and coat cut expertly to mold across the broad expanse of his shoulders. Her pulse hummed in remembrance of the muscles hidden beneath the coat.

He faced her, his eyes crinkling with amusement. Raising his champagne in the air, he saluted her and then downed the drink. He bowed in her direction, his gaze never wavering from her face. When he smiled, her lips pulled into a reluctant grin at his show.

No doubt, he'd practiced that smile on at least a hundred debutantes. He cocked his head to the side, as if he knew her thoughts, before starting across the room.

Was he going to find the woman he had been intending to meet behind a curtain? She glanced around the ballroom. There were at least a dozen windows with similar treatments. Good luck to him and the poor woman whose heart he would undoubtedly break.

Gillian turned to make her way around the edge of the ballroom to the terrace, but her gaze traveled back to him. He had stopped in the center of the room and stood speaking with a flame-haired woman who gripped his arm. Was she the woman he'd been searching for? She did have short hair. She was pretty in a cold sort of way, like a lovely bauble that was good for nothing but admiring for its beauty. Gillian gave herself a mental shake. It wouldn't do to be petty and judgmental.

The man's beautiful face became dark and fierce. He reached for the woman's hand, his irritation evident in the way he pried her fingers away. A reticent smile touched his lips as he executed a perfect bow to the red-haired woman, winked at Gillian and turned on his heel, making his way quickly through the crowd and disappearing through the terrace doors.

Well, she certainly could not search the terrace now. The stranger seemed just pompous enough to think she really was following him. She had wasted enough time standing here watching him like a fool. Time she had no right to waste.

She wove among guests, smiling as if she hadn't a care in the world. No one stopped her to introduce themselves, but then she hadn't been under any false assumption she, her sister, or her father would be warmly welcomed back into the bosom of the *ton*.

They may have lived as recluses for eleven years, but it had taken less than a minute to realize the *ton* had not forgotten the scandal or the speculation that Gillian's father had killed her mother. The four looks of disdain had been her first clue. And the two direct cuts and two silly debutantes who had stared in wide-eyed fear at her and her family had confirmed her suspicion. Whoever had sent the note threatening to expose her sister's role in their mother's death was not the only one who clearly remembered the past. Hopefully, the villain would be the only one trying to use it to keep them out of Society.

That was what he or she—after all the villain could be a villainess—wanted. The note had said so. *Don't return to Society or I will expose your sister.* The villain had to be someone who knew them—or Father, to be more precise, since he had surprised everyone by announcing two weeks ago he planned for them to return to Society. Or the villain could be one of the staff.

She ground her teeth. She'd been through all this already. Whoever the villain was, and whatever the reason the fiend wanted her family to stay recluses in the country, the person was a complete dolt. She had no control over her father. She had begged, pleaded, even conjured up tears, but Father had been resolute in his decision to drag them all back into the *ton*. Not even the threatening letter had swayed him. For a moment, she thought she'd convinced him, but then he'd gone and shocked her.

Father and his counterattack plans. Her head ached just thinking about his plan to marry her and Whitney off as quickly as possible, so if a new scandal did break they would already be wed.

Gillian neared the edge of the ballroom and paused when she spotted her sister standing to the left of the door in a row of forlorn-looking young women. Father was a bigger dolt than whoever was threatening them. No Englishman was going to offer for her or Whitney. Let alone dance with them. She crumpled her empty dance card into a small wad. The starchy lot of Englishmen would be far too worried marriage to the daughters of a man suspected of murder would taint their bloodlines with some unseen insanity. And if the men weren't worried, their mothers would certainly be concerned enough to not allow any such match.

Gillian gazed across the faces of the women who composed the line of wallflowers. The proof of her belief was in the line of beautiful women. Nothing was wrong with their looks. One of them had a drunkard for a father. One had a brother with a gambling problem. One had a sister who had lowered herself by marrying outside of the *ton*. And Lady Emma's father was a merchant. *The horror*! Her heart twisted when she got to Whitney.

She raised her hand and waved to get Whitney's attention. Her face lit up when her eyes met Gillian's. She rushed away from the other women with a backward glance. Gillian braced herself against displaying her worries or concerns. Whitney was blissfully unaware of the threatening note, and if Gillian could help it, her sister would remain unharmed by the foolish notions of the *ton*.

Whitney reached Gillian within seconds and clutched her arm. "Have you been dancing?"

Gillian fingered the crumpled dance card in her hand. "No. More importantly, have you?"

"Not yet." Whitney bit her lip. "Do you think it's this dress?"

She eyed her sister's white lacy confection. She looked perfect, like innocence on the verge of allure. *Not the dress, for certain.* It was their name, and it always would be. "You look lovely."

"If I look lovely, why not one request for a dance?"

"Because you are so breathtaking they are afraid to approach you," she assured Whitney. Finding their aunt was a priority. Surely she had enough sway to get at least one gentleman to dance with Whitney. Gillian wanted to skin all Englishmen. If she'd had any doubts about meeting and seducing Mr. Sutherland, they evaporated as Whitney's eyes filled with tears.

"Don't cry like a goose. I had no idea you pined to dance so."

Whitney sniffed and dried her eyes. "Don't you?"

The only thing she pined for was a one-way ticket out of England for herself and Whitney. If a dance could reduce her sister to tears, what would social ruination and the ugly truth do to her? She smiled indulgently. "Of course, I pine to dance," she lied.

"Gillie, there's an angry-looking woman headed towards us."

Gillian quickly turned and faced the crowd behind her. The redhead who'd been talking to the pompous Englishman stalked toward her. By the twisted look on the woman's face, her temper matched the color of her hair.

Gillian gave Whitney a little shove toward the refreshment table. "I'm feeling faint. Will you get me some lemonade?"

"I knew you were acting odd. I'll be right back." At least Whitney would be safe from the taint of a scene if it came to that. Surely the woman didn't think Gillian had set her cap on the Englishman.

The woman stopped directly in front of Gillian, spearing her with a slanted green gaze. "I thought I recognized you. You can't imagine the gossip your family's reappearance into Society has caused."

She could imagine quite a lot of things at this moment, but none of them were very ladylike. She pasted a smile on her face, though she doubted she looked friendly. "I'm afraid you have me at a disadvantage, as you know me, but I do not know you."

"I'm Lady Staunton. You no doubt recognize my name."

"I'm afraid not. But I haven't been in Society in a very long time. I am surprised, though, that the *ton* so lacks for entertainment they are reduced to speculating about age-old rumors regarding my family." That she professed the lie without so much as a quiver in her voice was an immense relief.

Lady Staunton smiled falsely. "But the mystery was never solved, now, was it? So the rumors are still delicious, and I hear you've the exact look of your mother. I've seen for myself you have her wandering eye."

So this was about the man. Blast him. She should have known he would cause her trouble. "I'm not sure what you mean," she said while she cursed *Lord Pain in the Neck* in her mind.

Lady Staunton gave Gillian a look that said they both knew Gillian was lying. "You should not stare at every handsome man you see, my dear."

"I only return the stares I receive, Lady Staunton. Now, if you will pardon me. I think I see my father beckoning me."

"I can see you're in need of some friendly advice," Lady Staunton said as she gripped Gillian's arm.

Beads of sweat dripped down Gillian's back. She eyed the gaggle of men and women who had stopped talking to gape at her and Lady Staunton. She could make a scene, but that would serve no purpose and would undoubtedly make matters worse for her family. "I'm all ears, Lady Staunton. I never turn down advice from my elders." Gillian smiled sweetly as she delivered the pointed barb.

Lady Staunton's lip curled back most unbecomingly. "Stay away from Alex."

"Who?"

"Don't play innocent with me," Lady Staunton snapped. "I saw him raise his champagne glass to you. Bow to you."

Gillian ground her teeth on a growl of frustration. It was just like a man to cause trouble and disappear. A black head flashed up ahead just as a man slipped through the wide doors that led to the entrance hall. That thick, wavy black hair was unmistakable. "Lady Staunton," Gillian said, struck with inspiration, "I have no interest in the man you are referring to, but if you wish to pursue him, I believe I just saw him rushing out of the ballroom toward the entrance hall."

"Really?"

Lady Staunton turned and fled before Gillian could answer her question. Gillian breathed out a shaky sigh of relief. Finally, she could search for Mr. Sutherland. She turned on her heel and nearly toppled into her fiercely frowning father.

Two

ALEX STRODE THROUGH THE milling throng of guests, not bothering to slow to speak to those who signaled him. If he didn't know Lady Staunton so well he'd think his mind was playing tricks on him, but unfortunately he knew her very well. Or he once had. That was definitely her voice calling behind him. She had always been the sort to believe no man could resist her, and it still smarted to think he had once given credence to her belief. He pretended not to hear her and lengthened his stride. The last thing he wanted was another encounter with her tonight.

He slowed his steps only when he reached the door to freedom. He signaled to the somber-faced servants standing ready near the door, and they scrambled to open it for him, their dark green and gold liveried coattails flying out behind them in their haste.

The heavy, dark doors swung open with a creak to reveal the black night beyond the mansion. Not even Lady Staunton was brazen enough to run after a man into the night. For a moment, he reconsidered when he recalled just how brazen she could be, but her husband was inside. Surely that would cause her to be more delicate in her pursuit.

His shoes tapped a descent against the marble staircase as the music of the waltz faded behind him. A sense of release seized him the moment the false twitters of the ballroom ceased. Before he reached the beginning of the pea-gravel drive, his coachman pulled to a halt directly in front of him.

"Was the evening good, my lord?"

"It was a ball," Alex replied, looking up at Jenkins.

"Ye need say no more. I know what ye think of those."

Alex bloody hated them, but his mother had begged his help in watching over Lissie, and he could not very well let his favorite sister down. And when he made the date to meet the willing and luscious Lady Beth behind the curtain, the ball hadn't seemed so tiresome, until he'd picked the wrong curtain.

A reluctant smile of admiration pulled at his lips. Whoever the black-haired beauty was who had emerged looking as innocent as a child from behind the curtain certainly had spunk. And a grand ability to verbally spar. Too bad she appeared to be a debutante. He drew the line of wickedness at innocent virgins.

He jumped into his carriage and rapped on the ceiling. "Take me to the docks, Jenkins."

Jenkins' ruddy face appeared upside down in the window, his brown hair hanging in a comical pointed fashion. "Do ye mean yer office or the Devil's Tavern?"

"The Devil's Tavern, good man. Sutherland's just in from America."

"Delayed, was he, my lord?"

"Three full nights. No doubt he's livid."

"Yer partner stayin' awhile this time?"

"I suspect so. We're buying another ship."

Jenkins smiled; then his face vanished, but his loud whistle drifted down to Alex's ears. "A celebration, then, is it?"

"Certainly," Alex said and stretched his legs out in front of him.

"Might I remind you, my lord, last time ye two gents bought a ship, the celebration got a mite too rowdy."

Alex grinned up at the roof of his carriage. "You're entirely too familiar for a driver."

"Aye, my lord. That's why you like me."

That was true, but he'd not admit it to Jenkins.

"How many ships does this make, my lord?"

"Twelve."

"I'll be getting a raise, then?"

"I suppose," Alex said with a chuckle, and then settled back against the cushion and closed his eyes while breathing deeply of the cool night air. He needed to clear his mind and concentrate on business, but the scent of magnolias drifted around him from the Devons' enormous garden, and the fragrance had him smiling.

The cheeky chit from the curtains had smelled flowery. Why in the devil would a debutante be hiding behind a curtain waiting to meet a man? Didn't she know she was courting ruin? Maybe she wanted to be ruined. *Likely*, given how a woman's mind worked. The notion of the tart-tongued woman as a schemer didn't fit. Maybe she'd been convinced by some scoundrel to meet him behind the curtain? Alex sat up with the insane impulse to go back, find the woman and make sure she was fine. He paused with his hand on the door.

He was a scoundrel. What was he thinking? She would doubtfully take any advice from him, however well intended. He sat back with a growl. What had come over him? He knew better than to involve himself with debutantes. They wanted husbands, not rakes to introduce them to the pleasures of the body. "Jenkins, what the bloody hell, man? *Go.*"

The door to the carriage flew open. His younger brother Cameron bounded through the entrance and snatched the door closed behind him, looking like a hunted bandit with his mussed hair and a darting gaze. Cameron tapped the carriage ceiling with his cane. "Go, Jenkins. Before the women run out to catch a rare glimpse of Lord Lionhurst. They'll tear me to pieces just to get at him."

"Amusing as always, I see," Alex growled as the carriage jerked to a start.

Cameron grinned in return. "I do try. Now tell me what induced you to break your vow."

"My what?"

"I seem to recall you swearing you would never attend another ball under your own devices again," Cameron said, clutching at the seat as Jenkins took them around an especially sharp curve.

"Mother," Alex said simply. Really he need say no more. Cameron was her son too, after all.

"Ah." Cameron nodded. "That explains everything. So this is a one-time favor?"

"Unfortunately, no," Alex replied, something black and sharp curling in his gut when he considered the possibility that he would have to encounter Lady Staunton again. "Mother has asked me to keep an eye on Lissie as she enters Society."

Cameron's eyebrows came together. "Why didn't she ask me? She knows you hate Society, and I love it."

"I suppose Mother doesn't trust that your attention will stay on Lissie and off whatever pretty face happens by you."

"You offend me."

Alex laughed. "Really? Why? You know it's true."

"I can be just as focused as you."

Alex considered the fact that he had told Lady Beth he'd meet her behind the curtain tonight. But he had only agreed to the secret encounter once he'd known Lissie was safely ensconced in their parents' carriage and on her way home. "I've more control," he said with a smile. "You would have been behind the curtain with some lady embraced in your arms while Lissie was still at the ball."

"Beg pardon?" Cameron said, looking like a bobbling head as the carriage bounced and jerked.

"Never mind," Alex replied testily as the carriage swayed down the road. Jenkins had clearly imbibed in some drink while waiting for Alex to leave the ball. Not that he blamed the man. It was a damned cold night. But Alex didn't want to end up overturned because his driver had drunk too much. A gentle reminder should do.

"I don't see how it's absolutely necessary you attend every ball Lissie goes to this season," Cameron said.

Alex studied his brother's frowning face. "Exactly how does my attending a few balls cause *you* any distress?"

"Five out of ten women who stopped to talk to me tonight wanted to talk to me about *you*."

"Ah, I do apologize for being the cause of your pride

taking a blow."

"As you should." Cameron let go of his seat cushion long enough to jerk his coat down and smooth out a few wrinkles. "I know I'm devilishly handsome." He flashed a perfect smile. "But I was starting to wonder tonight whether my looks are fading."

Alex struggled to hold in his laughter. Sometimes reading Cameron was difficult. His brother could be joking or he could be completely serious. He had been known to be sensitive, relegated as he was to the slot of youngest brother.

"You're not ugly *yet*," Alex said, deciding to reply with an answer that could be considered serious or facetious. "But you may want to slow down. Too much wine and women is bound to age any man."

"I don't think so," Cameron replied. "Look at you. Almost three and twenty, never married, and God alone knows how many women you've bedded and how much whiskey you've drank."

"I'm an exception to the rule," Alex replied, suddenly wishing to change the course of the discussion. "Besides, I'm only bedding one woman right now."

"Yes, the lovely Bess. How is your mistress? Attached, are you?"

"I do not form attachments, and you know it." He hadn't meant to snap the words, but each one resounded in the carriage.

"Settle down, old man. I wasn't implying you had softened in your view of women."

Alex scrubbed a hand across his face to hide the scowl pulling at his lips. "Sorry. It's been a long night."

"Yes," Cameron nodded. "I saw Lady Staunton ensnare you briefly. And then I saw you streak out of the ball as if the devil chased you."

Alex did laugh then. "More like a witch. Vile woman."

"Listen," Cameron said as he leaned forward in his carriage seat. "You should know that Bess is saying the two of you have a relationship with many strings."

Alex studied the river as they passed it. He'd have to talk to Bess. He'd thought she understood. Splendid. He did not want to hurt her, but he couldn't allow her to think there was more to their understanding than simply pleasure.

Cameron propped his feet on the seat next to Alex's leg. "So you don't care for Bess at all? I thought perhaps you had thawed a bit when I heard the news."

With a quick shake of his head, Alex shoved Cameron's feet away before leveling his brother with a narrow-eyed warning. "Don't be ridiculous."

The carriage jerked to a stop, and Alex glanced out the window to make sure they were at the Devil's Tavern. No telling where Jenkins might have taken them if he had drunk as much as it seemed. The peeling red paint and the broken black shingles of the dock's most famous drinking establishment told Alex they'd arrived just where he intended. He threw open the door and stepped onto the stairs. "Jenkins," he bellowed.

His driver popped down to the ground. "Sir?"

"Not so much whiskey next time, no matter how bloody cold it is outside."

"Aye." Jenkins had the grace to look properly humbled, though his coachman knew it would take a disaster for Alex to fire him. He had a soft spot for his driver, the man being the only one who had any inkling just how hard Alex's older brother's death had been.

Alex descended the carriage, Cameron close behind him. Cameron didn't speak, but the mumbling under his breath was clear enough. The lights from the tavern illuminated his younger brother's troubled face. Alex sighed. "You've something else to say, I take it."

Instead of answering, Cameron shifted back and forth, making Alex uneasy. Cameron was normally blunt to a fault. A ship's bell rang from the river, signaling its entrance into the Thames, followed by a raucous cheer erupting from within the belly of the tavern. "I need a drink," Cameron muttered.

"Then by all means let's make haste," Alex said, taking that as a signal that Cameron was not going to say anything after all.

Cameron shook his head. "My confession's best given out here in private."

The muscles in Alex's body tensed in response to the

word *confession.* "In my experience it's best to keep confessions to yourself. They rarely have the effect you desire." They both knew whom Alex was speaking of. They seldom mentioned their dead older brother, though Robert occupied a place in Alex's thoughts daily.

"Mother's asked me to watch you," Cameron said, having the decency to sound sorry about the matter.

"My, she's been busy. She convinced me to watch Lissie, but I suppose that was a guise so she could get me where she wants me and keep me under her scrutiny."

"Oh, I think her asking you to watch Lissie is genuine. She doesn't trust me to diligently guard Lissie's honor, I suppose. But since your honor was misplaced some years ago, my educated guess is she concluded I'd do to watch you."

"I wonder when she'll quit trying to manipulate me into marriage."

Cameron shrugged. "Don't be too hard on her. She *is* worried about you. So worried, in fact, that you have taken precedence on her reform list over Father's drinking."

"Dear God, I'm number one on her list?"

Cameron nodded.

"Well, *that* is something to worry about. I'll have to inform Mother tomorrow that you may well get the pox if you don't reform *your* ways."

"You wouldn't dare. She'd perish on the spot if her sainted ears heard the word 'pox.'"

Alex turned on his heels, relishing the worried look on Cameron's face. He'd let him worry a little more before putting him out of his misery. He pushed through the heavy tavern door whistling a merry tune. He hadn't felt this light since...He searched his mind and smiled. Since the wench behind the curtain had nearly boxed his ears for exploring her face. And what a face it was too. His loins stirred in remembrance. Best to dampen that right now. She was on the hunt for a husband, not a tumble in the bed.

He made his way through the crowded bar, which was packed. Not a surprise considering it was payday at the docks. The sailors always cleaned up on payday to come to the Devil's Tavern and spend their hard-earned money on mead and women. From the spilled mead, which made the floor slick, to the perfume, which tickled his nose, it was nice to know two things in life never changed.

He spotted Sutherland at the end of the bar with a big sappy smile on his American face. Sutherland was another constant. Always happy and unfalteringly reliable.

Alex wove through the drunken crowd and shrugged off the groping hands of eager, overly painted, scantily dressed women. Somewhere to the right of him, someone pounded on the keys of the piano, and soon a merry ballad about a rich nobleman and his daughter filled the tavern. The loud singing combined with the thumping of pewter ale mugs on the tables put a pleasant vibration in his ears.

The humming in the air reminded him of the intense notes of the country dance playing in the background at the ball tonight when he had huddled behind the curtain with the enchantress. Her glistening black hair, eyes dancing with merriment and secrets, and lips calling to him flashed in his mind. He might well need to end things with Bess, but he obviously did not need to dawdle in replacing his mistress.

Before Alex took his seat, a mug slid from Sutherland to him. Alex grasped the mug, indicated Cameron coming up behind him and signaled to the tavern keeper. "One more."

As Cameron took the seat by Alex, a mug slid past him and was snatched off the bar by his brother. Without a word of greeting, they raised their glasses, clinked them together and threw back the mead as if it was the last drink they'd ever receive. The sweet liquid coated Alex's throat and took off the edge that had sprung up since learning his mother had taken a renewed interest in seeing to his life.

"Tell me the news." Sutherland clasped Alex's shoulder.

"Alex was closeted up with an innocent-looking thing

behind a curtain tonight," Cameron said before Alex had even finished swallowing his drink. Cameron thumped his mug onto the bar and grinned.

"Quit glaring. I told you Mother wanted me to watch you. I had to have something to report and that was the most entertaining thing you did all night."

"Do not watch me and report back to Mother or I will drag you into the ring at Gentleman Jackson's and leave your sorry butt there after I pummel your face in."

"Fine. But you have to help me think of stories to feed Mother."

"I'm sure you can come up with something on your own," Alex snapped.

Sutherland raised his eyebrows at Alex. "I take it by your surly tone you were unable to convince the lady to loosen her corset for you?"

"Hardly. She practically shoved me out of the curtain. It was a simple mistake. I was meaning to meet an improper lady and stumbled upon a young miss no doubt trying to trap a man into marriage."

Sutherland raised his mug. "To Lionhurst for saving a hapless victim from marriage mart manipulations."

"God, you sound positively English," Alex said, amazed that his friend had managed to mimic an English accent so perfectly.

"I've been practicing so I can catch a proper English wife."

"Still stuck on that plan, huh?"

"Absolutely," Sutherland replied and held up three fingers to the tavern keeper to indicate three more mugs of mead. "I just need to meet a lady that sufficiently turns my head. Say, tell me about the lady from the curtains. If she's searching and so am I, we might be just the thing the other needs."

A flash of the woman's delicately sculpted face filled Alex's mind. "She was not attractive in the least," he lied, uncertain why he would do such a thing.

Three

WHOEVER WAS THREATENING HER family had to be a man. Gillian read the latest note in the string of seven, which had arrived daily for an entire week. *Cease your social outings or else.* She understood the *or else* perfectly. The fiend had spelled it out clearly. He would tell the *ton* her sister was a murderess. Gillian would gladly chance social leprosy for herself, but her sister was another matter entirely.

She folded the parchment into a tight square, threw it in her jewelry box and slammed the lid. She had to protect Whitney and keep her safe and happy.

That meant marrying a foreigner and getting herself and Whitney out of England as soon as possible. Drake Sutherland was a foreigner. And from what she had read in all the Society papers, his visit here would be brief. His home was in New York, and he was powerful and wealthy. He could whisk them there immediately and solve all her problems. Neither she nor her sister would be in English Society and therefore the threat should disappear. Father would be relieved of his hopeless goal to make his daughters proper English matches. She smiled. That was actually a benefit considering whom her father might pick out for them to marry. Someone like him or one of his friends would be worse than death.

She stood and ran a hand down the length of her silk

dress. What more could a lady ask for? She dismissed out of hand the foolish wish for love. Anyone who'd failed her sister as she once had didn't deserve to expect to marry for love. A truth made painfully apparent with each passing night that her sister stood on the wallflower line and people greeted them frostily at best. Blank dance cards did not a marriage make. Time to look happy for the next ball. Hopefully, disaster wouldn't strike before she could actually meet Mr. Sutherland.

She made her way down the hall and to the staircase. Whitney's voice floated up from below. Gillian forced the butterflies to cease their turning. She had to protect Whitney and give her a chance at real happiness. Only a man would think they could tell her not to appear in Society and assume she could obey the command. Women had little power, especially in England, and if they did have power, they had to wield it craftily lest a man should feel threatened and take it away.

Her father must be plagued by insecurity over losing his power. Why else would he not give her a crumb of say in her life? She had tried for a week to keep them at home, yet every night they were back at balls met with the same frosty reception and no names written on their dance cards. The threatening notes had arrived daily, but there was nothing she could do to ensure they stayed home as the gentleman threatening them demanded.

How much time did she have before this person spilled their secret? Her stomach clenched at the thought.

"Gillian." Her father's grip on her arm snapped her out of her musings. "Tonight I expect you to dance."

She nodded obediently so he would let go. As expected, he released her with a curt nod. Obedience was always the best way to stay on his pleasant side. Of course using the word "pleasant" to refer to him was a liberal stretch of the term. He'd been most unpleasant earlier when she showed him the latest note. He'd yelled at her to burn the thing and quit worrying. As if she could? And frankly, she did not understand his attitude.

She glared at his back as he strode down the steps. Did he really think it that simple? He could demand that tonight she dance, and *poof*, it would happen? Whitney fell in step beside her, slipping an arm securely around Gillian's waist. "You look lovely. I'm sure tonight our dance cards will fill."

Gillian nodded and tried discreetly to dislodge the lump of emotion that had formed with Whitney's naively hopeful words. "I'm sure we both shall dance," she lied. If wishing it to be so could fill a card, then theirs would be full.

The moment her father stopped and turned toward her she regretted the loudness of her tone. She hadn't meant for him to hear her. "You will dance, young lady." He wagged a finger in her face. "As eldest, you have to marry first. And since you can't seem to manage to secure a dance on your own, I've secured one for you. Smile prettily, make pleasant conversation and this may be the only dance you ever need."

"Whatever do you mean?" she asked, settling into the carriage on shaking legs. Did she sound as nervous as his statement made her feel?

"I've promised Mr. Mallorian you will dance with him. He fancies you."

"Father." She swallowed the bile that had risen in her throat. She could not very well repeat what she'd overheard about Mr. Mallorian's sexual pursuits or scream out her dislike of the man. "I don't care for him."

Her father reached across the carriage and patted her knee. "Your worries are unfounded. If it makes you feel better, I know he has a country estate, which you could reside at permanently if you were to marry."

Her father's words of assurance actually made her feel like retching. She swallowed convulsively. God help her, her thoughts had been selfish. Shame washed through her. She'd not even considered whoever was threatening them. Her worry was solely that she was positive marriage to a man like Mr. Mallorian would make her miserable.

The carriage jerked to a start, and as it rolled down the road she stared out the window. Her sister took her hand and squeezed. Gillian offered Whitney a quick reassuring smile before turning back to pretend interest in the scenery. The trees blurred by her. She was prepared to sacrifice marrying for love to protect her sister, but that didn't mean she wanted to marry a man she detested. Mr. Mallorian was not a good man. Angry tears burned the back of her throat at her father's willingness to pawn her off on anyone who may be interested, whether he was a good person or not.

The trip to the Primwitty ball was fortunately quick. The silence in the carriage had been deafening. As they ascended the stairs to the entrance of the ball, Gillian blinked in surprise at her Aunt Millicent's smiling face. "I thought you couldn't come tonight," she said and rushed over to give her aunt a hug. Auntie was just what she needed. Someone in her corner who might be able to talk reason with her father or at the very least distract him so she could find Mr. Sutherland. She knew for a fact he was supposed to be here.

She pressed her mouth close to her aunt's ear. "Auntie, can you distract Father long enough for Whitney and I to slip away unnoticed?"

Her aunt raised a silver brow at her. "Are you up to anything improper?"

"Shall I lie?" Gillian held her breath, waiting for her aunt's response. Auntie was the least conventional person Gillian had ever known, but she wasn't sure her aunt would approve of her plan to seduce Mr. Sutherland into marrying her. Then again, Auntie might approve if she knew about Whitney, but the only thing Auntie knew was the same as everyone else.

Whitney had lost her memory of the night their mother died. According to the doctors, the simple shock of losing her mother so young had been the culprit. The doctors couldn't say if her memory would ever come back. All they had ever said was it could be dangerous to Whitney's fragile mind to press the memories on her. And the doctors didn't know the half of it.

Auntie looked between Gillian and her father. "What's he trying to do?"

"I think he may be trying to arrange a marriage between myself and Mr. Mallorian."

Auntie's eyes narrowed into pale green slits. "That family is horrid. I'd sooner see you a spinster."

"So you'll help me?"

Auntie patted absently at her silver hair. The gesture always signaled when her aunt was deciding on something. Finally, she ceased her ministrations to her already perfectly coifed hair and waved a hand through the air. "Lucinda, dear, over here."

A muddy-haired matron in a flowing violet gown wiggled around Gillian's father and toward them. She stopped, breathless and smiling, her brown eyes lit with warmth. "I may dance tonight, Millicent," she announced before pointing down to her feet. "My toes are not bothering me in the least since I lost a bit of weight."

Auntie's chuckle made Gillian smile despite her concerns. Auntie's friend Lucinda looked as if the only thing she'd lost was her ability to quit eating when full, but the woman seemed genuinely nice. Auntie nodded toward Gillian. "Lucinda, this is my niece."

The woman looked her up and down, her cheeks rippling into folds when she smiled. "You are just as pretty as your aunt said. Take heart, dear. Millicent told me you were once friends with the Duchess of Primwitty. And she's the *ton's* darling. So you are already one step toward overcoming the nasty rumors."

Auntie slapped her friend on the arm with her fan. "I told you to curb your bluntness. How do you expect to catch a new husband with that tongue?"

"Posh." Lucinda waved at Gillian's aunt. "I don't want another husband. Thirty years with a man as wonderful as Hector is enough to keep me warm until I die. I just want to dance. I miss it."

"That's perfectly all right," Gillian quickly interrupted, seeing exactly why her aunt and Lucinda were friends. They both spoke their minds and strayed from the topic of conversation. "What you said is partially the truth. I was once friends with the duchess, but I've no doubt my aunt used a multitude of favors to get these ballroom doors opened for my sister and myself."

"Not true," Auntie protested, but her flushed face indicated otherwise.

The older woman glanced past Gillian to where Whitney stood gazing toward the ballroom and humming.

"Your sister?"

Gillian nodded.

"She's lovely as well," Lucinda said.

"Thank you. Auntie, my favor?"

"Ah, yes! Lucinda, dear, will you help me distract my brother-in-law so these two precious girls can have a bit of fun?"

"Just the thing to make my night interesting," Lucinda crowed. "Can he be enticed to dance?"

"Doubtful, but you never know."

"Come along." Lucinda grasped Auntie's hand. "You know I love a challenge."

The minute Auntie and her friend stood in front of Father, Gillian hurried to her sister. "Time to disappear," she whispered and nudged Whitney into motion. Giggling, they dodged into the crowd and across the threshold into the chaos and heat of the Duke and Duchess of Primwitty's glittering ballroom.

"Are we searching for Mr. Sutherland again?" Whitney asked.

"Of course." Gillian scanned and discarded each gentleman for being too short, too old, too fat, or their hair too dark. "Good grief," she grumbled as someone bumped into her back. "This could take all night, and this ballroom is too crowded and reeks of an overuse of perfume."

"You should depart at once if the perfume offends you," a feminine voice said to her back.

Gillian clenched her teeth at the high-pitched tone she had tried to wipe from her memory. Pasting a smile on her face, she turned to greet Lady Staunton. A scene was out of the question, but the idea of placating the woman who glared at her over a man Gillian didn't know nor cared to know made her stomach turn. Before she could make a false, cheery hello come from her unwilling lips, a melodic voice came close from her right.

"Lady Gillian and Lady Whitney, there you are, my dears. I've been looking everywhere for you."

Gillian blinked. Were her eyes deceiving her? Sally—no, the Duchess of Primwitty, Gillian corrected herself—reached toward her and pulled Gillian close. Gillian gaped, too stunned to speak. It had been years, eleven precisely, since she and her childhood friend had spoken.

Sally eyed Gillian before offering a placid smile to her curious guests. "Quit glaring, Serena," Sally murmured in a voice dripping with honey, "and run along before I have you shown to the door."

"You wouldn't dare," Lady Staunton said, "Your husband would be furious, and you know it."

"I know nothing of the sort." Sally squeezed Gillian's wrist just a bit. "And I'm very daring. Now off you go. And do try to be nice for the rest of the night."

They stood in silence, watching Lady Staunton depart. When her red hair was no longer visible, Gillian dipped into a proper curtsy. "Thank you, Your Grace."

"Gillian Rutherford!" Sally erupted into laughter before grabbing Gillian by the elbow and towing her fully into the busy ballroom. "Surely you jest! As long as we've known each other and you think to call me anything but Sally." She waved Whitney closer. "You too, Whitney."

Gillian studied her old friend, trying to take her measure. The years had wrought many changes in Sally. High cheekbones, a slender nose and full lips replaced the girlish features in a most becoming manner. Sally still barely reached Gillian's shoulders, but her friend no longer reminded Gillian of a fair-haired sprite. She was a regal queen, small in stature but commanding all the same.

Sally studied her. "We are still friends, are we not? Just because our fathers had a falling out does not mean I ever felt the same."

Gillian exhaled, surprised she had been holding her breath. She nodded, unable to speak past the large lump in her throat.

"Since I've been out from underneath Papa's repressive thumb, I've invited you both to every social function I've given. The response has always been no, until now. Your father, I presume?"

Gillian nodded, though she felt like gasping as Whitney had. A torrent of emotions coursed through her, but she held each one back as always.

"My dears, we can't change the mistakes of our

parents," Sally said. "Shall we pick up with our friendship as if it was never interrupted?"

"I'd like that very much," Gillian said.

"*We'd* like that very much," Whitney amended.

"Excellent!" Sally embraced them before shoving them back to study them. After a moment, she smiled. "Now that we've settled that, Gillian, you must tell me what you did to pique Lady Staunton's ire. I heard you were involved in a bit of a scene last week."

Gillian frowned. She'd hoped the incident would pass without remark. She should have known better. "I can't say for certain, but I've a fair idea. However, it seems so trivial. It must not take much to anger Lady Staunton."

Sally rolled her eyes heavenward. "Not much at all. She's a spiteful woman, though with her mother who can blame her? So what was your sin?"

"She thinks I have designs on a man she apparently has a deep affection for."

"Well, that couldn't have been her husband," Sally pronounced with a wicked grin. "He's rail thin, sloppily dressed, with a sallow complexion and thinning brown hair. She's smart enough to know you wouldn't want him, and it's common knowledge she holds no affection for him."

Gillian laughed. "The years have not changed your direct nature in the least."

"Were you worried they had, darling?"

"Maybe not the years, but definitely becoming a duchess."

"Oh, that." Sally thrust her hands on her hips. "That's changed me quite a bit. Now I put up with nonsense from no one."

"You were like that at eight."

"Was I?" Sally quirked her mouth. "I must speak to my husband, then. He promised quite a lot of benefits if I married him."

"You're incorrigible." Gillian laughed and it felt exactly as it had when they had been younger.

"I'm incorrigible? You're one to talk. One week back into Society and you're trying to pinch Lady Staunton's next victim out from her eager clutches. What does the poor fellow look like?"

Gillian opened her mouth to give his description, then promptly changed her mind. She could paint a vivid, exact picture of the man: black hair, dancing blue eyes, crooked smile and overwhelming presence. But how could she explain remembering so much detail about a man she had improperly met while hiding behind a curtain? She could not. She shrugged, choosing her words carefully. "He was tall with black hair and blue eyes."

"Darling, that describes half the men here," Sally murmured with a sigh. "You're no help. Then again, if he's rich, alive and holds a loftier title than the one Lady Staunton currently possesses, she would think you were poaching someone she might want to claim. Her poor husband's at death's door, and she's on the prowl for his replacement."

"That's despicable," Whitney said. "Surely you're mistaken."

"I'm never mistaken when it comes to matters of the heart." Without taking her gaze off Gillian, Sally returned the wave of a young couple who danced past. "She's awful, and she's after one of my dearest friends. I heard she made quite a scene chasing after him at a ball last week. Chased him right to the front door, which I'm told he dashed out of to escape her."

"I wouldn't worry about him."

Sally narrowed her eyes at Gillian.

Blast! She'd not meant to let anything slip, but the surprise of realizing Sally was talking about the man from the curtains had stolen her senses.

"Why?" Sally raised her eyebrows. "Is Lionhurst the man she thinks you're after?"

"Lionhurst?" Gillian frowned. The name unleashed an old memory. "Do you mean Alexander Trevelle?" She pictured the boy she remembered from childhood. Face streaked with dirt and hair filled with straw from the haystack he had been hiding in to avoid being whipped by his father, the duke.

"One and the same," Sally said. "I see by your frown you remember him."

"Oh, I remember him." Didn't all women remember the first boy who ever kissed them? She was no exception, even if the kiss had been when she was eight, and she had considered his warm lips extremely disgusting. The way he'd barged behind the curtain and thought she was a woman who had been waiting with bated breath to fall into his arms made perfect sense now. The little she recalled of the boy she'd barely known was someone who assumed everyone pined for his attention. "I can't believe after all these years he's not changed in the way he treats women."

"Oh, he's changed some," Sally said with a chuckle. "He steals quite a bit more than just kisses nowadays."

"What does he steal?" Gillian asked, intrigued by Sally's statement.

"Hearts, darling." Sally pulled Gillian to her side, their heads close together. "He steals hearts." She grinned at Gillian. "You've given me an idea."

Gillian didn't like the sound of that. Sally had never been known for her sound ideas. "What sort of notion?"

"You have to help me."

"Help you?" Gillian tried to extract herself from her friend's embrace. "How can I help you?"

"Why to save Lion from Lady Staunton, of course."

"What fun," Whitney exclaimed, a grin lighting her face. "I'll help too."

"I'll find a small role for you."

"A small role?" Whitney's lips poked out in a pout.

"Darling, you're gorgeous," Sally exclaimed to Whitney. "But Lionhurst likes dark hair."

Whitney and Sally both stared at Gillian. She ignored her sister and focused on Sally. "I can't afford to embroil myself in helping your friend. I've too much on my mind."

"You only need act if Lady Staunton comes near him."

"I'm sorry." Gillian shook her head. She could not slip into such an entanglement. "I just can't."

All the animation in Sally's face disappeared. "Why not? Are you afraid of losing your heart to him?"

"Don't be ridiculous," Gillian snapped, picturing the man he had become. She could imagine with his gorgeous smile and, no doubt perfected seduction methods, how a woman might be in danger of losing her heart to him, but she was not your average woman. She was on a mission to save her sister and herself. "My heart is in no danger."

"Then you're perfect. I don't have to worry you'll get hurt this way, and I can quit fretting about Lionhurst falling back into Lady Staunton's clutches. The last time almost killed him."

"From my conversation earlier with Lord Lionhurst," Gillian said firmly, "I suspect he can handle himself with any woman."

"You don't truly know him." Sally shook her head. "He never shows his true self when he is out in Society."

"No doubt because the women would run screaming," Gillian retorted.

Sally's eyes narrowed. "I don't remember you being cold and mean."

Heat flooded Gillian's face. "I'm not. It's just..." She trailed off. She could explain neither her situation nor the encounter behind the curtain with Lord Lionhurst. "I just already have something very important to see to tonight."

"Oh, darling. What a goose I am! What gentleman is in your line of fire tonight?"

"No one in particular," Gillian replied, not certain she was ready to divulge her mission to Sally just yet, or possibly ever.

"Have you forgotten about Mr. Sutherland?" Whitney interjected, a gleam of mischief in her eye. "I thought you wanted to marry him?"

"Whitney, hush!" How embarrassing and typical of Whitney to stir up trouble by blurting such a thing to Sally. Now Sally would ask questions that Gillian could not answer.

"How very interesting." Sally scrutinized her. "Why do you wish to marry Mr. Sutherland? He would take you away from England."

"I have my reasons for wanting him." She prayed Sally would accept her vague answer.

Sally's mouth tightened, but she nodded. "Well, I suppose I could assist you, though I really don't wish to help you capture a man who will whisk you away from

me."

A swell of emotions rose up to lodge in Gillian's chest, but she pushed the tide back. Sentimentality would have to wait. "How do you suppose you could help me? Do you know Mr. Sutherland?"

"Not personally. Lionhurst is business partners with him and has brought the man here tonight."

What a relief. After a week of trying to meet Mr. Sutherland, she was finally going to get her chance. Gillian couldn't stop the smile from coming to her face.

Sally grinned back. "I'm glad my information pleases you. Lionhurst can introduce Mr. Sutherland to us both."

"Couldn't you just introduce me to Mr. Sutherland yourself after you meet him?" Something about Lord Lionhurst made her think avoiding him would be best. So far, he'd caused her nothing but trouble.

"I would, darling, but there they are. *Together.*" Sally pointed toward the terrace door.

Gillian followed the direction Sally pointed. Her sight settled immediately on Lord Lionhurst's tall figure. His black hair shimmered under the light of the chandelier. His white shirt, cravat and black pants would have been commonplace except he wore a ruby waistcoat that fit him to perfection. A devilish grin danced across his face, as if wicked thoughts played out in his mind. He was the apple in the Garden of Eden. *Dangerous. Sinful.*

An involuntary sigh of appreciation escaped her lips. *Good God, she was a dolt!* She glanced around to see if anyone had noticed.

An amused smile stretched across Sally's lips. "Are you positive your heart is safe?"

"Completely certain. Mr. Sutherland is the only man for me."

"Truly? What is it about Mr. Sutherland's looks that draws you to him?"

Gillian quickly turned her gaze to Mr. Sutherland as Sally quietly chuckled beside her. Blast Sally! She somehow knew Gillian had not spared a glance toward Mr. Sutherland. As the men made their way through the crowd and toward them, Gillian found it hard to keep Mr. Sutherland in her sights with Lord Lionhurst there. The man was too tall, his shoulders too broad.

She forced herself to concentrate on Mr. Sutherland. He had brown wavy hair that did not shine as the marquess' black locks did and—oh, good heavens. This comparison was going badly and in a dangerous direction. She pasted a smile on her lips and kept her gaze planted on Mr. Sutherland until both men stood before her.

"Lionhurst, this is Lady Gillian, the Duke of Kingsley's eldest daughter. I'm sure you remember her," Sally finished with a throaty laugh.

Gillian shot Sally a glare.

"Of course, I mean after all these years," Sally finished with a shrug.

Gillian focused on Lord Lionhurst and prayed he would keep their meeting in the curtains to himself.

His blue eyes crinkled with amusement and something else—something possibly wicked. His bold gaze moved down her body and back to her face again. Little sparks of gold danced like flashes of light across his eyes.

Warmth suffused her body. "Lord Lionhurst," she whispered, though she'd meant for her voice to come out strong.

A slow, purely seductive grin spread across his face. "I remember you." He said no more, but she knew exactly what he was remembering. His hands on her face and at her waist. No doubt, the kiss he'd stolen eleven years ago had been long forgotten by a man who'd probably kissed more women than a legion of men.

Gillian's heart hammered, but she forced herself to speak. "You must have an excellent memory."

"Oh, I do." His eyes smoldered. "I never forget a woman I've kissed."

"You most certainly have not kissed me!" Gillian protested, glancing from her sister's shocked face to Sally's knowing one. Looking at Mr. Sutherland was out of the question. Her face might as well be on fire, for all the embarrassment she felt.

"I did kiss you. Of course, you were just a child—"

"Eight," she interrupted.

He grinned. "You remember too?"

"You scoundrel," she snapped. "You stole that kiss!"

He shrugged. "The slap was well worth it."

What must Mr. Sutherland think? She stole a glance at him. Was that amusement or horror? Before she could decide, Sally said, "I presume this is Mr. Sutherland, your business partner?"

Mr. Sutherland bowed to Sally. "I think we can skip the formal introduction." His gaze slid between Gillian and Lord Lionhurst. Thank goodness, the man appeared to have a sense of humor.

He bowed to Gillian. "I can see why Lionhurst remembers you."

Gillian's stomach tightened. He seemed nice enough based on ten seconds. Could she seduce this man into marriage? What choice did she have? Gillian curtsied. "It's a pleasure to meet you." As she was coming up, a hand pushed against her back.

"Get to the dance floor," Sally hissed, propelling Gillian into Lord Lionhurst's arms and away from Mr. Sutherland.

"Wait, no," Gillian protested, but her objection was drowned out by the lively notes the orchestra had struck up.

Surprise that appeared to match her own registered across Lord Lionhurst's face, but he slipped his hand around her waist and led her away.

Four

ALEX WANTED TO AVOID a confrontation with Lady Staunton, but he wasn't sure whisking Lady Gillian onto the dance floor was a better predicament than facing the woman who was making a beeline for him. One woman wanted him, and he wanted the other.

An innocent. A woman he had no right to want. He would never offer her the thing a debutante such as herself would be after—marriage. And what he did have to offer—pleasure and passion—was not something she would be shopping for.

He thought he knew better than to play with fire, so why was he leading the burning flame onto the dance floor? He should be a man, turn around and march her back into the safekeeping of the lady's sister and Sally.

Her hips swayed alluringly as she walked beside him, but he knew she did not intend to entice him into her bed. Her look of outrage as he propelled her onto the dance floor had made how she felt about him apparent. She had judged him as a rake and knew the best thing was to stay away. *Good for her. And him.* But one dance would not bind either of them to anything. And his attention would not harm her. He was an honorable man when it came to debutantes. Hell, any woman. He never got involved with a woman unless she was widowed and willing or a paid professional who knew better than to expect marriage and emotions.

He led her onto the dance floor while trying to ignore her scent. Was that freesia? He leaned close to her hair. *Definitely freesia.*

She swatted beside her as if he was a pesky fly.

She had spunk. He'd give her that. And she smelled good. No doubt, she would prove to be like all women of her lot—interested only in titles and wealth. He grabbed her gently by the arm and turned her to face him.

"Do you always sniff women like you're a dog?" Emerald eyes framed by long, sooty lashes glared at him.

He swallowed his laughter and desire. "No. Why didn't you want to dance with me?"

Her forehead creased at his question. "I think we both know why, Lord Lionhurst. You don't seem the sort of man to simply want a dance from a lady."

"I'm without reproach when it comes to debutantes," he snapped, unsure why her negative perception of him made him angry.

"Not true," she replied, placing a hand on his arm to position herself for the dance. "You stole a kiss from me, and I am a debutante."

He swirled them around the dance floor in silence, trying to decide what to say to that. She was right. He had stolen a kiss from her years ago. He'd never stolen another kiss since. Her slap across the face had left a lasting impression. Making sure the woman was willing was always necessary.

He hadn't the foggiest idea what to say. No witty rejoinder came to mind—a completely new situation for him. He forced himself to look at her and was surprised to find her studying him. "Are you going to keep our secret?"

"Of course," he replied, bothered at the frown of worry creasing her forehead. It had been fun to tease her earlier, but he hadn't meant to really concern her. "Relax and have fun. I promise to return you unscathed to your sister the moment the dance ends."

Her gaze traveled back the way they had come, the frown not lessening a bit. If anything, she appeared more concerned. "Are you concerned that dancing with me will harm your reputation?"

She bit her lip but didn't respond.

"I assure you, try as I might to dissuade mothers from pursing me, I am still a favorite pick as an eligible bachelor season after season."

"You're rather conceited," she said.

"No. I know very well it has nothing to do with me. Or rather anything they know about me personally. They want me for their daughters because of my title and my money. I could be daft and they would still want me. Dancing with me might actually help you garner attention. Pleasant attention, that is. So you can rest easy, unless your frown has nothing to do with being concerned about your reputation and is caused by something else entirely."

Her eyes widened a fraction.

"Ah." He swirled her around once and smiled down at her. Did she know how expressive her face was? "So what is the truth of your concern?"

"Do you truly wish to hear the truth?"

"The truth would be nice. I so rarely get it but generally prefer it. Don't you?"

She nodded. "Generally, though sometimes the truth can be hurtful."

"I'll take my chances."

"All right." She glanced to where Sally and Sutherland stood talking to Lady Whitney before settling her troubled gaze back on him. "I have someone I wish to become acquainted with, and I'm anxious that I'll miss my chance while on the dance floor with you."

"Well, that was refreshingly honest and ego crushing."

"I'm sorry." Her face flushed as her gaze trailed back to Sally. Or was she staring at Sutherland? Impossible.

"Is the person you wish to meet my business partner?"

She leveled him with a steady look. "If you want an answer, I think it only reasonable I get to ask a question first since I have already answered one of yours."

He believed in fairness. "Go ahead."

"Did you whisk me onto the dance floor because you didn't want to speak with Lady Staunton?"

"Yes," he clipped, regretting his agreement to answer

honestly. He did not discuss personal matters. No flirting with debs and no personal chitchat. He lived by those rules. Yet as he stared into her eyes, the way gold shot through the green fascinated him. Maybe it was the celebratory whiskey he drank earlier. More likely it was the leftover adrenaline rush of gaining another ship for his shipping company this morning, but whatever it was, tonight he would forget his rules for five minutes. Five minutes couldn't bring any catastrophic harm.

Decision made, he pulled Lady Gillian a little closer and tighter, enjoying the curve of her waist and the warmth of her skin. She sucked in a sharp breath, but did not fight his nearness, and his whole body tightened in response to her.

As they made a circle around the ballroom, she pulled back and looked at him. "I think it's admirable you are avoiding a married woman's advances."

"Thank you," he replied. He'd have to speak to Sally later about sharing his personal history.

The orchestra's music began to fade, signaling the dance was ending. He didn't want it to end. Not yet. He'd not had his five minutes of freedom from the life he'd made. "Would you care for one more dance?"

"I can't." She was already pulling away. He gripped the tips of her fingers to stop her flight. What was he doing? Stalling for time? A moment that would lead to nowhere. He racked his brain and seized what he could. "You never told me if it was my partner you wanted to meet."

She tugged her fingers out of his grasp, a smile pulling at her lips. "That's because I don't share personal information with men who lurk behind curtains."

Someone to the left called his name. He glanced to find the voice, but the crowd was thick. That could wait. He would much prefer to exchange witty barbs with Lady Gillian. "You're a cheeky chit," he said, turning back to see her response, but she was gone.

What the devil? He glanced around the dance floor but didn't see her. He quelled the odd sense of disappointment. He must be bored to even care she had fled. It was best, considering who he was and what she was. He started to weave through the crowd, but a flash of a woman with long black hair ascending the staircase caught his attention. *Lady Gillian.*

Before he considered the consequences to her or him, he dashed through the crowd, breaking another one of his sacred rules. *Never chase after a woman.*

GILLIAN'S HEART POUNDED IN her ears as she rushed up the stairs and down the candlelit hall. She leaned against the wall and doubled over. Curse whoever dictated women's fashion. Stays and a multitude of cotton and silk layers made running no easy task. She struggled for a few short breaths, and then she straightened and pressed her fingertips to her temples.

She was horrified at how much she had wanted to say yes to one more dance with Lord Lionhurst. What was wrong with her? Flirting with him would not get her any closer to her goal of saving her sister.

She pushed away from the wall and frowned. She really needed to come up with better escape plans. How was she going to speak with Mr. Sutherland now? She sighed. No telling what Lord Lionhurst would say about her. Hopefully, nothing.

She had to go in search of Mr. Sutherland, but her feet didn't want to move. *Coward.* It wasn't as if Lord Lionhurst would be lurking around the corner waiting for her. He was probably defending himself from Lady Staunton's advances at this very moment. That would actually be the perfect scenario. She could speak with Mr. Sutherland without Lord Lionhurst lurking about.

No more stalling. Mr. Sutherland could leave before she had the chance to find him. Or worse, he could meet someone else. The thought had her flying down the corridor toward the ballroom, but as she rounded the corner, the toe of her slipper caught under a turned-up corner of a rug. She careened forward, throwing her arms out to soften the coming impact.

Strong hands gripped her and pulled her to her feet. When she raised her head to thank her savior, her breath hitched in her throat. Lord Lionhurst stared at her in way that left her body tingling.

"I was looking for you. You dashed away so fast I thought you might feel ill."

Gillian blinked. His words, or what she thought he said, registered in her brain. It was hard to know, with his warm hands on her bare arms, and the scent of pine and rain invading her senses. She leaned toward him, a positively idiotic thing to do, but one she was helpless to stop. Mmm...not only did he smell nice, he had the loveliest smile, perfect white teeth. He grinned at her, and she grinned back.

"Lady Gillian, did you hear me?"

"Uh-huh." One superb smile and two dazzling eyes, and her brain was now mush. How disappointing. She had to do better. She pulled out of his grasp and stepped back to put proper distance between them.

His brow dipped down as if he knew exactly what she'd been thinking. She squirmed under his penetrating stare. He smiled, causing dimples to appear on his cheeks. "Are you unwell?"

"I'm perfectly healthy." Daftness did not constitute sickness.

He proffered his arm while inclining his head toward the stairs. "Oh, yes. You are acting like the picture of health. Not answering questions, your eyes are glazed and a sheen of perspiration is covering your brow."

"It's very ungentlemanly to point out such things." She slipped her arm through his and feigned a rabid interest in the floor.

"Something interesting down there?" he asked as he led them toward the steps.

"Just making sure I don't misplace my step again."

He walked toward the stairs, and when he reached the top, he paused. "Has anyone ever told you that you are a terrible liar?"

"A few times," she answered, too distracted by the way his fingers rubbed back and forth on her arm to guard her tongue. She needed to leave him before she said anything else foolish and he told Mr. Sutherland to avoid her. What could she say to part ways that would sound truthful?

"Gillian!" someone called, interrupting her thoughts.

Sally rushed up the stairs to join them. She looked between them as she heaved deep breaths. "I was wondering where the two of you ran off to." Her amused gaze moved from Gillian's face to her hand. Gillian tugged her hand free from Lord Lionhurst's grip and forced herself to meet Sally's smirk. How thoroughly irritating. Did Sally think her so silly as to fall for a man based on his remarkable looks?

"Did you decide to explain everything to Lionhurst?"

"She was just explaining," Lord Lionhurst declared.

Stunned at his blatant lie, Gillian gaped at him, unsure how to correct his claim without actually calling him a liar.

"Good, good." Sally leaned toward Lord Lionhurst. "So can you help her secure a marriage proposal from your partner?"

"Sally, please." Gillian glared at Sally then turned to meet Lord Lionhurst's gaze. She wished she hadn't.

He assessed her in a most unfriendly manner. "You surprise me, Lady Gillian." His tone was low and hard.

She really didn't want to know how she surprised him, but what choice did she have? "How so, my lord?"

"I had allowed myself to consider for a moment that you might be a genuine woman. Something I never do when it comes to your ilk."

His verbal flaying made her flinch. She was nothing like the debutantes here. She did not want Mr. Sutherland for his money, and though she did not love him yet, she believed in her heart she could. That had to count for something. *It just had to.* She swallowed back her emotions. Lord Lionhurst's unfair judgment could not be the undoing of her composure. "Lord Lionhurst, you don't understand."

Sally wagged a finger at him "You're being unfair. And it's quite unlike you."

If anything his expression grew colder. Gillian could not resist rubbing at the goose flesh that popped up on her arms. Silence stretched so that she wanted to bolt from his presence and never see the man again. It was vastly unfair that he was partners with the man she intended to marry. Maybe she could talk Mr. Sutherland into finding a new partner in years to come. One who didn't hate women.

Sally blew out a long sigh. "Darling, you should apologize."

His gaze locked on Gillian. "I'm sorry you pulled the wool over my eyes."

That was hardly an apology, but Gillian forced a smile. "And I'm sorry you're a cad."

His faced darkened, but before he could respond, Sally stamped her foot. "Play nice, children. You are both my friends, and I'll tolerate no quarrelling."

Gillian locked gazes with him once again. If he thought she would be the first to apologize, the man was mistaken. She'd stand here all night, even if these slippers did pain her feet to distraction.

"All right," Sally said, irritation lacing both words. "I see the two most stubborn people in the *ton* are standing before me. "Come along, Gillian. The challenge of who will outlast the other will have to wait. Your father sent me to find you."

Gillian's mouth went dry. She forced herself to swallow. "Why?"

"Something about an important announcement."

Blast her father. The possibility of what he might want to announce frightened her. Throwing decorum to the wind, she whirled around to race down the stairs to stop her father's madness. Two steps into her charge, her slick shoe slid out from under her, and she hurtled forward.

Warm hands slid around her waist, jerking her back and locking under her rib cage, dangerously close to her breasts. Hot breath tickled her neck. Lord Lionhurst pulled her close against the hardness of his chest and powerful thighs. She shook, but it was not from fear of her near fall. A bolt of desire streaked through her body, making her weak in the knees.

This night was not going at all as she had planned. She tried to wiggle out of his grasp, but he refused to release her. Why wouldn't he let go when he thought so little of her? Did he want her profuse thanks? Did he expect her to faint or blubber on and on? She straightened her shoulders and prayed she appeared composed and calm.

"Thank you for saving me."

Heat radiated from the length of his body to hers; his heartbeat tapped a fast rhythm against her back. He turned her around on the step and tipped her chin up, until she looked into his eyes. He did not look like he hated her. He looked like he might kiss her. Her pulse leaped at the notion. She forced herself not to move.

He leaned toward her, and she closed her eyes. His hand brushed her cheek and tucked an errant strand of her hair behind her ear. "You need to slow down."

Good God, but she really was a fool. What must he think about her standing there and closing her eyes? She shivered as his fingers traced a hot path down her jawbone. "There may not always be someone there to catch you when you fall."

It was not her fall she was afraid of, and the reminder slammed her in the chest. She stepped back, aware of their inappropriate closeness. "I'll be careful," she murmured.

"You've not changed one whit since we were young," Sally huffed beside her. "Disaster follows your every footstep. Lionhurst is correct. You *do* need to slow down." Sally gave her a stern look. "Especially on slick steps. Not every man here is as quick on the feet or as chivalrous as Lionhurst. It's ghastly to admit, but some of these fops wouldn't risk wrinkling their fine coats in order to save a lady from social disaster."

Gillian peeked at Lord Lionhurst and was surprised to find a blush tingeing the skin around the edges of his snowy cravat. He pulled on his collar while bowing to them. "As I've performed my chivalrous duty for the night, I'll bid you farewell."

He swept past Gillian and down the stairs, disappearing after a moment into the thick crowd of the ballroom.

"I wouldn't count on Lionhurst's help again." Sally linked her arm through Gillian's.

"Because he thinks I'm a despicable fortune hunter?"

"Are you?"

Gillian shook her head. "I swear I'm not."

"I believe you." Sally squeezed her hand. "I really do. Lionhurst will see he's misjudged you."

"You don't think he'll say anything to Mr. Sutherland, do you? Warn him against me, I mean."

"Darling, I hate to tell you this, but I've no doubt he'll warn Mr. Sutherland against you. Lionhurst detests treachery, and it appears he has decided you're treacherous."

"Then why are you smiling? We have to stop him." She grabbed Sally's hand and flew down the stairs, not pausing until she reached the bottom. "Do you see him?"

"All I see are stars. That descent left my head spinning."

Gillian wanted to shake Sally for her flippant attitude. Everything rode on getting to Lord Lionhurst before he got to Mr. Sutherland. She had to find a way to make him understand without telling him too much.

"There he is." Sally pointed.

Gillian craned her neck around a group of men to see the best path to him. But before she could judge the quickest way, her father materialized from the crowd.

"Finally," he barked. "Come along, my dear." He took her arm, but she dug in her heels.

"Are we leaving already?" Things could not get any worse.

"Certainly not," he replied. "Mr. Mallorian is waiting for you."

"*For me*?" Gillian gulped back her fear. "I feel ill, Father. I really can't dance right now."

"Good." Her father pushed her through the crowd. "He doesn't want to dance."

"What does he want?"

"Why, to announce your engagement, of course. It's all settled. The wedding is set for two months' time."

Five

ALEX MADE HIS WAY around the outer edges of the crowded ballroom, intent on reaching the card room before another woman waylaid him. He should have known better than to come into the den of schemers, otherwise known as the marriage mart. Women loved to play games, and he had decided long ago that he was no woman's prize, so why the blazes was he irritated with Lady Gillian? She'd admitted nothing shocking in her plan to capture Sutherland. Indeed, she had proven herself to be like all other women. He had expected it, hadn't he?

He yanked on the edge of his dangling cravat and wrapped the material around his fingers as he walked. It wasn't her bothering him. *Surely not.* He flexed and released his fingers against the soft material. *But what if it was? What did that mean*? He paused, unwound the cravat and stuffed it into his coat pocket. It would mean he was a fool who still held a farthing of hope that women were not inherently conniving. And he was no fool.

No, it was not Lady Gillian—it was dressing like a dandy and coming to a place where women plotted to catch him or some other unsuspecting sop for his title, money or land. He refused to spare another thought for the lady. The company was expanding faster than he'd ever dreamed when he concocted the scheme of going into a merchant trade to irritate his father.

He pushed through the door to the gaming room. Stopping inside the threshold, he allowed his eyes to adjust to the dim lighting. A pungent haze hung over the heads of the players. He located Sutherland at a small table by the window on the far side of the room. By the way Sutherland's opponent yanked his hands through his hair, Alex had no doubt his partner was winning. No surprise given his ability at *Vingt-et-un* was legendary at the shipping yard. Alex strode across the room, nodding to acquaintances but purposely not stopping.

His head buzzed with the roar of conversations in the room. He needed to talk to Sally about her card room set-up. It was too loud by half to think properly in here. *Bloody balls.* He longed to leave and go to a nice dark corner at White's.

Just as Alex reached Sutherland's table a chair scraped across the marble floor almost tripping him in his path.

"Watch it," Alex clipped, letting his dark mood slip through.

"Beg pardon," the man said and turned. Marcus Rutherford's ruddy face broke into a wide smile. "If I'd known it was you I'd not have apologized."

Alex grinned in return and extended his hand to Rutherford. "It's been a long time."

Thick fingers clamped around Alex's hand before he found his arm propelled up and down in an enthusiastic handshake. Rutherford had always reminded him of a friendly pup, but now the pup was grown.

"Come into Society more often and you'd see me," Rutherford said.

"I've better things to do than stand around while ladies decide if I'm rich enough, titled enough and stupid enough for them to snare me as their husband."

Rutherford chuckled. "I feel certain they don't think they can snare you. Unless your opinion of marriage has changed."

"Did something in my demeanor just now lead you to think it might have?"

"Not really, but since you were here I thought

perhaps..."

"I'm here because my youngest sister made her debut and my mother called in a favor from me."

"Ah, the fair Allysia is now on the market?"

Alex didn't like the gleam in Rutherford's eye. "My sister is under my watchful gaze."

"You don't have any worries from me," Rutherford said. "She's lovely but another lady has my attention at the present."

"Splendid." He clapped Rutherford on the back. He'd hate to have to meet his friend in the ring at Gentleman Jackson's. But he'd pummel any man who trod on his sister's heart.

He glanced back the way he had come. Maybe he should go back into the ballroom and watch his sister more closely. Father was here, but he was easily distracted. Until now, Alex had not really considered what it meant that Lissie was now counted among the grasping horde of Society misses. He turned back to Rutherford and found the man studying him.

"I know how you feel."

"Am I that obvious?"

"Only to a man in the same predicament. My cousins are like sisters to me. Gillian and Whitney have both been launched into the season by my uncle."

Alex frowned. It was unusual for two sisters to be launched at once, but who was he to comment about proper behavior? He was far from a rule follower. "I'd forgotten she was your cousin."

"Have you seen her tonight?" Rutherford adjusted his waistcoat as he looked at Alex.

The feel of her soft skin still warmed Alex's fingers. He offered a curt nod. "You could say I caught her."

Rutherford flushed a deep red. "Now, see here, Lionhurst. My cousin is not to be toyed with, same as your sister."

Alex clenched his jaw. Sometimes his reputation pleased him and sometimes it was a damn nuisance. "I doubt you need to worry about anyone toying with Lady Gillian. In fact, if I were you, I would be more concerned about her plans for her future."

"What the devil do you mean?"

At that moment, Sutherland glanced over his shoulder and motioned for Alex to sit. "Never mind. I spoke out of turn." Let the fair Lady Gillian have her game. It was not his concern. "The only thing I'll say is you may want to keep an eye on your cousin. If you'll excuse me?"

"Of course. I had better go find Gillian anyway." Rutherford moved away but immediately turned back. "Trent's coming home tomorrow, and Mother has planned a week-long house party in his honor."

"What exactly was Sin doing in Paris for the last year?"

"Who knows?" Rutherford shrugged. "He left in a cloud of mystery, and he returns much the same way. Care to join the hunt and welcome him back?"

"May I bring Sutherland?"

Rutherford flicked his gaze to the card table. "The American? But of course. We'll bet on the hunt and take his money before the day is over."

"Don't count on it," Sutherland called without turning around. "I'll take *your* money just as I did tonight."

"Nasty American," Rutherford said with a laugh. "I'll see you both on Friday at Ravenhurst, no later than sunrise."

As Rutherford departed, Alex took off his coat, sat down and motioned to be dealt into the game. He stared blindly at his cards, irritated that he couldn't focus. Guilt nagged at him for what he'd said about Lady Gillian. He didn't like to consider himself a snitch. To his right, Sutherland drummed his fingers on the table. Alex pushed thoughts of the lady away and glanced at Sutherland. "I do believe your patience is getting shorter the longer I know you."

Sutherland snorted. "And you, my friend, are becoming ruder. You left me sitting here while you chatted with Rutherford, and then you think to barge in on my game and not say a word to me?"

"I thought conciliatory silence was why we've remained partners and friends for as long as we have."

Sutherland tapped his cards on the table, his eyes narrowing. "It's unlike you to be distracted. What's on your mind?"

"A lady." Sutherland was the one person Alex could be partially honest with.

"Does the lady have a name?"

"Lady Gillian."

"Rutherford's cousin?"

"Were you eavesdropping on my conversation?"

"Of course. That's why I'm such a great partner. My ability to appear preoccupied while I soak in all the details. It throws off our competition."

"True. But you don't have all the details you need."

Sutherland raised his eyebrows and pushed a full glass of dark liquor toward Alex. "Let me guess. She intrigued you, and it bothered you because she is a proper lady and you only pursue improper women."

The statement brushed too close to the truth that he hadn't really admitted to himself. He set down his cards and shoved his chair away from the table.

"Are you leaving before you've even started?"

Alex nodded. "I've lost the desire to play."

"You've lost the desire to play your favorite game? This is a first. This Lady Gillian must be some woman."

"She's some sort of woman, all right. She's set her sights on you, so you better be careful."

"Me?" Sutherland grinned. "Is she beautiful?"

Her green eyes and olive skin flashed in Alex's mind. "She's passably pretty."

"Well, I suppose I could settle for passably pretty," Sutherland said. "What's her temperament like?"

Alex thought of the way she'd glared at him and refused to back down or be the first to apologize. "I don't know her very well, mind you. I've only seen her twice briefly in the last week. And the last time before that she was eight."

"Yes, fine, so temperament?"

"Tart-tongued, disagreeable and argumentative." He stood up and snapped, "Deal me out," at the dealer. Alex ran a hand over his face. What was wrong with him? He was normally such a calm fellow. It had to be this blasted, bloody awful ball.

"You're in a fine mood." Sutherland motioned for the dealer to deal him out as well. "Let's forget the lady if my meeting her is going to put you in such a disagreeable mood."

Alex clenched his jaw. "Meet her. Marry her. But don't say I didn't warn you." He jerked on his coat. He refused to argue over a woman he barely knew. "Unless you want to find your way back to my town house alone, let's drop this conversation. I have more important things to worry about than whether Lady Gillian traps you into marriage. You're a grown man. My sister, however, is a young lady in need of protection, and I can't very well protect her in here."

He turned on his heel and wound back toward the ballroom door. He had to find Lisse. Sutherland nudged him as they entered the ballroom.

Alex ignored his friend and scanned the room, determined to secure his sister in his sights.

Another jab dug into his ribs. "Do you know when you described Lady Gillian, you smiled? I'm wondering if you don't want her for yourself because your life is so pathetically lonely. You could use a wife. If you want her, I'm gentleman enough to ignore her, even if I am interested."

"Try to remember you're my business partner, not my mother. And spare me your opinion of what my life needs."

"I'm simply saying I've never seen you smile when you've spoken of any woman."

Had he smiled? He had felt as if he was scowling. "It was a smile of relief—relief that I no longer was listening to her chatter."

Alex scanned the crowd again for his sister. He didn't see her anywhere, but that was no surprise given her short stature and the press of bodies in the room. Sweat beaded on his forehead. He should have never quit the ballroom for the card room. Impatient, he wove through the people toward the front of the ballroom. If he could reach the dais, he'd have a much better view over the crowd.

"Lionhurst!" Lord Kettering slapped him on the back. "Good to see you."

Alex pumped the man's hand vigorously. "Likewise,

but I'm in a rush." He shot around the portly fiend and stopped. What in the world was Lady Gillian doing on the dais? She appeared deuced uncomfortable, standing beside a man who was no doubt her father, by the age and look of him. Beside the older gentleman, Harrison Mallorian glowered in Alex's direction. Alex grinned in return and nudged Sutherland nice and hard to pay him back for earlier. "Do you see Mallorian?"

"Yes." Sutherland rubbed at his ribs. "No doubt he's still fuming."

"No doubt." Alex didn't like how the blackguard moved close to Lady Gillian any more than he liked how the man had tried to buy into their company. Both actions made Alex want to crush Mallorian. Lady Gillian jerked away from Mallorian and turned to her father, speaking rapidly.

Good for her. At least she knew a devil disguised in gentlemen's clothing. Alex narrowed his eyes as he studied Mallorian. What was that weasel up to? Alex swept his gaze over the gathered party. Sally stood beside a woman whose pale, drawn face did not bode well for whatever transpired. He recognized the woman as Lady Davenport, the Duke of Kingsley's sister-in-law. That answered the mystery of who the older man was.

Alex moved close.

"What are you doing?" Sutherland fell into step beside him. "Do you see your sister?"

"No, but there's Lady Gillian."

"You said she was passably pretty. She's gorgeous," Sutherland accused.

Sutherland was right. She was beautiful, even more so when angry, and there was no doubt the lady was livid. She shook her dark head at her father, anger visible in her rigid shoulders, jutted chin and deeply pinked skin. Mallorian, on the other hand, appeared smug. *Too smug.* "What do you think Mallorian is up to?"

"Maybe he's trying to buy something else out of his reach," Sutherland quipped.

Sutherland was jesting, but there could be some truth in the matter. And while he hoped the lady failed in her plan to hoodwink Sutherland into marriage, that didn't mean he wanted to see her thrown to the sharks. Or shark, as it were.

Someone latched on to Alex's arm, breaking his focus on the scene. He glanced to the left. "Lissie." He drew his sister close to him.

"Alex! Thank goodness. I cannot find Mother and Father in the chaos."

Her white face alarmed him. "Are you unwell, Lissie?"

"No." She shook her head. "Just overly hot."

"Then let's go on the terrace."

"No!" Lissie reared back out of his reach, her brown-eyed gaze widening. "I have to hear the announcement."

"Why do you care what the Duke of Kingsley is going to announce?"

"I…I don't *care*." Lissie bit her lip. "I simply would be up on the latest news as everyone else."

Her twitching upper lip gave her lie away. Alex studied his sister. She had never lied to him, as far as he knew, but he did not doubt she was lying now. "Lissie—"

A bell rang from the front and the crowd fell silent.

The Duke of Kingsley stepped forward and grasped Lady Gillian by the arm, drawing her near.

As Mallorian stepped to her side, Lissie inhaled sharply. It was on the tip of his tongue to ask his sister what was the matter, but tearing his gaze away from Lady Gillian proved impossible. The color drained from her face. Her gaze darted, searched. For what? An escape?

Kingsley raised a glass. "It's my pleasure to announce the betrothal of my daughter to Mr. Harrison Mallorian."

Lady Gillian took the glass proffered to her with a trembling hand. Alex turned away from the spectacle and glanced at Sutherland. "Well, I suppose the lady has been outwitted by her father." He clasped Sutherland on the shoulder. "Don't worry, my friend, the *ton* is full of hundreds of beautiful debutantes who will want to marry you." He swallowed, his mouth suddenly filled with a bitter taste.

"Now, Lissie–" Where the devil? He glanced around them. What was wrong with that girl? "Where'd she go?" he grumbled more to himself than Sutherland.

"Your sister fled when they announced the betrothal."

"Odd of her to disappear like that."

Sutherland shrugged. "No stranger than you staring at Lady Gillian during the entire announcement and not noticing your sister fleeing from your side."

Alex sighed. Rising to his full height, he scanned the crowd once more but still did not see his sister. *Blasted unreasonable women.* He'd hoped that with her odd behavior she might be agreeable to go. Now he had no choice but to stay among this rabble until he found her. Maybe even then she'd want to stay for hours. "Damn," he muttered under his breath as he motioned to Sutherland to help begin the search.

Six

ALEX COULDN'T UNDERSTAND WHY he still felt so tense. His sister had been found and safely sent home with their parents after begging a headache. His chaperone duties were over for the night. He had a full glass of whiskey in front of him, and he was with his friend and brother, yet his shoulders bunched with tension.

And he couldn't get his bloody mind on the bloody *Vingt-et-un* game. Something was bothering his sister, and he intended to get to the bottom of her problem tomorrow. *Headache his arse.* Her eye had twitched with her second lie of the night.

After a moment's contemplation he knew what was bothering him, other than his sister, he just didn't know why. Lady Gillian had clearly not wished to become someone's soon-to-be bride tonight. But why the hell should that be on his mind? The woman was not his concern.

He shifted in his seat but still could not get comfortable. He had to get out of this place. White's hummed with an excited undercurrent he normally thrived on, yet tonight the buzz of business, drink and bets annoyed him. He needed a woman's soft touch to make him forget the tart-tongued Lady Gillian. Of course, he had no mistress now since he'd had to break things off with Bess. And he was not in the mood to try out a new woman tonight. These things took time and careful consideration.

"Lionhurst? Have you heard a word we said?" Sutherland demanded.

Alex glanced up. He was only just aware he had been staring mindlessly at the crowd of men gathered around the betting book at the front of White's. His brother and Sutherland watched him, no doubt expecting an answer.

"Not a word. Sorry." He picked up his drink and drained the liquid with one gulp before setting the glass down. The last thing he was prepared to do was spill what was on his mind. "The ball drained my ability to think clearly," he said as way of explanation since they appeared to still want one.

Cameron chuckled. "That sounds exactly like something Robert would have said."

Alex twitched at the mention of their dead older brother. He stared at Cameron in stony silence, until color flooded his brother's face. *Good*. His brother needed to be reminded of a few things. Alex leaned forward. "I will never be Robert. I never could be, even if I wanted to."

"Thank God," Cameron mumbled. "But I didn't mean to imply that."

"Whatever you meant, if you want me to take you seriously about buying into the company with Sutherland and me, then don't ever compare me to Robert."

Cameron leaned back in his chair, his embarrassment replaced with a frown. "Forgive me. I wrongfully thought the subject less prickly for you. Consider the matter dropped."

"Perfect." Alex forced a smile. His polite façade wasn't quite where it needed to be tonight. And getting it there seemed impossible. His face twitched with the effort to appear bored.

Damn Cameron for mentioning Robert. Keeping the demons away was easy as long as he didn't think of his older brother. Melancholy seeped over him. He was a betrayer. Whether he thought about it or not, the fact remained the same.

He grasped Cameron's full whiskey glass and chugged the liquid down to wash away the sour taste filling his mouth.

Cameron didn't say a word. His eyes expressed concern, but after a second his gaze slid away from Alex. He turned to Sutherland and asked him something Alex could not hear.

Alex signaled the waiter, got a refill of whiskey and swirled the honey-colored liquid around his glass. He'd never settle into being the marquess. It was hopeless. For everyone. Father was disappointed. Mother. No sense going through the whole bloody list.

At a commotion behind him, he glanced back toward the betting book, eager to turn his thoughts. "Do either of you know what the great interest in the books is tonight?"

Sutherland and Cameron exchanged a look. *What was this about?* "It's unusual for either of you to be mute on any subject."

Sutherland stilled with his glass to his lips, then slowly put it down. "There's a new bet on the books."

"You don't say. Well, from the way you two are gaping at me, I assume my good name, or lack thereof, is somehow the object of the bet."

Cameron grinned. "You're rather smart, old man."

"What is it now? Did I ravish a virgin? Split up a perfectly happy marriage?" It always amazed him the tales people concocted. If he'd done half the things he'd been given credit for he'd be dead from exhaustion.

Sutherland leaned toward him. "Personally, I put my money on you, but then I don't know this woman Lady Staunton, so I may be on the verge of losing a good deal."

Alex narrowed his eyes to control the twitch of anger. "You'd better give me all the details so I can ensure you keep your blunt."

Cameron scooted his chair closer. "I'll give you the details. It's the least I can do as your brother."

"Your concern warms my heart." A twitch in the side of his jaw joined the one in his right eye. This night was never ending. "Get on with it," he bit out.

"It seems Primwitty placed a bet against Randall and Franklin yesterday. They say you and Lady Staunton will be embroiled in an affair by the end of the season. Primwitty, smart chap that he is, bet against them in your favor."

Irritation washed over Alex. Was he not to find any peace tonight? He raised his glass and motioned toward the same servant who had just served him. The man appeared at the table and poured him another shot of liquor. Alex tapped the glass. "More."

"That's a lot of liquor," Cameron said.

Alex eyed his brother. "If you had my memories you'd need just exactly this much," he snapped and downed the liquid. He didn't bother to say that no amount of liquor wiped away the memories of Lady Staunton and Robert. But the whiskey did take the edge off when the memories were at their worst, and tonight was one of those nights.

"I'll need to thank Peter later for taking up my cause."

"It wasn't Primwitty," Cameron said. "It was Sally. Primwitty told me he placed the bet in your favor for her. She's your champion. Primwitty thought it would be better to ignore the matter, turn a blind eye, but Sally insisted your honor had to be defended."

Alex laughed at the news that his champion was none other than the petite blonde duchess. He could see her, now rosy with anger, blue eyes flashing and pushing her husband, Alex's dearest and oldest friend, out the door to play the defender. "Sally's daft. I don't give a damn about my honor. People will believe the worst no matter what." And the way Lady Staunton had been chasing him around despite her ill husband's presence was bound to make tongues wag.

Alex swirled the remaining liquor in his glass before setting the glass down. He'd had his limit, and he knew better than to have any more.

"Interesting that Lady Staunton has set her cap on you again," Cameron said.

"Not really. She knows I'll be duke someday."

Cameron's face relaxed visibly.

"Were you worried for me, little brother?" Alex asked

with a laugh.

"She is beautiful."

"And vile," Alex retorted. "Don't worry. Besides, Father will probably outlive us all."

"That's not what Catherine says."

"What has our dear sister been saying now?" Alex jerked his hands through his hair at the reminder of the duty he'd left untended. He had to get to Sheffield soon and speak to Catherine's husband about her constant gossiping and need for drama. He would stop in on his way to the hunt in Yorkshire. "Why isn't Forrester controlling her tongue?"

"You know as well as I Catherine cannot be controlled. She's taken it into her head Father's going to drink himself to an early grave, and she's apparently been lamenting about it all over Sheffield."

"Well that explains Lady Staunton's renewed interest in me." Alex glanced away from Cameron and toward the front door. He wanted to get out of here and forget everything, just for an hour. Catherine was right to worry about Father—he had been drinking too much. But he'd been doing it since the day Robert had killed himself and the old codger appeared none worse for the liquor.

The front door to White's slammed open, and Alex's friend Dansby loomed in the doorway. Alex raised his hand to wave him over. Judging by the way Dansby shoved through the crowd of men around the books and strode toward Alex, the visit must be urgent. He stood to greet Dansby.

"What brings you out at this late hour?"

"Your father sent me to find you and your brother."

Alex's gut clenched. His father never involved anyone in family affairs. "What's wrong?"

"It's your sister, Allysia."

"Damnation." He grabbed his coat and jerked it on. "I knew something was wrong with her. Is she ill?"

Dansby shook his head.

"Well, what is it?"

Dansby's gaze shot to Cameron and then Sutherland.

"Spit it out," Alex demanded, barely containing his temper.

"She's dead."

"I WISH I WERE dead!" Gillian fell backward onto her bed. She pulled the covers up over her head and stared into the darkness.

"Gillie, don't say such a thing, even in jest." Whitney plopped onto the bed and tugged the covers away from Gillian's face. "You know I couldn't get on without you. I've every confidence you'll manage to avoid marrying Mr. Mallorian."

Gillian struggled into a sitting position at the note of desperation in Whitney's voice. Whit needed her. "Don't fret, Whit. I'm just allowing myself a moment of pity that Father wants to rid himself of me so badly that he would betroth me to Mr. Mallorian."

Whitney shook her head. "Father loves you. He just..." Whitney gave Gillian a pleading look. "You know Father. He doesn't think things through when he's imbibed too much."

Gillian pressed her lips together on her retort. Father *had* thought things through, and that was the point, but Whitney needed to cling to her hope that Father adored them both. There was no point in trying to make Whit see the truth now when they were hopefully escaping soon.

A shudder ran through Gillian as she pictured herself posed for a Westonburt family portrait flanked by Lady Westonburt and Mr. Mallorian. The idea of Lady Westonburt being her mother-in-law was enough to make her ill, without even bringing the woman's son into the picture. As usual, Gillian got that funny creeping sensation over her skin when she thought of the baroness. When they happened to cross paths in church, the woman always looked at her as if she knew Gillian's secret. Lately, it had gotten worse. Lady Westonburt's sly stares had become scathing, direct looks. It was impossible the woman could know anything. *Completely impossible.* Even still, Gillian breathed deeply to calm her jangled nerves.

Whitney propped herself onto her elbows and kicked off her shoes. "I saw Lady Westonburt in Town yesterday when I was purchasing ribbon. She gave me the evil eye and turned away. She didn't even acknowledge when I said hello to her. Isn't that funny? She had to have known you were becoming her daughter-in-law. Why would she act so odd?"

"I don't know, Whit, but just try to avoid her if I'm not with you."

"Gillie, you cannot play mother to me forever. At some point, you have to let me take care of myself."

Gillian rested her hands underneath her chin. "Don't worry. The minute our feet hit American soil, you won't have me hovering over you anymore."

Whitney screwed up her face. "I don't understand your fascination with America. Do you really fancy yourself in love with Mr. Sutherland?"

"Not yet, but I'm sure I will be. He's perfect for me."

"Why?"

"Because, Whit." Gillian scrambled onto her knees and stared into her sister's eyes, hoping she would understand. "According to the gossip sheets, he wants a wife with a brain, not a woman to treat as chattel. I refuse to be stuck in an unhappy marriage like Mother and Father's, and I refuse for you to be stuck in that either. Is that what you want?"

"No, but perhaps you could get out of marriage to Mr. Mallorian and find someone here in England who would make you happy."

Gillian sighed. They couldn't stay in England. Not just because of the person sending the threatening notes, but also because of Father. She certainly could not mention the notes to Whitney, but she had to make her understand. "Father will not budge. I already tried to reason with him, and he fairly shoved me out of his study. It's pointless. He was standing beside me tonight when Mr. Mallorian told me my future duties, and Father didn't even raise an eyebrow."

"What did Mr. Mallorian say?"

"I'm to adorn his arm, silent and smiling at every *ton* function, provide him with children, ask no questions and run his household as he tells me to."

"Oh, that is bad, Gillie. What are we going to do now

that Father has made this move?"

Gillian rubbed her temples, trying to think clearly. "Father may have won the first round, but I intend to win the match. I've thought about it, and I'm going to send a message to Sally with an invitation to Auntie's house party in honor of Trent."

Whitney frowned. "How is that going to help you avoid marriage to Mr. Mallorian?"

Gillian scooted off the bed, feeling better by the second. "Sally can see that Mr. Sutherland attends the party. Then I'll have an entire week to get the man to agree to marry me."

"Oh, yes." Whitney nodded with a smirk. "That sounds utterly reasonable. Mr. Sutherland will surely jump at the chance to attend a week-long party for our cousin whom he doesn't even know."

"I disagree. He's an avid foxhunter and Vingt-et-un player, so I'll make sure Sally mentions both."

"Shouldn't you ask Auntie first?"

"I'll send her a note straightaway explaining the additional guests. You know how she detests Lady Westonburt."

"And how she's a firm believer in marriages of love. Given her and Uncle's."

Gillian nodded. "She'll help."

"Father will never forgive us for going against him."

A lump formed in Gillian's throat. Did she want or care about her father's forgiveness? Her heart squeezed. She loved him. It was useless to try to deny it. No matter what, she loved her father. "He may not, but we have to take that chance. To not take it..." Gillian glanced at the jewelry box that held the threatening letter. "That's simply not an option."

"So you say," Whitney murmured. "But I feel as if you are leaving out a piece of this puzzle."

Gillian grasped her sister's hands and squeezed. The only piece she was leaving out was the piece of the past that could irrevocably harm her sister and the piece of the present that would definitely harm her. "I'm not," she lied.

Seven

Cheapside
London, England

AT THE BREAK OF dawn, Harrison Mallorian stumbled out of the whore's bed to make his way to his parents' town house. *Damn his mother for being an early riser.* He'd have slept till noon if he didn't need to go home before she awoke. She'd make his life a living hell if he wasn't there with all the details of how her plan had gone.

He staggered down the creaking steps of Madame Lovelace's small establishment and raised a hand to shield his eyes from the first traces of sunlight streaming into the sky. Imbibing too much whiskey to celebrate his success and dull the image of Allysia Trevelle had not been his most brilliant idea. Cotton occupied the better part of his head, a nasty acidic taste filled his mouth and the sun hurt his bloody eyes.

He tripped down the last step, only maintaining his upright position thanks to his coachman quickly coming to grasp his arm. He straightened to thank the man but caught his smirk. Anger replaced any trace of gratefulness. "Need I remind you of the beating you took last week?"

Hallsworth shook his head. "Ye need not, sir."

"Good. Mind you to remember not many in London would employ a man dismissed on accusation of stealing from his former employer."

"I know it, sir." Hallsworth touched the fading bruise on his eye. "I don't reckon I'll forget yer generous nature after yer last lesson."

Harrison turned and settled into the carriage, trying to get comfortable. He pulled his overcoat tight to capture some warmth and blew into his hands. His breath swirled white into the air.

"Are ye ready, sir?"

"Yes," he snapped, rubbing his aching head. "I hardly want to sit here in the freezing cold."

The carriage jolted to a start, causing his head to jerk back with the force of sudden movement. He clenched his teeth, gripping the edge of the cushion. Hallsworth hated him, but that was perfect. The lower class often disliked their superiors. They begrudged showing the proper amount of respect. It may have taken several beatings for the coachman to learn his place, but the man knew it now and would not forget it. Everyone had a place in Society, like it or not. And he'd learned years ago only the strongest and smartest could possibly change their place. The coachman was mad because he was too stupid and too weak to change his own life.

Harrison was changing his life, though having to rely on his mother in order to accomplish his goals grated on his nerves. But that situation would change when he married Lady Gillian and his father succumbed to his sickness.

He ran a hand through his hair, trying to set it to rights. There was no need for his mother to know what he had been doing last night. She'd not approve, but soon she'd learn who was in control. As a matter of fact, his headstrong fiancée needed that same lesson immediately. She'd offered him little regard at the Primwitty ball.

He would show her he was more than a lowly baron's son. The carriage jerked to a halt in front of the town house. No lights burned in the window. Finally, things were going his way.

If he could just get a bit of sleep before facing his mother, he could tolerate her screeching. He was damn sick and tired of screeching women. Though Allysia had probably had a right to be so upset with him. He *had* used her to get back at her pompous brother just as she had accused him of doing.

He still boiled with anger at the way his attempt to buy into Lionhurst's shipping company had been so easily crushed by the man. Who was insignificant now? Not him. He'd bedded the pompous ass's sister. So why did he not feel better? Had he not made his enemy's favorite sister a whore?

His gut twisted on the thought. He smashed his fist into the seat. She was a weapon. A means to an end. There was no room for guilt. But it was there. Her pleading words rang in his ears. He pressed his hands to either side of his head. She was wrong. And he was right. Her pompous father would never have let her marry him. No, indeed.

He'd been right to discard her. That would wound Lionhurst all the more. Harrison took a deep breath and got out of the carriage. A lowly baron's son needed a secret to marry upward into the *haute ton*. He paused in his steps, considering yet again how Mother knew the Duke of Kingsley would consent to a match. It was a mystery she refused to unravel for him. Yet another reason he despised her.

Inside the town house, he rounded the corner to the stairs and cursed. The old witch had waited up for him.

"Hello, Mother." He tried to sound loving.

She cackled from the top of the steps, her gray hair shimmering silver from the glow of the candle in her hand. "I can smell a whore's perfume from fifty paces." She descended the steps, her gnarled hands gripping the banister. "Harry, you're a fool to risk your future with Lady Gillian. Remember, my secret will only take us so far in Society. I suspect the duke has his limits, and I'm not keen to test just where they might be."

"I'm sorry, Mother." He felt ten again. *Damn woman.*

"I take it by your stench that you celebrated your good fortune?"

He nodded and tried to quell the hatred swelling in his chest. Soon he would rule a woman; soon he would be his own master.

His mother pursed her lips. "The apple never does roll far from the tree. But you seek out a lower class of whore than your father did. At least his indiscretion made us rich. Weak fool. Go say goodbye to your father. He's finally dying." She pushed past him, sauntering along the hall as if the death of her husband did not affect her in the slightest.

Harrison trudged up the stairs toward his father's room. The sickly sweet stench of death filled the air, and he swallowed back the nausea threatening to erupt. He ambled over to his father's side. His eyes lay closed, but his raspy breathing filled the air.

Harrison dropped into a chair by his father's bed. Struck with an idea, he smiled and pressed his lips close to his father's ear. "Tell me your secret, Father. Tell me everything, and I'll make sure Mother knows who is in charge from here on out."

His father's eyes cracked open, and his gaze flickered around the room.

"We're alone, Father," Harrison whispered encouragingly.

His father nodded, then licked his cracked lips. "Isabella Rutherford, Lady Kingsley, was my life."

Eight

Two days later
Sheffield, England
Loxley Castle

ALEX STOOD WITH THE other mourners huddled at the top of the hill and stared down at Lissie's coffin. Everything was wrong. The air refused to warm, though it was near noon. The day should have been cloudless, but damnable clouds covered the sun. Shadows blanketed his sister's grave. She would have hated that. And if she had still been alive she would have bemoaned the hint of rain to come that filled the air. She would have disliked everything about this day, yet the conditions seemed fitting to him. Her death had stopped life around the place just as Robert's had years before.

Alex tried to focus on what the priest said about Lissie's sudden and tragic death, but the word "tragic" bothered him. The single word did not do justice to how his heart twisted. It was more than tragic that he would never see his poppet again or experience her smile or laughter. When in the blazes had she quit smiling? His head ached as the priest grew quiet and nodded to the caretaker to throw the first shovel of dirt onto his sister's grave. The dirt hit the coffin and resounded like a thunderclap inside his head.

His mother moaned beside him, her soft sobs filling the quiet. He stared at the smattering of dark brown dirt now covering Lissie's pale wood coffin. The air around him smothered him with the moisture beginning to fill it. He swallowed, every breath a struggle. Lissie could feel nothing, but he had the insane desire to jump into the grave, throw open the lid and allow fresh air to flow around her. The wind picked up and pushed a cold, invisible hand against his body. He stepped forward, only to be stopped by a firm grip around his arm.

Alex's gaze locked with Cameron's. Did Cameron feel the same? A sense of being smothered? They gripped arms until the final shovel of dirt was thrown. He clenched his teeth to suppress the bellow of rage in his throat. He could not think on what had befallen her now in front of all these people.

If Mother had not insisted on her family's bizarre tradition of inviting everyone who knew them to the graveside, he would have simply left the grave and be damned if his family got angry. But he would not embarrass Mother or Father in front of all the prying eyes surrounding them. It baffled him, his Mother's notion that a funeral was a time everyone should come together to say their goodbyes to the person. This was not a damned celebration. Lissie was not off to boarding school. She was dead, and she sure as hell was never coming back to them.

Someone coughed to his right, and he looked up to meet the slanted violet eyes of Lady Staunton. Her bold, flirtatious smile made him ill. Did she have no decency? *Stupid fool. You know the answer to that one.* He glared and pointedly fixed his gaze on her husband to remind the wretched woman she was still married.

Dear God, but Lord Staunton had declined. The man didn't look as if he would make it past this day alive. His gray skin and dull eyes did not bode well for his future. Alex's gaze flickered back to Lady Staunton and the small smile tugging at the corner of her lips finally disappeared as he stared. Within seconds, she brushed a few tears off her cheeks. He wanted to shake her to get her to cease her act. She had not changed a bit in the years since Robert's death. The need to be the center of attention was still at her core.

He refused to give her what she wanted. He glanced around the circle of people gathered to say goodbye and fought the urge to turn on his heel and walk away from the onlookers.

"Alex." His father spoke behind him. "Will you walk your mother down the hill, please?"

He didn't need any further prodding. Getting away would be a blessing. He threw his arm around his mother's tiny shoulders and supported most of her weight. As they descended the hill, she began to cry in earnest, and it took all his will not to let loose the emotions swelling inside him and join her.

ALEX STEPPED ONTO THE dark balcony, shutting the door firmly behind him. As the door clicked, the hum in the dining hall abruptly stopped, and he allowed himself to relax as he leaned against the railing. The bright moon filled the sky. *Funny that the moon would be so vivid on the night they buried Lissie. Maybe she'd get those good things in the afterlife she swore a full moon brought*. The little dreamer. He smiled. He could still picture her staring up at the sky, a look of intense preoccupation on her face. He'd sneak up on her, and she'd dissolve into fits of laughter before promptly telling him what was on her mind. Except lately he'd been too busy to notice if anything was on her mind.

He gripped the glass tighter and gulped down the last of the whiskey. Lissie would never see the places she had dreamed of exploring. And all because she had been afraid to tell any of them she was pregnant. He still could not believe it, but the hysterical servant who had helped her gather the pennyroyal and watched her ingest the oil until she was vomiting and doubled over in pain said it was so.

The voices in the dining hall erupted behind him once again. He tensed at the intrusion on his solitude. An elbow brushed his arm then Cameron leaned beside him against the balcony. "You have a murderous look on your face."

Alex nodded. "I was thinking how I'll find the blackguard who seduced Lissie and kill him."

"You're not a murderer."

"I know." He met his brother's gaze. "It's damn annoying. I'm not too good for revenge, though."

Cameron smiled. "I suspected as much. But you have a more pressing problem at the moment."

"What might that be?"

"Lady Staunton is looking for you. She's acting like a dog in heat. I bet she thinks you'll ask her to marry you once her husband keels over."

Alex could not raise his usual amused chuckle. "Ever direct, little brother."

"Everything I am I learned from you."

"God help you, then. I'd sooner marry old Lady Burrows than marry Lady Staunton."

"Really?" Cameron looked appalled. "You'd marry that wrinkled old bag before the delectable Lady Staunton?"

"Certainly. Lady Burrows may be old and wrinkled, but at least she has a heart."

"Good point. See, you are wise, and I can learn a great deal from you."

"Are you trying to lighten my mood?"

All playfulness left Cameron's face. "Well, when you walked out here you did look as if you might fling yourself off the balcony."

"No," Alex assured his brother, understanding Cameron's concern. Between Robert's suicide and Lissie's accidentally killing herself, Alex had the desire to draw his remaining siblings close and put them under lock and key. "I was thinking about throwing Lissie's seducer off a balcony. Not myself."

"Good."

"Now, on to more important matters."

"Lady Staunton?"

Alex shook his head. "She is not important. Where are Mother and Father?"

"Mother's upstairs with a migraine, and Father is locked away in his study drinking barrels of whiskey."

Cameron frowned down at his empty glass. “Catherine is in the dining hall playing the hostess. She’s twittering around the room, smiling and laughing. It appears she’s forgotten the occasion is our sister’s funeral.”

Alex pushed away from the rail and circled his shoulders, trying to work out the knots in his neck. “Don’t be too hard. That’s just how Catherine copes. Now how do you know Father is imbibing in a good deal of whiskey?”

“Because, old man, I watched the servant take a full bottle in, and just now when I came looking for you, I saw my good man Smitty bring out the same bottle, now empty. Smitty says Father is foxed.”

“That should give the guests something more to tantalize them.”

“They’re tantalized enough,” Cameron said. “I overheard someone whisper that our family is cursed.”

“Did you, now?” Alex looked at his brother. “What else are the guests saying?”

“They say two grown children dying out of five is a bad omen, a curse.” Cameron pushed off the rail. “I hate how people are so inconsiderate as to whisper loud enough for me to hear.”

“Yes, they should take care to whisper more quietly.” Alex glanced at Cameron. “Maybe we are cursed. First Robert’s death, now Lissie’s.”

“Lissie didn’t mean to kill herself. Her girl said so.”

“True. But Robert did. The fool. And no one knows that better than me.”

Cameron flinched.

“Sorry.” Alex sighed. “I didn’t mean to bring Robert up now.”

“No, I’m glad you did. You never talk about him. Do you want to?”

“You want me to lay my betrayal out nice and neat for you?” Alex growled.

“That’s not what I said nor, for the record, is it what I think.” Cameron took a swig of his drink. “Let’s forget it.”

“Forgotten.”

“How do you propose we find the fiend who seduced Lissie? And when we do, what are we going to do to him?"

"Since murdering him is out, I'll settle on heinous revenge."

"I'm helping."

"We'll see." Alex didn't want Cameron to get into any trouble.

When Cameron looked as if he were about to protest, Alex said, "I propose we start in Lissie's room. Maybe we'll discover something to point us in the right direction."

A few minutes later, he stood on the threshold of his sister's bedroom. He and Cameron slipped quietly into the space. The pungent odor of mint and sickness surrounded him, nearly gagging him.

"What the devil is that smell?" Cameron held his arm to his mouth as he rushed to open the window.

"That's the smell of death." Alex walked over to the dresser and opened a drawer. They worked in silence for close to an hour until they stood surrounded by scattered clothes, books, shoes and enough feminine trinkets to boggle the mind—but no clues.

"I don't know, old man. Maybe she didn't leave a clue."

Alex surveyed the room. There had to be a clue. His eyes burned as he swept his gaze over the room repeatedly.

Cameron walked toward the bedroom door. "Maybe we should get some sleep. Come back tomorrow."

It would be so easy to agree. In sleep, the pain would be forgotten, but when he woke it would still be there, consuming, throbbing and never really a memory. Just like Robert.

He shook his head, blinked and glanced around the room again. The old doll he had given Lissie on her eighth birthday still sat on a small green child's chair in the corner of her room. The decor of pastels and flowers could not have fit his sister more perfectly. He studied the dresser, cluttered with brushes, perfumes and hairpins. Nothing there that could help him. What kind of clue was he even looking for? Who was his sister? A dreamer, a writer. Perhaps a diary? Where would she hide a diary?

He walked over to the wooden jewelry box he'd given her for her birthday last year and tried the lid. Locked. He sifted through her belongings on her vanity, looking for the key.

"What are you doing?" Cameron asked, coming to stand beside him.

"Looking for a key."

"Why?"

"Maybe there's a diary in here." Alex tapped on the lid of the wooden box.

"Lissie didn't have any dark secrets to hide!" Cameron protested.

"Really?"

"Sorry. Stupid thing to say."

Alex picked up a letter opener and wedged it into the lock until it clicked satisfactorily. His hands trembled as he opened the lid and picked up the small leather-bound book. He ran a thumb over the cover of his sister's diary as he walked to the bed and sat. Cameron sat beside him. Opening the diary, Alex flipped toward the back.

March 20, 1818

Today I told him I wished to marry him, but he said it couldn't work. He's to marry another, has probably known for weeks and weeks that he will. Why didn't he tell me and stop our madness? What am I to do? The shame to me, the shame to my family. I'd kill myself, but how can I do that to Mother after Robert?

Alex gripped the paper between his clammy fingers and forced himself to turn the page. He cleared his throat and continued.

April 1, 1818

Marion is my best hope. She owes me since I know she's been playing the doxy to the stable master. Who am I to stand on propriety? Still, I must appear to be threatening.

Marion is all atwitter with fear that I'll tell her secret, so I told her mine. She'll help me gather the Pennyroyal to rid myself of M.'s baby. I shall never forgive him or myself.

Alex looked up from the paper. "Who do you think M. is?"

Cameron squinted down at the paper. "I've no idea."

April 2, 1818

Alex's hands shook so violently he had to grip one hand with the other in order to read the spidery writing. April 2 had been three days ago, the Primwitty ball. He should have known something was badly wrong when she had fled his side. He swallowed his self-loathing, storing the feeling for later, and gazed at the entry.

Now I know, and it is worse than I thought. I forced myself to stand and hear it all and watch it all. They announced his betrothal, and he appeared so very happy and she so very beautiful. Lady Gillian Rutherford. I hate her. I hate him. I hate myself most of all.

Alex snapped the book closed.

"Did you hear me?" Cameron asked.

"What?" A roaring filled Alex's ears.

"I said we need to warn Lady Gillian who she's to marry."

"Warn her?" He whipped up and loomed over his brother. "Don't utter a word. The lady's a schemer who had every intention of seducing Sutherland into marrying her. Besides, when I'm through the lady won't have to concern herself with being shackled to a monster."

"All right. I can live with that. But what exactly are we going to do?"

"You're going to do nothing."

"Alex—"

"No. This is my revenge. Mallorian seduced Lissie to get back at me."

"Why? Why would he do that?"

"Because." Alex said, "he wanted to buy into my company and I dismissed him like the piece of garbage he is."

"It's not like you to be cruel."

Alex nodded. "He happened to come to me right after Bess told me about a serving wench who'd said she'd been beaten and forced by him. But the woman had no witnesses. Bess took the girl in and wanted to make sure it was all right with me."

Cameron whistled. "That's bad. What do you intend to do?"

"The man's a social climber. I intend to take away his

ladder."

"The Lady Gillian?"

"That's right," Alex said, the roaring finally dying away in his ears.

"Are you saying you intend to seduce his fiancée into marrying you instead? A sort of public humiliation?"

He intended to seduce Lady Gillian into publicly leaving Mallorian, but marriage was not part of the bargain. He'd set her up nicely when he was done and ensure she had a better life than she would have ever had with Mallorian.

"Alex, you didn't answer my question. You do intend to marry the lady once you've ruined her, don't you?"

"I do not," he replied, giving his brother a look that dared him to protest. "The lady wanted to flee to America on Sutherland's coattails. Well, I'll send her there in grand style. She'll be fine. And in the end she'll thank me. She can find a man to marry that she actually loves."

Cameron shook his head. "Somehow I doubt the lady will thank you."

Nine

Two Days Later
Cheapside
London, England

ALEX CROUCHED BESIDE PETER Manchester, the Duke of Primwitty—the one man besides his brother that he trusted with this sordid mess. Alex pressed his back against the cold brick of the Merry Tavern and took another shallow breath. It was useless. The stench of rotting garbage filled his nose once again. "Sodding garbage."

"Exactly," Peter agreed, taking his own shallow breath with his hands over his mouth. "My legs are cramping."

"Quit whining." Alex rubbed at the knots in his own legs.

"How much longer do you think we'll be forced to crouch here?" Peter asked.

"Can't be that much longer." Alex eyed Madame Lovelace's establishment.

"We've been here for hours," Peter complained.

Alex glanced at the moon. "Probably three. Mallorian has to come out soon."

"I long for my clean, warm bed. And my wife," Peter said, his voice raising a notch.

Alex chuckled. "Marriage has made you weak. Keep

quiet or you'll blow our cover."

Alex would wait here all night to learn every sordid detail he could about Mallorian. He wanted to know the man better than his own mother did. Then he'd use that knowledge to completely destroy him.

Something rustled through the trash near his left foot, and in the little sliver of moonlight shining between the tavern and the madame's house, Alex made out the outline of a rat. *Loathsome creatures*. He hated rats. Peter bolted upright beside him, and Alex reached up reflexively and jerked Peter back down.

"Sit still, man. You'll get us discovered with your theatrics."

"Rats are vile," Peter growled, shaking off Alex's hand. "Got bit by one once when I was a child. Deuced nasty bite that almost killed me."

"Does Sally know you're afraid of rats?"

"No. Nor does my curious wife know I'm here playing spy with you, given you made me swear not to tell her. Keep annoying me and I may have to unburden all my secrets."

"You're bluffing. If I thought you would do that I wouldn't have asked for your help."

"Ask for my help?" Peter sputtered. "You told me I was helping, then swore me to secrecy. Sally would blister my ears if she knew we were crouched outside of Madame Lovelace's engaged in some harebrained scheme of revenge. You do know they have constables for this sort of thing?"

"I can't use a constable, and you know it. I'll not chance besmirching my sister's good name by allowing this sordid mess to come to light."

"You know, sometimes being your friend is a burden. Lucky for you, I'm a strapping young man, so I'm up to the challenge."

When Peter flexed his thin arm as proof of his masculine state, a smile pulled at Alex's lips, but allowing even a moment of levity so soon after burying his sister felt like the worst sort of betrayal. He looked away and rubbed his burning eyes.

"You do realize Sally would only protest because she is

not here with us."

"I do." Peter's white teeth flashed in the darkness. "However, I choose to forget my wife's adventurous nature in order to maintain my sanity." Peter slapped at his face, disheveling his glasses. He shoved his spectacles back onto the bridge of his nose. "These blasted mosquitoes are chewing on me like a savory piece of meat. Are you sure your mistress gave you the correct information about this man's habits?"

"Positive," Alex replied, not bothering to explain that Bess was no longer his mistress. He would save that conversation for later, or maybe never. It was his private matter. "I gave Bess a large purse to distribute as she saw fit to loosen some tongues, and she said Madame Lovelace's tongue would have detached from her body had it gotten any looser. Mallorian is here, as he is every Wednesday night. When he exits, you follow him, and I'll pay a visit to Mistress Caprice Mills—his regular choice for companionship, according to Bess."

"Are you sure this is the best course of action?"

"What would you do if someone seduced your sister and she died trying to rid herself of the child?"

There was a pause of silence as Peter took off his glasses and rubbed at the bridge of his nose. Finally, he put them back on with a sigh. "Same thing. I'd destroy the man, but I'd probably leave out ruining another woman."

"I told you, she will be better off with what I have planned for her. She wanted to seduce Sutherland. Clearly, she wants no part of marrying Mallorian and she wants out of England. I will be providing her both her fondest wishes."

"It's convenient for you to think so," Peter replied.

Alex clenched his fists. "If you won't help me without lecturing me, then go."

"I'll stay. And I'll shut up, but only because I have every faith your good nature will return, and you'll do the right thing by Lady Gillian once you've seduced her."

Alex gaped at Peter. "If you think I'm going to have some change of heart and marry the lady, you're sadly mistaken."

When silence greeted Alex, he glowered. "I will never marry."

"I know you say that. I think you've just not met the right woman."

"And you think a lady I already dislike, who I plan to seduce and then ship off to America, might be just the woman to change my mind about women and marriage?"

"I think she might," Peter snapped. "Sally's told me a great deal about Lady Gillian and her personality. I think she'd suit you."

"I didn't ask you to come here and think, and why the bloody hell have you been talking to Sally about Lady Gillian?"

"Calm down," Peter growled from the darkness. "The conversation had nothing to do with you. Sally was excited to see her friend after all these years, and we simply talked of the two of them and then the lady herself."

He was just about to tell Peter to shut up when Mallorian alighted from the house and shuffled down the stairs. Alex turned to motion Peter to retrieve the horse tied behind the house, but Peter was already stalking silently in that direction. After a moment, Mallorian's coach appeared at the same time Peter did with the horse.

Alex stood and moved through the shadows toward Peter. "Stay close, but not too close."

Peter nodded.

Tension mounted and coiled through Alex. He wanted to follow Mallorian himself, but he also wished to question the man's ladybird. He had to trust Peter. "Don't lose him."

"Bugger off, Lionhurst," Peter hissed before mounting his horse. A whistle rang through the silence, and Mallorian's carriage moved down the road with Peter following a good space behind. Alex waited until they were out of sight before he strode to the front door of Madame Lovelace's establishment and knocked.

The door eased open and a cloud of overpowering musky perfume filtered out. He swallowed his distaste and gazed down at the buxom redhead squeezed into the gaudiest creation of silk and lace he had ever seen. A pale blue gaze swept over him, moving from his shoes to what appeared to be his private region, then slowly to his face. Cherry lips parted to display slightly yellowed teeth. If he had been a man with a weak stomach, his evening meal would have departed. Instead, he smiled, slowly and appreciatively.

The redhead's eyes rounded with surprise. He bowed slightly to ease her suspicion. Every woman deserved deference no matter her occupation. "I'm Lord Lionhurst. May I come in?"

He didn't know what to expect. But he certainly didn't expect her to reach out and trace a finger across his chest, which was exactly what she did. He stood stock-still. He was prepared to do a lot of things to get his revenge, but sleeping with the madame was not one of them.

Opening the door wider, she motioned him in. "You are a lion, indeed. So strong." She squeezed his bicep. "So handsome." She ran a rough finger down his cheekbone, not stopping until she got to the top of his breeches. "So well-endowed, it would appear."

A man could only take so much. He grabbed her hand and pressed it gently back to her side. "You entice me, my dear, but I'm committed at the moment."

She winked. "I know. We *all* know in this trade how generous and cold you can be. Your former lovers talk, you know."

He clenched his teeth against the tic in his jaw. "I've always been honest about what to expect from a relationship with me." *Was he really standing here defending his honor to a madame*?

"But they fall in love with you anyway, don't they?"

"Not that I'm aware of," he said evenly.

"Well, let me enlighten you." She took his arm and pulled him through the door. An aged footman appeared out of nowhere and quietly closed the door behind Alex. He glanced around the dimly lit parlor in case anyone else was lurking in the shadows waiting to materialize. A pianoforte stood in the corner and several settees and some empty chairs were scattered about the sparse room. His eyes stopped abruptly on a girl flanked by two men. She looked young enough to be his sister. Hell, she resembled his sister with her pale blond hair and light blue eyes. His heart sped up.

Was this the girl Mallorian had come to see? *Sick bastard.* Bile rose in Alex's throat. The lady had a black eye along with a swollen, cut lip. This had to be Caprice Mills. "I'm here for the services of Caprice Mills," he said, aware he was contradicting his previous statement about being otherwise engaged.

Madame Lovelace raised a questioning eyebrow but pointed at the woman. "She's there if you still want her after getting a look at her. The blackguard before you has a fiery, mean temper. I've warned him. Now I'll not be letting him back in my establishment, because he can't heed a warning. No one harms my girls."

He had a newfound respect for Madame Lovelace. "I advise you to take care," Alex warned. From what he could ascertain, Caprice Mills was not the first woman to experience Mallorian's temper.

Madame Lovelace chortled with laughter. "Dearie, those two men right there are all the precaution I need."

Alex followed her gaze to the two tall men standing next to Caprice. By the bruises on Caprice's face, it was obvious the men had failed miserably in protecting what was Madame Lovelace's, but Alex held his peace. Stating his opinion would not gain him an audience with Caprice, and he needed that more than enlightening the madame to the failings of her paid protectors. Alex turned to Caprice. "May I have a moment of your company?" He produced a heavy bag of coins and offered it to her.

She snatched it from his hands, scuttling backward as her fingers clutched the material of the bag. "Easy," he said in a soothing tone. "I swear I won't harm you."

She shifted the coins back and forth between her small hands before handing the bag to Madame Lovelace. Alex noted her gaze stayed firmly planted on the money. She'd likely not see a dime of the coin. He'd make sure to compensate her without the madame's knowledge.

Madame Lovelace handed the girl a drink, which she

promptly downed and then took another. By the third glass full of what looked like whiskey, Alex stepped forward. He'd thought calming her might be a good idea, but he didn't want the girl so in her cups she couldn't answer any of his questions. "I think that will do her."

Madame Lovelace smiled. "Take the gold room."

Caprice took the full cup the madame handed her while gazing at Alex a moment before offering a tentative smile. He smiled back and noted her shoulders sag as she relaxed. Up the stairs and two doors to the right, they entered the gold room. Madame Lovelace had aptly named the room.

The small space fairly blinded him with the gold coverlet, curtains and pillows. Everything that was not wood was the color of gold. He would have laughed had he still possessed the ability.

Caprice glanced at him. "You hate it?" Her lower lip quivered.

Damn it all, he had not meant to embarrass her. "No. It's lovely."

"Yer a terrible liar. Anyone ever told you that?"

"No." But he clearly remembered telling Lady Gillian the exact same thing. *Blast her green eyes.* Caprice gave a shrill laugh before tilting her glass up and draining it. "It's awful, I know it. Ye know it. The only one who doesn't seem ta know it is Madame Lovelace, and she's the only one who counts. I don't matter a whit, except for when I hand over my money. And as you've already paid…"

She took his hand and led him to the bed. He sat on the edge, but when she reached down to pull up the bottom of her sheer gown, he stilled her hands. "I'm not here for that." He patted the space beside him. "Will you please sit?"

Worry etched her face. "You've nothing to fear," he said, trying to reassure her. "I simply want to ask you a few questions."

"Ye paid so much blunt only ta ask me some questions?" The disbelief was evident in her tone.

"They're important questions." He pulled her gently onto the bed beside him.

"Well, you've bought me, and so far ye're the nicest visitor I've ever had, so what do ye want ta know?" She hiccupped, and her skin turned a deep shade of red.

"Can you tell me anything about Mr. Mallorian?"

She turned her face away from his, but her hands twisted furiously in her lap.

He touched her shoulder with care. "It's quite all right," he reassured her again. "I mean you no harm."

"I could tell ye a great deal, sir." Her worried blue gaze came to his face. "Harrison's quite the talker. But ye see, he frightens me. I've got ta earn a livin' and this is where I earn it. I don't doubt he'd come for me if he thought I'd spoken any of his secrets. Unlike Madame, I don't believe her henchmen are any match for the likes of him."

Alex rubbed his chin. What could he do? She was afraid and rightly so. But what if...? Bess would help him. His former mistress would know just how to set Caprice up in her own business. Bess could do the work, and he would give the girl enough blunt to live on until she got started. He would not miss such a paltry sum. "I can offer you a new life."

"As yer mistress?"

He picked up her hand and squeezed it. "No, but you are very lovely. Unfortunately for us both, you remind me of my sister. So you see—"

"Gawds, yes." She wrinkled her nose. "I've a brother somewhere out there, and I could never let a man touch me who looked like him."

Alex nodded, relieved her feelings were not hurt. "I have a lady friend who can set you up somewhere quietly, and I'll provide the blunt you need until you get a protector."

Tears shimmered in Caprice's eyes. "You'd do that for me?"

"I wish I were as nice as that. I'll do it to obtain your information."

"I think you'd do it anyway. I saw the way your face darkened when you saw my bruises and cuts. Yer no man to leave a woman in need. Yer a real nice man."

She hugged him fiercely. "Ye could have just beaten my secrets out of me. Many men would. But you're good.

See?"

Alex untwined her arms. He was not comfortable being on anyone's pedestal. "Clearly, you have not known many truly virtuous men if you label me so, but I'll take the gratitude if it means you'll help me."

"Oh, I'll help you." Caprice scooted back on the bed and propped up several shimmering gold pillows. "He talked about a good deal of things, probably because no one else would listen. At first I felt sorry for him, almost liked him. Can ye understand?"

Hell, no, he did not understand, but he nodded anyway. "Did he talk about any women in particular?"

"One. Some poor girl related ta a man who'd made Harrison mad. Alice? No." Caprice shook her head. "Agnes?"

"Allysia?" It was hard to choke the word out past the anger constricting his throat.

"Yes, Allysia! How'd ye know? Is she why you're here?"

He'd come here for proof, and now he had it. He'd thought he was right, but he had wanted to make positively sure before destroying the man. "Yes." He struggled to keep his voice low and calm. "She's what brought me to you."

Caprice pulled her knees to her chest. She looked so young and innocent, like Lissie. Looking out the window, Caprice sighed. "I can't tell ye much, simply because he didn't say too much about her. He used her. I know cause he bragged about how easy she'd been to seduce."

Alex jumped off the bed and paced the room. He needed to destroy something or he would find Mallorian tonight and murder the blackguard.

"He fancies himself irresistible ta women." Caprice snorted. "But ye know, I think he likes her. I mean ta say liked her. She's dead now, ye know." Caprice tilted her head at him. "But ye must know this."

Unable to form a suitable inoffensive reply, he nodded. He knew his little sister was dead. He knew nothing else. The room closed in on him. Stalking to the window, he opened it and gulped in some cool air.

Caprice came up behind him and put her hand on his shoulder. "Ye loved her?"

"Yes." He'd been closer to Lissie than any of his siblings. They'd both dreamed of different lives. Her dream included the choice to marry whomever she pleased, and he longed to be free from the title that bound him, to make his own way in the world, so he could put distance between himself and his memories.

Caprice nodded, as if she understood his heartbreak. "I'm not sure if this will make it better for ye, but he did seem a bit remorseful. Of course, as much remorse as someone as twisted as he is can feel. The sadness lasted,"— Caprice snapped her fingers— "for this long. He's marrying a duke's daughter. *La-dee-da*, was all I could think as he sat on my bed naked as the day he was born and went on and on 'bout how his betrothed was so beautiful, and now he'd be getting the respect he so richly deserved. He was fair ta bursting with glee even with his father just dying."

Caprice pointed to a decanter on the nightstand. "Pour me another, would ye?"

Alex leaned over and filled the glass. So Mallorian was now Baron Westonburt. "Can you remember anything else?" Any small detail could bring down a man.

"This job makes ye want ta forget," Caprice said, slurping at the liquor.

Alex could only imagine all the things Caprice wanted to forget. "I'm sorry for your sadness."

Tears welled in her eyes. "Harrison was pleased as punch that he's now a baron. Imagine the shame, being pleased yer namesake's died. He'll rot in hell one day for sure. There's not much more ta tell."

"I can't thank you enough." Alex turned to Caprice and raised her hand to his lips. "I'll make sure Mistress Vicery is here to fetch you tomorrow. She'll speak to Madame Lovelace and have money for you."

"Will I see ye again, do ye think?"

Finding it hard to concentrate on her any longer, he shook his head. He had the glimmer of a plan, but would it work? "No, I'm sorry to say you probably will not." With nothing else to say, he strode from the room.

WIND WHIPPED HIS FACE as he rode Braun to his town house. His anger kept the chill of the night at bay. Upon entering the house, he stalked to his liquor cabinet and poured himself a whiskey, hoping to cool the burn of revenge. He gulped down some of the liquid, strode across the room and dropped into a chair, intent on working out the details of what he should do next. Yet all he could think on was how he would love to wring the life out of Mallorian. If only he could come to terms with killing someone, but he couldn't, and it was damned frustrating to feel so weak and helpless.

Anger, frustration and sadness vibrated through him. He'd held himself together to this point, but the strain was too much. With a roar, he reared his arm back and tossed his glass across the room. It shattered against the wall, sending glass and liquor flying through the air in a shimmer of brownish-gold liquid.

The door to his study flew open, and Peter and Sally appeared in the doorway. Peter looked first at the brown stain on the wall and then at Alex. "Tell me that was not the imported whisky you just wasted."

"It was," Alex said, feeling foolish. He wished he had known they were here.

"Well, I hope you at least feel better."

"I don't," he growled as Sally came to sit beside him.

"Oh, darling." Sally caressed his cheek with the back of her hand. "You appear to be teetering on madness. You must get hold of yourself. The rumors are already awful, and if anyone sees you like this…" She kissed the back of his hand as a sister or mother would.

"Sally, do quit mothering him," Peter said, pulling her to her feet.

Belatedly registering the fact that Peter was not where he was supposed to be, Alex narrowed his eyes. "Why are you here?"

"I lost sight of Mallorian." Peter turned a deep shade of red.

Alex glanced at Sally, then back to Peter. "That explains half of it."

"She was waiting for me when I went home to change," Peter mumbled. "She insisted on coming. I'm no match for her, Lionhurst."

"What did you tell her?" Alex demanded, coming to stand in front of Peter.

"Do be quiet, Alex," Sally snapped. "Peter told me nothing. I eavesdropped on your conversation, and I knew exactly what you two were up to. I *let* you go, because I could tell there was no stopping you." She shrugged. "Besides, I had an idea of who might be able to tell us a little about Mr. Mallorian as well."

"Sally, my dear," Alex said, "you continue to astonish me even after knowing you since we were in leading strings. But my astonishment does not mean I'm about to let you become involved in this sordid affair. Your husband" —he motioned toward Peter— "may not be able to say no to you, but I can. Tell me what you know, and then you're going to go home and tuck yourself into bed where you will be safe, if not sound."

Sally raised her eyebrows at him. "I'll do no such thing. You need my help. I loved your sister too. Besides, I'll not tell you one thing I have learned if you don't allow me to assist you."

"Allow you to assist me?" Alex sputtered. "Mallorian—I mean *Lord* Westonburt—is dangerous. You could be hurt."

Sally crossed her arms over her chest. "You know I'll help you whether you agree to it or not. If you would simply agree then you will be in a much better position to keep me safe. Otherwise, I'll be forced to proceed behind your back. *Alone. Vulnerable.*

"Fine," Alex growled. How was he supposed to argue against a woman's misguided logic? He glanced toward Peter, but Peter refused to meet his gaze. Alex gritted his teeth. Having friends could be a bloody nuisance.

Sally twined her arm through his and dragged him to the couch, pulling him with her as she fell back into the cushions. Peter was on her other side before Alex's backside hit the cushion.

Tears shimmered in Sally's eyes as she squeezed his hand. "I still can't believe she's gone."

He pulled his hand away, her concern rankling him. Sorrow would not help him now. He could not dwell on

Lissie's death or he would go mad. His focus must be on his plan. "Tell me what you've learned."

Sally nodded but sniffed loudly. "I called on my mother after the two of you left this afternoon."

"You did what?" he snapped. He couldn't have heard her correctly. "The whole *ton* will know now."

She rolled her eyes. "Don't worry. I didn't tell her anything about you. Mother detests Lady Westonburt, but she did say a prayer for the woman's poor departed husband. She says the baroness is a harridan. I once had the unfortunate experience of being seated beside her at a dinner and know this to be the truth. She may be exquisitely dressed, but under all that finery hides a woman who gets great joy from shaming her husband and son."

"Is that it?" Alex did not mean to sound so gruff, but he had been expecting something more, something he could use to bring Westonburt low.

"Darling, do try and be patient. Of course, that's not everything, but you did interrupt me."

"I'm sorry, Sally. Do continue."

"Let me see..." Sally tilted her head to the side. "Where was I?"

"I believe you were speaking on his mother's character flaws," Alex said, trying to control his impatience. At this rate, this could bloody well take all night.

"Ah, yes! Before you interrupted me" —Sally hitched her brows at him— "I was going to tell you that Mother chanced upon Lady Westonburt scolding her son in the garden of a party about a year ago. It seems she wanted him to pay attention to some chit, and he refused on the grounds the girl resembled a cow or some such nonsense as that. Anyway, Mother says Lady Westonburt blistered his ears, telling him to march back in to the musical and woo the girl even if he had to ruin her to get her to the altar. Apparently, Lady Westonburt desires her son to marry any girl who has the highest title and the biggest dowry." Sally shrugged. "Commonplace in the *ton*,really. What's not acceptable is to ruin a girl to achieve this."

He ignored the pointed stare from Peter. He had no intention of simply ruining Lady Gillian. He would be providing her an opportunity for a much better life than she would ever have as Westonburt's wife.

Alex focused on Sally's information and put himself in Westonburt's shoes. If he were Westonburt and wanted to marry a woman with a title and a large dowry, why not ask for Lissie's hand? Westonburt had been bent on revenge. Wouldn't the ultimate revenge have been marrying into Alex's family? So why would he not try?

He could think of only one reason. He slammed his fist onto the desk. "Father."

"Pardon?" Sally said.

"Sorry. I'm thinking out loud." Father's attitudes of rank and order were well known among the *ton*. Westonburt must have known his suit of Lissie would be met with disdain. The only thing that wasn't falling into place was Lissie's pregnancy. Westonburt couldn't have known about the child or else he would have approached their father. Father would have had no choice but to acquiesce.

Did she not tell Westonburt about the child? Possibly not. She was as prideful as they all were. If she had suspected the man had used her, she would not have said a word.

No matter what the answers were, Westonburt seduced his sister ,then killed her with his selfishness and callousness. The man would pay. "Sally, do you know if Lady Gillian is planning on attending her aunt's house party?"

Sally grinned slyly. "I was hoping you would ask me that."

"You were?" He had planned to threaten to spill all of Peter's secrets to Sally if that was what it took to ensure Peter did not tell his wife what Alex was up to, but things would be so much easier if Sally actually wanted to help him.

"Of course, darling. I'm very intuitive, you know."

"And what are your instincts telling you?"

"That you want to steal Lady Gillian away from Lord Westonburt to get your revenge."

Alex shot Peter a warning look when he coughed and sputtered. "My, you are intuitive."

"I knew it!" Sally clapped her hands together. "When I saw the two of you together at the ball, I positively knew you would suit, even when she told me she wanted to marry your business partner. *An American*. Imagine that! I can't think what led her to such a ridiculous notion. You would make a much better husband for her."

This time Alex nearly choked. He covered his cough with his hand.

"What is it, darling? Are you all right?"

He nodded, wiping at the tears seeping out of his eyes. "Air went down the wrong way."

"Alex," Peter growled from the other side of the room.

"Keep quiet," Alex snapped.

Peter strode across the room to stand by Sally. "You know I can't do that. I can't mislead my wife."

"Mislead me in what?" Sally demanded.

Alex sighed. He supposed Peter was right. It wouldn't be fair to ask a man to lie to his wife. "I've no intention of marrying Lady Gillian."

Sally's eyes narrowed on him. "What *were* your intentions?"

"The first part of my plan is to seduce her and get her to publicly break her engagement to Lord Westonburt, so he will be humiliated in front of the entire *ton*."

"That's your whole plan?"

"Well, no." Alex shook his head. "I'm going to take all the man's money, his house and his overblown pride. Everything he holds dear."

Sally waved her hand at him. "I didn't mean your plan in regards to that man. I was referring to your plan in regards to my friend."

What did she want him to say? "I'll provide her with plenty of money to live extremely comfortably for the rest of her life. I'll be saving her from a marriage she likely had no idea how to get out of. And she will be free to pursue her wish to live in America on the freedom my money will afford her."

Sally shook her head. "Men really are fools."

"Keep me separate from the anger you're directing at Lionhurst," Peter said.

She glared at both of them before resuming her usual

sweet smile. "I'm not angry. Why should I be? You"— she poked Alex in the chest— "are a fool. You underestimate Lady Gillian. She will never succumb to your seduction."

"I can be quite persuasive," Alex said.

"If you do manage to seduce her, I can promise you this— you will want to marry her. I know you. You just no longer know yourself."

"I won't want to marry her, Sally. But I promise you, I have every intention of telling the lady exactly what I plan to do. She will know I intend to seduce her. I won't bring an innocent down under false pretenses."

"How noble of you, darling. Just as I said, this will work out."

Sally's attitude was grating on his nerves. "Now, listen, Sally—"

"This is actually perfect," Sally said, interrupting him. "The *ton* will forgive her for running away and marrying you. The scandal will be salacious, of course, but everyone forgives you everything."

"Sally," Alex barked and raked a hand through his hair.

She paused in her pacing and looked at him. "What?"

"I am not going to marry Lady Gillian."

"You will. You'll see. Shall I tell you a bit about your future wife?"

"No."

"I visited her right after her mother died, but you wouldn't know this." Sally stared at him as she spoke. He shifted, uncomfortable with the pain in her voice and of learning anything favorable about Lady Gillian that might make him question what he was planning.

"It was the dinner hour, and Gillian was alone in the kitchen eating. Her father and sister were eating in the formal dining room. I've never forgotten it." Sally's blue eyes bore into him. "I have often wondered if her father made her eat every meal alone. *Wretched man.*"

These were exactly the kind of details Alex didn't want to know. He didn't want to like Lady Gillian or feel bad for her. Thinking of her as a schemer was easier. Damn Sally. Begrudging regard lodged in his chest. He understood loneliness and pain and what both could drive you to do in desperation. Was she desperate? So desperate that she would scheme to seduce a man simply to escape her life?

Should he ask Sutherland if he was amenable to the lady's plan? No. Alex dismissed the thought. The revenge was his to complete. He could not use his friend. Besides, Sutherland was a controller to a fault. Lady Gillian would regret her vows a month after she said them. Alex rocked back on his heels, considering his plan. He would be ruining her, but he would also be giving her freedom. Something she would never have without his money.

"Sally, I may need your help getting Lady Gillian alone this coming week."

Sally's gaze searched his for a second, and she smiled, more to herself than at him. "We won't be at the house party until Monday, but I feel certain you'll manage to find some way to get her alone on Sunday."

Several ideas, all inappropriate in the extreme, came to mind. Now the problem was which tactic to take. He smiled, settling on a plan and a backup, in case Lady Gillian proved difficult. It was a very good thing he had never minded breaking a few rules, because he was about to embrace the destruction of them all.

Ten

GILLIAN FINGERED THE EMERALD brooch pinned to her bodice as she examined her appearance in the looking glass. She traced the oval cut of the smooth stone, a little sigh escaping her lips.

When Whitney cleared her throat, Gillian met her sister's brown gaze over the edge of the looking glass. "You've never worn that brooch."

"No. I suppose I was afraid of losing it."

Whitney reached out and touched the stone. "You're not afraid anymore?"

"Yes, but it somehow seems fitting to wear Mother's brooch today." Gillian pushed her arms through her coat and arranged the material to cover the brooch. "Mother had a certain flair, and I need all the help I can get in catching Mr. Sutherland's attention." That half-truth was all Whitney would get. "Just look at this." Gillian pointed to her eyes, wanting to move away from her reasons. "Blue shadows. Not exactly the come-hither look."

Whitney's lips curled into a smile. "I hardly think Mr. Sutherland will notice your face."

"What's that supposed to mean?"

Whitney lowered her gaze to Gillian's bodice.

"Is it too much?" Gillian tugged the deep plunging neckline of her riding habit up a bit, but no matter how she pulled on the material her breasts still swelled above the rich, dark fabric.

"I'd say it's not enough. Material, that is. But I suppose you have to display your wares in order for the man to buy the goods."

That did it. She strode over to her wardrobe. She should never have listened to Madame Beaupont and allowed the modiste to make this special "French-flair" riding habit. Her sister's quiet snicker stopped Gillian. She whirled around, took one look at Whitney's smiling face, and threw the hairbrush gripped in her hands. The brush knocked Whitney on the side of the head.

"That hurt!"

"It was meant to hurt," Gillian replied, retrieving the brush from the floor. She tugged the brush through her tangled mass of hair, which hung heavily down her back. "I'm dreadfully self-conscious in this clothing, but Auntie and Madame Beaupont assured me it was necessary to get Mr. Sutherland to come to heel immediately. And frankly, after the dazzling displays of creamy white flesh I saw at Sally's ball, I quite agree."

"I was only teasing you. You look lovely. Well, except for your hair." Whitney snatched the brush from Gillian's hand and yanked it through her hair.

"Ouch! You little vixen!"

"Oh dear. Did that hurt?"

"Truce," Gillian declared with a laugh. "Now help me dress my hair."

"Why me? Where's Clara?"

"Toothache," Gillian mumbled, trying to get a pin in her hair. But the pin popped right out, and her hair fell back into her eyes. How did Clara make dressing hair look so easy? She would have to praise her lady's maid more when she next performed the service.

"Perhaps you should wear your hair down for the hunt?" Whitney suggested. "Look at my hair."

Gillian obliged, then stifled a giggle. Whitney's hair was a wild mass of blonde curls with a few pieces plopped on top of her head in the most haphazard fashion Gillian had ever seen. "Did you fix your hair this morning?"

"Indeed I did. Do you now see my point?"

"I do." Gillian ran a hand through her hair, thinking on the matter of her attire and hair. "It's one thing to make a bold statement with this outfit, but if I wear my hair down to boot, I'm afraid Mr. Sutherland might proposition me for a night of pleasure instead of contemplating marrying me."

"I see your point. Come closer."

Gillian moved toward her sister and leaned her head back. "How's this?"

"Good." Whitney began pulling up sections of Gillian's hair, twisting them into some unknown creation and then jabbing Gillian's head with sharp pins to hold the masterpiece in place.

Gillian grimaced as the last pin stuck her especially hard. "I think you enjoy inflicting pain."

"Not at all," Whitney declared, her voice trembling with laughter. "It's just that your hair is so thick, and I'm dreadfully bad at dressing hair." She patted Gillian's head. "Do try for once not to ride so recklessly. This up do is likely to tumble down with too much motion."

Gillian nodded, but she could already feel the wind in her face and the strength of her horse underneath her as they soared across the countryside.

Descending the stairs with Whitney beside her, Gillian paused at the bottom and took a deep breath. Everything rode on this week. Sally's note assured her Mr. Sutherland was coming for the entire week, and Father's gout was bothering him, so maybe he wouldn't attend any of the functions.

She tried to suppress her smile, feeling slightly guilty that she considered her father's ill health fortunate. It wasn't his ill health precisely, but rather that she needed a bit of luck and having his keen gaze off her was very lucky. She said a quick prayer that he would recover—*next week.*

Today was the beginning. If she was going to get Mr. Sutherland alone, there was no better time than in the woods amid the underbrush and confusion of the hunt.

Male voices drifted from Father's study as she strode down the hall with Whitney on her heels. She did not pause at the study door; instead, she inclined her head to Mr. Percy, who scrambled to open the door for her. Sweeping into the sunshine, she called over her shoulder, "Tell my father we've gone to my aunt's and that we shall see him later in the evening."

As she neared the stable, she motioned to the groom. "Mr. Ganter, please replace the saddle so I can ride astride." The groomsman gaped at her, but to his credit, he recovered quickly and rushed to do her bidding.

"What are you doing?" Whitney cried, looking truly concerned.

"I have no hope of keeping up with Mr. Sutherland if I ride sidesaddle," Gillian answered as she shoved on her gloves and tried to appear more confident than she felt. "Therefore, I'll ride astride just as the men do."

With the help of the groom, Whitney swung her legs over the slowest mare in their stable and clung for dear life, though the mare was standing still. The horse moved and Whitney's eyes grew round. "Blasted beast. Don't move." She glared down at Gillian. "Quit smirking at me. You know I hate horses."

"She senses your fear," Gillian replied, employing the soft tones she had used for years to soothe her sister's worries. "Just relax." Gillian patted the mare's nose. "May is perfectly harmless. She's so old she can barely get a trot going."

"I do hope you know what you're doing. Father will have an apoplectic fit if he sees you riding astride. Besides" —Whitney swept a hand toward Gillian— "how do you hope to ride astride in that get up?"

Grinning, Gillian mounted Lightning. "These new French riding habits are actually quite the thing for the bolder set of women. See?" She pointed to her split skirt. "Isn't that wonderful?"

"I suppose," Whitney said, looking doubtful.

"Don't worry over Lady Gillian's attire or her riding ability," Mr. Ganter said, stepping toward Whitney and resituating the reins in her hands so she held them properly. "It's you that has me concerned, since you never would let me teach you about riding. Your sister there" —he hitched a thumb at Gillian— "is a fine horsewoman, better than most men I know. But you, little lady" —Mr. Ganter shook his head— "need to just hold on tight and go real slow."

Gillian chuckled at the blush staining Whitney's cheeks. It served Whit right for being so impudent. Mr. Ganter winked, and she winked back. She adored the old stable master, and he knew it. He had indeed taught her everything she knew about horses when Father had flatly refused to take the time. But more than that, Mr. Ganter had tried to soothe her wounded feelings by telling her Mother had loved her horse more than her husband, and Father couldn't forget that. She would never forget how Mr. Ganter tried to make her think that it was not that Father didn't love her, but that it was bad memories of her mother that made him act so coldly.

She tightened her legs against Lightning's muscular sides, and a fierce desire to ride recklessly into the wind shot through her and stole her breath. Whit would be fine. May knew the path to Aunt Millicient's even if Whitney didn't. Gillian caught her sister's gaze. "I'll see you there. Just do as Mr. Ganter said and allow May to lead you."

She tapped Lightning's sides, and he dashed down the dirt road, kicking up dust as he gathered speed. Sweeping around the large iron gate that marked the entrance to their home, she raced toward the open green space before her.

Rows of magnificent oak trees lined the countryside, and their sturdy presence comforted her. She took a deep breath, appreciating the heady freesia swirling around her. Burning wood and apple mingled with the freesia, and her mouth watered with memories of Cook's apple tarts.

An enormous sense of freedom and exhilaration swept over her as the crisp air caressed her face. The pounding of Lightning's hooves caused the few pins binding her hair to loosen. She did not care. She encouraged Lightning into a faster gallop and laughed with the explosion of happiness coursing through her.

As the countryside flew past, a bit of anxiety built within her, squelching some of her enjoyment. Her seduction of Mr. Sutherland needed to be fast. Each day she and Whitney were out in the *ton*, Gillian felt sure that was the day their enemy would reveal their secret and her sister's life would never be the same. Whit never need know how their mother had really died. She never need live with the guilt. The long drive of Trent's country home came into view, forcing Gillian to dismiss the possibility of her plan failing. How hard could it be to get a man to want to marry her?

The sun glared down, and a little beads of perspiration stung her eyes. She swiped at them, trying to clear her blurry vision. The sun reflected off a stained glass window, blinding her, and she raised her hand in an effort to block the glare. Just as the path came back into focus, a rider loomed before her. With a gasp, she tugged on Lightning's reins. The horse stopped with a jerk, and she hurtled over his head, landing with a jarring thud on her bottom. Her teeth clanked together with the force of her fall, but her senses returned swiftly, and she scrambled out of the oncoming rider's path just as he veered the stallion to the right to avoid trampling her.

Her heart beat a painful rhythm and every muscle in her body quivered. She pinched herself. Still alive. No thanks to the fool who almost got her killed. She struggled to gain her feet as heavy boots stomped toward her.

"Well, well, well, look who we have here," a baritone voice said above her.

She knew that voice. Surely, it could not be. She glanced up and bit her lip on a cry of outrage.

The sun outlined Lord Lionhurst's tall frame in a golden glow. Against her better judgment, she glanced at his broad chest, where his white shirt hung casually unbuttoned just enough to show the ripple of tan skin underneath. Her stomach flipped at his show of flesh. Blast the man. She disliked him, but he was gorgeous.

He gazed down at her and jolts of unwanted, but undeniable, desire sparked through her. "What are you doing here?" she demanded, irritated with her reaction to the fiend and at him for being here.

That slow, seductive grin of several nights before spread across his face. "Looking for you."

Eleven

ALEX HAD A MILLION ways to woo a woman, but as he stared at the voluptuous creature before him, he could not remember a single one he had mastered in all his twenty-two years. Penetrating green eyes met his and a jolt of lust shot through his body. He had to keep his wits about him. He was on a mission of revenge, not pleasure. But if the mission should end up being pleasurable, he didn't mind that.

He smiled at her, and she glared in return. Sally's prediction that Lady Gillian would not be easily seduced rang in his ears. "Are you hurt?"

"You almost killed me."

"Actually, you almost ran me over." He leaned over and grasped her under the arms, lifting her onto her feet. "We need to talk."

She gazed up at him, lifting one perfect black eyebrow. "Are you ready to apologize?"

"For what?"

"Misjudging my character."

Between the smell of freesia surrounding her and her soft body within his hands, he had the distracting wish to cover her full, pink mouth in a deep kiss that had nothing to do with a purposeful seduction and everything to do with learning what she tasted like. Instead, he gently set her away from him. "You are the woman who was planning on seducing my partner into marriage, weren't you?"

"Yes, but you don't understand."

"Then make me."

Her mouth parted, closed and then opened again. "I'm afraid I can't."

"Then I'm afraid I can't apologize."

She turned on her heel so fast that the weight of her hair swung behind her and whipped across his chest. Stunned, he watched her march to her horse. Surely the little vixen did not plan to rudely dismiss him. She grabbed the reins and placed her foot in the stirrup. Women did not walk away from him ever, let alone *hurry* to get away.

A perfect, slender calf peeked from beneath her skirt as she swung her right leg over the horse and mounted it as a man would. By all the saints, this woman intended to leave him standing in her dust. She reached around her and shook the folds of her skirt over her exposed legs before turning to fix him with a severe glare.

So much for his legendary charm. Obviously it only applied to women he had no interest in whatsoever. Now that he actually wanted a woman to fall under his spell, she disliked him. So bloody typical of those of the female persuasion. He stalked toward her and pulled her off the horse.

She struggled, attempting to move from his grasp, making it painfully obvious she did not wish to hear what he had to say. This was not going well at all.

"Let go," she demanded, squirming in his arms before twisting around to gaze up at him with blazing eyes. "You aren't even supposed to be here."

"Just who are you hoping is here?" he demanded, though he had a fairly, if rather astonishingly, good idea.

"Mr. Sutherland, of course."

"Have you considered that your betrothal should have put a halt to your plans to seduce my friend?" The lady had audacity. He'd give her that.

Her eyes formed dangerous slits, and her lips pressed together in a hard white line. "I've considered nothing of the sort. My father betrothed me to Lord Westonburt despite my wishes."

"There's hardly anything abnormal in that. You are under your father's control." Blood rushed to her cheeks, giving them a most pleasing pinkness, except Alex knew by the way her arms folded across her chest and her eyes shot daggers at him that she was livid.

"You would think that, Lord Lionhurst. You are a typical Englishman."

"I think I'm beginning to understand you." He had the perfect opportunity to present the problem and his case.

"Pray tell me what you think you understand."

"You're pursuing my partner because you don't wish to marry a controlling Englishman. You want to get out of England and go to America, where you think you will have more freedom."

Her eyes rounded to twin saucers. "You are partially correct. Are you going to tell your partner?"

"I've already warned him."

"You're a horrid man."

"Why? Because I didn't stand idly by and let you seduce my unsuspecting friend?"

"I will make him an excellent wife."

Her surety that she was still going to be Sutherland's wife irritated the hell out of Alex. "He won't fall for your tricks." Yet as Alex stared at her perfectly sculpted face and her worried eyes, he had doubts. Sutherland wanted a beautiful wife with backbone, and Lady Gillian definitely fit both of those requirements perfectly.

"Is he here?" She glanced around him.

"He is," Alex snapped. "Don't you think people will question you chasing after one man when you are betrothed to another?"

"I'll be very discreet."

"Aren't you worried I won't be?" He couldn't resist. Her unwavering focus on Sutherland was annoying him.

Small, slender fingers gripped his arm. "You mustn't say anything to anyone."

"Why?"

"If my father knew what I was up to…" She shook her head.

One glance into her wide, pleading eyes melted his resolve to use whatever means necessary to seduce her.

He'd simply seduce her before she could accomplish her goal. And he'd better do it quickly. One bat of those pretty eyes and Sutherland would probably drop to one knee and ask for her hand. "Don't worry. I'll not tell your father or anyone else, for that matter. Your impending marriage is why I'm here."

"It is?"

He nodded. "I agree you should not marry Westonburt."

Her brow creased as she gazed at him. "You do? Well, thank you, I suppose. But I must say, I'm confused."

"For the sake of time, may I be blunt?"

"I hadn't realized you could be otherwise," she replied with a smile. "By all means." She waved a hand at him. "Try and shock me."

"Westonburt has wronged me in a way that can only be righted by revenge."

"I can't say as I'm shocked, since I know the man. He's vile. But do continue."

Alex chuckled. If she wasn't a woman in want of a husband he might like to truly get to know her. "He wants to climb the social ladder, and you are his rung."

"That's funny, since my family is practically outcasts from the *ton*."

The trembling of her lips jerked on his heart. Fragile women would be his undoing. He raked a hand though his hair. He would not embarrass her by remarking on the unfairness of it all. She was right, her family was whispered about, but Westonburt was hated by many in the *ton*. Marriage to her would help him. She was beautiful and an object of extreme curiosity. That alone would open doors previously closed to him. "Outcasts or not, you can still get him what he wants."

"What do you propose to do to Lord Westonburt?"

"Take away his rung."

For a moment, she stared at him, her lovely mouth parting. "You wish to marry me?"

"No. I wish to seduce you."

Lady Gillian burst out laughing, but after a moment, likely because he didn't join in, her laughter died. "You're serious."

"Completely."

"You think you can just stare at any woman with those blue eyes, and we will all fall at your feet? Reputations be damned?"

"Considering that you're intending to still try and seduce my partner, I doubt your reputation is of much concern to you."

"I can't afford to be concerned, Lord Lionhurst. But my problems do not concern *you*. And I fail to see how seducing me will help you get your revenge."

"You'll break your betrothal once you're ruined. And Westonburt will know I'm the one that took the one thing he wanted most. His public humiliation is just the first step. I plan to destroy the man."

"And what of me? I'll be ruined and stuck here. Not a very good bargain."

"I'll supply you with enough money to live comfortably in America for the rest of your life. And I'll supply the passage for you to get there."

Something flashed in her eyes that he could not read. Her lips pursed together and she took in a long breath. "My favors are not for sale, Lord Lionhurst."

"You misunderstand me." But damned if she did, he realized. He was proposing to buy her. The thought sickened him. In his grief and anger, he hadn't considered the ramifications completely.

She cocked an eyebrow at him. "I don't think I've misunderstood. Let me propose a different solution."

"Such as?" Was there a way to get what he wanted without being so vile?

"You could just help me win your partner's hand. You would've helped to take me from Westonburt, which will give you what you want, and I will secure a marriage to a good man who does not live in England, which will give me what I want."

Could he do that? He had considered it. Why had he dismissed it?

"I'm afraid our time alone is ending, Lord Lionhurst." She stuck out her hand. "Are we partners or enemies? My sister is coming up the drive, so you must decide quickly."

Twelve

GILLIAN TRIED TO CONTROL the trembling of her outstretched hand. She couldn't believe she was striking a deal with the devil, but what choice did she have? He would no doubt make it impossible to capture Mr. Sutherland if she did not get Lord Lionhurst to help her. And there was no way she would ever allow the man to seduce her and send her packing to America without a husband. The main point was to flee England with a man who had the means to protect her sister from any harm that may follow them across the waters, and Mr. Sutherland's good name would do that.

He took her hand. "Deal. But seducing you would have been more pleasurable I think."

An amused grin tugged at the corners of his mouth. Heat spread up her neck and over her face. *Blast him.* She wished he did not ruffle her so.

"Have you forgotten how to speak?" He flashed a dazzling white smile that caused her heart to flutter. He cocked his head to the side, waiting, she knew, for her to speak.

"No," she managed to get out before clearing her throat at the sound of her husky voice. Good heavens, she was a simpleton. He reached out and ran a finger down her cheek, lingering for a moment on her lips. She jerked away, but self-consciously brought her fingers to her lips. They tingled as if swollen from too much sun or tart fruit.

Every time she encountered this man, he had the ability to make her forget herself. First things first, she had to get control of this situation. It would not do for Mr. Sutherland to think she wanted Lord Lionhurst or encouraged any special attention from him. From this moment forward, she would not be alone with this man. She took a step away from him and squared her shoulders, hoping to appear unshakeable in her resolve.

Gillian glanced around Lord Lionhurst, relieved to see Whitney's slow horse finally approaching. Trying not to appear as desperate as she felt, she casually waved for Whitney to come closer. Instead, Whitney shook her head and pulled up on May's reins, causing the mare to come to an abrupt stop. Of all the times to be obstinate! Surely Whit could see Gillian's need. Gillian narrowed her eyes at her sister.

"Poor May is terribly hungry," Whitney called out. "I'll just take a minute and let her eat some grass."

Gillian would blister Whitney's ears when she got her alone. For now she settled on giving Lord Lionhurst a tight smile, which she prayed conveyed annoyance and not befuddlement. "Good day to you, my lord. I'll just go help my sister."

His hand whipped forward and gripped her arm. "Don't you think we should discuss details and strategy? By the way, if we are to be partners, you should call me Alex."

"Absolutely not. That's much too informal."

"I insist."

The man was too stubborn by half. "No," she snapped.

"Yes. And I'll call you Gillian."

He was too sure of himself, but the loopy grin on his face made her smile in return. "You will not call me by my given name as I've not given you permission."

"But you will."

He sounded so sure that she almost believed it.

Voices sounded in the distance from the area of the stables. The last thing she needed was to be seen standing so close to Lord Lionhurst. They probably appeared to be engaged in intimate conversation. "Lord Lionhurst, simply sing my praises to your partner. I'll do the rest. Now please go. This conversation looks too…"

"Cozy?"

A breath of air rushed out of her lungs. He understood her at last. Of course he would. Why had she doubted it? "Yes, it would seem quite improper."

He stepped toward her and leaned in so his lips almost touched her ear. "Jealousy is a sure way to attract another man." Lord Lionhurst's breath caressed her neck, making her want to lean toward his warmth. Instead, she forced herself to lean away. "Really?"

"Absolutely."

"You're quite sure?"

"Trust me."

She snorted. "How many times have you told a woman that?"

He pulled back from her, a dark scowl marring his face. "Never."

Her stomach fluttered at his serious expression. "Are you sure it will work on Mr. Sutherland? Surely all men are not exactly the same?"

"Of course we're not. But it will work."

"All right. I'll trust you. To an extent."

Lord Lionhurst's finger came under her chin. The scent of grass, pine and earth surrounded her. His hands cupped her face, and she could scarcely breathe. She swallowed, sure he could hear the sudden rapid beating of her heart. "I think a public kiss is too indiscreet."

His hands twined into her hair, tilting her head back. "I completely agree. Good thing we're still alone."

A protest sprung to her lips just as his mouth came down upon hers.

Thirteen

HIS LIPS MELDED WITH hers instantly, deliciously massaging her good senses away. His tongue swirled inside her mouth, sending her pulse into a rapid beat. Ordering her thoughts was impossible. He wrapped his arms around her waist and drew her against the length of his hard body. He thrilled and frightened her. She wanted nothing more than to explore him and the desire he displayed for her. Yet the intensity of her feelings frightened her and cut through the haze in her mind.

She tried to push away from him, but her body shook, and instead of putting distance between them, she now clung. His mouth softened, signaling a new, eminent attack. The kiss gentled, like the swirling lap of the tide, beckoning to her and showing her a different side of this man, one that pulled at tender emotions. She feared she could not battle them in her present condition.

This realization, alongside the fact that a throat cleared beside her, finally propelled Gillian into action. Bracing her palms against Lord Lionhurst, she shoved away, nearly losing her balance in the process.

"You must be quite the kisser," Whitney chirped, clasping Gillian's arm before leveling Lord Lionhurst with a look Gillian could only describe as admiring.

Heat flamed from Gillian's neck to her cheeks. How mortifying! If he had an ounce of courtesy, he would ignore Whitney's statement.

"What would make you say that?" Lord Lionhurst questioned with a chuckle.

Gillian groaned. She should have known the man didn't possess even a speck of gallantry.

Whitney nodded toward Gillian. "Look at her."

Self-conscious, Gillian touched her hair and grimaced at the wild disorder.

"Ah, I do see your point," Lord Lionhurst said with such a salacious undertone that Gillian looked at him despite her resolve not to. He winked, and she hastily glanced away.

"It's not just the flush and the swollen lips," Whitney crooned, clearly enjoying herself. "Last I spoke with Gillie, she was coming here today to make Mr. Sutherland fall in love with her, but by the looks of your embrace, I'd say she's quite forgotten him."

Gillian flung Whitney's hand off her arm and whirled on her sister. "I have done no such thing. Mr. Sutherland is at the forefront of my every thought. Now, do be quiet before I remove my stocking and stuff it in your mouth." The widening of Whitney's eyes and the slight paling of her formerly rosy cheeks gratified Gillian.

"Does she mean it?" Lord Lionhurst posed the question directly to Whitney as if Gillian were not even present. She ground her teeth at the man's continued audacity.

"She means it," Whitney replied. "She's little patience and no sense of humor."

That was unfair and untrue. With a gentle shove, Gillian moved Whitney out of her way. "Go on ahead or I'll show you just how ill-tempered I can be."

"Are you sure you don't want me to stay and chaperone?"

"I'm sure," Gillian snapped. She could not for the life of her understand what had gotten into her sister. It was as if Whitney were deliberately trying to sabotage the plan by encouraging Lord Lionhurst. Gillian shook her head and turned back toward the source of her problems, the blue-eyed devil himself.

"Fine, I'll go," Whitney huffed. "But don't expect me to

cover for you if you two don't show your faces in the next few minutes."

Gillian faced Lord Lionhurst, intent on laying down some ground rules. "That is the second time you have kissed me without asking."

"Are you angry?"

The question gave her pause. She was angry, but at herself for responding to him and not stopping him. "Do not kiss me again."

"I won't, unless you ask."

The audacity of the man! "I won't be asking."

"Then I won't be kissing you. But I promise you will ask."

"You!" She pointed a finger at him. "We made a deal. You help me win the hand of your partner, and I'll help you gain revenge on my unwanted fiancé. Either stick to our deal or the bargain is off."

"And how far do you think you would get with my friend if I told him you only wanted to marry him for his money?"

"That's not true," she said with a gasp.

"How do I know? I could be leading poor Sutherland into a life sentence of a terrible marriage."

"No." She shook her head, her pulse skittering in panic. "I swear I mean to make him a good wife. The best. A true and loving wife."

Something darkened Lord Lionhurst's face, but he looked away, making it impossible to read what the man was thinking.

"I may be a fool, but I think I believe you."

"Thank you!"

He turned to her, a half smile stretched across his lips. "The only other time I believed a woman's declaration I lived to regret it. Don't make me regret this."

"I won't. I swear."

"Straighten yourself up, peach. I think we have company."

"What?" She didn't see anyone coming down the path, but now that she was really listening she heard men's voices. She glanced toward the stables, knowing that at any moment the hunting party would probably round the bend to find her mere inches from a well-known libertine. The thought sent her flying backward in haste. Lord Lionhurst raised an amused eyebrow at her, but made no move to advance in her direction.

She tidied her hair and smoothed the wrinkles out of her dress. When she was done, she looked up and was surprised to find Lord Lionhurst's gaze boring into her. "Do I look presentable?"

"You look delectable."

"Who's delectable?" The deep voice behind her caused her to flinch. She spun on her heel and met the inquisitive gaze of Mr. Sutherland.

Fourteen

MR. SUTHERLAND STARED DOWN at her. His coffee-colored eyes, she noted, wishing to heaven above that she could ignore it, could not compare to the blue of Lord Lionhurst's gaze. Of all the people to come up behind her, it had to be him. She had no idea what to say to his inquiry.

His gaze flickered from her face to Lord Lionhurst's. Lord Lionhurst stepped beside Mr. Sutherland and motioned to her. "Lady Gillian was worried the ride over here mussed her hair. I was just assuring her she still looks lovely." His mouth quirked into a smile.

If that ludicrous explanation was an example of how Lord Lionhurst intended to help her, she'd do better without him. "Lord Lionhurst is teasing me."

"Have I interrupted something private?" Mr. Sutherland asked.

"Of course not. I was actually hoping to have a chance to speak with you today. Would you care to escort me to the hunting group?" She pasted her sweetest smile on her face. The one she had practiced to get her father to rethink going back into Society. Of course, it had not worked, but maybe she'd have better luck with Mr. Sutherland.

His throwing his head back and laughing seemed like a good sign. She wanted to share in his mirth, but she was too annoyed with herself. It was taking all her will not to glance at Lord Lionhurst. She wished he'd go on ahead. His presence made flirting difficult. Finally, Mr. Sutherland's laughter died to a low chuckle. "I do believe you are a woman after my own heart."

"Your heart and everything else," Lord Lionhurst snapped, pushing past them, untethering his horse from the tree and leading it down the path.

"Shall we join the hunting party?" Gillian quickly asked, watching Lord Lionhurst walk away. What on earth was wrong with him? He needed lessons in being helpful.

Before Gillian and Mr. Sutherland had taken too many steps, her cousin Trent rounded the corner. Recognition flashed in his eyes and a smile spread across his face. "My favorite cousin," he said with a wink and stepped forward to embrace her.

Gillian gasped at the changed man before her. Trent had gone to Paris a man in the prime of health with shining eyes. Yet one look at his slight body, drawn face and dull eyes told her this was not the man she had said goodbye to a year ago. No, indeed. This man had a fresh, angry red scar about three inches long, running down his right cheekbone. She quelled her desire to question him and reached out to return his hug. As her fingers splayed over his hard back, she noted his loss of flesh was even greater than she had thought. What had happened to him?

"Gillie, I missed you."

She felt rather than saw Mr. Sutherland move past them. She would have to thank him later for giving them a moment of privacy.

"I missed you too." She squeezed his hand. "Why are you so thin? Did the food in Paris not agree with you?"

"You could say that. Come, you don't want to hear my boring Paris stories. Moreover, those men are ready to hunt. We can catch up tonight." Trent held out his arm, and they walked toward the men mounted on the horses in a semicircle.

Making it a point not to look Lord Lionhurst's way, she concentrated on the stable boy as he held Lightning steady. The moment she sank into the saddle, Lord Lionhurst moved his beast beside her.

"I'm surprised to see you're not riding sidesaddle."

"Why? I'm an excellent rider."

"Really?" His eyebrows rose in an arc of incredulity.

Situated between the man she meant to catch and the man who apparently meant to drive her to insanity, she gripped Lightning's reins, determined not to be baited.

Lord Lionhurst smirked. He knew, blast him. The devil understood the price her silence was causing her.

"Do you care to make a wager?" he asked, taunting her.

She gritted her teeth, until she thought she might crack one. Mr. Sutherland would think her utterly scandalous if she took a wager. "No, I—"

"Never mind. I see you have reconsidered your claim." He turned his back, dismissing her as an unworthy opponent.

Maybe this was all part of a grand plan he had? If he led her astray may he suffer the pox. "I'll wager you I can reach the fox first."

The group fell silent, including her sister, which was never a good sign. Gillian kept her gaze firmly on Lord Lionhurst as he faced her. An amused smile quirked his mouth.

"A bold claim. Since we're both confident in our abilities, why not raise the stakes?"

She swallowed. Backing down in front of a group of people would kill her, and somehow Lord Lionhurst read the weakness of pride in her eyes. A simple pox was too generous for him. He deserved a thousand. "How do you propose we obtain a winner of the booty if not by who reaches the fox first?" She was grateful her voice did not betray her mounting anger. Had he lied to her? Did he mean to help her or ambush her?

His eyes bore into hers. "Simple. We reach the fox, *and* we jump the fence."

"You're mad," Gillian's cousin Marcus blurted. "Have you seen the new fence? It's a good four inches taller than it used to be."

"I've seen it," Lord Lionhurst said. "It can still be

cleared, but only by a rider with superb skills. Do you still care to take my wager?"

"She does not," Trent said.

"I do." She met Lionhurst's gaze. He did not say a word, but his eyes held a dare in their depths. "I most certainly do." She could barely contain her smile. She was a superb jumper. She would teach that man never to underestimate a woman.

"It sounds like this group is more than ready," the hunt master said. "Shall I release the fox, Lord Davenport?"

"The sooner the better."

"Tally-ho!" the hunt master yelled, causing her to jerk in surprise. By the time she got her wits about her and tapped Lightning into a start, she coughed and spit in a most unladylike manner, glaring at Lord Lionhurst's departing back and the wake of his dust billowing around her. It was not until she went around the first bend that she realized she had completely forgotten about Mr. Sutherland and her plan to spend the day making him fall in love with her.

ALEX PRESSED LOW AGAINST his horse's neck, getting as close to Braun as possible. The beast snorted but did not slow his frantic pace in the least. Wise beast. Tension strummed through Alex, making him clench his legs tighter than he normally would. No doubt Braun was reacting to the signals.

Swiftness was a must. Gillian appeared to be very smart. He had no doubt she would quickly surmise he was leading her deep into the woods, and he wasn't entirely sure the lady would follow. He knew Sutherland, though. If he thought Alex might be interested in the lady, that would make his business partner all the more fascinated himself.

He tossed a quick look over his shoulder to make sure she was still there. She was bent low over her horse, concentration furrowing her brow. She'd gobbled up the bait of the challenge more easily than he'd expected. The dogs yelped as they raced across the trail in pursuit of the reddish-brown coats. Hooves pounded behind him, and with a quick snap at Braun's reins, Alex urged his horse to let loose. In seconds, the wind blew harder in his face.

His instincts sang like lightning through his veins. He pulled Braun's reins to the left onto a narrow path, hardly wide enough to be called a trail, but the passage would do for his purposes. Braun did not hesitate as he descended the rocky incline toward the water in the distance. The jarring motion clanked Alex's teeth together, causing him to bite down hard on the inside of his cheek. His mouth filled with the metallic taste of blood.

Branches loomed from every direction and trees passed in a swimming blur. He ducked just in time to avoid being knocked clean off Braun by a low, gnarly limb of a gigantic oak tree. Was he endangering Gillian by leading her down this steep path? He pulled up on Braun's reins to turn his horse and warn her.

Braun took objection and whipped his head back around, causing the beast to misstep. As they slid down the path, Alex braced his legs and threw his weight back. Approaching hooves beat an ominous tempo behind him. Saints above, the woman would kill them both if she intended to pass him on the narrow trail. Before he could move, noise exploded and Gillian brushed past, so close their horses' flesh whispered a greeting.

She maneuvered down the steep embankment with the ease of water sliding down bare skin. At the bottom, she paused where the slope met the edge of a stream. The sun shone on her, highlighting auburn streaks in the shimmering black of her hair. She grinned up at him, and Alex swallowed against a strange catch in his throat.

She raised her hand to her eyes. "You should see the look on your face. Clearly, you're astonished to find I am the superior rider."

What astonished him was the realization that she excited him. A tug of jealousy that Sutherland would likely soon be sharing her bed pulled at Alex. *Let it go, old man. Everything is settled for the best.*

"If you're so superior, why have you stopped when you

have yet to corner a fox?"

The smile slid from her face, and she turned toward the stream. He regretted the loss of her smile, but he knew by the way she reached for the reins but then hesitated that she only now realized she did not hear the dogs, nor see any fox.

She faced him, black brows furrowed together and lips pressed in a firm line. "Where are the dogs?"

"I do believe," he said, surveying the landscape to decide which way to send them, "the fox and dogs went upstream." The rocks led to a trail cast in deep shadows by swaying branches of willow trees—a perfect place to get lost for a bit.

She cocked one eyebrow up before plunging her horse into the stream to follow the path. She fascinated him. Steely determination underlined everything she did, but she appeared a delicate creature with her fine bones and luscious curves. His experience with the opposite sex had taught him there was nothing fragile about their minds, which turned, plotted and hurt a man foolish enough to forget this fact.

He blinked and tapped Braun, signaling the beast to move. The horse plunged into the stream, soaking Alex's pants leg with ice-cold water. "Damnation!" With the weather a bit warmer, he had not expected such freezing water.

Gillian chuckled from the other side on the embankment, but as he drew nearer, he could see her lips had a slight blue tint to them.

He arched his eyebrows. "You might have mentioned the temperature of the water to me."

"I might have, but this is so much more amusing."

Sutherland was lucky. The unexpected thought astonished him. *Keep your mind on the goal. Make Sutherland want the lady so you can get revenge.*

"I don't hear the dogs anymore. You're sure they came this way?"

"I'm sure they didn't."

"What are you up to, Lord Lionhurst?"

"Planting seeds and strategizing."

Her eyes narrowed on him. "I beg your pardon?"

“We men are like children.”

She nodded. “I couldn’t agree more.”

She had a beautiful smile. He couldn’t believe he hadn’t noticed until now.

“Lord Lionhurst…”

“Um, yes?”

“Your thought. Men are like children…?”

He cleared his throat. “We want all the toys in the playroom.”

Her brow furrowed in an adorable way. He had the urge to reach over and rub his thumb over the crease. Instead he gripped his reins tighter.

“Am I the toy?” she asked.

“In this analogy you are.”

“Do you mean to say you think Mr. Sutherland will want me more if he thinks you want me?”

“Precisely.”

She huffed out a breath. “In the future, just say what you mean and skip the analogies.”

He loved her witty banter. Working with her would be amusing. “I did just say what I meant. And might I point out you understood me perfectly.”

“Only because I’ve had practice getting to the real meaning of my sister’s nonsensical ramblings. So, did you challenge me on purpose?”

“Of course. I meant to lead you away from everyone else.”

“Then why didn’t you just whisper that in my ear?”

“Because I suspected you wouldn’t have followed me. Was I right?” The wind around them picked up and blew loose strands of her hair across her face. She pushed them away.

“Probably. Why did we need to leave the group to make Mr. Sutherland jealous? Wouldn’t it be better if he witnesses you flirting with me?”

“No.” A drop of rain hit Alex’s hand. He glanced up at the dark sky and frowned.

“Lord Lionhurst?”

He looked at her and almost laughed. A raindrop had plopped on the end of her nose. She wiped it away and stared at him expectantly. “This way is better,” he said.

"Sutherland doesn't know what's going on, and when he finds us, the curiosity will drive him nuts. We'll flirt a little and make him wonder."

"I suppose that makes sense." She cocked her head and glanced up at the sky, then refocused on him. "And what of strategizing?"

"That's simple. I'll make sure to reiterate to Sutherland that you do not wish to marry Westonburt, and then I'll nudge him in your direction. He asked me about meeting you previously, so it shouldn't be that difficult to reignite his interest."

"He wanted to meet me?" A grin spread across her face, lighting up her eyes.

Alex was suddenly, unaccountably annoyed. He was glad things had worked out as they had, so why did he feel jealous of the lady's enthusiasm over Sutherland? He pushed the question aside and forced himself to concentrate on the matter at hand. "So you know your part?"

She nodded. "Flirt discreetly."

"Excellent. We better get going. The rain's not going to hold."

Lightning illuminated the sky as she turned her horse toward the path.

"Damnation," he cursed under his breath. "We better take cover. The sky's about to let loose and if your horse slips on the embankment and you break your pretty little neck, my plan will be ruined."

She turned in her saddle and looked at him. "Your concern for my neck warms my heart. But I know this trail, and I'm not worried. As I said before, I'm an excellent horsewoman."

Just then thunder vibrated the air, and a streak of lightning came down with a crack. Her horse reared up on his hind legs and neighed wildly. Alex's pulse jumped. He was beside her in a flash and took hold of the horse's reins. She couldn't mask the look of surprise on her face, but she tried. He'd give her that. Before he could suggest again that they wait, the sky opened up and rain came pouring down.

He jerked her horse around and led them both back to

flat ground. He knew she was protesting by the outraged look on her face, but the rain muffled her exact words. “We need to dismount,” he yelled over the thunder.

She shook her head, but as she did lightning came down again and the horse jerked as if to bolt. Lady Gillian pushed her wet hair out of her eyes. “I think I’ll dismount now.” He held in his smile. Amazing how the lady acted as if the idea had just occurred to her. If he wasn’t trying to help her marry his partner, getting to know her could be enjoyable.

Fifteen

LORD LIONHURST GRASPED HER around the waist as she slid off her horse. When she turned, he was so close she could see the vein pulsing near his right eye. “Should we tether the horses?” she asked, taking a discreet step backwards

“I’ll do it. Why don’t you see if you can find us somewhere to take shelter?”

She nodded and started up the path. About six or seven feet up, the path turned and the rocky cliff jutted down from above to overhang the trail on the side nearest to the woods. One overhang came out particularly wide, and if she and Lord Lionhurst scrunched together, they would probably remain dry, or drier than they were now.

She wrapped her arms around herself. She was already starting to shiver from being wet. She raced back down the way she had come and met him halfway. “Shelter’s up there.”

He nodded and gripped her around the waist to help her back up the slippery trail. She’d never been held so intimately by a man, and her insides swirled in response. Once under the protective covering, she dropped to the cold, hard ground and scooted as far away from Lord Lionhurst as the meager space would allow. She didn’t like the peculiar way he made her feel.

The wind picked up in intensity, swaying the branches

of the trees until the thinner ones looked as if they might snap. She had a sudden recollection of the night her mother had died. A storm had been brewing that night. Shivering, she rubbed her arms with her hands.

Beside her, Lord Lionhurst shifted closer until his leg pressed against her hip. She was uncomfortably aware of the hardness of his leg and the strange pulling in her stomach. “Cold?”

She nodded. She was chilled from the rain and her memories. “What are you doing?” She gasped as he took off his overcoat.

He flashed a grin but didn’t respond. Once the longer coat was off, he pulled off a shorter coat. “Lean forward.”

She quickly obliged when she realized he was offering her his dry jacket. She expected to feel the weight of the dark blue coat dropped onto her shoulders. The material did fall like a warm blanket across her shoulders, but then his arm came around her back and his fingers curled around her waist before drawing her near. She started to protest, but when she looked at him she stilled and stared in admiration at the picture of perfect ease he presented.

His eyes were closed and a beatific smile lit his face. He was beautiful, masculine, and she wanted him to kiss her. How horrifying and wrong. He was the best friend of the man she intended to marry.

Lord Lionhurst was not for her; he would never be for her. He could not take her far enough away from her problems, to a place her sister could never be harmed by the past. And even if she didn’t have the pressing need to leave here, she would never allow herself to fall for a man who clearly put marriage in a category with leprosy. *Avoid at all costs.*

She should thank him for his coat and ask him to move his arm. The weight and strength of it pressed into her back. His eyes snapped open before she could utter a word.

He turned his head toward her. “Did you want to ask me something?”

“How did you know?”

“People inhale sharply when about to speak.”

She frowned. Had she drawn a sharp breath? How could he hear such a thing over the rain? "You're very observant."

"Usually."

She leaned forward and glanced pointedly behind her at his arm.

He slid it slowly out from behind her and smiled. "You'll be less comfortable and colder."

She ignored his words, especially since he was right. "I bet your keen observations drive your sisters mad. I can just see you stalking their suitors at the balls."

He grimaced, scrubbing a hand over the black stubble of his jaw. "I don't have a sister on the market anymore. The eldest is married, and the youngest—" He stopped talking and dug his hand deep into the dirt between them. "We buried her last week." Dirt fell from between his fingers.

"I'm so sorry for your loss," Gillian whispered. "I had no idea. Was she very ill?"

"No, she wasn't ill."

She knew she should drop the subject, but the glint in his eyes prodded her to continue. "Did she have an accident?"

"Yes. She fell in love with the wrong kind of man. The worst sort of accident a woman can have, wouldn't you say?"

His light blue eyes transformed to dark and gleaming. His grief filled the air between them. Her stomach twisted with his pain. She was not so sheltered that she didn't know the implications of what he meant. His sister had fallen in love with a dishonorable man. Had she been compromised? Taken her life? "Alex." She touched a hand to his shoulder.

"So it's Alex now, is it?"

"Only since we're partners," she lied, moved into letting down her guard by his grief. Grief she understood. She would have tried to comfort anyone she saw who had as much pain as was reflected in Alex's eyes.

"Does this mean I can call you Gillian?"

She pulled the soft material of his coat tighter around her. She really should say no, but that didn't seem right.

"All right. I hope the blackguard who hurt your sister pays with his life."

His eyebrows shot up, and for a moment he stared at her, unblinking. "He'll pay. Don't worry. Lord Westonburt will never harm another woman again."

"*Lord Westonburt*?" The implications of what Alex said chilled her blood.

He nodded. "My sister is why I want revenge."

She scrambled onto her knees and faced him. "If there's anything you could tell me I might use to convince my father to release me from the engagement, I would forever be in your debt."

He shook his head. "My sister's good name would be ruined and that would kill my mother."

"No one need know the reason for my broken betrothal." Things would be so much less nasty between her and Father if she didn't break her betrothal and flee to America. Maybe he would forgive one transgression, but two seemed insurmountable.

"You're being fanciful," Alex replied. "If your father didn't give a reason, then your reputation would be compromised."

"I don't give a whit for my reputation," she said, slapping her hand against the dirt. "I don't plan on being here much longer, and Mr. Sutherland hardly seems the type of man to be influenced by gossip. I wish to ease the tension between myself and my father."

Alex grasped her arm. "You may not care about your reputation, but what about your sister's? Would you ruin her chances for a good marriage?"

"No," she replied, brushing his hand away from her arm. She would never do anything to hurt Whitney. "Whitney's going to come with me when I marry Mr. Sutherland and leave."

"You may think you have it all planned out, but what if you fail to capture Sutherland's heart, and you and your sister are both stuck here? What then?"

"I thought you had faith in me," Gillian snapped and scooted away from him.

His gaze moved slowly down the length of her body, pausing for a moment at the décolletage she had taken great pains to display this morning. His stare meandered back to her face, a wicked smile parting his lips. "I'd say it's probable you will make Sutherland fall in lust with you and that will do for your purposes." He sounded angry, but she had no idea why. She pressed her lips together. *Let him be angry.* As long as he helped her, he could act unaccountably grouchy.

She stared out at the rain, the slanting sheet of white wetness reminding her, as it always did, of the night her mother died.

Alex shifted beside her, his leg brushing hers, and then moved quickly away. "Does the river rise quickly here?"

"Why?" She tilted her head to look at him. She'd been thinking of how the river had risen so quickly the night her mother died, but there was no way he could know her thoughts. Still...

"It seems like it would, based on what I've seen of the property so far."

"It can rise very rapidly. And become very cold." Her mother had been tinged blue when pulled from the river.

"Swim here much? I mean, when the weather's warm."

"Never."

"Too ladylike to swim, are you?"

"No." She glared at him. "The river holds bad memories."

The smug smile slid from his face. Small satisfaction for her stupid mistake. It wasn't her habit to remind people of the rumors circling her family name.

His eyes met hers. "I don't believe the rumors, you know."

"I hardly think if you did, you'd agree to help me capture the attention of your friend."

"You're wrong." He reached out and tucked a drying strand of her hair behind her ear. The intimate gesture made her stomach clench. She barely knew Alex, yet this was the most personal conversation she'd ever had regarding the rumors.

"Even if I believed your father killed your mother, I wouldn't treat you differently. Murder is hardly catching."

She swallowed the thick emotion making her throat

constrict. “You hold a minority opinion.”

“I may, but most of the *ton* is filled with nitwits and popinjays.”

She laughed until tears came to her eyes. “I’ve never laughed *or* talked to anyone about this.” She took his hand and squeezed it. “Thank you.”

“Are the rumors why you want to leave?”

“Yes.” She told the partial lie without guilt. She refused to feel guilty about protecting Whitney.

“You know your lower lip quivers when you lie.”

She snatched her hand away. “I am not lying. I just don’t care to go into detail about all the sad reasons I want to leave.”

“That’s fine. Disliking personal conversations is nothing to glare about.”

“You’re one to talk.”

“Me? Ask me anything you want. I’m honest to my detriment.”

“I doubt that,” she said with a snort.

“Try me.”

“All right. Why are you afraid of marriage?”

“I am not afraid of marriage. Is that what they say about me in the *ton*?”

“No. I drew my own conclusions. They call you ‘the heartbreaker.’”

“That’s bloody unoriginal. Like I said, nitwits and popinjays. If I’ve broken anyone’s heart, it was her own fault. I tell any woman I become involved with exactly what they can expect from me, and marriage is never a choice.”

“Because you’re afraid,” she said triumphantly. What was it about Alex that made her want to needle him? She’d never felt this way before.

“No, Gillian. Because I don’t repeat the same mistake twice.”

“You’ve been married before?” She couldn’t seem to keep the surprise out of her voice.

“No, never married. But I was close until the woman told me she’d rather marry my brother.”

“Oh, Alex. I am sorry.” She took his hand again and squeezed it. How cruel and simple-minded she’d been.

Just like all the people in the *ton* had been to her. She'd not even allowed for the possibility that a woman had broken his heart. "She loved your brother?"

His bitter laugh made her heart twist in response to his pain. "No." He pulled his hand away from hers. "That would have been bearable. She wished to marry my brother because he was in line to be the next duke. It had nothing to do with love."

"But you can't avoid marriage all your life because of one horrid woman. Not all women are like that."

"Aren't they? Do you want to marry for love?"

Heat scorched her cheeks. She couldn't say yes, and he knew it. She hated him for making her feel ashamed of something she had to do. She looked away toward the rain, surprised to find it had stopped. "We can go now," she said coldly.

"Anxious to capture your quarry?"

"You know how we women are," she snapped, meeting his steely gaze. "It's one thing, as you well know, to capture a man's lust, but it is quite another to entice him into marriage."

"True. If you do not make Sutherland a good wife, I'll make your life miserable."

She didn't doubt him for a moment. "I swear I'll be devoted."

ALEX LOOKED AWAY FROM her shining eyes. He believed she was sincere. And it angered him. Why the bloody hell would that anger him? He should be glad she wanted to make his friend a good wife.

He had to snap out of this. The first part of his revenge was within his reach. Westonburt would be deprived of Gillian as his wife—a goal Alex knew the man coveted above all else. All he had to do was help Gillian capture Sutherland's attention enough to get the man to marry her.

The task would be simple. Sutherland wanted a beautiful wife who could brave America. Gillian was the perfect match, the answer to all his problems. Alex stared at his hands and tried to order his thoughts. Why was he so bothered that Gillian was the answer to all Sutherland's problems? Simple selfishness.

He glanced her way. She stretched her arms out to the side, parting her jacket and revealing thin white material stretched across her swell of breasts. An emerald broach pinned above her right breast caught his eye. Without consideration, he reached out and touched the cool stone.

She drew back, a frown marring her beautiful face. "What are you doing?"

"Obviously not thinking." He smiled, trying to lighten the moment, but she did not return his smile. "I'm sorry. Your brooch caught my attention. It's beautiful."

"Thank you. It was my mother's. It's the only thing I have left of hers."

A slow, dull anger mounted in his gut. "The only thing?"

Gillian nodded. "My father got rid of everything but this. He wanted to wipe her memory away, but of course fate had the last laugh."

"How?"

"I look just like her. And he couldn't rid himself of me." She touched the brooch. "Until now."

Alex wanted to hit the duke. The duke had tried as best he could to rid himself of Gillian—devil take the man. That explained why Gillian was forced to eat alone. The duke had wanted her out of his sight. And now she was trying her hardest to give her father his wish.

How could he make her pain better? He didn't know any way but the physical one he'd been relying on to wipe away his own pain for years. Without hesitation, he laced his hands through her hair and brought her lips close to his. She gasped and tried to pull back, but he held her firmly.

"Sometimes," he said, by way of a preemptory apology against her anger, "it's better to ask forgiveness than permission." He swooped down and claimed her mouth, releasing himself to the kiss and the small tug of strange need her soft lips awoke in him.

Sixteen

ALEX'S GENTLE KISS SHOCKED Gillian more than his earlier plundering one. His lips brushed over hers, teasing, leading and showing her the promise of how he would be as a lover. A lover? Dear Lord above, what was she thinking? She shoved him back and scrambled to her feet. "I'm sure everyone must be looking for us."

"I doubt it," Alex said as he stood to face her.

"You swore you wouldn't kiss me again unless I asked."

"I'm a rake, my lady. Don't believe a word I say."

"I'll second that," a voice said from behind her.

She whirled around at the familiar voice. "Trent!" she exclaimed, her gaze going immediately to the coat she wore. "I can explain."

He cocked his eyebrow up in a way that could only mean disbelief. "This should be interesting."

"It's not," Alex said blandly. "We followed one of the foxes, lost its trail and then got caught in the thunderstorm."

"You expect me to believe that? I may have been gone for a year to Paris, but I didn't leave my memory there." Trent yanked Alex's coat off her shoulders and threw it at Alex. He caught it mid-air and slowly put it on before facing Trent with the casual air of someone about to discuss the weather.

His ability to appear so blasé about Trent's anger impressed her. Her heart thundered in her ears. Trent could ruin everything. She cast Alex a pleading glance, which he returned with a wink. “I’m not trying to seduce your cousin.” Alex flicked a grin her way, which made her breath catch. “Well, not anymore, anyway. She informed me rather blandly that she wished to be married and not seduced. A desire I’m afraid I cannot change nor fulfill.”

A smile pulled at Gillian’s lips. Lord Lionhurst was full of surprises.

The material of Trent’s jacket, which pulled tight across his shoulders, relaxed as Alex’s words took effect. Gillian breathed a sigh of relief.

Trent rubbed his hand over his brow. “So you two weren’t just—”

“No!” Gillian interrupted, scrambling forward. “We were not *just* anything.” She slanted her eyes at Alex, daring him silently to contradict her white lie.

“I may have had designs on your cousin—after all, who wouldn’t?— but she—”Alex waved a hand toward her—“has her sights set on my partner.”

Gillian groaned at Alex’s admission, but he took little heed of her annoyance, choosing instead to keep spouting her secrets like water bursting from a busted dam.

“In fact”—Alex rocked back on his heels, surveying her—“she means to marry Sutherland. Believe it or not, which you may not since I’m still having a hard time believing it, I’ve agreed to help her with her suit.” He appeared proud as a peacock as he finished his sentence. Did the man actually think he’d just done her a favor?

“Men are obtuse,” she grumbled before turning to Trent. “Before you think to unleash the tirade on the tip of your tongue, let me tell you something. Father has gone and betrothed me to Lord Westonburt against my loud protest. I’ve tried to reason with him, but he won’t listen. Now, I’m forced to drastic measures.”

“Good God, that is awful, since Lord Westonburt is already married,” Trent replied with a snicker.

“It’s not funny,” Gillian snapped, irritated that Trent was not taking her seriously. “The former Lord Westonburt has passed away, and his son—you may remember him as Mr. Mallorian—now carries the title.”

With a frown, Trent turned to Alex. “Is this the chap

who tried to worm his way into your shipping business?"

"How the bloody hell did you know about something that happened while you were gone? Especially since I can count on one hand those privy to that information."

Gillian was all ears for what either of them might let slip next. Trent appeared to be holding his own full bag of secrets, and Alex had failed to mention he had multiple reasons for wishing revenge against Lord Westonburt. She studied the angry set of Alex's jaw and his narrowed eyes. What else had he forgotten to tell her? Typical English know-it-all bull of a man.

"What have you been up to in Paris, Trent?"

"Let's all keep our little secrets, shall we?"

"That sounds perfect to me," she snapped. "Don't you dare say a word to Father or anyone else, and I won't question you, or better yet, I won't whisper in Auntie's ear that she should be questioning you."

"Deal." He stuck his hand out and for the second time today, she sealed a bargain with a man. "Now, where can I find Mr. Sutherland?"

Trent smirked at her. "No doubt with your sister."

"Why are you smirking at me?"

"While you were idling your time away here with Lionhurst, the man you've set your sights on has set his sights on your sister."

"What?" She could not have heard correctly.

"Yes, indeed. I'd say Mr. Sutherland is fairly bewitched by Whitney. Of course, who wouldn't admire a girl who cleared the jump over the fence with the grace that Whitney exhibited and then plucked off her jacket and stockings to wade in a stream, showing her ankles to the drooling men blessed with her company?"

What in the world was Whit up to? Gillian whirled away and ran toward her horse. She yanked the rope away from the tree.

"Where are you going?" Trent called merrily behind her.

She swung up into the saddle, not bothering to respond. She didn't know whether to be worried or grateful. Was Whitney trying to help Gillian's plan or hinder it?

Seventeen

GILLIAN'S HORSE HAD GALLOPED halfway across the stream by the time Alex caught up with them. He yanked Braun's reins to the left and brought his stallion up next to Gillian's horse. Reaching over, he snatched the reins out of her hands with his left one and gently urged her horse to a stop.

Her thunderous face did not surprise him in the least.

"What are you doing?" she demanded.

"Saving your arse, my lady. You'll look the fool if you go charging in there and demanding your sister keep her hands off your future husband. You're already betrothed, if you care to pause and remember."

"Oh, I remember," she mumbled darkly. "It's not possible to forget. And you needn't worry that I would have made a fool of myself. It's not as if I planned to charge in screeching."

"What is your plan?"

"I was working on that."

"Then let me be of service."

A smirk quirked her lips and her gaze wandered to his mouth before darting away. "I think I've had enough of your personal services."

"I'm sorry. I was definitely out of line. I swear it won't happen again."

"I've heard that from you before."

He laughed. "You're absolutely right. But I swear it won't happen again." It couldn't. It wasn't his place to want her or soothe her. She incited his lust, but he could control himself. Regulating his emotions was his life.

"Trent." She waved a hand at her cousin.

"Remarkable timing as always, Sin," Alex said.

"Have you two worked everything out?"

Gillian shot Alex a narrow-eyed look. "We were just discussing Whit and what she might be up to with Mr. Sutherland. What do you think?"

"Whitney probably doesn't want you to leave England. Maybe she thinks she can sabotage your plan."

"She knows I'm planning on taking her with me."

"Maybe *she* doesn't want to go. Perhaps she has concluded there is a better man to help you get out of your unwanted engagement." Sin leveled Alex with a fierce frown.

"Quit glowering at me," Alex snapped. "I offered to provide Gillian enough money that she need not marry any man and could move to America and live exactly as she pleased."

"Did you?" Surprise resonated in Sin's voice; then his face darkened. "Why the hell would you do that? You don't even know my cousin. Have you—"

"I have not," Alex interrupted. He knew exactly what Sin was going to ask. "Gillian is still perfectly innocent." Except for a few kisses. "I already told you I *tried* to seduce her. The money I offered was in hopes of enticing her to agree to my plan."

"What the hell is going on here?" Sin roared.

Alex explained quickly. And when he was finished Sin stared at him with his mouth hanging open. "By God, you should put a bullet through Westonburt's heart."

"I want to," Alex said, feeling that dark hole opening up in his chest, "but I'm no murderer."

"Morality is tiresome."

"I couldn't agree more."

Sin moved to stand directly in front of Gillian. "Is it so bad here that fleeing to America seems the only option?"

"It's worse than bad," she replied, her voice quavering.

Something inside Alex's chest tugged. He shifted

uncomfortably.

"Let me talk to Uncle." Sin said.

"No!" She gasped. "Don't you dare. It won't do any good. He'd simply have me married off within a week by special license. Promise me."

The vehemence in her voice and the stark whiteness of her skin surprised Alex. It was as if she feared Westonburt or her father. If she did, she no doubt had good reason.

"No one will say a word," he said, hoping to soothe her.

"Did Westonburt harm you?" Sin demanded. "I'll kill him today if he did. I don't give a damn about my mortal soul. It's already tarnished beyond salvation."

Alex surveyed his friend's unblinking eyes and tense face. "Later, we need to talk about Paris."

"Much later," Sin snapped, not even sparing Alex a glance. "Did Westonburt harm you, Gillie?"

She shook her head. "No. But I've heard rumors of things he's done to other women." A shudder ran through her body and her gaze darted to Alex. "More women than just your sister."

Alex nodded. He suspected she was speaking of the serving wench. The black hole in his heart opened wide. He wanted to kill Westonburt.

"Surely, if you tell Uncle—"

"No." Gillian interrupted Sin. "I won't live here the rest of my life. I can't. I…I can't stand it. I'm done discussing this."

Alex had seen enough of the woman to know simple rumors would not drive her away, but who was he to question her? "She's right," he said. "If we don't move soon, the hunting party will notice us missing. This is what I propose you should do, Gillian. Jump the fence, fumble a fake fall and let Sutherland race to your rescue. He loves to be the hero. Once you are comfortably ensconced in his arms, turn on all the feminine charm you possess. I've experienced a bit, so he should be yours in no time."

Hell, had he really just said that? Alex took in the two openmouthed stares. Yes, he'd said exactly what was in his thoughts. What a damned stupid thing to do.

“Um, er, thank you, Alex,” Gillian stuttered, blushing furiously.

“I always compliment where it’s deserved. Now, then,” he said, working to turn the conversation away from his idiocy, “in case you don’t capture Sutherland this week send your social calendar to Sally, and I’ll make sure Sutherland is everywhere you are.”

“Oh, that’s good,” Gillian said. “But what if I need you this week and beyond for interference and what not?”

“I hadn’t thought of that.” Alex scrubbed his hand over his face. He didn’t care to stick around and watch the seduction of this woman by his partner, or would it be the other way around? It didn’t matter who seduced whom; he’d rather not be a witness. Yet he needed to be here to ensure all went as planned. “I’ll be wherever Sutherland is, don’t worry.” What the hell was he getting himself into?

“Perfect.” Gillian offered a slight smile.

“Get going.” He slapped the hindquarter of Gillian’s horse. “We’ll be right behind you, putting on a big show to make everyone think the race is still on between us.”

Gillian nodded and sped off in the direction of the fence. Alex moved to go, but Sin gripped his arm.

“Do you think she’s hiding something?”

“Hell yes,” Alex replied, grasping Braun’s reins. “What do you plan to do?”

Sin gave Alex a strange look. “Absolutely nothing. I’ve a feeling it will all work out.”

“You’re just going to let her go? Run off to America?”

“Why do you care?”

The question slammed him in the chest. His brother had asked him the exact same thing the day Robert had shot himself. Alex ground his teeth. He knew better than to meddle in anyone’s life. “I don’t care,” Alex finally replied, tapping Braun’s reins to gallop away.

Eighteen

GILLIAN GOADED LIGHTNING INTO a faster speed as she squinted against the sun to judge the height of the fence. It certainly wouldn't hurt to be a little showy. The earth trembled under the pounding of Lightning's hooves, bringing the fence closer by the second. Was it four feet or five?

They would sail over it with no problem. Together they had hurdled heights of six feet before. The faces of the hunting party sharpened as she drew nearer. She leaned forward in preparation to soar, counting the paces. The mechanics of what she needed to do ran through her mind—tighten the legs, brace the body, jump and land. But then what should she do?

She must fake a fall to bring Mr. Sutherland to heel. She could alight and pull the reins taut. Without the beast having the proper amount of time to slow his momentum, he would fight against the control and most probably jerk her around a bit. This would present the perfect opportunity to slide off her horse. She would lean to the left, away from the group and toward that nice patch of hay calling her name.

The thought of purposely fumbling a perfect leap left a sour taste in her mouth. Hooves approached behind her, their building tempo letting her know that Alex closed the distance between them. So he planned a good show, did he? She grinned and tapped Lightning. "Give me everything, old boy."

The beast responded with dizzying quickness. The forest flew by in a green blur on either side of her and exaltation poured through her veins. She loved the speed, the freedom and the thrill of the unknown.

In a flash, Alex whizzed by her on his black beast. Her heartbeat exploded, and her gasp filled the air. He had not said a word about besting her. *The devil.* The man was really not to be trusted.

He was reckless. He landed in one fluid motion on the other side of the fence and swung the steed around to face her, a gleaming smile lighting Alex's face. Greek tales of Bellerophon and Pegasus that her mother had once told her filled Gillian's head. She could well imagine Alex as the descendant of the great Greek hero who rode the flying horse.

She had to clear her thoughts. There was no more time for fanciful musings. One deep breath and every muscle tensed as she signaled to Lightning, and they vaulted up over the fence, through the hissing air and down toward the ground rushing at her. They landed in an explosion of speed and jarring movement, which sent waves of numbness ricocheting through her body and clanked her teeth together with a force that left her wincing. That was not her smoothest landing.

Her reflexes took over and she wrenched the reins upward instead of using the tight, controlled pull she had intended. Lightning reacted violently to his speed being abruptly ended. He reared back and up, hooves kicking in the air. Time ticked to a stop, save the twisted faces matched in their horror at the doom displayed before them. Her head roared, and her pulse soared. Too late to correct her mistake and soothe her steed. His hooves sang through the air, met the ground and paused long enough to bend his neck and send her flying forward.

She landed without any grace whatsoever but with a bit of luck. Instead of meeting her death against a tree or sharp rock, she alighted in the semisoft hay she'd meant to aim for. Of course, she had not intended to land with her feet in the air and her split skirt bunched up at the top of her legs, but at least she was not dead. She would have moved and set herself to a respectable position if she could have even wiggled a pinkie. As it was, the act of breathing hurt her chest. Her state of dishabille would have to be dealt with in a moment.

Perhaps Mr. Sutherland would find her legs pleasing and marry her on the spot for her lovely calves. She started to chuckle, but abruptly stopped to spit out some stray hay stuck in her mouth. Noise erupted around her, and she brushed the locks of hair hanging in her eyes away so she could see if her plan was working.

First a black boot appeared, followed by a rather muscular leg clad in tight tan riding britches, which dropped into a kneeling position beside her. If these were the consequences of botching her jump then she could live with them. She inspected the powerful muscles swelling underneath Mr. Sutherland's riding breeches. Her future husband had nice legs.

Fingers grabbed at her skirt and pulled it down toward her ankles, and she could not help but hope Mr. Sutherland liked her legs as much as she liked his. A heavy, warm arm lay over her ankles and pushed down as a hand grasped her under her arm and pulled her up into a sitting position. Alex's amused blue gaze met hers.

"That was quite a show," he whispered.

She grinned, happy to see him even though he was the wrong man. "You did say put on a 'big show.'"

"Not one that would make my heart stop."

Gillian gaped at the intensity of his statement. Recovering herself, she smiled cheekily. "I didn't know you truly cared," she teased.

He brushed a finger down her cheek. "It surprised me as well."

Before she could respond to his statement or his tender touch, Whitney and Sutherland walked up. They knelt on the ground beside Gillian. With a frown, Whitney pressed cool fingers to Gillian's cheek. "Are you all right?"

"I'll recover."

"I wish I could say the same," Whitney snapped, abruptly changing her demeanor. "You just aged me five years. I've never seen you take a tumble or miss a jump."

"And I've never seen you clear any jump," Gillian snapped back, slapping her palms against the dirt and pushing into a standing position. Her head swam with the rush of blood through her body, and she rocked backward with dizziness. She reached out blindly and gratefully grasped the arm offered to her. "Thank you." She turned and expected to see Alex's familiar face. Instead, Mr. Sutherland smiled at her.

"My pleasure, doll. Nothing a man likes better than rescuing a damsel in distress."

Gillian met Alex's eyes, understanding passing between them. He tilted his head, a small smile curling the corners of his mouth up, and then he turned the full force of his gaze onto Whitney. Gillian clenched her teeth against the unfounded jealousy streaking through her.

Alex tucked Whitney's hand into his arm, and she leaned toward him as he led her away. They appeared as two lovers sharing a secret. Gillian fought the urge to jump up, run to them and place herself in the middle of their pretty little picture. What on earth was the matter with her? Mr. Sutherland was beside her, ripe for seduction, and she stared at Alex as if he was the forbidden apple in the Garden of Eden.

She snapped her gaze to Mr. Sutherland and was surprised to find Trent looming over her. Where the devil had he come from?

He clapped a hand on Mr. Sutherland's shoulder. "Do you mind giving Gillian a ride back to the house? I don't want her back on her own horse after that fall. Mother and the staff are there and can take her off your hands."

Gillian stared in awe at Trent. Her cousin was a brilliant liar. Apparently, whatever else he had done in Paris, he had also mastered the art of subterfuge. He had not blinked an eye or missed a breath as he wove his tale. She really needed to learn his tricks for any upcoming confrontations with her father. Not becoming tongue-tied and flushed would come in quite handy if she needed to have a secret rendezvous with Mr. Sutherland.

"My horse is over there," Mr. Sutherland said, taking her hand in his. His hand was nice, though not nearly as large as Alex's. Mr. Sutherland had long, thin fingers, whereas Alex's fingers were long and—curse her wandering mind and the devil who invaded her thoughts. Why were unwanted images of Alex causing havoc in her head?

Mr. Sutherland raised her hand to his lips, brushing a light kiss over her knuckles. She waited for an explosion of emotion, an awareness in her gut or a tingling *anywhere*.

"I'm not used to all the rules and regulations that dictate your Society. I hope I've not offended you by holding your hand."

"It would take a good deal more than you taking the liberty of holding my hand to offend me, Mr. Sutherland." She batted her eyelashes at him, determined to regain her focus.

"Call me Drake. All my intimate acquaintances use my Christian name."

She nodded as he leaned toward his horse and helped her to mount. He settled behind her, and she rested against his chest. Leaning into her ear, he whispered, "Is this proper?"

"Not in the least," she replied, catching Alex staring at her from across the way. His gaze probed, questioned, and as Drake's hand slid around her waist, she was sure Alex's eyes narrowed with a dangerous glint. Was he jealous? A thrill pounded through her at the thought.

Curse him! She raised trembling fingertips to her lips, lips Alex had kissed into a tender, swollen state earlier. Confusion muddled her mind as Drake set his horse to a trot. She was going to ruin everything if she could not keep her mind on Mr. Sutherland.

Nineteen

Road to the Kingsley Estates
Yorkshire, England

EVEN WITH THE BREEZE created by the speed of Abigor's gallop, the midday sun glared down on Harrison's head. His good mood threatened to evaporate. He hated being hot almost as much as he hated his mother. He kicked Abigor in the hindquarters, and the steed snorted in return but quickened his pace. His beast knew better than to cross him or risk the whip, and after last night, Harrison's mother knew better too.

With his father's dying secret, he had the weapon to be the man he was meant to be. Mother could take her shrewish ways and disappear if she didn't behave.

He grinned as he entered the immaculate grounds of the Kingsley estate. Soon he would be part of all this, and then the men at his club would never be condescending to him again. He would be the one to look down on them, gifting them sometimes with a tale or allowing them to share in a card game.

First things first, though. Gillian's education as to exactly who reigned as lord and master needed to begin today. He was not concerned about Kingsley trying to stand up to him. In eleven years, the great and mighty duke had not managed to break the hold Harrison's mother had over him, and she was just a bent-over, beady-eyed woman with a sharp tongue.

God, he loved this feeling of finally having control over his life. He jumped off Abigor and bounded up the steps. Just as he raised his hand to rap on the door, it swung open and a butler, dressed better than he was, *damn him*, glanced over him once before resting cold gray eyes on his face.

"Help enters at the rear entrance," the butler said, brushing past to shake out a rug.

"I am not a servant, you fool."

The butler paused mid-shake and turned to face Harrison. "You're not the stable master's new man?"

Harrison clenched his fist at his side. Luckily for this idiot, he didn't want to ruin a perfectly good shirt. "I am Baron Westonburt, Lady Gillian's fiancé."

"I apologize for my mistake," the butler hastened to reply, but the man did not make a move to show Harrison into the house.

"Go announce me to Lady Gillian and His Grace." He brushed past the butler and into the foyer. He wanted to break the man's nose, but what if Kingsley was one of those weak men who opposed violence and decided sacrificing Gillian *was* actually wrong?

He stopped in his tracks, stunned and pleased by the splendor of the home. Obviously, blackmail had not put the tiniest dent in the Kingsley coffers. *Good.* He glanced at the arrogant butler. What would the good man say if Harrison swung from one of the enormous chandeliers singing his good fortune for having a mother who followed her brainless husband into the woods eleven years ago? The servant would likely faint dead and show himself to be the fop he really was.

"Lady Gillian is not home at present. Would you care for an audience with His Grace?"

"Didn't I just say that?"

The butler inclined his head and turned on his heel, but Harrison reached out and grabbed the man's arm. "What's your name?"

"Mr. Percy."

"Well, Percy." Harrison towered over the man, intent on intimidating him.

The butler gazed at him with a blank expression. *Fool. Soon he would understand his place.* "Do you always leave company standing in the entranceway? How about a drink and a seat?"

"I beg your pardon," Percy replied. "I'm afraid I'm still recovering from learning you were not the new help."

"Why you miserable little—"

"See here, what's this about?" a voice boomed from the top of the stairs.

Sure that the voice belonged to the duke, Harrison stepped back from Percy and genuflected as Kingsley descended the stairs. The necessary show of respect curdled in his stomach like sour milk. "Your man needs a lesson in respect."

"Go about your business, Percy." Kingsley waved at his butler, then turned dull blue eyes upon Harrison.

"Follow me." Kingsley did not wait for a reply but walked away. Left with no choice, Harrison followed along, though he hated feeling as if he was a puppy trailing after his father.

Kingsley shut the door behind him as Harrison situated himself into a deep, comfortable chair. He gazed around at the hundreds of books lining the walls, the full liquor cabinet and the ornate, expensive looking mahogany desk. This was a rich man's haven with the view of the enormous gardens, lush rugs and an open box wafting the scent of foreign cigars in his direction. He settled back with a contentment he had never experienced. He was home, and nothing short of death would prevent him from claiming everything here as his.

Of course, he'd never have Kingsley's title, but that left a lot of other treasures for the taking. He was in the mood to take. He needed to make sure Lady Gillian's dowry was indecently huge.

"Thanks," he said, taking the drink Kingsley handed to him. The strong aroma of whiskey made his mouth water. Just what he needed to relax a bit.

Over the rim of his glass, he studied Kingsley. The duke took a swig of his drink before setting the glass down with a thud. "Was it the ride that put you in such a foul mood?"

"Your butler thought me a servant."

With one eyebrow raised, Kingsley hardly appeared appalled. Fine. Let the duke play this game. The man's turn would only last a minute.

"I don't know how you get on with your servants, Westonburt, but I don't manhandle mine. Percy made an honest mistake. You're covered in dust and sweat and not exactly dressed in finery."

"Well, I guess you'll have to remedy that once I marry your daughter. You wouldn't want me to bring shame to the family name with my shabby attire, now, would you?"

Kingsley scrubbed his hand across his face. The man's increasing weariness was pleasing.

"Why are you here? I told your mother—"

Harrison came out of his chair to tower over the duke. "You'll no longer be dealing with my mother. I know what your agreement was with her, but I have some terms of my own."

"Who the hell do you think you are?" Kingsley choked out.

The man was angry. It was plain enough to see by his mottled complexion and the spittle that had sprayed out of his mouth when he spoke. Harrison smiled evenly. "I am the man that knows your darkest secret."

Blanching, Kingsley pressed down into his chair. "Roberta swore never to tell you. It was part of our arrangement."

Pleased with Kingsley's shaky tone, Harrison dropped down in the chair beside the duke and slapped the old man's back. "Don't worry, Kingsley. Mother didn't break her promise to you, though she shouldn't have tried to keep me in the dark. Father told me everything, rest his pathetic soul."

"Have you been sending the threatening letters to Gillian?"

"That was Mother. She was worried someone else might catch Gillian's eye when you returned to Society, but I've told her to stop."

"You've gotten everything you want, so why are you

here now?" the duke whispered.

"I want you to add more money to Gillian's dowry. And I want you to come fully out of seclusion and make sure I'm accepted into Society." He settled back and crossed his legs. This day was getting better by the moment.

"Is that all?" the duke sneered, raising a shaking hand to his temple.

"Oh, I almost forgot. I want to spend some time alone with Gillian, so we may properly get to know each other."

The duke lunged at him. With little effort, Harrison stopped the old bugger's laughable attempt and sent him flying with a grunt backward into his seat. "Careful, Your Grace. Your temper could be the death of you. Gillian's virtue is safe with me until our wedding night."

"And if I've changed my mind and I don't agree?"

"Then I suppose your secret will have to come out, and we shall see what consequences the past reaps for the future."

"You wouldn't."

He caught Kingsley's gaze and held it. "I would. Make no mistake about it. Now tell me—where is Gillian?"

A few short minutes later, he was back on Abigor and riding hell-bent toward Davenport's home.

Twenty

GILLIAN SAT IN BROODING silence as she swayed with the motion of Mr. Sutherland's—drat it all—*Drake's* horse. She did not know why it was so hard to think of him on intimate terms. It hadn't been difficult to think of Alex on personal terms. She gritted her teeth and struggled simply to relax into Drake. Loosening up enough to seduce him was proving no easy task. A persistent image of Alex staring at her as she rode off with Drake kept popping into her mind no matter how she tried to concentrate on the man behind her.

After nearly half an hour she shook her head. This line of thought was not helping. She studied the broad expanse of Drake's back. Was it sneaky to pursue a man who she truly believed in her heart would make her a good husband and who she fully planned to make an excellent wife? Even if it was, she could not see how she had a choice. Drake had the power to help her take Whitney far away from here. Gillian touched his shoulder. "Do you mind stopping for a moment?"

"I thought you'd never ask," he replied and brought the horse to a slow stop.

Her jaw fell open at his comment. Thank goodness he could not see the surprise on her face. He had been waiting for her to say something. Wasn't it a man's place to take the initiative?

He dismounted, then reached up and grasped her around the waist to help her off the horse. She gulped a deep breath and concentrated on the man before her. He was not as tall as Alex, but that would make dancing easier. Instead of her gaze being level with the base of Drake's neck as it had been with Alex's, she stared at his chin. It was a nice chin, not too pointy, but his jawline was not nearly as strong as Alex's.

She twined her hands in Drake's hair and brought his head close to hers. "Kiss me," she demanded, throwing caution, decorum and hopefully the images of Alex clouding her observations to the wind.

A smile lit Drake's face, and he wound his hands into her hair to tilt her head back. "You're an unusual woman, do you know that?"

"So I've been told," she murmured, wishing he would just get on with the kiss.

His lips came over hers, soft, warm and timid. Why weren't her toes curling? Why wasn't her heart pounding? Maybe kissing was not his greatest accomplishment. When the kiss ended, he drew her toward his chest. She wrapped her arms around his waist. She refused to compare their kiss to the searing one she had shared with Alex. The cad had probably kissed hundreds of women, whereas Drake may have only kissed a few. She would teach him how it was properly done, given enough time. His embrace was warm, solid and comforting. The spark would come later.

He tilted her chin back, and she met his eyes. Before he could say anything, the sound of horse hooves broke the silence. His arms dropped from around her, just as she whirled around to face whoever approached. Narrowed obsidian eyes were trained on her. All the warmth left her body, replaced by a bone-chilling cold. Lord Westonburt's dark scowl made him look as if he wished to wrap his hands around her neck.

"Who is that?" Drake squinted in Lord Westonburt's direction.

"That would be my fiancé." Gillian shuddered involuntarily as the words left her mouth.

Drake's eyes narrowed slightly; then a smile tugged at

his lips. "Your fiancé has terrible timing."

"My sentiments exactly," she replied, wanting to kiss Drake then and there for the casual way he handled her betrothal. Lord Westonburt jerked up on his steed's reins and slowed the foaming-mouthed beast. He dismounted and strode toward them, gaze flickering from Gillian to Drake. She held his stare, though her stomach turned. How dreadful. She didn't even have time to explain her complicated situation.

"Who is this?" Lord Westonburt snarled, coming to stand so near she could smell the stench of sweat that emanated from him. She swallowed convulsively before settling herself.

"Lord Westonburt, may I introduce Mr. Sutherland."

"We've met," Drake said. "Business is business," he said and stuck out his hand. "No hard feelings?"

Lord Westonburt wrapped his fingers around Gillian's arm and drew her near. She had the urge to kick out at him and flee his side, but he was certain to tell Father if she did. Fleeing to America would be deuced hard if she was locked in her bedroom.

"I don't abide men standing so near to what is mine," Lord Westonburt said.

"Your horse?" Drake waved a negligent hand in the horse's direction. "The beast is over there."

"You know perfectly well I meant Lady Gillian."

"You don't own her," Drake said.

Gillian had to bite the inside of her cheek to restrain her grin.

"She's mine," Lord Westonburt snarled.

Drake's eyebrows rose upward. "Then I've misunderstood. The two of you are married?" He glanced from Lord Westonburt to Gillian.

She could not resist shaking her head.

"We are engaged," Lord Westonburt said. "And in England that makes her mine."

"It may make her yours here, but in America the lady is fair game until she's wedded, bedded and bound for the birthing chair." Drake winked, and Gillian coughed to cover her laughter. Had he just declared he wanted to court her?

Judging by the near purple color of her fiancé's face, he did not think it nearly as funny as she did. Lord Westonburt had never had a sense of humor, even as a child. Simple teasing had always sent him into a tizzy and ended with him trying to beat the other child to death. And she knew from the rumors what violence the man was capable of now. A shiver tingled over her sensitive skin, and she reached up to rub her arms.

"Take your leave, Mr. Sutherland. *My* fiancée has no further need of you."

How dare this man think he had leave to rule her life before they had ever said any vows? "There's no need for Drake to leave. We can all ride back together."

"The need is a simple one, my dear." The cad trailed his finger across her cheekbone. She flinched despite her effort not to move. "I wish to be alone with you."

"That's highly improper," she retorted, choosing to ignore the fact that she had been alone with Drake.

"I'm in agreement with the lady," Drake added.

Lord Westonburt took her hand in his and pressed his lips against the material of her glove. "Your father granted his permission for me to spend some time alone with you today."

She snatched her hand away. Tonight she would discard the gloves she wore. "When did you see him?"

"At your house. No doubt he's here now with your aunt if you care to ride back and gain his consent for yourself."

The air released out of her lungs, leaving her deflated and sad. What had she done to deserve the cold, uncaring treatment her father continued to lavish on her? She was trapped, and she knew it. She wanted to curl up and hide. Instead she straightened her spine. Whatever lingering misgivings she possessed about fleeing to America and abandoning her father no longer mattered. But until she could leave, she had to be very careful. Father didn't like disobedience, and she wasn't at all certain what he might do if he found out about her plan.

"Drake, please go ahead. Lord Westonburt and I will be along shortly."

Drake's eyes held a world of concern, and she was grateful to see he was a caring man. Hopefully she could steal a moment alone with him later and explain everything. Perhaps he would think too many complications came with pursuing her. A tiny sliver of worry wormed its way into her head.

He raised her hand to his lips and brushed a soft kiss across her glove. "Will you be coming back to your aunt's tomorrow?"

She dearly wished he had not asked her that question in front of Lord Westonburt. She didn't want her betrothed to stay for the house party, but she felt certain he now would. Undoubtedly, father had mentioned it to him.

"Of course," she replied, left with no choice but to tell the truth.

"Then I look forward to seeing you tomorrow," Drake said, proffering a quick bow, mounting his horse and riding off. It did not escape her notice that Drake had purposely ignored Lord Westonburt, and based on the stony silence coming from her betrothed she knew the slight had not escaped him either.

As Drake rode out of sight, Lord Westonburt turned her to face him. "You'll not speak to that man again, do you hear me?"

She wrenched her arm free. "I hear you." She'd never hated a man before now, but surely it was hatred coursing through her veins, making her see red.

He reached out and crushed her to his chest, locking her against him. "You need to take care with your tone." His mouth came down on hers in a bruising kiss while his hand found her breast. But before she could react, he was wrenched away, and she stared openmouthed at Alex's fist connecting with a crack against Lord Westonburt's nose.

Twenty-One

"ARE YOU HURT?" ALEX asked, assessing Gillian.

"I'm fine." She ran a hand through her hair, attempting to tuck the escaping wisps back into order.

The knot inside Alex's chest loosened, but the red veil over his vision remained. Losing his soul in exchange for Westonburt's death seemed a fair trade at this moment.

Westonburt whipped out a handkerchief and pressed it to his nose. "Why the hell did you charge in here and punch me? I'm her bloody fiancé."

"You appeared to be mauling the lady," Alex replied, thinking of Lissie.

"I was not mauling her. Passion swept us away. Ask her." Westonburt flicked his gaze to Gillian. "She'll tell you we're to be married, and we were simply getting to know each other."

"I know you well enough already," she replied blandly. "And if you call what you just did to me passion, I'd hate to ever feel the touch of your anger."

Alex grinned at Gillian's show of spirit.

Westonburt removed his handkerchief. "You're my fiancée and soon you will be my wife. So watch your shrewish tongue lest you anger your father or me. You'd be wise to remember I've every right to discipline you once we're married."

Alex surged forward to wring the man's neck, but

Gillian scrambled in front of him and shook her head. Her hand pressed hard against his chest. Her eyes held his a long moment, her silent plea for him to stand down obvious.

"Heed the lady, Lord Lionhurst. You caught me unaware with that first punch, but that won't happen again. Why the hell do you even care what transpires between me and my fiancée?"

"Because it's clear to me you have no clue how to make a woman happy," Alex answered.

"And you think you can make my fiancée happy?"

"I'm sure of it," Alex replied, allowing his gaze to roam over Gillian's face, her breasts and down lower to where he would dearly love to part her creamy thighs and plunge within. He tensed at the unexpected thought.

"You bloody sod," Westonburt snarled before he barreled toward Alex and threw a punch. Alex ducked and stepped to the side.

"Tsk—tsk—tsk, Westonburt." Alex wagged a finger. "Don't you know I'm the reigning boxing champion at Gentleman Jackson's five years running now?" Alex flashed a smile meant to irritate. "But if you really want to try me—" He began to remove his jacket, praying and hoping that Westonburt would take him up on the offer. Just as he got one arm out of his coat, a lone rider came bumping down the road, waving an arm in the air. *Who the blazes was that*? Alex squinted, trying to get a clear picture of the face, but the late afternoon sun made it hard to see his hand in front of his eyes.

"Oh, good!" a familiar voice called. Alex ground his teeth.

Lady Staunton flourished an arm draped in an absurd creation of purple bejeweled silk at them. Her ability to seek him out was amazing in a most unfortunate way.

Before he could ask what she was doing there, Gillian spoke. "Lady Staunton, how surprising to see you here."

Alex jerked his gaze to Gillian. He'd already deduced she was clever, but her ability to make a general statement while filling her tone with disgust was brilliant.

"Your aunt invited me, and I could hardly refuse when I heard who would be in attendance."

Alex longed to drag Lady Staunton off her horse and shake some sense into her. The woman was married. And even if she wasn't, there would never be a future that involved the two of them again. "Where's your husband?" he asked, giving her a pointed look.

"Not feeling well. I suppose he's napping or something. He's always ill."

"Your compassion is astounding as usual."

"You're being cruel, and here I came looking especially for you."

"During the middle of a hunt?" Gillian said. "How very odd."

Alex had never known Lady Staunton to be embarrassed about anything in her life, but a blush stained her cheeks. He'd already developed a liking for Gillian, but anyone who could put Lady Staunton in her place had his utmost respect.

"Your aunt assured me the hunt should be concluding, and there are several games of whist going on in the card room. I simply had to find Lord Lionhurst. I must have a partner as my husband has begged off. No one will do but Lord Lionhurst." She wrapped her possessive fingers around Alex's arm. "We used to play all the time. Remember? Remember what fun we had and how good we were together?"

Alex brushed away her hand. "Your recollections are different than mine. I detest whist."

"I'm unbeatable," Westonburt said. "Maybe we can partner tomorrow?"

"Tomorrow?" Gillian repeated, the color leaving her face. "You're staying for the house party, then?"

"Certainly," Lord Westonburt replied, taking her arm and putting it through his. "Wherever you are, my pet, I'll be."

Her flinch made Alex want to toss Westonburt away from her. "I'm going home to rest," Gillian said. "I feel a headache coming on."

Alex really needed to teach her how to lie properly. As soon as he got her alone he'd give her a lesson.

"Shall I ride with you to introduce you to my aunt and secure your room?" she asked Westonburt.

"I thought I'd stay with you," he replied.

Alex clenched his fists. He could only imagine what Westonburt was scheming.

Gillian shook her head. "Oh, no. That wouldn't be proper, and Auntie would be offended as well. You are *her* invited guest, after all."

Alex suppressed a chuckle at Gillian's overt slight of Lord Westonburt, but his amusement died on his lips as his enemy led Gillian to her horse and hoisted her up.

Gillian smiled in Alex's direction, but he could see by the lines between her brow that her smile was forced. "Until tomorrow," she said with a wave.

He watched helplessly as Westonburt rode off with Gillian. It wasn't until they were out of sight and Lady Staunton's fingers touched his hand that he remembered the lady was even standing beside him.

"Alone at last," she purred.

He flicked her hand off his and quickly mounted Braun. "Quit seeking me out," he snapped and rode off before she could utter a word.

Twenty-Two

GILLIAN DRESSED WITH CARE the next morning. She wanted to keep Mr. Sutherland's notice, but she could not afford to alert her father or Lord Westonburt to her game. She came into the breakfast room prepared to be lectured by her father, but found Whitney sitting alone at the long table.

"Where's Father?"

A smiled tugged at Whitney's lips. "Too much riding yesterday. He's in bed with both feet propped to ease his gout."

"How awful," Gillian said, working to control her own giddy relief as she piled eggs on her plate. Sitting next to Whitney, she met her sister's gaze and worked to control her smile. It was useless. They both burst out laughing.

"We should say a prayer for his quick recovery," Whitney said between gales of laughter.

Gillian nodded and glanced up to the ceiling. "May he recover *next week*."

"Amen," Whitney added, taking a bite of her bacon. They both burst into a fit of laughter again. Once their noise died down, they ate in congenial silence, until Whitney set down her fork and said, "You still have Lord Westonburt to contend with."

Gillian set her own fork down and studied her sister. "I've thought about that. I think I have just the answer."

"What?"

"Auntie has two activities planned for today. I want you to make sure Lord Westonburt thinks I am going to tour the village with the other guests. Tell him I had to take care of Father, but that I will be joining all of you in the village."

"But of course you won't be."

Gillian smiled. "Of course not. I have every intention of hunting with the men again. By the time Westonburt realizes I'm not coming, he certainly won't be able to leave Auntie's touring party without appearing completely rude."

"That's brilliant!"

"Thank you. Let's just hope it works."

An hour later, full of excitement for a chance to finally be alone with Mr. Sutherland, Gillian rode Lightning up to the group of men gathered at the stables and glanced around, puzzled. Her gaze drifted from Trent to her cousin Cameron and their friend Lord Dansby. Finally, she met Alex's eyes, and her heart lurched a little. Anyone's would, really, she assured herself.

An easy smile stretched his lips and his eyes bore into hers as if he wanted to know the secrets of her heart. *He looks at all women that way, you ninny.* She licked her suddenly dry lips. "Where's Mr. Sutherland?"

"Your aunt insisted he come with her on a tour of the village since he'd never seen it."

She turned an accusing glare on Trent.

"I tried to talk her out of it," he said.

Gillian gritted her teeth in outrage. She certainly couldn't protest in front of Cameron and Lord Dansby.

"Do you wish to join the village party?" Alex asked gently. "You can probably still make it."

It would do her absolutely no good to join Mr. Sutherland on a tour of the village since her betrothed would be touring the village as well. In fact, it could harm her. "No." She shook her head. "I prefer to best the three of you in hunting."

"That's the spirit," Alex said.

A few short minutes later, the four of them were off racing through the wind and following the dogs once again. Alex quickly took the lead, but Gillian was determined to beat him.

She took an unused path to gain a lead and charged over some rocks. As she crossed the last rock, Lightning jerked to a halt with a loud neigh. Gillian cursed herself for her recklessness. She jumped off her horse and bent down to inspect the leg Lightning was bending.

Blast and damn. His shoe had come loose. She glanced around, listening. Not a sound but the normal ones of the woods greeted her. *Now what?* She couldn't ride Lightning like this. The only choice was to walk back to her aunt's and have someone take her to get Mr. Ganter so he could fix Lightning's shoe.

With a sigh, she found a sturdy tree to tie Lightning to, and once the task was complete, she started walking back the way she had ridden moments before. Within twenty minutes, perspiration rolled down her back and beads of sweat dampened her scalp. Grumbling to herself, she pulled off her riding gloves, rolled up her sleeves and yanked off her jacket. That was better. At least she wouldn't perish from the heat this way. At a noise rumbling in the air behind her, she whipped around, surprised and grateful to see Alex riding toward her.

Her stomach fluttered at the sight of him. With his black hair fanning away from his face and his powerful shoulders bunched over his horse in determination, he looked more like a dark god than a noble Englishman.

He pulled his horse up in front of her and jumped down. "What happened?"

"In my excitement to win the race, I got careless and rode Lightning where I shouldn't have."

"Over the rocks?"

She looked at him in surprise. "Did you do it too?"

He nodded. "I did. I was just luckier than you. I saw your horse. He'll be fine. He just needs a new shoe."

"I know."

Now he looked surprised. "How do you know?"

"I checked. My stable master taught me long ago all about horses."

"I'm impressed. Most women don't know the first thing about horses."

"I'm not most women, Alex."

"I already know that, peach."

Nothing he'd said was scandalous, but it was the *way* he said it. His tone held the promise of illicit actions. Heat unfurled in her belly and made her curl her toes. Her eyes wandered to his lips. What sort of forbidden things had he done with those lips?

His chuckle broke her musings, and she hurriedly drew her gaze farther up. Big mistake. His eyes burned into her, and she felt as if he undressed her layer by layer.

"It's hot today, isn't it?"

She nodded. There it was again. Something forbidden in his tone. Maybe she was imagining it. "Why did you call me peach?"

"Because your lips are full and pink like a ripe, juicy peach."

Heat not only uncurled in her belly this time, it engulfed her entire body. She had never experienced desire, but she desired Alex. She was certain of it. She was also certain to act on it would be the greatest folly and act of selfishness. "You mustn't call me peach."

"I know. I won't again. It slipped out." He grinned like a mischievous child.

"Do you call all your women by nicknames?" Dear God, why had she asked that?

A hard look crossed his face. "I don't have a harem of women, Gillian. I usually keep one mistress. I am loyal when I'm with her. And no, I never give any of them nicknames."

For some inane reason, his admission pleased her. It was stupid really to be pleased. His words meant nothing for her. She was not special to him. She did not want to be special to him. "Can you take me to my stable?"

He nodded and without warning lifted her off the ground and swung her onto his horse. Within seconds he was settled in front of her, and they were galloping back toward her house. She had no choice but to wrap her arms around him or risk falling backward off his stallion.

Heaven help her, but touching him sent an unwelcome thrill through her. He'd taken his jacket off, like her, because of the unusual heat, and the only thing separating her bare fingers from his bare skin was his shirt.

The muscles of his stomach rippled underneath her fingertips, and she found herself wondering what he would look like with his shirt off. No doubt breathtaking. She tried very hard to think on anything other than him, but it was hopeless. Nothing else held the appeal he did. His broad shoulders and powerful thighs fascinated her. How did a man who stood in line to become a duke become so fit? Most Englishmen were soft and not well developed. "Do you work at the shipping yard a lot?" she asked. She had to press close to his ear to ask him the question, and when she did she got a whiff of pine and leather. He smelled just as manly as he looked.

"How do you know about the shipping yard? My working there is supposed to be a secret."

"Trent told me. He finds it admirable that you took the time to learn what the men you employ actually do."

"I'm glad he doesn't consider me a fool as most in the *ton* do."

"Does it bother you that they look down upon you for owning a company?"

"No. Their opinion doesn't concern me at all. But your cousin's does. He is one of the few people I admire. He's done exactly what he wanted with his life, regardless of what Society expected."

"I admire him too," Gillian admitted.

"Is your father about?" Alex asked as her house came in sight.

"Yes. So if you don't mind, we'll go straight to the stables and not the house."

Alex swerved his horse to the right. "I don't mind. I thought as much."

As they approached the stables, Mr. Ganter appeared. "My lady, where is Lightning?"

"He's got a loose shoe because of my carelessness. Can you come fix it?"

"Certainly, I'll just get my tools. But I'm surprised at you. I taught you better, didn't I?"

"You did. I'm sorry."

"Yes. Well, don't be telling me, tell Lightning."

As Mr. Ganter disappeared into the stable, Alex turned in the saddle to look at her. "Your stable master is very familiar with you. Does he always dress you down?"

"Only when I need it," she said. "He really is like a father to me."

"Strange since your real father is alive."

Mr. Ganter thankfully came out at that moment and saved her from having to explain herself to Alex. They returned to Lightning at an even quicker pace than they'd come, which prevented conversation with Alex. No doubt a good thing since the more time she spent with him, the more personal information she seemed to reveal. She didn't want him asking too many questions.

Once Lightning's shoe was fixed, they rode back quickly to her aunt's house and parted ways with Mr. Ganter as they entered the courtyard.

Gillian was surprised to see her aunt pacing there. Auntie rushed toward them as they approached, sending dread ricocheting through Gillian.

"Stop the horse," Gillian demanded, sliding off the steed the moment he stood still. She ran to her aunt. "What is it, Auntie?" Gillian asked, grabbing her aunt's hands. Alex's boots clopped to the ground as he dismounted. Then he stood behind her, a calming, reassuring presence.

"You need ask?"

"Is it Whitney?"

"Whitney? No. Your sister is being rowed in the boat by that American."

"Mr. Sutherland," Gillian supplied, fully aware that her aunt was not pleased with the idea of Gillian wedding Mr. Sutherland and moving so far away. But her aunt had seemed to settle to the idea when Gillian had refused to be swayed.

"Your betrothed is livid. We returned, as did the hunting party. But guess who was not here."

"Me," Gillian whispered, knowing exactly where her aunt was going.

"Yes. How clever you are, my niece. That wouldn't have been so terrible except he"—Auntie cut her eyes at Alex—"was missing as well. And your dolt of a cousin told your betrothed that he"—she cut her eyes at Alex again—"had raced into the woods to find you when you hadn't shown up at the hounds and neither of you had come back."

Gillian glanced at Alex. "You raced to find me?" Had he been worried for her?

He shrugged. "I couldn't let harm come to my secret weapon."

"What do you mean?" Auntie demanded.

"Nothing," Gillian assured her. "He means nothing." How stupid of her to think for a second that he'd been concerned for her actual welfare. Of course he was only concerned that she be fit to help him carry out his revenge. "Shall we go in and get refreshments, Auntie?"

"Not quite yet." Aunt Millicent was staring hard at Alex. What on earth was her aunt up to? "Lord Lionhurst, why is it that you are approaching the age of—"

"Three and twenty," Alex supplied.

"And you are not married?"

"Auntie, please," Gillian scolded.

"Luck, I suppose." He offered the answer with a casual shrug and a wink in Gillian's direction. Her stomach fluttered in response.

Auntie smacked his arm and served him a scowl. "Be serious, young man."

His eyes flicked to Gillian and held hers. "I asked a woman to marry me when I was but a green boy of eighteen. She taught me that women prefer titles to love."

"A foolish woman," Aunt Millicent murmured. "You seem to attract foolish women, Lord Lionhurst."

Gillian blinked at her aunt's cool green gaze, which was not focused on her. "Must you speak so plainly?" Gillian moaned, rolling her eyes heavenward.

"I must."

Judging by the chuckle Auntie's response drew from Alex, her aunt had failed to shock him with her bluntness.

"Your uncle loved my direct nature. He always said so. Since he passed, I strive to practice it every day."

"Oh, I daresay it's perfected, Aunt. You are as direct as the straightest line."

"Lord Lionhurst, do you love direct women?"

"I love a woman who knows what she wants and goes after it."

She should not look at him. She should murmur an excuse and hurry away. Leave her aunt and Alex to this pointless banter. But she did look. His eyes held hers, and she was sure he had been speaking of her, and she was once again inexcusably pleased.

"Well," Auntie said. "You're rather handsome. Maybe you'll yet meet a woman who wants you."

"That's unlikely," he said. "Unfortunately, I have deficiencies in my character that appear to be irreparable"

"Such as?"

"Well for one, I'm not American."

Auntie pierced Gillian with an assessing look. "In my experience, the best laid plans usually somehow go astray and lead the planner down a far better path."

Her aunt was up to something, but Gillian wasn't sure what. "We better go, Auntie. I'm sure I need to explain my whereabouts to Lord Westonburt."

She practically dragged her aunt away from Alex, and when he was out of distance to hear her, she hissed in her aunt's ear. "Stop whatever it is you think you're doing. Lord Lionhurst is not interested in marrying me."

"He is. He just hasn't accepted it yet."

"Auntie!" Gillian blew out a frustrated breath. "Even if he was interested in marrying me, which he most certainly is not, I have to marry Mr. Sutherland and move to America."

"Whatever for? I just don't understand your insistence on this course of action."

"I hate it here," Gillian lied. "I will not live one more month under the *ton's* whispers and scrutiny. I'll perish if I don't get away." The stricken look on her aunt's face was like a knife in Gillian's heart.

"I see, dearest. Well then, I suppose you are doing what you think you must."

"Yes. That's right. So just let me do it."

"Fine." Her aunt gave her a quick hug. "I promise I'll do nothing to jeopardize your future."

"Thank you," Gillian whispered and parted ways with her aunt once they got in the house.

It was not until the next afternoon, when after a series of unbelievable events that left Gillian sitting alone by a stream in the woods with Alex, that she recalled her aunt's promise and realized her aunt had never actually agreed *not* to interfere.

Twenty-Three

"I THINK MY AUNT has decided we will suit," Gillian said bluntly.

Alex leaned back on his elbows and stretched his long legs out in the grass. She watched as he casually propped one boot on top of the other. His coat fell open, and with his shirt stretched tight across his chest, her fingers tingled in memory of the corded muscles she had felt under his shirt yesterday when they were riding his horse.

He turned his head to look at her, amusement making crinkles at the corners of his eyes. "What makes you say that? Was it the fact that she insisted Sutherland had to be the one to take your sister back to the house?"

She opened her mouth to respond, but he continued. "Or was it that she refused to let me accompany her back for her supposedly twisted ankle and insisted Westonburt accompany her, though you and I both know she does not care for the man? Or if it was neither of those things, maybe it was the fact that she insisted your cousins had to go straightaway to check on the tenants, even though your aunt was the one to plan this excursion of exercise into the woods. Which one of those things clued you in to your aunt's plan to throw us together?"

Gillian lay back in the grass and laughed. By God it

felt good. When she was finished, her belly ached and her eyes were filled with tears of joy. She turned her head finally to answer Alex, and her breath caught in her throat. He had propped himself on one elbow and he faced her directly. Butterflies flooded her stomach. "I think perhaps it was the last—the rushing my cousins away despite their protest that they'd already visited the tenants—that was the deciding factor for me."

"Yes." Alex reached out and plucked something out of her hair, his fingers gently touching her scalp. Instantly, her body tingled in awareness of his touch.

"You've grass in your hair." He picked out a few more blades, then smiled a devastating smile at her. More butterflies flooded her stomach until she found she was squirming.

"Do you think anyone else noticed?" she asked, turning her head and looking up at the sky. White puffs of clouds dotted the blue expanse. She concentrated on the shapes to take her focus off the blue eyes in her head.

"Doubtful. Your aunt is stealthy. If she wasn't a woman, I have no doubt she would be a spy for the King."

Gillian nodded. "She'd be the best."

"Shall we continue with the excursion for a bit, to satisfy your aunt that we have spent sufficient time alone? Then you can go back and charm a proposal out of Sutherland, while I run interference against your aunt and your betrothed."

Gillian winced. The whole affair sounded so awful when put so bluntly. "Can we just lay here for a few minutes?"

It seemed like ages since she had simply relaxed. Trying to keep her father and Lord Westonburt in the dark as to what she was up to while batting her eyelashes, smiling continuously and laughing at everything Mr. Sutherland said was exhausting. The only time she had not felt on edge in three days was right now lying here in the sunshine. She frowned, realizing with a start that she had also been relaxed yesterday when riding back to her aunt's house with Alex. And the day before, when she and Alex had chatted while waiting for the storm to pass. Oh, they had exchanged barbed banter back and forth, but it had been fun, until he had stolen that kiss.

Her pulse quickened in memory of his lips against hers. She concentrated hard on the shapes of the clouds.

"What are you doing?"

Was that her imagination or was his voice husky? She would not turn her head his way. As long as she didn't look at him, she would be perfectly fine. "It's silly, but I like to study the shapes of the clouds."

"Me too," he said so casually that she turned to gape at him without thinking. He was not looking at her though. He was on his back, his gaze focused upward and his head propped up on his rolled up jacket. Her eyes trailed to his chest. When had he taken off his jacket?

Her heart thumped wildly. As he raised his hand to point at the sky, she was helpless to do anything but stare at him.

"I see a dog, a knight and a lady-in-waiting. What do you see?" He turned his head to face her, his lips parting and his breath swishing out in the softest exhalation.

All she could see was him. She was too mesmerized by his aching beauty to even unscramble her brain and turn her gaze back to the clouds. The wind blew a cool breeze just then. She shivered. Perhaps it was the temperature. She had dressed for warmer weather because yesterday had been unusually warm, but today it was cool again.

She opened her mouth to say they should get going, but when he reached out and ran his hand up and down her arm, all her thoughts left her head.

"Your teeth are chattering." He said the statement simply, as if putting his hand on her arm to warm her was the most innocent thing. His hand slid back and forth over her arm, warming her not only there but in every part of her body. His touch was incredible. She could not pull her gaze away from his bicep, where his muscle bulged underneath his shirt every time his hand stroked the length of her arm.

Belatedly, she realized she had not responded to his statement and she was staring. She did not know what to say. She should protest, demand he quit, but she did not want to. This was desire. Real desire. Maybe she would never feel it again. She had not yet felt any sort of spark with Mr. Sutherland.

With her heart thumping loudly, she parted her lips. She knew what she wanted. For one moment in time, she wanted to pretend that she was a normal debutante and that Alex was courting her because he wanted to marry her. And she wanted to say yes.

She swallowed thickly, trying to find her voice. Taking a deep breath she said, "Kiss me."

ALEX DID NOT NEED to be asked twice. It had taken every ounce of restraint he possessed not to kiss her. Being around Gillian for these last three days and denying his natural desire for her had been more punishing than any boxing match he had ever fought at Gentleman Jackson's. Her simple plea was all the encouragement he needed.

He tugged her to him until their lips were so close, he could smell her sweet breath. Her scent intoxicated him. He breathed deeply and slid his hand to the back of her neck. Her skin felt like silk under his fingertips. He tilted her head back and moved in to press his lips to hers. Desire poured through his veins.

He knew he should end the kiss. Their desire for each other could lead nowhere good for her or him. But he could not do it. He wanted to deepen the kiss, not end it. He kissed the corner of her mouth and then trailed kisses across her jaw. When a moan escaped her, his heart quickened in response.

He found her mouth again and pressed his lips harder to hers. He needed more of her. He had never wanted a woman this much. He wanted to taste her. Taking a chance, he parted her mouth with his tongue. She met him tentatively, and then more boldly, until their tongues danced together. His hand moved from her neck to her back, and he pulled her body up against his until the swell of her breasts crushed against his chest.

He knew he had to stop where this was going, but when her hand clutched at his arm and she threw her head back to give him further access to her neck he was lost. His fingers went to the buttons at the back of her dress. He had one thought in his head—to feel her bare skin against him. That would be heaven. He could be alone for the rest of his life, if he had that memory.

He fumbled with the first button, his own ragged breathing filling his ears. A twig snapped beside him and brought reality crashing down around him. He pushed her away as he rolled up to his feet prepared to explain, fight or offer for her hand—whatever it took to protect her.

Gillian's sister smirked at him. "Auntie sent me to find the two of you. It's time for lunch, and Gillian's betrothed is becoming quite irritated by her absence."

Gillian scrambled to her feet. Her sister scrutinized her, and Alex knew what she saw. The rosy lips, the disheveled hair, the dazed look. Had his kissed really dazed her? Satisfaction flowed through him. "Our hike through the woods was most invigorating."

"I see that," Lady Whitney said. Her voice dripped with disbelief.

"And I see your ankle is all better," Alex commented, wishing to turn her attention.

A blush colored her cheeks. "Good as new. Quite amazing."

He tried to capture Gillian's gaze to convey his apology with his eyes, but she would not look at him. He did not blame her. She had asked for a simple kiss, and he almost ravaged her. He battered himself with recriminations. What had he been thinking, touching her arm to warm her?

He had started to seduce an innocent, when he knew perfectly well she wanted marriage. He was as bad as everyone thought. Except, he had—he realized with numbing shock—been prepared to offer for her hand if the person who had stumbled upon them could ruin her reputation. What was happening to him? "Shall I escort the two of you back to the house?"

"No," Gillian said sharply and finally met his gaze. "Please don't."

"She's right," Lady Whitney agreed. "Besides, Auntie's lady's maid is waiting at the edge of the woods where you left her to come back and fetch your coat."

"I did?" Alex asked, trying to figure out where Lady Whitney was going with this.

"You did." She nodded. "And Lauren, who was sent by Auntie to escort you and Gillian on your hike, waited with Gillian at the edge of the woods for you to retrieve your coat, which is why the three of you have been gone for so long."

"Of course," he said. He understood perfectly now. Gillian's aunt had made sure his excursion with Gillian appeared perfectly proper, though he suspected the lady was hoping it was anything but. What did Gillian's aunt think? That Gillian would be so befuddled by him that she would abandon her plan to marry Sutherland and let herself be seduced instead? Then what? Did she suppose he would then offer for her niece's hand and Gillian would stay in England as the aunt obviously wanted?

He ground his teeth together. The aunt clearly did not know how stubborn Gillian was or that he had vowed—after Lady Staunton had taught him that women wanted the best possible match over love—that he would never marry anyone. He proffered a quick bow. "I believe my services here are over for the day."

At Gillian's sharp inhalation of breath, he cursed himself. Why had he chosen those words? He did not want to hurt Gillian. Hell, he had just been prepared to break his vow to save her. But she would never know that.

GILLIAN WAS NOT SURE if she took more care to avoid Alex the next day or if he took more care to avoid her. Either way, their not spending any more time alone was for the best. Her desire for one simple kiss had almost been her willing ruination.

With great effort, she put Alex out of her head and spent the day with Auntie and Mr. Sutherland. It was a simple matter of good luck that Father had been called away to deal with a problem on their estate, and Auntie had suggested Lord Westonburt accompany him, so they might have an opportunity to bond.

Gillian giggled, thinking of both men's flabbergasted faces. Neither had been able to refuse the suggestion, though it was apparent both had wanted to. Gillian expected her aunt to beg a headache or some such excuse and leave her and Mr. Sutherland to their own devices, especially after the thorough dressing down she had given her aunt the night before for interfering, but Auntie stayed with them all day.

It was just as well, Gillian decided that night as she lay in her bed and tried to fall asleep. She had been rotten company, and Auntie had carried most of the conversation with Mr. Sutherland. Hopefully, he would not notice she had been sullen today.

She tossed and turned in her bed. She knew what was wrong with her, but she wanted to deny it. Alex was her problem. He had occupied the better part of her thoughts all day. His eyes. His lips. The wonderful way he kissed. The way he rode a horse. The wounded look in his eyes when she had asked him not to accompany her back to the house yesterday, and then the clear anger at himself.

As much as that man was a rake, he was good. She was sure he was playing at being something else to hide deep wounds, and the thought that some woman would someday come along and help him accept who he really was made Gillian jealous. She squeezed her eyes determinedly shut and forced his face away. He was not her future. She had no right to be jealous. Tomorrow was a new day, and she would concentrate all her efforts and attention on Mr. Sutherland.

Twenty-Four

"WHAT DO YOU MEAN he's gone?" Gillian demanded of her aunt.

Auntie set down her needlework and pinned Gillian with a look that could only be interpreted as exasperated. "Gone. As in not here. I determined your sister needed a new dress for the ball tomorrow night, and you know perfectly well the only one who can create something sensational in such a short time here in the country is Madame Beaupont."

"Auntie," Gillian growled, not caring that Alex was sitting on the couch. He wasn't paying much heed to her anyway. A scowl marred his face, and he was staring, it appeared rather incomprehensively, at a paper in his lap. "I don't see what Whitney getting a dress has to do with Mr. Sutherland."

"She couldn't very well go into town without a chaperone," Auntie said with a roll of her eyes.

"And you consider Mr. Sutherland a proper chaperone for an unwed girl?"

"Don't be ridiculous, dear. He's driving them."

Gillian pressed her fingertips to her aching temples—that was what having no sleep would do to a woman. She took a deep, calming breath. "Auntie, please explain—*slowly*."

Her aunt paused with her needle in mid-air. "The Duke and Duchess of Primwitty finally arrived this morning. The duchess insisted she needed a new bonnet for walking around out of doors. Their driver was indisposed, and you certainly cannot expect me to allow the Duke of Primwitty to drive himself around. I may not be conventional, but I do try to retain some social graces."

Gillian flopped into a chair, exhausted from trying to obtain a reasonable explanation from her aunt. Her aunt was speaking in confusing circles on purpose. "What about your coachman?"

"The poor fellow is indisposed."

Gillian snorted. No doubt his illness had more to do with her aunt telling him to feign sickness than anything else. "So you're telling me Whitney has gone into town with Sally and the duke as her chaperone and Mr. Sutherland as her driver?"

"My, your thoughts are elsewhere today, dearest." Auntie glanced meaningfully at Alex. Gillian had the urge to kick and scream like a child would, except it would do her no good. "I would never ask the duchess to assume the role of chaperone. Social graces, remember?"

"I remember," Gillian said wearily.

"My lady's maid has gone along as the chaperone, which worked out perfectly because poor Lauren had not been able to see her mother in ages, and now she can."

Gillian was almost afraid to ask, but she had to know. "Whatever do you mean?"

"The duke and duchess graciously agreed to allow Lauren to stop at her mother's house in the village for a visit. They should all be back by nightfall."

"Nightfall," Gillian repeated, seething. Her aunt had effectively managed to keep Mr. Sutherland away from her for the entire day, and there were only three more days left until the house party was over. She didn't bother to remind Auntie that she had promised not to interfere, because of course she had promised no such thing. The woman was too clever. Gillian would have to think of a way to outwit her aunt for the next two days, and as much as she did not want to risk spending any more time alone with Alex, she needed his help.

She glanced at him, surprised to find his blue eyes

assessing her. A small smile pulled at his lips. "It's not all bad."

"How?" she snapped.

"Now you can spend the day hiding from your betrothed."

Gillian groaned. In her haste to arrive here this morning and see Mr. Sutherland, she had not spared one thought for Lord Westonburt.

Gillian scrambled to her feet. "I think I feel ill. I better go home and lie down."

Auntie snorted. "Business called Lord Westonburt away today. He will be back tomorrow in time for the ball. I imagine a note is waiting for you at your home."

"Our butler did try to give me one this morning, but I waved him away."

"Perhaps you'd like to go home and read it, since there is no need to stay here now," Auntie said.

Gillian's eyes involuntarily darted to Alex. He was staring down at the paper again, but she could have sworn he was on the exact same page he had been on when she had come in. What was wrong with him today? Her aunt smiled at her. "Or maybe you would care to stay?"

Drat her aunt. She was purposely reading more into the situation than there was. "Well, I do feel a tad better."

"That's good, dearest." Aunt Millicent's head was already bent, and her eyes were focused on her knitting. "I'll just be right here, if you need me."

Gillian needed a way to talk privately with Alex that would not lend credit to her aunt's suspicions. But going off alone with the man was out of the question for more reasons than mere propriety's sake. She glanced around the sitting room, the pianoforte catching her gaze. That was perfect. It was across the room, would create noise, and she and Alex would be close enough together to discuss strategy. "Lord Lionhurst, would you care to play the piano while I sing?"

He glanced up, surprise evident in his confused gaze. My, he was preoccupied. She had not seen him like this. "Pianoforte, did you say?"

She nodded.

"I don't play."

Drat him. Why was he being difficult?

"Do you sing? I can play."

"I don't sing either. How about a walk outdoors?" He was looking at her, but it almost seemed he was not seeing her.

She shook her head. "Too cold." She wanted to believe she could trust herself around him, but what if she slipped again?

"Why don't you play chess?" Auntie suggested.

"Perfect!" Gillian exclaimed, wanting to kiss her aunt for the suggestion. The chess table was on the opposite side of the room by the pianoforte, and they could easily pretend to play while forming a plan of attack.

Alex shook his head. "I no longer play chess."

"Why ever not?" Gillian protested.

A dark look crossed Alex's face. "I have my reasons."

She didn't want to push him, especially because he for once looked vulnerable instead of like a carefree rake, but she simply had to speak to him. *Please.* She mouthed the word silently, so he could read her lips.

With a jerk of his head, he rose and strode to the chess table. He pulled out a chair for her and stood tensely, until she crossed the room and sat. Once he was seated, she studied his face for a moment. His jaw ticked and his fingers drummed a rapid beat on the table. "We don't really have to play chess. I just needed an excuse to speak with you."

He nodded and pushed the chessboard away from the table as if touching it might burn him. "How can I help you?"

She wanted to ask the same of him but was certain he would deny the need for any assistance. "My aunt is obviously still working to throw us together."

"Yes. If only you could make her understand you detest me."

"You know that's not true." Why had he said that? He didn't want to marry her or anyone else for that matter.

"I'm sorry. I'm being unpardonably rude."

Impulsively, she reached over and grabbed his hand, and as she did, she knocked a chess piece over.

He picked it up and set it down with a thump. "Today is the anniversary of my brother's death."

"Oh, Alex." She squeezed his hand. "I'm so sorry. How did he die?"

"Don't you know?"

She shook her head. "Should I?"

"I suppose you might not with your absence from Society. If you stayed around long enough, I'm sure someone would fill you in. He killed himself."

"Oh, my goodness." She didn't know what else to say. "How awful for you."

"It's worse for him, really. He's the dead one. Of course I'm left here with the guilt, so there is that."

"Why would you feel guilty? It's not as if you killed him." Alex's hand twitched under hers.

"I may not have pulled the trigger, but make no mistake about it, I'm the reason he's dead."

His face was taut with pain. Suddenly, it dawned on her why he lived as he did. Alex was punishing himself for his brother's death. Was that why he tried to be bad? Because he thought he was? Was he not allowing anyone to get close because he didn't think he deserved love? Her heart ached for him. She understood all too well how it felt to think you had failed someone you loved. "You can't possibly be responsible for your brother taking his life."

His eyes cut into her, making her shiver. "Forget it." He raked a hand through his hair, and when his hand came down, his smile of perfect nonchalance was back in place. "What can I do for you?" His tone was that of suggestive rake once more.

She sighed. He had put his façade firmly back in place. Still, she had to try. "Alex—"

"I said forget it."

"All right. I'll let it go, because I suspect if I didn't you'd leave me sitting here without a backwards glance."

"You're very astute."

"If you ever need someone to talk to—"

"I'll employ another mistress," he finished for her.

She knew he was lashing out more in anger at himself than her, but his words hurt. She was nothing to him, and he had put her in her rightful place. She swallowed her embarrassment. “Will you run interference for me tomorrow night at the ball, so I can have some time alone with Mr. Sutherland?”

“Of course. Make sure your aunt has her card room open.”

“Do you have a plan?”

“Of course I do. Don’t you know rakes always have a plan? Now if you’ll excuse me?”

“Where are you going?” There wasn’t much more to discuss since he had a plan, but she hated to see him go somewhere alone on this day in his mood. “Let me come with you.”

“Aren’t you worried about what might happen?”

She bit her lip at his reminder. She was worried, but not that he might take advantage of her. She was worried she would beg him to kiss her again. The man made her senseless.

His finger brushed down her cheekbone and fell away before she could comprehend the intimacy. She shivered at his touch.

“You’re right to worry, peach. Don’t allow yourself to be alone with me again.”

Her heart thundered at his words. “Why?” she whispered.

“Because I’m not sure I could restrain myself next time.”

He turned on his heel and left her standing there, gaping with longing and surprise. He wanted her. He desired her. Silly, foolish woman that she was, she was inordinately pleased because she didn’t think his desire had a thing to do with wanting revenge.

After spending the afternoon going over all the details of the ball with her unusually quiet aunt, Gillian rode Lightning home. In the twilight, she allowed her thoughts to drift back to Alex. It was then, in the cool air that crystallized her thoughts, she realized he had become a rake right before her eyes rather than allow her inside his personal pain.

And she had let him. Disarmed by his lethal smile, she had failed him. Was that what all women did? It was no wonder Alex dismissed the idea of love, if all women became simple minded as she had when faced with his seductive ways. He no doubt had never been pushed to open up and share his heart and pain. She prayed a woman would come along and help him. Then she prayed one would not. She felt awful and confused. Her last prayer was for a good night's sleep to straighten out her muddled thoughts and calm her turbulent emotions.

AFTER A DAY OF hard riding and a night of holing himself up alone in his guest room, Alex emerged the next day to the sound of Gillian's laughter. Her merriment filled his heart until Sutherland's loud guffaw joined her soft chuckle. Alex turned on his heel and made his way toward the stables. He passed a footman on the way, and after ordering a quick lunch to be packed, he gave the footman instructions to tell Lady Primwitty he had gone riding for the day. Let them think what they would. He would make sure do his part tonight, but today he needed to reorder his thoughts and push Gillian out of them, except for how to help her catch Sutherland.

The riding was exhausting, which was exactly what he needed. He made it a point to stay away for most of the day. When he arrived back at the house, servants were bustling about to prepare for the ball and most of the guests were in their rooms preparing for the evening. He made his way to his room and called for a bath to get the layer of dust off his body.

After undressing, he pilfered through the stack of notes by his door. As expected, Peter, Sally and Sin had all asked him to seek them out before tonight. Sutherland had left a blunt note that he thought he had found the perfect woman to be his wife; now all he need do was convince her to leave her betrothed. Alex crumpled the note and threw it across the room.

He jotted a quick note to Peter explaining the plan for tonight, called for a servant to deliver the note and then he ignored the other requests opting instead to soak in the bath until the last possible moment while trying not to think about Gillian in Sutherland's arms.

By the time he was properly attired for the evening, he thought he was in control. But as he wound his way through the crowd of people already gathered in the Rutherfords' ballroom, he found himself searching for Gillian in the sea of guests.

Everything about her enticed, beckoned and drugged his senses. And her eyes... Alex inhaled deeply. The way they displayed her emotions fascinated him. When she was excited, her emerald eyes turned at least two shades brighter, almost the color of teal. And when she was angry, they deepened to remind him of the dark green trees in the forest, sheltering and secretive. And when she felt pity—he shoved the memory away, as it reminded him of Robert.

As Alex walked by a group of people gathered in conversation, a hand reached out and grabbed his arm, snapping his attention away from his ridiculous ruminations and back to where it belonged, his surroundings. Lady Chastain smiled at him, showing teeth tainted yellow by her years. She curtsied, smacking him in the face with a large—was that a blasted feather? Swiping a hand over his tingling nose, he squinted at the purple plume sticking out of the woman's hair. "Ah, Lady Chastain."

Why in God's name women felt the need to adorn themselves so ridiculously he would never understand. He preferred simple beauty. Even if the woman was not lovely, trying to mask it with feathers—Alex glanced down the bumpy length of Lady Chastain's bejeweled gown—and so many sparkling gems that hurt a man's eye was not a good idea. Hardly the way to draw attention, at least the favorable kind.

"Lord Lionhurst, I want to introduce you to my daughter." Lady Chastain reached behind her and yanked a poor, unsuspecting chit from the circle. She pushed a girl with mousy brown hair and dull brown eyes toward him. The girl tried to hold back her forward motion, but Lady Chastain was a mother hunting a husband for her daughter, and nothing would stand in her way, including her embarrassed daughter.

Alex sighed and shifted his weight to his back foot just

in case the mother hurtled the girl at him. This was exactly why he avoided balls. If the mother schemed hard enough and his guard slipped, even just a bit, he could find himself trapped in a room alone with a girl who could—and devil take them all—*would claim* ruination. Then he would have no choice but to marry the chit.

Honor was a damned nuisance, especially now as he felt the tug of it. He could not abandon this poor girl, though he longed to throw himself into his plan to get his mind off Gillian. He bowed deeply and smiled into the girl's widening gaze. Her face flushed an amazing shade of red and a very slight smile turned up the corners of her lips. Ah, here stood an unblemished treasure. This was a green girl new to the hunt, not yet keen to the ways of the world and most likely still dreaming of falling in love, not being matched with a husband as one matches a stallion to mare. Nothing required beyond impeccable lineage and the ability to procreate.

"My Marion's dance card is empty," Lady Chastain said from behind her daughter.

Marion's lower jaw dropped open, and Alex suspected she wished the floor would open up for her as well. Who could blame her? He could not change who her mother was, but he could help launch the girl into Society by creating a buzz.

As ridiculous as it was, the fact remained the young fops would dance with her if *he* did so now. *Blasted honor.* He glanced in the direction of the dancers and saw that two long lines of couples gathered to perform the longways Country Dance. What a bit of stunning bad luck. He'd be at least an hour on the dance floor before he could continue his search. No hope for it, though.

"Dancing with your daughter would be my pleasure, Lady Chastain." Alex took Marion's clammy hand in his and led her onto the dance floor toward the middle of the line. Just as they neared the couples swaying on the marble tile, musical laughter filled the air. Gillian smiled, and her beauty stunned him in all its simplicity. She wore green silk, cut low and fitted to show all her charms, which he fully appreciated.

Her black hair drifted over her shoulders in alluring

waves, a simple white magnolia tucked behind one ear. He stared, as did every man around her. *Blast their lustful souls.* A generous display of sun-kissed flesh swelled up at the top of her dress. Well, the lady had pulled out all the stops tonight. Sutherland was a goner. Alex shifted with the desire throbbing painfully through every inch of his body, right to his fingertips, which flexed uncontrollably and squeezed the hand he held in his.

A gasp resounded to his left, and he glanced at Lady Marion just in time to see her hesitant smile turn to one of joy. He dropped her hand at her hopeful look and immediately put a good foot between them. What could he say so as not to hurt the girl's feelings, yet make her understand he did not harbor those kinds of feelings for her? "Lady Marion—"

"Darling, there you are," Sally chirped in his ear. "How goes your plan?" she whispered.

"Not accordingly. There have been some changes."

Sally raised her eyebrows in question.

"Later," Alex said. "I'll explain later."

"Very well, darling." Her voice raised to conversation level. "Peter and I have been looking everywhere for you. Haven't we, Peter?" Sally glanced behind her and Peter stepped forward.

"I tell you, the woman has dragged me back and forth across this dance floor till my shoes now have holes." Peter lifted his foot and pointed. "See. She's worn out my favorite pair all in search of your sorry self." Peter shook his head. "All I want is a drink and a good card game."

"I know just what you mean," Alex mumbled, then winced, remembering Lady Marion.

Sally whipped out her fan and smacked Peter on the arm, then turned and whacked Alex. "Men are so tedious at times," she said to Lady Marion, linking arms with the girl. "Don't mind their grumbling. Finery never can hide the naughty little boys they truly are." Sally led Lady Marion right next to Gillian in the dance line, leaving Peter and Alex to follow.

"I feel like a puppy who's been scolded for chewing up a shoe," Peter said, frowning. "A perfectly natural thing for a pup to do, mind you."

"I'd say so," Alex replied, staring at Gillian. She met his gaze, and his heart gave an odd tug. He put his hand to his chest to rub the ache away. Maybe he was getting ill.

For a moment, Sally and Gillian huddled together, making a show of exchanging a greeting, but their lips moved in a flurry of hurried, whispered words. What were those women up to?

"Lady Gillian, how did your game go this afternoon?" he asked. "Do you have a good strategy?" Was that enough of a hint for her to know he meant the game of seduction?

"The beginning of the game went well enough, but my strategy needs improving." Gillian cut her eyes to the left, and Alex followed her motion. *Bloody hell.* Westonburt was a leech at Gillian's side. Alex would have to remedy that. "Evening, Westonburt."

The man unclenched his jaw enough to say, "Same to you, Lionhurst."

Westonburt genuflected toward Peter. Alex nearly laughed, but Peter's well-placed sharp jab to his side stopped Alex's mirth.

"Your Grace, it's a pleasure to see you."

Peter pushed his glasses up the bridge of his nose and managed a superior look. "Likewise."

Peter's ability to suffuse disinterest into his reply impressed Alex. How had he never noticed that particular talent of his friend's?

It was time to begin his plan. He had played a little game of bait and catch many times with Peter in the past before his friend had become married and boring. Alex turned to Peter just as the notes of the music softly filled the room. "Cards after this?"

"What do you have in mind?"

The tempo rose and Alex's pulse sped up with the beat. "Vingt-et-un, of course. Dockside play."

"Those are high stakes, but I'm game," Peter replied with a nonchalant shrug. "But we need three more players."

On cue, Alex stepped forward and met Lady Marion in

the middle. She curtsied and as her head dipped, he took advantage of her distracted state to glance at Gillian. Her hair fell forward as she curtsied to Westonburt, and as she came up, the view of her décolletage made Alex swallow convulsively. It was the pure joy she displayed when her gaze locked with his that tripped him up, though. He missed a step as he stared at her and almost bumped into his surprised partner. Was she happy to see him for himself or because he was her distraction?

When her eyes cut to Westonburt and her brows rose in question, he had his answer. When had he become such a dolt?

The men moved back in line and Alex threw out the bait that he needed to. "I'll ask my brother and Lord Dansby. Who else?"

"Say, Westonburt," Peter fairly shouted over the rising crescendo. "Do you play Vingt-et-un?"

"Better than anyone I know," the man replied with the smuggest smile.

"Care to prove that and play in our modest game?"

Something shifted in Westonburt's eyes, making them darker, challenging. Alex recognized the burn to win at all cost. He'd seen it in his own face when he was younger and very foolish. Westonburt finally nodded. "I'd love to."

Adrenaline pumped through Alex's veins as he danced Lady Marion down the long lane to the end. The bait was cast. The game was on. And he meant to play for the stakes of ruination. Pray God, not his own.

Twenty-Five

TOWARD THE END OF the dance, Lady Struthford called for a change of partners, and Alex quickly grabbed Gillian's hands as she passed while guiding Lady Marion in Westonburt's direction. The wolf would hardly attempt to devour this girl. She was no beauty and possessed a lowly title. Alex refused to worry about her. He had his own problems. Yet as she danced away with a smile on her lips, he second guessed his selfishness.

"Developing a tendre?" Gillian whispered as he bowed to her.

He came up, wrapped an arm around her waist and twined his other hand with hers. "Hardly. Since you trod on my heart, I've quite given up on females."

Gillian chuckled as they danced down the line. "I'd say your low impression of females was formed long before our encounter."

Her words were so true that hearing them felt like he'd been pricked by something sharp. But he wasn't here to try to figure out anything about himself. "How goes the seduction? I don't see your target anywhere around."

"Quit calling it a seduction," she hissed. "It sounds so sordid put that way."

What else could he call it? He frowned. She was trying to capture a marriage proposal from his partner who she barely knew and certainly did not love. Although she wasn't after Sutherland's money, she was pursuing him based on where he lived. Didn't that make the whole affair sordid? One he couldn't quibble over since he was helping to lead the lamb to the sacrificial altar. *Deuced honor.* It kept rearing its ugly head tonight.

He squeezed Gillian's hand. "How's the merry chase going, then?"

She rolled her eyes heavenward. "You are incorrigible. It's a courtship."

"A what?" He gaped. Now he had heard it all. A woman courting a man? An interesting concept and one, he realized with surprise, he would not mind having tried on him. Not that he wanted a wife. Besides, he could not think of a single lady he would wish to court him. Now, seduce him… He glanced away from Gillian and forced his mind back to the task at hand.

"Call it what you like," he said, hearing the growl in his own voice as he danced her back down the line. "Just as long as it is a success. And judging by the fact that I do not see Sutherland anywhere around…"

She raised one beautiful black eyebrow. "But you underestimate me. Here comes my future husband."

Alex looked toward the direction she indicated. Sure enough, Sutherland strolled their way. Gillian tapped Alex's shoulder, drawing his gaze back to her, and nodded at the approaching figure. "If you really mean to help me, now is the perfect time."

He stood rooted to his spot, absurdly jealous that Sutherland would be dancing with Gillian while Alex sat in a smoky room full of men in their cups telling bawdy jokes. Funny, but he usually loved just that sort of thing.

"Don't you have a card game planned?" she offered.

"I'll take over from here, Lionhurst," Sutherland said, winking at Gillian while clapping Alex on the back.

As Westonburt ambled toward them, Alex sprang into action. He clasped the man around the neck. "Let's go, old boy. I'm dying to see just how good you are."

Westonburt hesitated, indecision flickering in his cold eyes. It was obvious that the man sensed he should stay and protect what was his, but Alex would bet his life that Westonburt's desire to climb the social ladder would win over good sense.

"They're waiting for us," Alex said, pointing to Peter and his friend Dansby. "Are you in or not?"

"I'm in."

Without a reply, Alex walked away from Gillian, though her tinkling laughter followed him, teasing him with what would never be his.

THE FIVE MEN SETTLED into their seats as a servant scurried toward their table with a silver tray containing liquor, their deck of cards and chips. Lady Davenport's husband might have been dead, but Gillian's aunt had obviously not forgotten what men wanted from a ball—a place to gamble and good liquor to drink. Apparently, this was exactly what her aunt wanted too.

She sat several tables over, holding court among eight other matrons. Lady Davenport shone like a diamond of the first water among the drab older women surrounding her. Her old cronies dressed as if they already had one foot in the grave in their dull gowns buttoned up to their necks with firm scowls on their faces. Not Lady Davenport. She wore royal-blue silk, which came to a rather daring plunge to expose her charms. The blue flowers in her hair made Alex smile. Her attire was a blunt, silent statement that she was not dead nor did she care to be old. Gillian must have learned how to express herself by mimicking her aunt.

Picking up the cards, Alex ran a finger over the smooth surface as he surveyed the table of four friends and one enemy surrounding him. Peter and Cameron knew the stakes were far higher than blunt, and Dansby would realize something was amiss very quickly as Alex planned to lose the first hand. He never lost at cards.

"Should we draw for the first dealer?" Alex spread the cards face down across the table with a fumbling stroke. One card flipped up, and Alex smiled ruefully. "Sorry. My fingers aren't warmed up yet."

"That's obvious," Westonburt said with a smug smile.

Dansby raised both eyebrows at Alex but said nothing.

Each man drew a card, then laid it face up in front of

them. Westonburt smiled, then reached for the cards to deal them. "It seems my luck has already begun."

Peter fiddled with his card as he stared at Westonburt. "Seems so. But I'm feeling rather lucky too. Why not make the minimum bet thirty pounds and the maximum five hundred?"

"Good God, man." Cameron smacked the table with a snort. "We are not all dukes with a king's ransom at our fingertips."

"Poor excuse," Peter replied with a grin. "If you're afraid to test your skill against mine, simply say so."

"I'm not, you bloody peacock," Cameron bellowed.

Peter flicked his card toward the pile Westonburt was gathering to shuffle. "Then you agree to the terms?"

Cameron blanched but nodded.

"If I lose five hundred pounds, I'll have pockets to let for the rest of the month," Dansby said, picking up his glass. He leaned back in his chair and took a long swig of the drink.

Alex hid his mirth by taking a drink of his whiskey. Dansby had plenty of money, but not many people knew it. The man was a friend indeed to play along so beautifully.

After a minute of drumming his fingers against his glass, Dansby finally nodded. "I'm in, but only if Lionhurst agrees to loan me some blunt if I end up in dire straits. Quarter Day is a long way off and a man has to eat. What do you say, Lionhurst? I'll pay you back if it comes to that."

Alex shrugged. "I suppose I can afford to do that. But if you end up without the money to pay me, I'll take it in property."

"As it should be, my friend, as it should be," Dansby replied.

Peter tapped on the table in front of Alex. "I take it this means you're still in the game?"

"I suppose I can't pull out since this was my idea, though I am now regretting the suggestion," Alex said.

All the men chuckled at his comment—all save one. Westonburt stared into his glass with a scowl. The stakes were high, so high Alex would bet if Westonburt lost enough hands, he would not have the money to pay into the pot. But then, that was the point. Alex stared at his foe.

"I'm in," Westonburt snapped.

"Then by all means, let's begin," Alex replied, pleased that his fish had bitten the bait meant to drag him to the surface and strip him of the ability to breathe.

Twenty-Six

ALEX FLICKED HIS FINGERNAIL over the edge of the card, causing it to pop back into place. It barely made a sound, really. And if you had good concentration, you would never even notice the noise.

No one spared him a glance but Westonburt. Testing the man's mettle, Alex flicked the card repeatedly until Westonburt slammed his fist against the table. The glasses rattled with the force.

"Do you mind?" he snapped, spittle flying out of his mouth.

Alex cocked his head to the side. "Do I mind what?"

"That racket." Westonburt flicked his own card in a mimicking gesture and glared at Alex. "I cannot think."

"Really? So sorry. I didn't even realize."

"Place your bet," Westonburt said through clenched teeth.

Alex pushed his chips forward and waited.

Peter thumped his glass down in front of him. "I can see I'll have to get the game going in earnest. I'll see your measly thirty pounds, Lion, and raise a hundred."

"Damnation, man." Dansby picked up one of Peter's chips. "I might actually need that loan before the night is through, Lionhurst."

"Of course." Alex nodded.

"All right, you addle-pate," Dansby snapped. "I'll

match you."

Peter grinned. "Then I'll let you slide for calling me stupid."

"I call 'em as I see them, Lord Primwitty. You're a fool if you think your wife isn't going to notice you skulking about after losing so much money tonight."

"She'll not notice," Peter replied.

Dansby shut one eye and squinted at Peter. "She's blind, then?"

Peter glared. "She won't notice because I plan on winning."

Cameron tossed his chips into the pile, matching Dansby and Peter's bets. "Seems we are at cross purposes, Primwitty. That's my plan exactly."

Westonburt dealt the next card. All joking stopped as each man studied his hand once again. Westonburt leaned forward and spread his two cards face up. "Twenty-one, *gentlemen*."

And so it went for three hands that Westonburt won two and lost one. On the fourth hand, Cameron, who had lost every hand, bowed out, shoving away from the table and storming off to weave around the other card tables in the direction of the door. Alex watched his brother stride out of the room. He favored his right leg as he went, yet managed easily to grab a glass of champagne off a tray before quitting the room. A grand exit by a grand actor. If only Mother would let poor Cam join the stage.

"It's your deal, Dansby." Alex held the cards toward his friend, but Dansby pushed them back. "I've lost five hundred pounds already. I'm out."

"Do you need a loan?"

Dansby shook his head. "I'll squeak by. Just expect me for dinner every night until the end of the month."

"Off with you, then. Sparring tomorrow?"

Dansby rose from his chair. "Make it day after. I'm otherwise engaged tomorrow."

"Do tell, Dansby," Peter crooned.

"Never." Dansby turned on his heel and strode away from the table.

Alex caught Peter's gaze and blinked three times fast and once slow. Time to go in for the kill. "What do you both say to the winner getting double what we staked?"

"I expect my luck to last," Westonburt said, tossing chips worth five hundred pounds into the center.

Alex whistled. "I should hope so. Just so you know, if it doesn't, I'll take property from you for payment."

"You're offering *me* some sort of reprieve? *You*, who've won but one hand? I've no concern of you. If there's any competition, it's *him*." Westonburt pointed to Peter.

Peter matched Westonburt's bet. "Thanks for the compliment. I hope I can be obliging."

After dealing, Alex glanced at his hand. He smiled. Really, he could not have stopped it even he had wanted to, and he did not. "Pontoon," he said simply.

Westonburt's cards fell to the table in front of him. "Let me see."

Alex flipped the cards onto the table, taking extra care to give them the snap he knew his enemy hated. "Don't forget you owe me double your stake."

Westonburt threw the chips at him from the pile he had accumulated. Alex eyed the remainder and quickly calculated. Two hands to take the winnings and two more to put the man into debt of unrecoverable proportions. Funny he did not feel any rush of excitement for the prospect. Maybe when the game came to a conclusion?

"I'm out," Peter said, sliding the rest of what he owed toward Alex.

"But you've all those chips left," protested Westonburt.

"I like to keep some money," Peter replied as he pulled his jacket from the chair and shrugged into it. "I'll leave it to the two of you." He met Alex's gaze for a brief second, then strode away from the table.

Alex eyed Westonburt. "Your deal."

Precisely two minutes later the man was bust. And so began the downfall. Alex drew the chips toward him. "Bad luck. Care to play again, or are you now afraid?"

"Your deal," Westonburt snarled.

In school years ago, the teachers would marvel at Alex's ability to see something once and remember exactly where he had seen it. He could look at a page and tell you everything on it, word for word. "Special" they had called him. A gift from God. Now he used this so-called gift. The old cards went to the bottom of the deck without shuffling. Without having to glance at the cards, he knew every card that was out of play. Pity every man could not do this.

Four lost hands later, Westonburt dripped sweat and he shook in his chair. Alex took a long sip of his whiskey, allowing the liquor to wash over his tongue. Anger was a powerful thing. Tricky too. It could make a man dominant or very, very careless. Westonburt had used up his winnings two hands ago.

Alex leaned toward his enemy. "You should stop. You owe me"—he looked down at the paper where the calculations had been scrawled, though he did not need to— "six thousand pounds."

Alex had never seen a man turn green, but there was a first for everything. He shoved Westonburt's glass at him. "Let's call it a game."

"No. The next hand is mine. Has–to–be."

"And if it's not? Can you pay me in blunt?"

"I'll give you my house."

Alex shrugged. "It's yours to give, but I suggest you stop. What will your mother say if you have to make her move?"

"I'm no mama's boy. Deal the damn cards."

The noise around Alex dulled to nothing as he concentrated. He heard only the beat of his heart, the hiss of his breath and the slide of fate as the cards swished across the table. One for the enemy. One for him.

Westonburt pulled out a handkerchief and wiped it across his glistening forehead. Alex watched him. Strange, but he felt oddly cold. Just to make sure things went smoothly, Alex leaned in to tighten the line. "I hate to see a man lose his house. Perhaps you should quit."

Westonburt glared daggers. The man would not quit. He was backed against the wall. Alex had hold of his enemy's Achilles' heel. Westonburt felt inferior, the weakness shimmered in his eyes. Westonburt wanted to prove he was the best. Whatever the cost. Reason was gone, and in its wake, disaster remained.

"I'll buy another."

"A mere thousand again?" Alex asked.

Westonburt's gaze snapped to his. A bead of sweat slid down the man's forehead and dropped onto the table. "Make it three."

Alex flipped the card. "You're bust, and you owe me twelve thousand." Where was the feeling of joy from the first strike?

Westonburt tore at his cravat. "A three," he spat. "I was sure it would be a three."

The man was clever, but not quite clever enough. Alex picked up what would have been the next card dealt and flipped it over. A three. He allowed a slow smile to curve his lips. "It seems you're unlucky tonight."

Twenty-Seven

WESTONBURT'S HAND CLAMPED DOWN on Alex's arm. "You bloody sod."

"Do you mind?" Alex gazed at Westonburt's fingers. "You're mussing my coat, and my valet will have a fit. He is not a man I care to anger. Irish, through and through."

"You played me for a fool," Westonburt growled.

"Did I? Seems to me you did that all on your own. Now, I suggest you unhand me, unless you now care to test my skills as a boxer, in which case, I'd be happy to oblige."

"I'll test you anywhere you like."

"Out there." Alex jerked his arm away, motioned toward the terrace and stood to accommodate his enemy.

Before he could take a step, a hand clamped on his shoulder and pressed him down. He glanced up into Sin's shadowed faced. Sin motioned him to sit back down. Alex hesitated for a moment, caught between anger and good sense. Robert's voice rang in his head. *No man worth his salt acts without thinking,* though apparently, Robert had forgotten his own worth. Alex dropped the rest of the way into his seat while appraising Westonburt. Judging by the man's open mouth, Sin's sudden appearance had dumfounded him as well.

Sin leaned in with both elbows on the table. "Though I love a good boxing match as well as the next chap, I promised my mother I would keep all my gentleman friends in line tonight. It seems she had some concern about my old chums all coming together in one house to greet me. Some dribble about us busting up the hunting lodge before I left for Europe."

"We are not friends," Westonburt hissed through clenched teeth.

"And here I thought we'd gotten off to such a fine start," Sin replied casually.

"How? By you helping your friend to swindle me?"

"I did not swindle you," Alex said. "Vingt-et-un is a game of bluffing. I bluffed. You failed to see it. Now you owe me twelve thousand pounds. I'll take it in cash or property, but I want it by day after tomorrow."

Alex leaned back in his chair, watching Westonburt's color deepen and the man's hands curl into fists on the table. What must it feel like to lose your home? Bloody awful. Alex had a twinge of pity for a moment, but shook it off with Lissie's memory.

"I'll have my man deliver the paperwork giving you ownership by noon day after tomorrow." Westonburt's words came out in jerky spats.

"That'll do nicely. I'll give you a week to remove your belongings."

Westonburt shoved back his chair and stood. "I won't forget what you've done, Lionhurst. I always repay my slights." Westonburt turned to leave; then he stopped. Slowly, he faced Alex once again. "You already knew that, didn't you?"

Yes, Alex wanted to say and grind the man's stupidity in his face, but it was far better to let Westonburt wonder. The doubt would eat at the man's soul in a way the truth could not. And Alex had personal experience with what doubt could do. "Are you referring to trying to buy into my company?"

"Of course."

"And how did you repay me for my supposed slight?" Alex asked, rising to face Westonburt. Would the man admit the truth?

"Watch yourself," Westonburt snarled, then stormed off.

Alex slumped into his seat. He was tired of revenge, yet the game was not over.

"Care to talk about it?" Sin asked while motioning a servant to bring two more drinks.

"About what?"

Sin took the two glasses from the waiter who now hovered at the table. "Why your revenge isn't bringing you any joy?"

Alex stared into the shadows of the ballroom. Why hadn't his first success with revenge brought him pleasure as he had thought it would? "Damn," he murmured. The only thing that had brought him any happiness tonight was when he had danced with Gillian. Not the game, nor the winning of it.

Sin reached over and gripped Alex's shoulder. "May I tell you what I learned in Paris?"

"Do I have a choice?"

Sin chuckled. "You know me too well." His fingers curled tightly around Alex's arm. His piercing gaze clouded. "Revenge is never as sweet as you imagine."

Alex studied his old friend. "What happened to you in Paris?"

"Nothing I'd like to see happen to you. I have no doubt Gillian will have an offer from Sutherland soon."

Alex nodded, his heart constricting.

"Don't let her leave for America and take your only chance at happiness with her."

Was Sin right? Could they actually make each other happy? Could he be happy? He hadn't thought so. But with her, things were different. He felt different. Like he had before Robert's death. "I have to go."

"I hoped you might," Sin said.

Alex left Sin sitting there and strode out of the room toward the ballroom. He had to see her. He didn't know what he would say or if he would say anything, but he had to see her.

HARRISON PUSHED HIS WAY through the crowd, fixed on getting the hell out of there before he killed someone.

Lionhurst would pay for what he had done. Or maybe the man would simply meet with a dagger in his back one dark night. As Harrison walked, he noticed people staring and snickering. Was it directed at him? He ran his hands through his hair, over his coat, straightened his tie, and then he finally let them drop to his sides where he clutched at the material of his britches.

They couldn't know what a fool he had been. Not yet. He paused midstride. How would he explain losing the house to Mother? What would he say? Damn her. That's what he would say. She could go rot on the side of the road where she belonged.

After all the years of making him feel less than worthless, she was now the worthless one. If she was very good and begged, he might let her come and live with him in the house Kingsley would be giving him. The marriage couldn't happen soon enough. How many weeks? Four! Bloody hell. No, three. Three weeks. He sighed with relief.

Three weeks. That left him two weeks to live where? Paying Lionhurst what he owed him would take everything. Kingsley was going to have to give him some money to live on until the marriage.

All he had ever wanted was to be one of them, but these people in this room had never accepted him. But one person had. Allysia had accepted him, maybe loved him. He stopped, grabbed a glass of champagne off a passing servant's tray and downed it. He wanted to drink her memory away. He had not killed her. Even so, he woke at night drenched in sweat, remembering how she had begged him to break off his engagement to Lady Gillian. He could not get Allysia's desperate voice out of his head.

He spotted Lady Gillian across the ballroom floor, dancing in the American's arms. Anger surged through him, and he quickened his pace to reach her. The little fool did not understand the power he wielded over her family. His secret made him invincible. There was no better moment than now to remind his forgetful fiancée exactly who she was engaged to. And he knew from experience just how to teach a woman a lesson she would never forget.

Twenty-Eight

TOO LATE, GILLIAN SAW Lord Westonburt approaching. If she turned and fled, it would be obvious she was running from him, which did not bother her, except for the fact that she did not know where her father was. For all she knew, he could be watching her at this very moment. There was no sense in alerting him to anything being amiss. That would only make her plan for escape more difficult.

Drake, as he had reminded her to call him, continued to talk to her, unaware her doom was walking their way. Gillian nodded and watched Lord Westonburt weave through the crowd, or rather push through the hapless people. His unwavering gaze held hers.

She squared her shoulders and made a quick decision. She had to face him and try to reason with him. If Lord Westonburt would just listen and see that they did not suit, they could end this engagement. Then her father would be spared the public humiliation of her running away from her fiancé. He would be humiliated enough when she and Whitney fled England.

Despite his lack of love for her, she owed him for his sacrifice in letting everyone think he had murdered Mother. He could have cleared his name, but he had chosen to protect Whitney, just as Gillian had.

She put a hand on Drake's arm. "I'm afraid you should

take your leave."

"Don't tell me I'm boring you?"

"No," she hastily replied, though she had been halfheartedly listening long before she saw Westonburt coming. Try as she might, her mind kept drifting to Alex.

"What is it, then?" Drake pressed a kiss to the back of her gloved hand.

"You shouldn't do that," she chided, suddenly irritated with his American obliviousness. But that was unfair. He had no idea about her father or the constraints he could place on her. She smiled faintly, hoping her concerns did not show on her face. "I'm sorry. It's just my father is watching me, and my fiancé is approaching, and he looks less than happy."

"Do you care? I was under the impression that you didn't want to marry him. Am I wrong?"

"No, but I have to be careful. I've no doubt my father would force me to it if he knew I was challenging his wishes." Talking about this in the middle of the ballroom made her uncomfortable. She found her father across the ballroom near the gaming room door. Just knowing he was nowhere near, where he could overhear or read her lips, made her breathe easier.

Drake reached out and lightly caressed her arm before letting his hand fall. "What do you want, doll?"

Such a simple question. One that she had asked herself for years and years. What she wanted—truly wanted—hardly mattered, because the past could not be relived and her choices mapped out her future. "I want to flee England and start a new life."

"A lofty goal for a woman. You may need a man to help you."

She breathed in his offer of redemption. It floated on the air between them. "Probably I will need someone," she murmured, distracted by the thought that she did not know Drake, not really. The realization caused her to break out into a sweat.

"Gillian, do you think it's possible we will run into each other again? I would very much like to see you."

"Yes, more than possible," she said in rush and pushed him away from her. "Just ask Alex where to find

me."

"Alex?" Drake frowned. "Why would he know?"

"Because I'll tell him where to find me so that you may be where I am." She curtsied and came up to meet the dark obsidian gaze of her intended. "Lord Westonburt." She inclined her head. "Mr. Sutherland was just telling me all about America. Fascinating, really, but I'm afraid I need some fresh air. Would you join me on the terrace?"

"I wasn't aware I needed an invitation." He clasped her arm and dragged her away from Drake and toward the terrace door.

"Wait a just a damn minute," Drake protested.

Gillian threw a glance over her shoulder, silently begging him to cease his protest. His gaze narrowed, but he nodded his agreement. Lord Westonburt did not pause. Either he had not heard Drake, which she doubted, or her fiancé deemed Drake unworthy of his time—the more likely choice.

She quickened her step to keep up with Lord Westonburt's clipped pace. The rigid set of his shoulders and the viselike grip on her arm made his anger clear. This was not a good time to try to reason with him, but this was the only opportunity she had left.

He jerked the terrace door open and shoved her out the door. Thank God the night was cool. The veranda was deserted and that suited her intention of speaking plainly. Before she could turn to face Lord Westonburt, his hand clamped on her arm once again, and her body twisted toward him.

Her heart raced, but she forced herself to breathe slowly. "I wished to speak to you."

He leaned toward her, his face moving out of dark shadows and into the red light shining from a blazing torch. The anger in his eyes blazed as fiercely as the torch beside him. She moved to step back, but his fingers curled tightly into the sensitive flesh of her arm. "What a coincidence, sweeting. I, too, wished to talk with you. You seem to forget you are betrothed, and I brought you out here to help you remember."

PAUSING IN HIS PURSUIT to find Gillian had been Alex's first mistake. But he had needed a fortifying drink to wipe out the guilt of destroying a man, even if Westonburt was his enemy. His second mistake was responding to Lord Staunton's polite greeting, which had caused his colossal failure to see Lady Staunton lurking behind the potted palm. He would have ignored Lord Staunton and marched past them both if he had been paying close attention.

"Lord Lionhurst, won't you dance with my wife? She's complained all night about my inability to dance. My health has declined rapidly, I'm afraid."

"I'm sorry to hear it, Lord Staunton." Alex glanced at the man who appeared to have lost a good deal more flesh since Lissie's funeral, if that was possible. "If there's anything I can do for you in the future..."

"You can dance with my wife."

Lady Staunton smiled like the cat she was—cold, cunning and likely to pounce on any prey with a lofty title. And now that her husband was on death's door, it was clear to Alex that he was her new prey. Funny that his title, or rather Robert's by rights, now brought him the woman he had wanted so long ago. Staring into her maliciously intentioned gaze, he could not recall why he had ever thought he loved her.

She grasped his hand as she led him away from her dying husband to the dance floor where the waltz played. He followed, but only because he did not want to create a scene.

They glided in a way that was at once familiar yet different. He had waltzed with her many times before in public and when they met clandestinely at his parents' stables. But alone, they had danced to a very different tune of lust while dressed simply in the skin God gave them.

She pressed her head to his shoulder with a sigh. "I've missed you."

He remained silent.

Lady Staunton raised her head and peered up at him as they circled the room. "Did you not miss me?"

"No." If she intended to ask blunt questions, he was

happy to give her direct answers.

Her hands gripped his arms. "Liar. I know you have at least missed how we were when we joined."

"Our joining was no different than all the other women I bedded. The real difference was that I was foolish enough to think I loved you."

She threw her head back and laughed as they twirled. Unlike Gillian's joyful melody, Lady Staunton's laugh was cold and brittle. "I see you've developed a taste for cruelty, love."

He tensed. Had he become cruel?

"After all these years, you still refuse to see what we really were to each other."

"I know what we were," he snapped, irritated that he had not been paying closer attention as he searched for Gillian.

Lady Staunton's eyes narrowed. "Do you still think I was the only one using someone? You used me too. You could have walked away from me after I became betrothed to Robert, but you slept with me once more to get back at him."

Alex swung toward the middle of the ballroom. He could not deny what she said. How he hated himself. Bile rose in his throat. She was right, he had used her. Robert had hurt him and Alex had retaliated without hesitation. There was no way to make up for his sin. He would pay for the rest of his life. He would make sure he did.

He did not need to see Gillian. He could never deserve her. He had to get out of the ballroom. He needed to be alone and get some air. "We have no future, Lady Staunton," he said simply, before releasing her and making his way toward the terrace.

He frowned when he spotted Sutherland across the dance floor smiling like a besotted fool at Gillian's younger sister. Why the devil was Gillian not with Sutherland? Alex dodged around the outer edges of the dance floor and grabbed Sutherland's arm just as he was leading Gillian's sister to the dance floor. "Sutherland, sorry to interrupt."

Sutherland stopped and faced him. Alex bowed to Lady Whitney and gave Sutherland a nod.

"It's amusing how formal you are here, Lionhurst."

Alex returned his friend's smile while trying to control the impatience building with each second. "Glad I can amuse you with my manners. Have you seen Lady Gillian?"

"Why do you ask?" A mischievous smile twitched at Lady Whitney's lips. What the devil was the chit smiling at him like that for?

"I need to speak with her."

"I just left her," Sutherland supplied. "Or rather she was dragged away from me."

"What do you mean?" Whitney grabbed Sutherland's arm. "Who dragged her away?

"Her fiancé."

"Which way?" Alex demanded.

Sutherland pointed toward the terrace doors. "Out there."

Blood rushed in his ears as he raced through the crowd toward the terrace. He wanted to run, but how the devil would he ever explain himself? He had to make sure she was fine. And then he would leave her alone and keep his distance as much as possible.

He grasped the handle, eased the door open and stepped out onto the darkened terrace as the smack of a hand against skin filled the silence. A woman's cry punctuated the air. For one stunned moment, he stood, squinting into the darkness. His eyes adjusted. Gillian's back was to him, her hand raised to her cheek, and Westonburt loomed in front of her.

Without hesitation, Alex charged, intent on killing the man.

Twenty-Nine

GILLIAN'S ANGER EXPLODED THE second her shock wore off, but before she could react, Alex barreled past her and straight into Lord Westonburt. They flew backward and hit the stone wall with loud grunts. In the dark shadows near the ground, the men were nothing more than blurs, their grumbles and shoes scuffling against the tiles joining the roaring of blood in her ears. She raced toward the men and reached them just as a fist flew through the air and connected with a sickening crunch against bone. A guttural roar filled the space where the men crouched.

She lunged into the fray and grabbed blindly in front of her. She pulled back on the powerful arm she clutched. "Stop it," she demanded, unsure who she was pleading with.

Before she could take another shaky breath, she was propelled onto her feet and stood facing Alex. His eyes burned in a way that made her shiver. Gone was the trace of the gentleman he was born and bred to be; a dark and dangerous man bent on vengeance stood before her.

Her heart twisted painfully. She wanted to throw herself into his arms and kiss him senseless for wanting to rescue her. Instead, she gathered her control and her wits. "Stop this. A scene is the last thing that will help

me."

Alex jerked his head in a nod. She could see the effort the self-control was causing him. His hands were bunched by his side into tight fists. Lord Westonburt lumbered to his feet, groping the wall.

Gillian's heart rose and plummeted, caught between a strange joy at Alex's display of concern and a wariness of her fiancé. "Please, Alex." She pushed him toward the door. "I need a moment with Lord Westonburt."

"I'm not leaving you alone with that sorry excuse for a man, no matter how prettily you plead. I'll stand over there." Alex pointed toward the terrace door before he brushed past her and advanced toward Lord Westonburt.

He grabbed the front of the man's shirt and jerked him up and away from the wall. "If you so much as breathe wrong, I'll be back at her side in a flash, and this time, so help me God, when I finish pummeling you, you won't recognize yourself in the mirror."

Lord Westonburt shoved at Alex's chest. "Leave go, you bloody bastard. You're insane. You interfere where you are neither needed nor wanted."

Gillian prayed Alex would just walk away, and when he finally moved toward the terrace door, she exhaled the breath she had been holding. Alex's shoes tapped against the tile, and as he walked past her, his gaze met hers. "If you need me..."

God, did she ever, and that was a problem. She nodded, and he brushed his fingers against hers as he passed. The man was scandalous, even now. Had he been unable to resist touching her or did he simply want to annoy Lord Westonburt as much as possible?

It had to be the latter. She faced Lord Westonburt and closed the distance between them, refusing to allow an ounce of fear to remain in her. He stared at her with his frigid gaze, one that probably instilled fear in many people. Yet somehow the blood smeared across his face made him seem pathetic to her.

He had hit her. He had actually thought he could. She reared back and slapped him across the face. "Do not ever lay your hands on me again. You are mistaken if you think my father will force me to marry a man who has struck me."

He stepped so close to her, she could feel the heat radiating from him, but he did not touch her. "You're the one that's mistaken," he whispered, a vein in his jaw jumping with his anger.

The surety with which he spoke sent waves of doubt through her.

"Your father will keep our contract. I've no doubt. Don't upset me again, sweeting, and behave while I'm gone. I was raised under the principle that to train a disobedient dog, you must first banish the litter. Isolation breeds devotion to the new master."

With that warning, he stalked toward the terrace door and shoved past Alex. Gillian stared at his departing figure. What did he mean, banish the litter? Was he talking about her sister? Why did he think he had the power to do anything to Whitney?

She gripped the banister, trying to make herself breathe and expel her ridiculous fear. All this wide space lay before her, but the heavy air smothered her. She could not draw a proper breath. A vine of fear sprang to life in her belly, unfurling and growing rampant through her insides.

She had to see her sister and make sure Whitney was all right. Gillian raced toward the door. "Alex, I have to find my sister. I...well, thank you." She wanted to say so much more, but what good would it do either of them? She tried to pull her wrist free, but he held tighter.

"What did he say to you?"

"Nothing. Nothing that affects you. Please."

Alex released her, but his gaze hardened. "I'm coming with you."

"Fine." She shoved through the door. She did not have time to argue. She entered the ballroom and scanned the area for Whitney. Gillian stopped so suddenly that Alex bumped into her back.

"What the devil?"

"I'm sorry," she mumbled, staring with shock at her sister. She was not in Lord Westonburt's angry clutches. Whitney twirled on the dance floor in Drake's arms. Her head was tilted up and her eyes were lowered in a coquettish half-mast. Her sister looked utterly happy. Lord Westonburt was nowhere to be seen. Gillian sighed with relief.

Gillian moved her gaze to Drake. His arm was wrapped tightly around Whitney's waist, and his hand was splayed protectively across her sister's back. He peered down at Whitney with an admiring smile. Gillian almost laughed. What was wrong with her? Shouldn't she feel a twinge of possessiveness toward the man she intended to marry?

Confusion flowed through her fast and furious. How could she pursue a man she didn't hold an attraction for? She had not counted on this lack of feeling in all her careful planning. She turned toward Alex, and he stared down at her, his eyes filled with concern.

Her heart leapt and the recklessness that had driven her in the woods consumed her once again. This could be the last time she was ever alone with him. "Follow me," she whispered, wincing at the breathiness of her tone.

A slow smile spread across his face. "Where to?"

Her heart tapped a dangerous rhythm of desire. "Does it matter?"

"Not in the least, peach."

She nodded and wove along the outer edge of the dance floor and into the darkened corridor that led to her aunt's library. At the door, she paused, suddenly unsure of what she was doing. He quirked an eyebrow up at her. "Afraid to be alone with me? I promise to behave."

She was more worried about whether she could behave, but she grabbed his hand and pulled him into the library. She shut the door and turned around straight into the hard wall of his chest. The desire to touch him overwhelmed her.

She took a step back and fell against the locked door while praying for her senses to return. He leaned toward her, closing the paltry distance between them. His masculine scent filled her senses just as his gaze found hers.

He reached toward her, and she closed her eyes, not caring he was the wrong man, not caring he did not fit her plan. She wet her lips in anticipation of his kiss. When he pressed his chest to her breasts, heart to heart, his heat enveloped her body and every nerve clenched in anticipation. A lock clicked and his heat vanished. Her eyes flew open, and so did her mouth.

His broad, quite lovely back moved away from her, along with the rest of his equally perfect form, toward the settee, where he dropped down and folded his long legs. A devilish smile crossed his lips, and the embarrassment and anger that had just begun to work their way to the surface to replace her shock disappeared as he directed his smile on her. He patted the settee with a resounding smack. "Come. Sit by me."

Based on her willingness only a moment ago to abandon all her plans in the heat of desire, she was certain she should say no, yet she walked over to the settee and sat beside him. When their legs brushed, she immediately scooted toward the other end of the settee before turning to face him once again.

"You're not going to tell me what Westonburt said, are you?"

She shook her head, afraid her voice would tremble with her desire if she spoke.

He dropped his arm over the back of the settee as he turned more fully toward her. She was acutely aware of his body touching hers and his fingers resting still against her shoulder. Suddenly, his fingers traced back and forth across her skin, and an aching need for his touch overwhelmed her. When she started to squirm, he stopped and glanced at her with both eyebrows raised before moving his arm. "If you're not going to tell me what he said to you and you appear to be perfectly fine, then I have a demand."

"A demand?" she croaked, finding it hard to speak at all. She cleared her throat. "What sort of demand?"

"I demand a kiss as my reward for rescuing you."

"You did not rescue me. I was on the verge of slapping him when you barreled through the door. I'm perfectly capable of rescuing myself."

He moved toward her and cupped her chin. "I still think I should be rewarded for my effort."

He pressed closer, delving his hand into her hair. His mouth came over hers, warm and consuming. From the first touch, the kiss was frenzied. Their tongues met and circled only to retreat as his lips moved down the sensitive skin of her neck. She hissed with pleasure, her fingers curling into the thick locks of his hair. His lips massaged her skin until she could scarcely think. A moan escaped her, and she threw her head back and pressed her chest forward to get closer to him. He trailed light kisses down her throat over the exposed expanse of her chest, then crept lower into the deep plunge of her dress. When his tongue flicked between the valley of her breasts, she gasped and pressed her fingers against his head to make sure he stayed there.

A deep, amused chuckle reached her ears. Gillian opened her eyes and glanced down in time to see his fingers catch the edge of her gown, then pull and tug until the tip of her breast spilled out and his warm hand scorched her bare skin. She gasped when his fingers touched the sensitive tip, but as he started to rub the bud, a strong, aching need filled her. She wanted only for him to make the need go away. All her embarrassment was gone and her doubts set aside for later.

His lips returned to tease, stroking the fire burning inside her with every flick of his wicked tongue. When he lapped with slow, gentle strokes, the madness inside of her rose to block out all else. Another moan escaped her control. His hand stroked lower, and her dress came up over her legs until his fingers brushed between her parted thighs. Her eyes flew open. What was she doing? Would she give herself to this man while pursuing another? Where was her honor? She pushed at his chest. "Stop."

He suckled her breast harder, faster. God help her, she wanted him to continue, but she twined her hands into his hair and yanked his head back. "Stop. Please. You must stop."

She released him as he pulled back with a harsh groan, and sat up before pulling her dress up to cover her.

He raked his hands through his hair as he stared at her with desperate eyes. "God, I'm sorry. I'm the worst sort of lecher. When I'm near you, I feel—"

She met his stricken gaze, then pressed a finger to his lips. "I feel it too." How else could she explain allowing him to fondle her so?

He dropped his gaze to the floor. “It won’t happen again. Unless you want it to.” His voice was ragged and possibly hopeful.

The hope tore her apart. She could not let him hope when she owed Whitney her life. Gillian reached for him, but thought better, and drew her hand back. “Never again.” She was foolish and selfish to risk her sister’s future for a moment of pleasure with this man. Now, if her sister was developing a tendre for Drake, things could possibly be different. Gillian stood, shook the wrinkles out of her skirts and set her hair to rights. Gillian did not know her sister’s heart. Until Whitney’s feelings were clear, things had to stay as planned.

Alex met Gillian’s gaze. The rigid set of his jaw told her he was upset. At her or himself, she couldn’t tell. Yet when he took her hand, again he squeezed it. “This was nothing. Don’t think on it again. I’m a rake and a cad and could lead the most virtuous woman astray.”

God, she was a fool. She was a whirl of confusion over a man who played the same game with her he played with every woman. She forced herself to smile, though her face felt like cold marble. “Don’t be silly. You’re not leading me astray or anywhere else, for that matter. We got carried away. We won’t do it again.”

She wanted to hate him for the way he made her burn and hunger for him, but she focused on being disgusted with herself. She could not trust her judgment when he was near. The blame was hers. “I’m going out now. Wait and follow me after a few minutes. If anyone were to see us…”

“You’d be ruined, and then you would have to marry me.” He grinned at her.

Gillian swallowed at the little thrill the thought of marrying him gave her. “A tragedy, indeed.”

Before he could reply, someone pounded on the door.

Thirty

"GILLIAN CLARE RUTHERFORD, OPEN this door at once," Auntie hissed from the other side of the dark paneling.

Rolling her eyes heavenward, Gillian moved toward the door. But before she could unlock it, Alex grabbed her hand and motioned toward her hair.

He ran his hands through her tresses. "You've quite a mess there." She shivered as his fingertips brushed lightly over her scalp. Longing sprang up in the pit of her stomach, warming every inch of her body. Warming places that had no right to be warmed by any man's touch, save her fiancé. And heavens, her aunt stood on the other side of the threshold. She raised her hands to still his, though she wanted more than anything to allow him to keep caressing her. His touch was the very thing she had always longed for—gentle, undemanding and loving. But that couldn't be right. Her brain must still be addled from his kiss.

She gently pushed his hands away. "Thank you."

He smiled while shaking his head. "I seem to be having a bit of trouble keeping my hands off you."

She laughed aloud at his innocent admission, then slapped her hand over her mouth.

"I'm waiting," chirped Auntie.

"Me too," came Whitney's voice.

"It seems I have a loyal, nosy following." Gillian flung

open the door.

Aunt Millicent brushed past her and stopped in the middle of the study. "Ah-ha! Just as I thought," she pronounced, looking at Alex.

If it wasn't so embarrassing, Gillian would have laughed at Alex's completely disheveled appearance. His shirt was half-untucked, his cravat hung loose, and his hair looked as if someone had run their hands through it repeatedly. Which was exactly what she'd done. Dear God above, what Auntie must think of her now. "Auntie, I can explain."

"Explain what, dear?" Aunt Millicent strode past Alex to her desk. She reached over and picked up a book, which she waved in the air. "I just came to get this book. I positively cannot ever go to sleep without reading, and I'm right in the middle of a chapter. Starting something else would be unthinkable."

Gillian shook her head. She knew her aunt was lying by her twitching right eye, but she would confront her when they were alone. Whitney was another matter. She crossed her arms and stared at her sister. "Why are you here and no longer dancing with Drake?" She wasn't jealous, but she did want to know what Whit was up to.

"He's retired for the night," Whitney murmured, blushing furiously.

Gillian barely held her own smile inside. If Whitney was interested in Drake and he in her, then they could marry. That would solve a great deal. Drake could whisk Whit to America, and Gillian would break her betrothal to Lord Westonburt without having to fear the repercussions to Whitney. Whatever else happened, if Whit was safe, Gillian could survive.

"So Drake went to bed without saying good night? He must have been quite befuddled from his dance with you." Gillian studied her sister, looking for a hint of interest or happiness.

"He was very tired." Whitney's face took on the mutinous look Gillian knew well from their childhood. If Whit did like Drake, she certainly wasn't going to announce it here and now.

A broad smile covered her aunt's face, lighting up her green eyes and reminding Gillian of how Auntie used to look when she was pulling the wool over Uncle Gene. Her aunt was still scheming, and now she had Whitney involved. Gillian rubbed her head, which was beginning to pound.

"I think I'll follow Drake's lead and depart for home and bed. I'm rather tired."

"I bet Lord Lionhurst is tired too," Whitney said.

Gillian glared at her sister. "I'm sure you are too. Jumping fences, wading in streams and vigorous dancing must surely wear a young lady to the bone."

Whitney's eyes nearly popped from her head. Good. Maybe she understood that Gillian saw the attraction Whit had to Drake.

"You're testy tonight, niece."

Gillian frowned. Her aunt had no idea.

Auntie moved in a blur, pushing Alex toward the door. "I've had your things moved, Lord Lionhurst. You'll be in the last room on the right tonight."

"Why did you move Alex's things?" Gillian demanded.

"Because, dearest. You and your sister are sleeping here tonight, and I could not very well have the two of you in the room next to him. Highly improper."

A small smile tugged at the corner of Alex's lips. "Do you think I'm not to be trusted?"

"You? Heavens no, dear. You're not one of the lovebirds, are you? But I couldn't move Mr. Sutherland and not you. Though you are simply an innocent bystander caught in their game. Or am I confused? Are you part of the game?"

"I'm part of the game." Alex caught Gillian's gaze.

"Oh?" Auntie waved her hand out the study door and Perks, her butler, magically appeared. "What's your part, Lord Lionhurst?"

"Helper."

Aunt Millicent gave him a shove toward Perks. "It does appear you are helping. But whether it's yourself or your friend remains to be seen."

Before Alex could respond, Perks tugged him out the door.

Aunt Millicent faced Gillian as the men departed. "I sent your father home."

"You're full of surprises, Auntie. How did you get him

to agree to go without Whitney and me?"

"It was simple enough."

Whitney rushed to their aunt's side. "You're being modest, Auntie. It was brilliant, Gillie. Father had come to fetch me, and Auntie was with him. I was just about to come find you when Auntie swooned in Father's arms. He was flabbergasted. When she insisted she needed both of us to stay and attend her, he readily agreed. You know how Father hates weak females."

Gillian nodded. She knew too well. "What game are you playing at, Auntie?"

"I'm giving you the time you wanted to get to know Mr. Sutherland. He'll be here in the morning and so will you. You two can go for a ride or a picnic. Won't that be lovely?"

She did not believe for a moment her aunt was doing any such thing but arguing would be pointless. She would spend tomorrow with Mr. Sutherland if it was the last thing she did.

Auntie yawned. "I'm exhausted. Off to bed with the two of you, but not without a hug and a kiss."

Gillian embraced her aunt, clinging for a moment. She inhaled her aunt's scent of roses. This woman had been her true mother since the day her own mother had decided she didn't really want the position. "Auntie, I've never understood why you and Mother were close. You were so different."

"Not so different, dearest. Your mother was a woman who loved greatly and never recovered from the loss. I loved greatly too, so I understood."

Whitney scrambled to Gillian's side. "Are you saying Mother loved Father greatly?"

"No, but that's all I'll say for now."

"But Auntie—" Gillian and Whitney cried in unison.

"Don't bother pleading. There's a time and a place for the past to be set to rights. Now is not the time, nor the place, and I'm still undecided as to whether I'm the person to shed the light."

Gillian glared at her aunt. "I refuse to leave this room until you have told me what you know."

Thirty-One

GILLIAN PUNCHED THE PILLOW on her bed in anger and frustration. Her aunt was a stubborn, unpredictable woman. Who would have thought she would make good on her threat to have the butler forcibly remove Gillian from the study and deposit her in her bedroom? Who could Auntie have been referring to? Who had Mother loved greatly?

"Gillie, are you thinking about Mother?"

Gillian turned onto her side to face Whitney. "Yes, but I'm thinking about you too."

"Me?" Whitney flopped around with her covers and settled back into her own bed.

Gillian took a deep breath. "Do you fancy Mr. Sutherland?"

"No."

Disappointment flooded Gillian. "Then why the jump on the horse, the wading in the stream and the dance with such evident devotion earlier this evening?"

Whitney turned her face into the pillow. "The jump was accidental. May got spooked by something and just took off. I couldn't stop her."

"Well, that's certainly more believable than you suddenly turning into an expert horsewoman."

"I'm glad you take my near death so lightly."

"I take nothing regarding you lightly," Gillian murmured.

"What's that supposed to mean?"

"Nothing. I'm just tired." Gillian prayed her sister wouldn't question her further.

"Gillian Clare Rutherford, if you're mad about me wading into the stream you don't know me very well at all. I only went into the stream because I developed a huge blister on my foot that was bleeding. And as for me dancing with Drake, he spent the entire time asking me questions about you. I don't want him, and he certainly doesn't fancy me, so quit worrying."

Wrinkling her nose, Gillian flipped onto her back and groaned. It had been ridiculous to hope for such an easy solution as Whitney caring for Drake.

"Gillie, what's wrong?"

Gillian drew the covers over her head. What could she say? I have to marry Drake to protect you, but I think I may be falling in love with Alex? Dear God. She gripped the sheet to her. Was she falling in love with a man she absolutely knew she could not allow herself to fall in love with?

"You like him, don't you?" Whitney asked.

"Of course," Gillian automatically responded from within her cocoon before tugging the covers down to her shoulders. "I like him. I'm trying to get him to fall in love with me, aren't I?"

Whitney snorted. "I don't mean Drake. I was referring to Lord Lionhurst. You can deny it, but I know you like him. And so does Auntie."

"Quit scheming with Auntie. I intend to marry Mr. Sutherland."

"But you like Lord Lionhurst!"

Gillian wanted to spill all her secrets, but she had to keep protecting her sister. "Good night, Whit."

"I've one more thing to say."

When Gillian didn't answer, a pillow hit her head. "What is it?"

"You know the painting in the great hall downstairs? It's the one where Mother actually looks happy."

"Yes." Gillian knew the exact painting of which Whitney spoke. It was completed five days before Mother died. She wore an emerald-green gown cut deep to show a vast amount of olive skin. She displayed no jewels except a choker of blood-red rubies. Not even her wedding ring adorned her hands, which were folded serenely in her lap with a deep, red rose clasped between them. Her beautiful shining eyes, which the painter had captured to perfection, took Gillian's breath away every time she passed the painting. They reminded her of summer moss.

"Are you picturing it?"

"Yes." Gillian's heart thumped against her ribs.

"I think Mother must have already been in love with the man Auntie referred to," Whitney whispered as if someone besides the two of them were around to hear the secret.

Gillian squeezed her eyes shut, remembering her mother in the dark night by the river with a man. Who had that man been? Mother loved him. She must have loved him desperately.

Tears slid down Gillian's face, and she quickly swiped them away. She never once stopped to consider how their mother must have felt in love with one man and married to another. How wretched it must have been. Remorse and understanding filled her.

"When you look at Alex, your eyes look just like Mother's do in that painting," Whitney said softly. "And you have just met him. Just think how it could be between the two of you in time. I don't want to see you end up like her—married to the wrong man."

Gillian didn't want to end up like Mother either, but even if Alex was the right man for her, he did not want her. Besides, her fate was set—sealed by a secret she shared with her father.

SHE AWOKE IN THE morning bleary-eyed, grumpy and alone. She frowned as she stumbled out of bed toward her clothes, surprised that Whit was already up. Where was her sister? By the rays shining through the window, it had to be early morning. Possibly nine. Whitney hadn't risen early on her own accord before the hour of ten since she was a child. So where on earth had she sneaked off to now? And sneak she surely had. Her little sister was knee-deep in a desire to make mischief. A behavior she definitely learned from Auntie.

Gillian shoved her arms in her dress, her feet in her slippers, and was four steps to the door before she paused. She didn't want to chance running into Drake with mussed hair. With a quick glance in the mirror, she winced at her pitiful reflection. A brush was definitely a must. A few quick strokes later and she was out the door. She had to find Drake, and if possible, avoid Alex. In the sleepless hours of the night, she had decided she simply needed more time alone with Drake and less time with Alex.

Of course she was attracted to the devilish man. He was handsome, suave and an astonishingly good kisser. And she had spent a great deal of time alone with him, more than Drake. She had not had time to develop a tendre for Drake. That was all. Simple and fixable. She hurried down the stairs toward the dining room intent on fixing her problem.

She strode into the dining room and stopped at the sight of Alex leaned back in his chair, shirt hanging casually open to reveal the top of his chest and his hair disheveled in a way that made Gillian want to go to him and run her hands through his tresses. He looked lovable, kissable and rakishly handsome. Gillian frowned. How was she supposed to avoid Alex when he was the only one in the room? "Where is everyone?"

She strode to the opposite end of the table, where a servant hovered, and motioned him to pull out the chair. The farther away she was from Alex, the better. "Eggs and bacon, please," she said, sitting down and adjusting her dress. When she finally looked up, Alex stared at her with a furrowed brow.

"And a good morning to you too," he drawled. "Are you always this friendly in the morning?"

She picked up her own cup of steaming coffee, which had just been poured for her, and took a small sip while thinking exactly what to say. "I'm sorry. I was hoping to run into Drake first thing this morning. I want to arrange some time alone with him."

"That'll be difficult," Alex replied, walking toward her, plate in hand.

"What are you doing?" Alarm raced through her as he advanced toward her. She set her coffee cup down for fear she would spill the liquid. He could not sit near her with his shirt undone, where she could see the tan skin of his chest and the hint of muscles she felt last night. She trembled just thinking of how those arms had felt around her.

Alex's eyebrows shot up, but he did not cease in his advancement. He set his plate next to hers and waved the appalled servant out of the room. He settled into his seat, his masculine scent invading her senses as it always did. "I'm merely making conversation more manageable. Is there a reason you chose the furthest seat from me?"

She shook her head, snatched her fork off the table and attacked her eggs.

"Hungry?"

"Famished," she murmured between mouthfuls of egg. The faster she finished, the quicker she could get away from him. Every second near him made her pulse beat faster, her breath come quicker. At this rate, she would have an attack and die. Did people die from desire? If not, she'd be the first. Immortalized forever in some book because she was an oddity. She took a deep breath to calm herself, but instead she breathed him in. This morning he smelled of rain, grass and the earth. She wanted to run before she attacked him.

She shoved the last bite into her mouth, while her stomach rolled in protest. Her fork clattered against the plate, and she shoved her chair back to leave. "Where did you say Drake was?"

As she rose, Alex clamped a hand around her arm, holding her in place. "I didn't say. Sit down, Gillian."

It was a command, and by the thread of steel underlying the tone, it was one she guessed pointless to try to ignore. She sank back into her chair, and he released his hold at once.

"Look at me, please."

She turned her gaze toward him and sighed. Black stubble covered his unshaven face and the blue of his eyes blazed brighter because of the contrast. Lord, but he was lovely. She wanted to run a finger over his stubble, down the line of his strong jaw, and end at his full lips. She shivered but did not look away.

"Are you trying to avoid me?"

"Certainly not," she lied. She was not about to tell him the effect he had on her, though after she let him caress her last night, he probably had a fairly good idea that he left her senseless. Of course, he did. The man left all women senseless. Devil take him.

"Then why did you sit at the other end of the table, refuse to look at me, and shovel food into your mouth? At a rate, by the way, that I've never seen a man match. And after that amazing performance of consumption, you attempted to dash out of here like a fire licked at your heels."

"I suppose I'm a trifle embarrassed about what occurred between us last night," she whispered, offering a partial truth. She studied him, trying to discern by his features how he felt about last night. But his look was unreadable.

"I've forgotten about it. So should you."

She picked at a nonexistent piece of lint on her skirt while swallowing down her hurt and embarrassment. His blunt words left a hole of disappointment in the middle of her gut. How silly of her. She should be glad he had forgotten the kiss. She forced a smile to her face. "I expect you find yourself with women in your arms quite a bit."

"Let's not discuss other women."

She nodded.

"There's no need to avoid me. We got carried away. But we won't again."

"No, we won't. I'm going to marry your best friend, after all. *I hope.*" Something flashed in his eyes, but it was gone so fast she could not fathom what the spark had been.

"Of course you are. And you will love him."

She nodded at his words. "Of course I'll love him." Her words sounded unsure to her. She peeked at Alex in the hope he had not noticed. His gaze met hers, and it felt as if he could read her secret thoughts. Her cheeks warmed, and after clearing her throat, she spoke again. “I will love him,” she reiterated.

The words were strong, but her tone rang false. *Blast and damn.* This time when she glanced at Alex the look of satisfaction that crossed his face was unmistakable.

Thirty-Two

"YOU DO NOT NEED to accompany me to my house," Gillian insisted for the fifth time. "I have ridden from Auntie's home to mine all by myself for years."

"Indulge me." Alex swung up into his saddle as Gillian mounted her horse. "It's not as if I can leave your aunt's until Sutherland returns. So since you insist on going home, I might as well escort you."

"I don't need an escort." It was the truth, but the bigger truth was that she was afraid to be alone with Alex. She was attracted to him, despite all the reasons she should not be. The last thing she wanted to do was give that attraction any more room to grow.

"I know you don't need me, Gillian, but I need you. You must save me from complete and utter boredom. I don't abide sitting idly. Never have."

"Fine." She laughed. "I hate to sit with nothing to do as well. You can accompany me, but only as far as the path by the river. I don't want Father to see you. After all, the whole reason I'm leaving now without seeing Drake is to avoid that very possibility."

"Yes, yes, I know. You've already explained."

Taking up her reins, Gillian blew out a frustrated breath. "I can't understand why Auntie won't stop meddling. What was she thinking, taking Whitney and Drake on a tour of her estates again?"

"That we'd fall into each other's arms," he said matter-of-factly.

"But we won't," she murmured, wishing her pulse had not leaped at his words.

"No, peach. We won't."

"Actually, I'm glad I got you alone," she said, just realizing she might be able to help him with their time together.

"Are you?" A devilish smile tugged at his lips.

"Yes," she said tartly. "I want to talk to you about your older brother."

His smile was instantly gone, replaced by a foreboding frown. "I don't talk to anyone about Robert."

"You talked to me about him yesterday," she reminded him gently.

Alex's eyes bore into hers. "That was a mistake," he said as he clicked his heels against his horse and raced ahead of her in a swirl of dust.

She watched him ride ahead, shoulders bent like demons were chasing him. Her heart ached for him. He was wounded, and she had a soft spot in her heart for wounded people. He was not going to talk to her or tell her any more about his older brother. That much was obvious. But she would say her piece. She tapped her heels against Lightning and raced to catch up with Alex. In seconds, she pulled up on Lightning's reins and slowed to the pace Alex's horse had fallen into.

"No matter what you think, you deserve happiness. You're warm and have a good heart. You're helping me, and you are trying to right a wrong done to your sister. Whatever you did in your past that haunts you, you should let it go. Let it die. And let yourself be happy."

He pulled his horse to a stop and turned to look at her. "Is that what you're doing? Letting your past die?"

"My past won't die," she said, dismounting and walking toward the river where her mother had drowned.

Alex's boots hit the ground and he fell into step beside her. The moving water called to her as it did so many days. At the edge, she stared down into the murky depths. Rocks jutted above the surface, and long, tangling weeds floated like green fingers, swaying with the river's movement. Those weeds had wrapped around her mother's kicking feet and dragged her to her death.

As Gillian leaned forward, Alex grabbed her arm and pulled her backward, pressing her against his chest. His arms encircled her body in a tight embrace. She welcomed his presence and his strength.

"Are you running to get away from your past?" he whispered in her ear.

She was running from the past, but not just hers. She couldn't share her secrets with anyone because they were not only hers to share. But she wouldn't lie. Not to Alex, not now. When she had asked him to tell her the truth about his past.

A connection ran between them, for better or worse. Instead, she quoted his own words back to him. "I would tell you if I could, but some secrets must be kept to protect those we love. I know you understand."

He turned her around and tipped her chin until she was looking at him. She may not know much, but she knew she wanted this man with every heartbeat, every breath and every bone in her body. Her desire curled in her belly.

"I understand," he said and traced a finger over her lips. Her pulse skittered in response.

She stepped away while staring at his lips. God, how she wanted him to kiss her. She craved it so much she ached. Forbidden fruit. That's what he was. And she was weak. "You better go."

His own face was flushed as he nodded. Did he feel it too? The uncontrollable desire. The pull like metal to a magnet. "Don't forget to let Sally know what *ton* events you'll be attending. Where you are, we will be also."

"You mean *Drake* will be," she corrected.

"Yes. I'll be in the background like a worried chaperone. Except I'll be worrying about how to get the two of you alone. You just use your charms, and let me do the rest." Alex mounted his horse and looked down at her. "You can count on me."

She watched the road until Alex disappeared back the way they had come. She needed to get home, but she didn't want to go yet. Instead, she sat at the edge of the riverbank and studied her surroundings. This spot had not changed much in eleven years. More brush, fuller trees, but nothing pretty ever grew here. It was as if the earth remembered her mother's death and refused to make the place beautiful because of it. Gillian kicked off her slippers and drew her knees to her chest. The water hissed below as it moved downstream, and she found herself once again staring into the murkiness.

You can count on me, he had said. Yes. She drew her toe back and forth in the dirt. She thought she could. Though she had never counted on anyone in her life but herself. Putting her faith in Alex had become too easy this week. It was time she got herself back on course.

FROWONING, HARRISON PAUSED OUTSIDE the modest yellow house with the neat lawn and black iron gate. This could not be the right place. He shoved his hand in his pocket and pulled out the crumpled piece of paper upon which Madame Lovelace had scrawled Caprice's new street number. This was indeed 3225 Magnolia Street. He couldn't imagine Madame Lovelace daring to lie to him after he had shown her what would happen if she did.

Harrison had tried to be nice, but no one would ever let him. The old woman wanted more coin than he could give her for the information he needed. He didn't have a lot of bloody coin. Not right now, anyway. Damn Lionhurst's lying hide to hell. The man was going to pay with his life for everything. The question was when and how.

As Harrison climbed the stairs to the home where Caprice was supposed to reside his desire mounted. He was angry, and his anger always fueled his desire. Anger had driven him to find Caprice. He needed to plant himself inside her and use her. She was not Allysia, but Caprice looked so much like her, he could imagine that she was. She would scream his name as Allysia had done and beg him for more. He wished Lionhurst knew how his little sister had pleaded to be plundered again and again.

Harrison fingered the heavy gold lion hooked to the

door. What the hell was this? This bloody knocker had to be worth a fortune. So his little Caprice had found herself a rich benefactor and hightailed it out of Madame Lovelace's with no intentions of saying goodbye to him or ever seeing him again.

He ran a finger down the intricate mane of the lion, his anger throbbing within him. That little bit o' muslin lived in a house with a nicer door than he had. Of course, he now owned no door, so that was not hard to accomplish. But that wasn't the damned point. He raised the knocker and banged, beating iron against wood with the force of all his pent-up rage. He banged until a deep, satisfying dent appeared in the slick black wood, leaving an imperfection that a mere coat of paint would never fix. Whoever owned this house would have to buy a new door if they wanted it to appear perfect once more.

He felt good. So good that he imagined doing the same sort of damage to Caprice's face for wanting to leave him for another man, a richer man. It didn't matter that he intended to give her up once he married Lady Gillian. Caprice did not know that.

He reached to touch the mark in the wood, and as his finger caressed the jagged indentation, the door flew open to reveal a skinny, gaping man. One who peered at him with that same bloody look of disdain Kingsley's butler had used.

Shoving past the man, Harrison swept into the main entrance. The house may not be as big as the home he had lost, but inside, the white marble floor gleamed, silk chairs lined the walls and an enormous table filled with all manner of colored flowers stood in the middle of the room under a blazing chandelier. "Get your mistress, and get her now," he snarled.

"She's not in, sir."

He eyed the older man. This butler may be haughty like the Kingsley's butler, but he didn't possess the same bothersome mettle that characterized that other old codger. He reached out, grabbed the front of the man's black livery and jerked the bag of bones toward him until the servant's face rested only inches from his own. "If you don't get your mistress now, I'm apt to lose my temper. I cannot say for sure what may happen then, but I lost my temper last night and a man lost the use of two of his fingers." Harrison held up the butler's right hand and grabbed two long, bony fingers. "Fingers, especially ones as frail as yours, are quite easy to break. You simply apply enough pressure right to the bend." The butler gasped.

The man's fear was a balm after this long week. "Let me demonstrate," he offered, feeling a genuine smile pull at his lips. He added a bit of pressure to the man's knuckle. Just enough to make him squirm, but not enough to break the bones. Not yet, anyway. "I can stop if you get your mistress, or I can continue if you persist on denying my request. Hurts, does it not? Where's your mistress?"

"Mistress Vicery is not in at the moment."

He shoved the man away, watching as the butler stumbled and flailed his arms out in an effort to right himself. The man had no chance. He reached for the table but grasped a handful of white cloth, which did nothing to stop his fall. The arrangement of flowers atop the table whipped through the air in a satisfying blur and landed on the servant's head before crashing to the floor. Glass shattered and splintered, reminding Harrison of the sound of the man's fingers breaking last night. The butler groaned and raised a shaking hand to his head, where a cut trickled a bit of blood.

The scene pleased Harrison but not enough to wipe away the irritation of his confusion. He knew Bess Vicery was Lionhurst's mistress, but what did she have to do with Caprice? Why was Caprice living here? Why would Lionhurst care to bring Caprice under his protection? There was no bloody reason. He stared at the shards of glass surrounding the dazed butler. The broken pieces reminded him of the punch glass Allysia had thrown at him the night of the Primwitty ball when he told her he would not risk his future with Lady Gillian for anything.

Harrison curled his hands into fists. Lionhurst must know about him and Allysia. What was the marquess up to? Revenge? That was what Harrison would do if the situation had been reversed. His fury at being such a fool exploded inside him. He kicked out at the glass, wanting to break it more and break the man hovering on the floor. He had to hurt someone because he was hurting.

Bending down, he grasped the butler by the arms, intent on pummeling the man's face to a bloody pulp.

"Lord Westonburt!" A strangled cry came from behind him.

He dropped the butler and swung around. Caprice, dressed in the layers of a fine lady, flew down the stairs toward him. Her rounded eyes and her trembling mouth pleased him. She still feared him. He would get the answers he needed.

She stopped in front of him, chest heaving from her running. "How did you find me?"

He reached toward her and touched a lock of her silky hair. So smooth, just like Allysia's had been. "You can't hide from me, even with Lionhurst protecting you."

Caprice pulled back from him, eyes narrowed, chin raised in defiance. "I don't know what you mean."

Anger flooded Harrison. How dare Caprice give his enemy loyalty? The tide of fury would drown him if he did not find release. He grabbed a fistful of her hair, bringing Caprice to her knees where she belonged. Fear blossomed in her eyes. It wouldn't take much for her to betray Lionhurst. He pushed her delicate pinkie back until it touched the back of her hand and a scream ripped from her lips. Smiling, he released her finger and cupped her chin. "Do you know what I mean now?"

She nodded, tears streaming down her face.

"Excellent. You can tell me everything upstairs." He scooped her into his arms and carried her up the stairs to the first bedroom he came upon. Laying her gently on the bed, he came down beside her, rubbing away the tears on her cheeks. When she quieted, he kissed first her lips, then her neck. She didn't respond, but she would. Soon, she would.

He undid her dress and pushed it off her shoulders to bare her glistening skin. She was lovely. Not as lovely as Allysia or Lady Gillian, but lovely. "Tell me why Lionhurst helped you, and I promise I'll be gentle from this moment forward." He could see her gaze flickering and wavering as she tried to decide what to do.

She needed more prodding. Quite a shame. He picked up her hand, and she winced, a hiss of breath escaping from between her clenched teeth. “I’d hate to break another one of your delicate fingers,” he said.

“No need,” she replied, cradling her hand protectively.

He lay back and brought her into the crook of his arm to cuddle her as she spoke. When she finished, he smiled, ripe with the knowledge of just how to destroy the man he hated.

Thirty-Three

ONE MORE MOMENT OF watching Sutherland court Gillian, and Alex might very well go insane. Had it only been two weeks since he had agreed to this ludicrous bargain? It felt like forever. Two blankets over, Sutherland sat in the shade of an oak tree. Gillian sat opposite of Alex's partner under the brilliant blue sky that matched her dress. Sutherland reached into the picnic basket, procured a bottle of wine and poured Gillian a glass, which he handed to her, taking his bloody time letting go of her hand.

Alex groaned. He wanted to look away, but he had to see Gillian's reaction. She smiled, brushed a discreet finger—one would only notice if staring as Alex was—over Sutherland's hand, and then she brought the glass of wine to her lips.

Her pink tongue darted out to lick her lips before she took a long swallow of the wine. She lowered the glass, her dark lashes rising as her gaze met Sutherland's. Something she said caused Sutherland to laugh. Alex hated his partner. That was not going to be good for their working relationship. He had to get over this jealousy. It was eating at him, just as it had the day Robert had stolen Lady Staunton. Where was the resolve that had carried him through the almost five years since Robert's death?

Thou shall not covet. He'd rebuilt his life on this command and had promised until his dying day to try to make amends.

He squeezed his eyes shut, and Gillian's face filled his mind. His wanting her had everything to do with her and nothing to do with trying to best Sutherland. It was completely different from what had happened years before between Lady Staunton, Robert and himself, yet it was still wrong.

He breathed deeply. Was he no better now? He clenched his teeth together and opened his eyes to find Sally standing over him. She gazed down at him with a furrowed brow. "May I sit?"

"By all means." He straightened the blanket for her.

Sally lowered herself and faced him. "Darling, do you mind if I speak frankly?"

"If I did, would it stop you?"

"Probably not." Sally gave him a cheeky smile. "I've known you too long to mince words."

"I suppose that's true. What do you want to say?"

"Don't you think you've punished yourself for what happened between you, Robert and the witch long enough?"

"I assume the witch is Lady Staunton?"

"Don't be obtuse." Sally frowned at him. "You know it is."

"Then no. I've not punished myself long enough."

"Darling." Sally grabbed his hand and squeezed. "I'm going to tell you something you won't want to hear."

"Then don't say it." He was not in the mood for one of Sally's well-meaning attempts to get him to forgive himself and forget the past.

"I wish it were that simple. I'd hoped you'd eventually snap out of this, but it's almost been five years."

"I don't want to talk about Robert," he snapped.

"I know. But Peter, Cameron, Dansby and I discussed it, and we decided there are some things that must be said."

He stared at her astonished. "You four sat around and discussed my personal life?"

"We love you, Alex."

"Don't do that," he said, squeezing her hand back. Her eyes were filling with tears. "If you're the appointed messenger, I promise to be good and listen. Just don't cry."

Sally nodded and swiped at her eyes. He expected her to start with a lecture on how he was really a good person. How everyone makes mistakes. How he'd grown. How he had been under Lady Staunton's spell. He'd heard it all before. He leaned back on his elbows and crossed his legs. "Well?"

"It's like this, darling. Robert was mean, jealous and impulsive to a fault."

Alex gaped. Of all the things he had been expecting, an attack on his brother had not been one of them. "You're wrong."

But as he denied what she said, he thought of the countless women he had been interested in that Robert had taken from him. The horse races Robert had cheated at to win. Robert cheating in school to get better grades than Alex. Robert drinking all the liquor in their father's study and blaming it on Alex. He had taken the blame and the disapproval from their father because he had loved Robert. He had worshipped his older brother. "I slept with his fiancée. I drove him to kill himself," he said. He would not take the easy way out.

Sally pursed her lips at him. "Yes, you slept with his fiancée after he stole her from you by dangling his title in front of her greedy little eyes. But, darling, I swear none of us believe Robert was driven to kill himself."

"He shot himself in the heart," Alex said drily.

"He loved himself too much, darling. He was impulsive and reckless. I don't think he meant to kill himself. I think he meant to make you feel horrid for the rest of your life by wounding himself, but for once he fired too true."

Robert had never possessed good aim with a gun. But that didn't change what had driven him to such drastic measures. "He shot himself because of me," Alex said stubbornly.

"Wake up," Sally demanded. "He shot himself to get back at you. He was jealous of you. Everyone knew it.

Robert had the title, but, darling, you always had the brains, the looks and the personality that drew everyone to you. Robert couldn't stand it, and that's why he was so horrid to you. That's why he always used his title to snatch away the women you were interested in. And you—" She rolled her eyes. "Such a typical man. You always chose women who *could* be taken. All fluff no substance. *Gillian* has substance. Don't let her get away."

With a sublime effort, he controlled his surprise at Sally's words. "I don't know what you mean. I have a bargain to help Lady Gillian and nothing more."

Sally shook her head. "You're lying and you know it. You've come to care for her. I see it in your eyes. *We all do.* You're afraid. If you let yourself be happy, you can no longer punish yourself. You've done your penance."

Havoc reigned in his head. Was Sally right? No. He had vowed to atone forever. He could not take the easy way out. Besides, the lady did not want him. "She wants Sutherland," he denied.

Sally waved a hand at him. "She wants to escape London; I just wish I really knew why. I believe she really wants you. I've seen her watching you when you're not paying attention."

He immediately glanced across the space to where Gillian sat with Sutherland. Their heads were close together, as future lovers' would be. He pushed away his desire for her. "Whatever her reasons, she has chosen Sutherland, and she's made the right choice."

"You're wrong. I know you're afraid. I know you don't want to quit punishing yourself, but what if she truly does not want to marry Sutherland? What if she's in love with you?"

Alex jerked his gaze away from his wineglass toward Gillian. Their eyes met a moment before she jumped up and walked away from the picnic and toward the stream. His heart thudded against his ribs.

"Go now, while everyone is preoccupied and talk to her. Take a chance, Alex, before it's truly too late."

Alex glanced around the group. Sally was right—everyone's attention was elsewhere. Sutherland was now deep in conversation with Lady Whitney, and Cameron appeared to be regaling Peter and Dansby with some story. Alex jumped up and brushed a few pieces of grass off his breeches. "I'll just go see if she is feeling all right."

Sally raised her eyebrows. "Whatever you have to tell yourself to make yourself go, then by all means, do so, darling. Just go."

Was Sally right? Had Gillian fallen in love with him? Was it possible he could forgive himself and claim some happiness? He was not sure, but he knew he wanted to be certain she was doing what she really wanted. He strode across the grassy knoll and paused just as he neared her. If she left tomorrow and he never saw her again, this moment would be forever in his head, putting him to sleep every night. Her face was raised to the sky, her black hair flowing down her back and a smile on her face.

Driven by a desire just to be near her, he moved toward her, his boot crushing a twig with a loud snap.

Her eyes flew open as she whirled to face him. "I thought I was alone."

"I saw you leave the picnic. Is everything satisfactory with you and Sutherland?"

"Of course." She sank onto a log and looked out at the stream. "He's a very nice man."

"A nice man?" Alex sat on the log beside her, their legs brushing against each other. Hope he had no right to feel filled his chest, yet he could not quash it. "That's a bland way to describe the man you mean to marry."

"Is it?" She turned to look at him, a cynical smile on her lips. "I suppose it is. Don't mind me. I'm melancholy about leaving the only home I've ever known. I didn't think I would be."

The moisture in her eyes undid his resolve to remain detached.

He grabbed her hand and pressed it to his chest. He didn't deserve her. He didn't know what he could offer her, but he couldn't just let her go. "Don't go."

Her eyes rounded. "What? Whatever do you mean?"

What did he mean? Could he make the plunge back into life? Before he could respond, her sister ran up to them.

"Gillie! I've been looking everywhere for you. Drake's proposed a horse race, and I knew you wouldn't want to miss it."

Gillian extracted her hand from his, giving him a curiously sad look as she rose. "My future husband beckons," she said brightly.

He watched her walk away until he could see her no more. If he'd had a chance, it was lost. So be it. This was for the best. Now he had to put the ridiculous notions Sally planted in his head out of his mind.

Thirty-Four

EVEN THOUGH TWO WEEKS had passed since that afternoon when Alex had grabbed her hand by the stream, Gillian could not forget the way his heart had hammered beneath her fingertips. Had he been worried for her or upset? She rubbed her aching temples. She would never know, and she simply had to quit rehashing their short conversation. Her head nor her heart could take it.

He had had his chance to declare himself, and he had met her question with silence. Thank goodness. She was worried she might not have had the strength to deny her heart and do what had to be done. She'd fallen in love with the wrong man.

She sighed as she passed through the entrance of the Primwitty house and tried to drum up some excitement for dinner with the man she intended to marry. Instead, she yawned.

"Darling, I saw that," Sally chided, gliding toward Gillian as if the frenzy of party rounds the last month had not tired the duchess one bit.

Gillian smiled and grabbed Sally's outstretched hand. "I'm exhausted. I've not laid my head on my pillow before two in the morning in an entire month."

"Don't you sleep in?"

"I've been having trouble sleeping lately."

"Thinking about your love?"

That was just the problem. She'd been thinking about Alex when she should have been thinking about Drake. She frowned.

Sally leaned in until their heads almost touched. "Perk up. He's already here. Looking quite handsome, I might add."

"Who?" She scanned the outer corridor for Alex.

"What an odd question, darling." Sally gave Gillian a funny look. "Drake, of course. Your future husband."

Gillian nodded. "Of course. I'm just so tired." *And preoccupied with another man. Blast him.* There had not been one night in the last seven he had not arrived at the ball, or dinner party, or opera without a beautiful woman on his arm. A different woman every single night. She dreaded who he might bring tonight.

Sally tapped her arm. "Have you heard a word I've said?"

"I'm sorry." Gillian shook her head. "I was daydreaming. It must be the lack of sleep." Or the fact that Alex had her heart in his fist. Blast him again and blast Drake. An entire month of countless kisses and the greatest desire Drake inspired when he held her in his arms was the longing for it to be over. She liked him, but she did not desire him. And she did not think love would come without desire.

Sally poked Gillian in the arm.

"Am I doing it again?"

"Darling, you are going to make me wonder if I have become a bore unless you start listening to me."

"You could not ever be called a bore. It's me, truly it is. What did you say, Sally?"

"I said, I think Drake is going to offer marriage to you tonight." Sally studied her with narrow eyes then waved her toward the settee. "Isn't that wonderful? He plans to leave in a week to go back to America, and you and Whitney can go with him. It will all be settled. Your plan has worked out perfectly. It makes me feel so sad."

Gillian felt queasy. "Might I have a refreshment, Sally? I feel rather light-headed."

"What would you like?" Sally waved a servant over. "Tea?"

"Claret, please."

A small smile curled Sally's lips. "Jonsey, bring Lady Gillian some claret. Oh, and I'll take a glass too."

She settled back into the settee and tugged on Gillian's arm until they both leaned far into the cushions. "Now, be a good little girl and tell me what's going on while it's just the two of us. Your aunt and sister will be back from the gardens any moment, and the men are likely to burst in from whatever mischief they're up to at any time."

Gillian took a breath to speak, but Sally cleared her throat, indicating that the servant was present. Gillian took her drink and started with a few tentative sips. The warm liquor slid down her throat and pooled in her belly, loosening some of the knots on contact. That was nice. She didn't usually drink, but tonight she would make an exception. Tilting the glass up, she gulped the wine in four swallows.

Sally took the empty glass out of Gillian's hands and set it down on a side table next to her full, untouched glass. Sally waved Jonsey away when he appeared before them with another glass for Gillian. She was inclined to reach for it, but her head already hummed quite nicely, and she was afraid one more glass might turn the nice hum into a noisy chorus.

"Darling, you don't love Mr. Sutherland, do you?"

Gillian grimaced. "Dear God, is it that obvious?"

The front door slammed and a booming male voice carried down the hall. A masculine voice. A soothing voice. Alex's voice. Gillian smiled. And then a woman's shrill, grating laughter joined Alex's rich baritone. He had brought another woman. Gillian frowned, then caught Sally looking at her with a grin.

"I believe Alex is here," Gillian murmured.

"Yes. I think you're right," Sally replied, continuing to stare.

Gillian fidgeted under the Duchess' probing gaze. "Darling, I'd like to tell you a story." Sally eyed the hallway with a frown. "It will have to be the abbreviated version."

Gillian nodded.

Sally pressed close to her. "Once there were two young men named Alex and Robert."

Gillian's gaze went immediately to where she had

heard Alex's voice.

"That's right, darling, I mean Alex and his brother. Robert had the title, but Alex had everything else that Robert longed for. Do you know what I mean?"

"I can imagine," Gillian murmured, thinking of Alex's smile, his wit, his dancing eyes and magnetic presence.

Sally eyed her knowingly. "I'm sure you can. Robert was never nice. Even as a child he was greedy and jealous, but Alex worshipped Robert as younger brothers are wont to do. He forgave Robert every slight and overlooked all his flaws. Until one day, because Alex is human, he snapped. And decided to fight back."

"What did he do?"

Sally's eyes darted to the hall, and then back to Gillian. "He was having a rather steamy affair with Lady Staunton—of course then she was unmarried and was Lady Granton. She chased Alex until he gave her his attention. I can attest to that."

"I don't doubt it," Gillian replied, her stomach turning with jealousy that the woman had experienced an intimacy with Alex that Gillian had spent the last month dreaming about.

"As soon as she had Alex embroiled in her web, Robert came after her."

"Because she wanted Alex?"

"Of course," Sally said. "She later bragged, though, about using Alex to capture Robert. She knew exactly what she was doing. We all had witnessed for years how Robert wanted to take everything away from Alex. Belittle him, if you will."

"His brother took Lady Staunton?"

"In more ways than one," Sally said with a cynical smile. "He offered her marriage—the only thing that would induce her to leave Alex, and of course she accepted. I think she must have fallen in love with Alex, though she loved the idea of being a duchess more. I don't know the exact details, but she ended up back in Alex's arms the very night she became betrothed to Robert. Robert found them—how shall I say this delicately?—naked as the day they were born."

Gillian clutched at the material of her dress. She

should tell Sally to cease the story, but she wanted to know the rest. She needed to understand what was driving Alex. "Did Alex tell you this?"

"Don't be absurd. The man is as communicative as a dead fish. One night when he was rather sloppily filled with whiskey, mead and I do believe whatever else he could find, he told Peter, and Peter told me. Alex doesn't remember the night whatsoever. So you see, Alex is like he is because he was once human. He feels guilty for sleeping with his brother's betrothed even though his brother stole the wretched woman from Alex."

"What happened to Robert? Alex said he drove his brother to his death."

"Of course not, darling, but if he doesn't blame himself, he would have to face who Robert really was. Then Alex would have to do the hard thing and take chances on life and love once more. As for Robert, he shot himself. But not one of us believes he ever meant to actually kill himself. Just wound himself to wound Alex."

"How terrible," Gillian whispered as she stood and went to the door where she might have a better view of the hallway. Sally came next to her just as Alex appeared, swaggering down the hall with a tall woman clinging to his arm. Her long, silky black hair swayed as she walked, and Gillian had the urge to go up to the woman and yank a chunk out of her head.

"He's punishing himself for what he did." It made perfect sense to her. She wished it did not. She loved him even more now. Gillian moaned, retreating into the room, trying to prepare herself to greet the man she loved with a woman who had his undivided attention. "I had such a perfect plan."

Sally patted Gillian's hand. "Perfection is overrated. Alex would keep you in England with me if you were to marry."

That was exactly what she didn't need, but he was everything she wanted. Her head was a disaster and so was her life.

Thirty-Five

SEVEN DIFFERENT WOMEN IN seven nights, and not for one second had Alex's thoughts turned from Gillian. At the sound of her voice, he turned away from the parlor and headed in the opposite direction toward the terrace, dragging Maria with him. Maria was his latest attempt to erase the feel of Gillian's lips under his, her soft skin beneath his fingertips and her heartbeat against his palm as he had touched her bare skin. Gillian was everything a woman should be and more than he would ever deserve.

"Why did you turn us, chéri?" Maria questioned with a pout on her painted red lips.

"I need some air." He glanced down at the woman clinging to his arm. He had always thought Maria Moreti enticing. Perhaps it was her lovely operatic voice and her stage presence, but more than likely, it was her exceptional skills in bed. But as he looked into her slanted cocoa eyes, he had no desire whatsoever to taste the charms he had once found so alluring. In fact, he wished he had not brought her here tonight to Sally and Peter's dinner party. How could he have thought this wise?

Maria could never distract his attention away from Gillian. Tonight, he would have to suffer through every agonizing moment of Gillian sitting across from him and staring into Sutherland's eyes. Maybe she would touch

Sutherland or laugh with him. Alex ground his teeth.

He wasn't at all sure he could contain his hands from wrapping around Sutherland's throat if his friend played the besotted fool. And choking his business partner would not be good for their company or their friendship. Not to mention Sutherland had done nothing wrong.

He just had the fine fortune to be in the position to whisk Gillian and her sister away from England. Sutherland deserved a good woman. Alex deserved nothing. He proceeded past the study door and the men's voices raised in conversation and turned Maria toward the terrace overlooking the gardens. Fresh air would clear his head and give him some perspective and, with any luck, the ability to make it through the night.

This would be the last bloody night he played chaperone to the two lovebirds, since Sutherland meant to propose marriage tonight. The thought brought a bitter taste to Alex's mouth, but he was glad the deed would be done. Maybe then he could forget Gillian and get back to his life.

He pushed the terrace door open and swore. Rain poured from above, driven in a slanting motion by the wind. Looking up at the overhang off the terrace, he judged it sufficient to keep them dry. He stepped down the first step, but Maria held back. "We'll stay dry," he said, pointing up to the ledge.

"No, chéri. My makeup and hair will ruin from the spray. I'll not stand out here. Take me inside to the other women, or even better, let us join the men."

He examined her face in the pale moonlight. She was not a fresh beauty as Gillian was. Gillian wore no paint, nor did she need to. Suddenly, he could not stand the thought of touching Maria or her touching him. "Show yourself to the men in the study. I'm sure they'll be glad to receive you. But try not to get into too much trouble before dinner."

As Maria left, he closed his eyes and allowed the breeze to surround and calm him. The night wind howled and hissed while rain splattered against the tiles of the terrace. He breathed in the scent of wet dirt, trees and grass. Lissie would have loved this night. She had always adored a storm. His throat tightened with her memory, and he opened his eyes to find Sutherland staring at him.

"I brought you a whiskey," Sutherland said, pushing a glass toward Alex. "Thought you might need to be warmed out here since you sent Signorina Moreti inside with us."

"She is a rather useful blanket at times, but I felt the need to be alone."

"Is that a hint?"

"I suppose, but don't take it the wrong way. I'm just feeling nostalgic."

"For what—or is it whom?" Sutherland tapped his glass against Alex's.

Alex turned up his glass and downed the entire contents. Maybe if he drank enough, the ache in his chest would go away.

"Have I done something?" Sutherland asked.

Well, old friend, you stole the woman I desire but have no right to. Alex would keep that to himself. He shook his head. "No. I'm just thinking of my sister. Her death has been on my mind a great deal."

"I understand."

And he did. Alex knew he did, because three nights ago he had told Sutherland all the details about Lissie and Westonburt. Alex did not think it fair for Sutherland to walk blindly into the situation with Gillian. Westonburt would likely be dangerous when provoked too far, and there was nothing like taking away a man's greatest hope to bring his anger to the surface. The man was sure to lash out. Alex was prepared, but Sutherland needed to be ready as well, especially to watch out for Gillian's safety.

"Have you seen Westonburt since the card game?" Sutherland asked.

Alex rolled his empty glass back and forth in his hands "I've not seen him, but I now hold the deed to his family's home, and my man was there yesterday to confirm they had cleared out."

"What will you do with the house?"

"I've arranged for it to be torn down starting tomorrow." He had no idea what he would do from there, but he would never step foot in the house where Westonburt once lived, breathed and plotted to seduce Lissie.

"That'll drive that man crazy. He'll know you never wanted the house."

Alex pushed away from the wall. "That's the point. I want him to know I took his money simply to throw it all away. Simply because I detest the air he breathes." His stomach turned at the sound of his own voice. He needed another drink and quick. Revenge made him ill. "I'm going inside."

"Wait a minute, would you?"

Alex forced himself to stand still. "What is it?"

"Can you provide one more distraction tonight?"

"Will felicitations be in order?" Did he sound as angry as he felt?

"I sure as hell hope so," Sutherland replied. "It remains to be seen. Gillian is, after all, already betrothed, but we both know she doesn't love him."

"Do you love her?" It was none of his damned business, but he had to know.

"Well, not yet, but hopefully someday. She's everything a man could want in a woman. She'll be the perfect wife for me, and I know that everyone back home will love her. What's not to love? She's smart, she's beautiful and she comes from a good family."

"You sound like you're speaking of a brood mare you want to buy," Alex growled.

Sutherland elbowed Alex in the side. "Is there a difference?"

There was a difference with her. Alex struggled to control his anger. Gillian was life, breath and happiness for any man who would be lucky enough to claim her. The fool didn't see it yet, but devil take it, Sutherland would have enough years to figure it out. The chance was his for the taking. Not Alex's.

"Good God, Alex, I'm just joking. I'm sure we'll get along fine. You act like she's your damn sister or something, the way you're so protective." Sutherland started to leave, then stopped and turned back. "You don't care for her, do you?"

Hell yes, he did. But he shouldn't. Alex forced a slight smile. "I care for her as a friend." For a moment, he actually felt good about himself. He had given away the one thing he wanted more than anything in this world. He had given Gillian to the better man.

Thirty-Six

SEATED AT THE PRIMWITTY'S dining table directly across from Alex and the woman who clung to his arm, Gillian had a hard time forcing herself to eat, let alone concentrate on the conversation flowing around her. It required all of her willpower not to stare at Alex and Signorina Moreti. If the woman would keep her hands off Alex for even a moment, perhaps being able to swallow one bite of food without worrying it might come right back up would be possible.

Gillian wished she could stop looking at Alex, but his obvious enjoyment of the garish display of affection made her want to scream. The least he could do was act like a gentleman, but she held little hope that he would remember his manners. He seemed quite happy with Signorina Moreti's shameful groping.

Gillian had to look away. Really she must. But just as she started to pull her gaze to Drake, Signorina Moreti squealed with delight when the servant put a dessert down in front of her. As Gillian's lemon custard was placed before her, she studied the confection. Certainly, it smelled delicious and the thick white cream on top looked inviting, but to squeal over it? A million scathing remarks filled her head, but instead of opening her mouth and getting herself into trouble, she dug her spoon into the dessert and plopped a mouthful of custard in where a biting comment waited to come out.

She would get through this final course, then excuse herself, claiming a stomachache. It was true enough, given how her stomach turned each time Signorina Moreti put her hands on Alex. When the woman drove her spoon into her custard with gusto then raised it to Alex's lips, Gillian frowned. Surely, he would not allow himself to be fed. When he opened wide, Gillian set her spoon down with a clank. Alex's gaze met hers, and his right eyebrow shot up.

She returned Alex's stare with what she sincerely hoped was a look of disdain. "It seems you have forgotten how to feed yourself."

The hum of conversation around her abruptly stopped. Why in the world could she not hold her tongue? Now that she had said it, she refused to act remorseful. She held his cold gaze that did not flicker from her. He quaffed down his wine, set his glass down and leaned his elbows on the table. "Jealous?"

"Certainly not," she bit out, though heat flamed her cheeks, displaying her lie for the whole table.

"Well, I'm certainly jealous," Auntie commented, poking her spoon in her custard and then shoving it into Alex's gaping mouth. The tension around the table died away, replaced with laughter and comments from men and women alike that they all wanted a chance to feed Alex. Everyone roared with laughter except her and—she noted with grim satisfaction—Alex.

He scowled at her, and she forced herself to smile widely. Her cheeks ached from her effort to pretend merriment. Let him think she did not care.

When her aunt cleared her throat, Gillian drew her gaze away from Alex and met Auntie's probing look. Auntie tilted her head and tapped her fingers against her glass as if in deep thought. Gillian got the feeling her aunt was about to embark on another of her blunt shows.

"Mr. Sutherland, do tell us all about America. I wish to know every little detail about your home and the culture."

Gillian slumped in her chair with relief.

"My home"—Drake leaned back, a wistful look on his face—"is on one of the busiest streets in New York. All hours of the day you can hear carriages rumbling by. The city is alive and noisy. I love it."

"Sounds dreadful," Auntie remarked. "But I'm a country lady at heart. Tell me about the culture. What do you do for entertainment?"

"Much the same as here. We go to the opera, balls, dinners, horse races and picnics. Do you want me to categorize all of our pastimes and give you a detailed description?"

Gillian suppressed her grin. Drake was on to her aunt's mechanisms. Gillian sat forward on the edge of her seat to see what would happen next. She welcomed any distraction that would take her mind off Alex.

"Well, certainly you can," Auntie chirped. "I'm sure Gillian and Whitney would love to hear all about America." Her aunt smiled directly at Whitney. "Don't you want to know all about America, dear?"

"Not particularly," Whitney said, apparently borrowing some of Auntie's bluntness. "I've no interest in hearing about a land I'll never see."

"You never know," Drake said, turning to face Whitney. "You may end up there yet." When he winked at Gillian, she nearly groaned aloud. She had planned and plotted to catch this man, and now that she had his attention, she was finding it hard to be happy.

"I don't mean to sound rude," Whitney said, giving Gillian a sharp look, then turning her attention back to Drake, "but I will never end up in America. I've quite made up my mind. I love England and couldn't imagine living anywhere but here."

Gillian spit out the sip of wine she had just taken. The red liquid flew all over her plate.

"Heavens, Gillian." Whitney plucked Gillian's wineglass out of her hand. "I'd say you've had quite enough of that. Here." Her sister shoved a glass of water into her hands. "Drink this."

Gillian took a gulp of the water. "But of course if I were to go"—she could not believe she was being so bold as to actually act as if Drake would certainly propose—"you would go. You would have to."

"I certainly would not go. I've quite made up my mind."

"Does anyone know what Martha is planning for her costume fete?" Auntie asked. The conversation around Gillian buzzed with speculation of the costume ball to come. Gillian stared at Whitney, ignoring the meaningless chatter.

She had never asked Whitney what she had wanted to do. She had told her and not given her sister one chance to voice how she felt. And now that Whit had been given the chance to speak, she was taking it. *Dear God.*

She leaned toward Whit's ear. "What do you mean you won't go to America? What of our plan?" she whispered.

Whitney moved her head enough so that her mouth pressed against Gillian's ear. "*Your* plan. It was always your plan, and I've decided I simply cannot go through with it. I don't want to leave England, I don't want to live with you and Drake and I doubt you want to marry him. I won't go. Nothing you say will move me to reconsider."

Gillian's world shifted. Whitney's voice dripped with stubborn defiance. There was no one more obstinate than Whit when she set her mind to it. Gillian sat back in her chair. Conversation continued to swirl around her, but she did not hear a word. She no longer had a plan or a way to protect her sister if she refused to leave.

She was dreadfully afraid for Whitney. There was no way to force her sister to go unless she told her the truth, but that might not even do the trick and it could seriously harm Whitney.

Across from her, Alex raised his glass and downed his wine. "Three cheers for good old Mother England."

As everyone raised their glasses to toast, Drake touched Gillian's shoulder. "Would you walk with me in the garden?"

She nodded and blindly reached for her glass to get a fortifying drink. Cool water slid down her throat, making her frown. Blasted meddling sister. Glaring at Whitney, Gillian pushed back from the table with a pounding heart.

How could she refuse Drake if he offered her marriage after she had plotted and schemed just for this? How could she not refuse him since her sister had just declared she would not leave? Gillian's stomach rolled with queasiness. Lord, she was a coward. She threw one last searching glance over her shoulder before stepping out of the room. No one noticed them, especially not Alex. The curve of Signorina Moreti's shoulder was too enticing for him to take note of Gillian's departure. As he leaned in to whisper something in the signorina's ear, Gillian bumped into the door jamb.

"Ouch." She rubbed her shoulder and forced herself to turn away from the scene.

Giving her a queer look, Drake took her hand. "Doll, if you actually look where you're walking, it will help you to avoid doors and walls."

Gillian nodded, feeling more alone than ever.

THE MOMENT GILLIAN AND Sutherland disappeared out of the dining room, Alex slumped in his chair, exhausted from the effort to keep his mouth shut and his desires to himself. It took all his reserves, but he'd done it. He let her go. He didn't need to worry about dying and going to hell for his sins, because he was already in hell. The next time he saw Gillian she would be engaged to not one, but two men. *Neither of them him. Bloody hell.* He was not drunk enough for this night.

"Alex," Maria purred, sliding her hand up his leg under the table while leaning toward his ear. "I want to come home with you to your bed."

He shoved her searching hand away, unable to stand his charade any longer. "No. I'll be going home alone tonight." And every night for the rest of his life. He wanted no woman but the one he couldn't have. He stood and clutched at his chest. The aching pain he was getting used to shot through the center of his heart, making him wince. Could longing kill a man? Peter motioned toward the door, and Alex nodded, following his friend out of the dining room toward the main entrance.

"I take it the lovely Maria will not be escorting you home?"

"No." Alex offered a slight smile. "Will you see she gets home safely?"

"My coachman can. If I tried to even put my big toe into a carriage alone with Maria, Sally would throttle me."

"Yes, she's rather possessive of you," Alex said, shrugging

on his overcoat.

"We're all possessive of those we love."

Waving the footman away, Alex opened the front door. He wanted to possess Gillian. He wanted to wrap his arms around her and never let her go. Did that mean he loved her? Or did that mean he was a fool? Perhaps it meant both.

As Alex's driver scrambled to open the carriage door, Alex stepped into the rain. He stood for a moment, letting the cool water drench his coat and seep cold into his skin. In the gazebo to the side, candlelight cast shadows on Sutherland and Gillian. They stood face-to-face. Alex forced his legs to move and get into the carriage, then he signaled his coachman to go.

As his carriage pulled away, a sweat broke out against his scalp, despite the frigid air. He had thought nothing could feel worse than knowing he was to blame for Robert killing himself. Damn it if he had not been grievously wrong. Not fighting for Gillian was the worst pain he had ever experienced.

DIM AND FAIRLY DESERTED, White's was perfect for Alex. He didn't want to make conversation or play cards or even pretend to be happy. He wanted to get bloody sopping foxed and by the swimming in his head, he had a damn good start.

Several hours later, he was sure he had perfected the art of feeling sorry for himself. "To Robert," he mumbled, turning up his glass of whiskey. As the liquid slid to his stomach, he closed his eyes, savoring the oblivion only truly good whiskey could bring.

A chair scraped beside him, and he growled in response. "Go away," he commanded, not caring who he might be offending.

"I can't do that, Lionhurst."

Unsure if his ears betrayed him, Alex opened one eye. Nope. His head may be soggy, but his ears still worked. He slowly opened the other eye and focused both on Sutherland. "There are two of you."

"No. Just one."

"What the hell are you doing here? Shouldn't you be celebrating your impending wedding with your intended?" If *he* had just proposed to Gillian, he would first kiss her lips, then her neck, then perhaps her shoulder or that little hollow place between her shoulder blades where she had a tiny scar. He shook his head with a groan.

Sutherland eyed him but said nothing.

"Go celebrate," Alex hissed, closing both eyes.

"Well, I would if I had a fiancée, but as the lady in question said no to my proposal..."

Alex bolted upright in his seat and the room swayed. "Bloody hell." He took a deep breath. "What did you say?"

"Gillian refused my offer of marriage."

"She refused you?"

Alex tried to concentrate on appearing concerned for Sutherland, but he could not get past the fact that Gillian had refused the man. "Why'd she refuse you?"

"It's customary to tell one sorry when they pour out their troubles to you."

Alex scrubbed a hand over his face. "I am sorry. Truly."

"She said something about attraction or lack thereof. And attraction leading to love. Oh, and men with blue eyes who refuse to wear their cravats properly." Sutherland's gaze fell to Alex's untied cravat. "And sisters who won't listen. And her being helpless, but sure she could no longer marry me. Honestly, I couldn't follow half the things she babbled about."

Alex grinned. He followed her perfectly. She cared for him. No denying the proof of her babbling. What to do about it? She deserved better than him. But he was a selfish bastard, and he no longer cared. He met Sutherland's eyes. "I can't let her go twice."

"I suspected something was between the two of you." Sutherland shrugged. "I chose to ignore it because she would have been the perfect wife for me, and I never dreamed you would marry anyone. Then Sally sat me down an hour ago, told me a story about you and your brother and lectured me on finding a woman who really loved me for me."

"What the hell does Sally know about Robert and me?"

Alex sat in stunned silence as Sutherland told him all the details that Peter had told Sally. "I don't remember telling Peter any of that."

Sutherland nodded. "You loved your brother. And then you betrayed him. And he betrayed you. Time and again. He was an ass. And so were you. It's time to forgive yourself."

"I can't," Alex said, pushing his chair away from the table. "But because I am an ass, I can't just let her go, though she deserves better than me."

Alex stood and swayed with the sudden motion. His effort to get foxed had been a supremely good one. He put his hand on the back of his chair to steady himself. "Was she still at Peter and Sally's when you left?"

"Yes. From the sound of it, she was arguing with her aunt about something. Primwitty said he thought you might be here, so I left to come find you."

"I should go find her."

"Not tonight, my friend."

"Why not?" Alex blinked his eyes to clear his vision.

"You're foxed. Go see her when you can talk coherently."

Waiting was out of the question. Alex wanted and needed to see her now and talk to her or even just look at her. He had no idea what he was going to say or what he could offer her, but he had to say something.

He took a step forward and the room tilted. He slapped his palm on the table. "I am not drunk," he protested, more for his own benefit. He had never been foxed over a woman in his life.

Chuckling, Sutherland asked, "How do you know you're not drunk?"

"If I can walk, I'm not foxed," Alex replied smugly, taking a step forward and pitching face-first onto the cold, hard floor. Hands came under his arms, and he would have lifted his head to protest, but the blasted thing weighed a ton. Instead, he decided to sleep since someone turned out the lights.

Alex woke with a pounding headache, a dry mouth and sweating from the bedcovers piled on him. After a brief inspection of his surroundings, he ascertained he was in his own town house. Thank God for that, or he supposed, he should thank Sutherland. With a quick change and a barked command to his butler, Alex was on his way to Peter and Sally's, praying all the way that Gillian had been detained by the rain that still plagued them this morning. He arrived at Sally and Peter's, and discarding all social graces, he did not bother to knock and charged into the house nearly running over the poor butler.

"Lord Lionhurst, I do believe you are expected," the butler stated politely, ignoring the fact that he had almost been shoved to the ground. "If I may escort you to the study?"

Alex nodded and followed the man, trying not to push him out of the way in his eagerness to get to Gillian faster. When the aged butler finally crept to the study door and opened it, Alex couldn't contain himself any longer. He brushed past him and stopped short, disappointment nearly choking him. Sally, Lady Whitney, Lady Davenport and Peter were in the room, but not Gillian.

"Where is she?" Alex asked, directing his question at Peter since he was closest to him.

"I assume you mean Lady Gillian?"

"You know who I mean," Alex snapped.

"She's gone."

Ready to shake his best friend, Alex advanced toward Peter. "What do you mean, she's gone?"

"It's as Peter has just told you," Gillian's aunt said. "She wanted to leave, so she left."

Alex dropped into a chintz chair, put his head between his hands and took three long breaths. When he thought he could talk without yelling, he sat up. "Let's try again, shall we?"

The women nodded in unison.

"Are you telling me she had a coach take her home in this driving rain?"

"Not precisely," Lady Whitney said.

Alex turned his glare on Peter. "I tried to stop her, Lion. She insisted she could drive the carriage herself, and when I flatly refused to allow her, she sneaked out of the house and took my favorite coach with the red and black top. How was I to know a lady would do such a thing?"

"Darling, really?" Sally chuckled. "After all these years married to me, you truly don't know an independent woman when you see her?"

"I thought your outlandish behavior was yours alone," Peter replied. "I'd no idea other women were afflicted so."

"You must not know many women with their own minds," Lady Davenport said with a shake of her head.

"Truly he doesn't," Sally confirmed. "Though I do maintain like-minded friends for myself as Gillian."

"Enough," Alex grumbled, coming to his feet. "How can you all sit here so calmly when she's alone out there in this abominable rain?"

Gillian's aunt stood up and crossed to him. "Because we only just realized she left. And working ourselves into a tizzy won't help her. We were just deciding if Whitney and I should go or if His Grace should take another carriage. She's going home, so we will find her. But she's quite capable with horses."

"Why would she go now in this rain?" Alex glared at all three women. "You women make no sense." He just wanted to see her and tell her…what? *I'm so glad you still only have one fiancé?* He groaned and raked his hand through his hair. When he found her, he had to know exactly what to say.

Thirty-Seven

STANDING IN THE POURING rain, Gillian kicked at the wheel of her carriage until her right foot throbbed from her effort. *Blasted rain.* When would it end? She ran a hand over her eyes to wipe away the water and stared at the offending wheel sunk deep into the brown muck. With one last burst of anger, she braced her hands on the wheel and dug her feet into the mud behind her, but as she slid forward toward the brown, soggy ground, all her determination slipped away as her hands sank into the mess.

She couldn't do it anymore. Whatever fight she possessed was gone. She had failed her sister, and her sister did not even know it yet. The only choice now was to protect Whitney as best she could from whatever may come.

Fearing she was about to end up face-first in the sludge, she tried to bring her knees forward and push herself up to stand. Instead, she tilted over and landed on her back, stuck in the mire. Her predicament echoed the past that haunted her, a mire of lies and mud brought about by rain. The river had killed Mother on a rainy night.

Weighed down by years of secrets, guilt and duty, Gillian relinquished the fight and dropped all the way back into the muck. The belief that she could one day figure this problem out drove her forward every day of her life, but now that belief was gone. Drake had been her only solution. She was left with nothing except her desire for Alex.

What kind of fool was she to want a man who had only offered to ruin her in order to hurt his enemy? Alex did not love her. If he had, then he would have stopped Drake from taking her from the dining room last night. Alex had known Drake meant to propose marriage. Drake had told her so. Blast her stupidity for falling in love with Alex.

He was not going to come charging up the road and rescue her from all her problems. What did that leave? She stared up at the gray sky and let the rain pelt her face, cold drops of confusion and defeat covering her skin with a wet layer. What to do now? Pull herself out of the mud? No. She was too tired to move just yet.

She would have to marry Lord Westonburt. She could not leave Whitney, and staying meant marriage to that man. Her stomach turned in protest. She lay in the muck until she was soaked to the bone, a deep chill settling into her soul along with the brutal truth.

Gillian dug her fists into the mire. Perhaps if she held tightly enough to the earth, she could maintain her senses as well. She closed her eyes and breathed in the wet dirt and rain. There was no good solution; there was no happy ending.

Her throat constricted, and every defense she gathered around her to make herself strong through the years slipped away. She felt like she was eight years old again, the longing to be loved as fresh as the moment she realized Mother was leaving them. But no longer did Gillian crave her mother's touch. She craved Alex's, and the longing made her angry. "I hate you, Lord Lionhurst," she hissed, slamming her palms into the dirt and pushing herself up.

"Don't say that, peach. I would hate to think I came all this way in the driving rain to find a woman who hates me."

Gillian's eyes flew open. She wasn't woolgathering. There was Alex, kneeling in the mud and gazing at her.

He shook his head, then swooped his arms under her legs and brought her against his chest while rising.

She didn't stop to think. She crushed her mouth to his. His arms tightened around her as he returned her kiss, gently massaging her lips with his own and breathing life back into her with the warmth of his breath. His lips sucked and nipped at her neck until his warm breath hit her ear, unraveling her at the center of her core with a pulsating need to be one with him.

Her fingers curled into his shoulder. He drew back to look at her, cupping the side of her face with his hand, then sliding his fingers under her chin. "Did you think I wouldn't come to find you once I heard you had turned Sutherland's proposal down?"

She laughed shakily. "I suppose I should have known you'd come looking to seduce me. Go ahead." She crushed her mouth to his once again. Embracing recklessness. Embracing her desire. Wanting to know his love for one moment. "I no longer care. If I'm to be forced to marry Westonburt, then just once I want to know what it feels like to be with the man I love."

"YOU LOVE ME?" HIS heart thudded as he pulled back and looked at Gillian.

"Yes," she replied, her teeth chattering.

He pressed her to him and wrapped his arms tight around her. "You're willing to let me seduce you because you love me?"

She nodded. "I cannot help you gain your revenge before my marriage. But I promise you he'll know you had me once I'm wed. I have to protect my sister above all, but I will get you your revenge."

"Damn it, Gillian." He clomped through the mud toward the hunting cabin he saw in the distance.

"What are you doing?"

"I'm getting us out of the rain. I prefer to talk to you without *my* teeth chattering."

"Put me down." She pushed on his shoulder as he continued to walk. With every step toward the cabin, her resistance grew. "Please, put me down. I can't go in there.

Not there."

"Why?" He stopped and met her rounded eyes.

"My mother," Gillian moaned. "She died there. Not five feet from that place."

"I guess we both need to banish our pasts." Alex strode up the steps and set her down in front of the door. Gillian did not move.

Alex rattled the door handle, then stepped back and kicked the door open. It flew back and hit the inner wall with a whack. She scrambled backward, but his arm looped around her back and his fingers splayed to become a barrier. He pushed her sopping hair off her shoulder, and she met his gaze. "Trust me."

Hell, he could not believe he was asking her to trust him. Until she had declared she loved him, he had not known what he was going to say. But now, he had no doubt.

She nodded and followed him inside. Once he closed the door, he turned to face her. "Promise you won't interrupt me."

She nodded.

He took a deep breath. "I'm not worthy of you."

"Alex—"

"You promised." He wanted to tell her everything at once.

She clamped her mouth shut.

"I'm not worthy of you. But I want you. I love you. And I'm selfish enough not to care that you deserve better than me."

"Alex, I—"

"Gillian, please..."

"Sorry." She pressed her lips together.

"You need to know some things about me." He started to pace the room. "I slept with my older brother Robert's fiancée, and that's what led Robert to kill himself. His death is on my hands. I've tried to atone, I vowed to never take a wife since I deprived Robert of the chance of ever having one, but I want you."

"You mean you want to *seduce* me."

"No, Gillian." He crossed the room and cupped her face in his hands. "I want to marry you. If you'll have me after what I've told you, I want you to be my wife. I swear to God I'll spend the rest of my life trying to be better than I've been."

SHE WANTED TO CRY at his declaration and pain. Instead, she ran her hands up the curves of his forearms and over the broad expanse of his muscled chest. "I already knew about your brother. Sally told me everything."

"Well, hasn't the duchess been rather chatty lately."

Gillian arched her brow. She didn't know what he meant by that, nor did she particularly care about Sally at this moment. Gillian slid her hands up his arms until they rounded his shoulders. She grasped the material of his soaking wet coat and tugged until it slid down his arms and dropped with a smack against the floor.

Her heart thudded in her chest. "What you did was wrong. But what Robert did to you all your life was wrong as well. You made a mistake, but you did not kill your brother."

His eyebrows lifted. "I slept with his betrothed."

"And he stole many of the women you were involved with. He stole Lady Staunton from you with his title."

"She used me."

Gillian gritted her teeth. The man was stubborn. She deftly unlaced his shirt and tapped his arms. He raised them above his head, and she swallowed back a wave of lust at the muscled flesh displayed before her. "Either way, your brother knew you were sleeping with her, did he not? He knew you cared for her, did he not?" She reached for the waist of his trousers, but his hands came to hers and held them.

"No one has ever tried to convince me quite like this."

She smiled, her heart pounding. "I want you to accept the truth. Robert was jealous of you. You had everything he wanted. When his title secured him Lady Staunton's hand in marriage, but not her love, he wanted to punish you."

Alex frowned at her for several seconds. "I never thought of it that way."

"You wouldn't. Let me ask you something. Would you

not have died for Robert?"

Alex stared at her, his dark eyes lightening. "Gladly. He was my brother."

"There's your answer. Let go of your guilt. You loved Robert. Despite everything between the two of you, you loved him."

He pulled her close and ran his hands up into her hair. Tilting her head back, he placed a light kiss on her lips. "Thank you."

"You're welcome." She kissed him back, relishing the tingle of desire simply kissing him could cause.

He took her hand and led her to the bed. "There's something I want to know before we go any further.

She smiled. She was sure he wanted to know if she would marry him. Of course, she would. She loved him. She could not save her sister from what may come, but maybe Alex could help control the damage if the truth came to light. And he was saving her from Westonburt. She would marry Alex no matter how her father protested.

She wrapped her arms around his neck. "What do you want to ask me?"

"What are you running from?"

Thirty-Eight

HIS QUESTION SHOCKED HER, but she took a deep breath and spoke. “My father didn’t kill my mother as most people think.” Just saying the words lifted something heavy and cumbersome off her shoulders.

“No?” Alex pushed a strand of her wet hair off her forehead. “Then it was truly an accident?”

“Yes, but my sister caused the accident.” She studied Alex to see if he grimaced or showed any signs of surprise, but he did not appear the least concerned or surprised by her statement.

She released her hold from around his neck and sat on the bed. “It was my ninth birthday, and Mother was nowhere to be found. After my party, Father sent us to bed and went looking for her. Whit and I followed him to the river because we were afraid Mother was going to leave us, and we were right. Father found her in *this* cabin with another man.”

The bed dipped beside her as Alex sat. “Who?”

God, how many times had she asked that same question? “I don’t know. I couldn’t see the man’s face, and Father refuses to speak of it.”

“So if your father didn’t push your mother to her death…”

“Whitney did,” Gillian rushed out, wanting to tell him everything before she turned coward again. “Mother and Father were arguing, and Father was waving a pistol around, and it seemed he was going to shoot her."

Gillian could see the sliver of moon and her mother with her hair flowing freely around her shoulders. She frowned. She had forgotten that until now. "Whit ran screaming through the dark toward them, and I think she must not have been able to stop. Or maybe she thought to grab Mother and pull her out of the way, but she did neither. She ran straight into her, and Mother simply teetered over the embankment and fell."

She paused, nausea washing over her.

Alex squeezed her hand. "Tell me the rest."

She studied his open blue gaze and saw no judgment there. "I ran when I saw her fall. I ran all the way back to the house. I didn't go to help Whit or Mother. I ran like a coward and sat crying, huddled under my covers until I heard Whit return. And when she did, she wouldn't speak or tell me anything. Father came hours later and told us Mother was dead. She'd drowned in the river. He showed us her body."

Gillian pressed her fingertips to her lips. "Did you know freezing cold water really does make lips turn blue?"

Alex shook his head. "I didn't know that."

"After we saw her, Whitney became very befuddled, and when she awoke the next day, she did not remember the night before. We had to remind her Mother was dead. It took weeks for her to believe."

Gillian rested her head against Alex's shoulder. "She never remembered. Father and I are the only ones who know the truth. We agreed never to tell her. I was glad not to tell her because I'd failed to protect her, *and* I blamed him."

"Gillian." Alex wrapped his arm around her shoulder and pulled her to his side. He placed a kiss on the top of her head. "You reacted as any child would have."

She clutched at him, wanting to hold on to him and the compassion he offered. He did not understand the worst. "I'm supposed to always watch out for Whitney. Mother had told me so."

"Gillian, she's a grown woman now. Maybe Whitney should hear the truth. Does this have something to do with why you wanted to leave England?"

"Yes." She swiped at the tears running down her face.

"Shh." He reached out and stroked her head. "I'll never say anything. No one will know. If you want to keep the secret, I'll keep it with you."

She clutched at him, desperate to feel his strength. "It's not that simple."

His hand stilled on her head. "What do you mean?"

"Someone already knows our secret. They've been sending me notes for months, threatening to expose Whitney unless we all stay out of Society."

Alex's finger came under her chin and turned her head until she met his gaze. "So you concocted the idea to enter into a loveless marriage to save your sister?"

"Yes." She swallowed, fearful. "Do you hate me?"

"God, Gillian." Before she knew what was happening, his mouth had come to hers in a demanding kiss that heated her from head to toe. He pulled back and stared at her. "I don't hate you. I love you *more*. I love you more than I knew was possible."

Before she could second guess her actions, she stood and unfastened her dress. His eyes devoured her as she bared one shoulder and then the other.

"God, you're beautiful," he whispered as he stood. He slid a finger up and down the hollow of her spine. His arms circled her, and she rested her head against his pounding heart.

Gillian took his hand and placed it over her bare breast to let him feel the pounding of her heart that matched his. "I love you. I think it started the moment you stepped behind the curtain and invaded my hiding place."

A slow smile spread across his face. "Lucky I picked the wrong curtain."

"Very," she murmured as his fingers traced a slow circle around the outer edge of her breast, then settled over the tip, lightly brushing back and forth across her skin. She moaned and he grinned, looking exactly as he had the moment she had first seen him, confident and devastatingly wicked.

He ran a thumb over her lips, and she captured his hand in hers, excited and afraid for what was coming.

Thirty-Nine

ALEX LAID GILLIAN DOWN and sucked in a breath of appreciation at the picture she presented. Creamy flesh. Dark hair. Slumberous eyes and enticing curves. He came down above her, hovering over her body.

"You're shaking," she whispered, caressing his chest.

"Like a green lad before his first time."

Gillian pushed a hand onto his chest until he rolled over and she rested on top of him. Her soft, warm body pressed against his hard, burning skin. She brushed her lips against his. "Why?"

"Because I love you." When tears filled her eyes, he brushed a hand over her cheek to wipe the dampness away. "Here, now. What's this? My declaration's not supposed to make you cry."

She shook her head before burying it in the crook of his neck. "Tears of happiness," she whispered into his shoulder, her breath caressing his bare skin.

He stroked her hair for a moment, relishing holding her. Having her naked body pressed so close made him want to ravish her, but he wanted to do it slowly, learning every curve of her body as he went.

He slid his hands to her smooth back and ran his fingertips up and down her spine, memorizing every dip. When he kneaded his hands down her back to her bottom, she groaned and ground her pelvis into his. Lust shot through him, and he gripped her hips to stop her movement. "If you move that way, peach, I'm not sure I can control myself."

She rose up onto her hands, the tips of her breasts touching his chest, her green eyes blazing with such unmistakable desire it made his heart ache. "I don't want you to keep your control."

"You're sure?" God, he sincerely hoped she was sure.

"Do I seem unsure?" She splayed her hands across his chest, her eyes challenging him.

SHE WAS ON HER back before she knew what happened. His mouth sucked and retreated at her neck, then her breasts, and farther down until his hands pushed her thighs apart. She tensed for a moment at the unknown, but when his tongue flicked over the most sensitive part of her body, nothing else mattered but getting closer to him.

Something inside her mounted and coiled. She pushed her pelvis up, clenching the sheets for support. His ministrations came faster and harder. She couldn't stand this teasing. What she needed was him. She grasped his shoulders and tugged, but he refused to come up. His tongue laved slowly back and forth, and then faster until she thought she would come undone.

"Please."

He came up sweating, panting and tense as a bow. He needed her too. She saw it in his eyes. "Take me."

Instantly, he hovered over her and settled between her thighs, his hands braced on either side of her shoulders. He gazed down at her. "I love you." His soft-spoken words reverberated with intensity in her heart.

She reached up and traced a finger over the pulsing skin of his chest. "Then make me yours."

He lifted her bottom and plunged inside her, then stilled. She clenched her fingers into his shoulders at the momentary twinge of pain, but as they lay locked as one, her body grew accustomed to him. Warm sensations swirled in her belly. He moved slowly, and the intensity started to build again as a fire rekindled. The flame grew brighter and stronger until a burning heat engulfed her.

His slow strokes became fast and hard. He panted—his skin slick from his efforts, the muscles of his arms bunched from holding back. She wrapped her legs around his back and rose to meet his thrusts, pushing her to the frenzied edge. And then she was no longer in control. She rode a wave that carried her up and rolled her in its powerful embrace, then dropped her down toward the earth, spent and helpless.

They lay face-to-face, listless. Only their mutual panting, which faded to a whisper, broke the silence. After a long while, he stirred, and she forced her eyes open. He was watching her with an intense look. "What is it?"

"I want to tell you about my sister and Westonburt."

She nodded, and Alex began to talk. When he finished, tears wet her eyes and hatred burned inside her. Lord Westonburt was a despicable beast. "I'm so sorry."

He nodded, and Gillian could see he was struggling to control his own emotions. They lay in silence, each lost in their own thoughts. After a bit she fell asleep. When she woke, shadows filled the room and a lone candle burned on the table.

"I hope you don't mind I searched the room and found the candle."

"No, I don't mind." Alex lay facing her on the bed. His skin glowed from the candlelight. She wanted to say here forever, but she couldn't. Sighing, she said, "I have to go."

He reached out and ran his fingertips over her breast. Her body tingled to awareness immediately, but she batted his hand away and rolled off the bed before he could stop her. "We'll have a lifetime together. Right now, I need to see my father."

Alex rolled off the bed and reached for his trousers as she slid her dress over her head. She turned her back to him. "Will you play my lady's maid?"

His hands curved around her shoulders while his lips brushed the sensitive skin behind her ear. "Gillian, my love, I'll be anything you want me to be as long as I'm with you."

The promise heated her to her core. She leaned against him as his hands cupped her breasts, and his mouth worked magic on her neck. Heaven help her. She would never leave at this rate. She could not force herself to pull away from this man. Turning, she wrapped her arms around him and met his mouth in a hungry, plundering kiss.

He lifted her and she wrapped her legs around his torso, as he bent his head and tugged at the material of her dress with his teeth. He just about had the left shoulder completely bared when behind them, something rattled, and the door to the cabin burst open.

Forty

A GASP FILLED THE room, followed by a snicker. Gillian would know that laugh anywhere. “Put me down,” she demanded in Alex’s ear. He slid her body down the length of his, and as he did so, she tugged the left shoulder of her dress back in place before swinging around to face Whitney.

Her sister stood with her hands on her hips and a smirk on her face. “I don’t know what I expected to find the two of you doing, but I must say, that acrobatic move I just witnessed surpassed my wildest expectations.”

Alex crossed to the foot of the bed and retrieved his shirt. “I do pride myself in my unique abilities to boggle a woman’s mind, so I thank you.”

“What are you doing here, Whit?” Gillian tried to force herself to concentrate on her sister’s face and not the way Alex’s muscles rippled as he maneuvered into his clothing.

“I came to fetch you before Father sets out to find you.”

“Father?”

“Yes. You know, the man whose house you live in?” Whitney crossed the room to Gillian and started tugging a hand through her hair. Gillian swatted her away. “What are you doing?”

“Making you presentable.” Whitney jerked on Gillian’s

bodice and then pulled on the folds of her dress. "Father's about to go stark raving mad, and your fiancé is there as well. He's come for the wedding, which is to be tomorrow, since apparently your betrothed cannot wait to make you his."

"The hell he will," Alex growled from the bed as he put on one of his boots. "I'll kill him first." Alex shoved his other foot in the boot and stood up with a ferocious glare on his face.

Already Gillian could feel her peace slipping away. She pressed her fingertips to her forehead in an effort to think. "Does Father know where I am?"

"No. I knew because I saw your carriage several hours ago when I rode past with the Primwittys."

"Sally and His Grace know I was in this cabin with Alex?" Gillian groaned.

Whitney raised her eyebrows, her smirk deepening until both her dimples pierced her cheeks. "Well, none of us knew for sure, but we all suspected when we saw your carriage and Alex's horse tied to the tree beside it. Auntie said you probably sought shelter from the rain in the cabin."

"You mean Auntie knows as well?" Gillian cried.

"Mm-hmm. She's the one that insisted we just drive right past and leave the two of you alone to figure each other out. The plan was to come fetch you after Father was to bed. Auntie told Father you were at her house visiting with Trent, but Father wouldn't be deterred. He said you had to come home straight away and was having his horse readied when I left. I don't know what the major ruckus is about, but from the bits and pieces I heard outside Father's door, Lord Westonburt is very angry."

Gillian squared her shoulders. "Time to face Father."

Whitney clutched Gillian's hand. "What are you going to do?"

Alex was across the room and beside Gillian before she could answer. "She's going to marry me."

"Thank God," Whitney said. "But how will you convince Father to give you his permission?"

"She's going to tell your father what Westonburt did to

my sister."

"I am?" Gillian locked gazes with him. She could hardly believe he was willing to sacrifice his sister's name for her. "Are you sure? What about your sister's reputation?"

"My sister would want this," Alex said, putting his arm around Gillian's waist and pulling her close. He pressed his lips close to her ear. "I love you."

"I love you too," she whispered back.

"Father can't help but agree when he sees the two of you," Whitney exclaimed.

Gillian shook her head. "Not the two of us. That might enrage Father to think I defied him and then brought Alex to rub my defiance in his face." She took a deep breath and turned to face Alex. She knew he was going to disagree, but she also knew her father. "I have to go alone."

"Not a chance," he said flatly.

"Please." She pressed a hand to his chest. "You have to trust me. My father will be unreasonable enough. Your presence will make it worse."

"Trust you, huh?"

She nodded. She knew how hard this was for him. He had not trusted anyone in so long, and here she was asking him to trust in her right after they had just settled matters between them. She had not exactly given him much time to get used to putting faith in her. Then again, she had no choice.

"I trust you," he said. "But that doesn't mean I like you facing Westonburt alone," Alex growled.

"I won't be alone."

"I won't leave her," Whitney interjected.

Gillian did not comment on Whitney's statement. Instead, she wrapped her arms around Alex. "I'll talk to Father, break my engagement with Westonburt, and when I have done everything I can to smooth things over, I'll send Whitney to retrieve you."

"Two hours. Not a second more," Alex grumbled, crushing Gillian to his chest and putting his mouth to her ear. "I mean it. If your sister is not back here in two hours, you can expect me to come crashing through your door."

Gillian didn't doubt his words. She stood on tiptoe and

brushed her lips to his. "Don't worry. Everything will be fine." As fine as it could be, considering what she was about to do and say.

In tense silence, Gillian drove the carriage Whitney had brought to retrieve her. When they neared the house, Gillian saw that Sally and Peter were getting into their coach. Thank goodness. The fewer people she had to worry about the better.

"Sally and Peter are leaving," Whitney cried.

"That's probably best." Gillian smiled reassuringly at her sister. "I'd hate for them to hear Father if he gets too angry when I break off my engagement."

"I suppose," Whitney replied, fidgeting in her seat. "At least Auntie is there, and I'll be there too. We won't leave your side. Don't worry."

Gillian was worried, but not about Auntie or Whitney staying with her. She had to think of a way to get them to leave the house. She needed to speak freely to Father and let him know that Alex knew about the past and was more than willing to stand behind Whitney, even if whoever was threatening them spilled the truth. Gillian pulled back on the reins of the horses to slow their speed.

"Whit, I want you to go home with Auntie."

"Why?"

"I don't want Father to blame Auntie for any of this, and he will if she's there."

"I suppose you're right, but I don't think I should leave you alone."

"Don't be ridiculous," Gillian said, trying to infuse a calming, cheerful note into her quavering voice. "It's not as if Father would beat me."

Whitney raised an eyebrow.

"He has never beaten us," Gillian admonished.

"Not yet. But Lord Westonburt does not seem the type of man to mind hitting a woman. What if they try to force you to marry him today?"

"Then I'll leave the house. I'll be twenty-one in one month. After that Father will have no control over me, and I'll marry Alex."

"You'd be ruined!"

"I hardly think Alex cares about my reputation."

Whitney sighed. "I wish there was someone who loved me so fiercely that nothing and no one in the world could make them relinquish me."

"I love you that way already." Gillian reached beside her and grabbed her sister's hand.

"Thank you, but I was speaking of a man. Anyway, you cannot love two people so much that you would never abandon either of them."

"I can and I do," Gillian replied as their carriage passed the Primwittys' departing one. Gillian waved in response to Sally's grin. She had no doubt Sally would want all the details later.

Before the door to the house was closed behind her, her father appeared in the hallway, lines of anger pulling at his mouth. "Gillian, I want to see you in my study," he snapped, causing her heart to skip a beat.

"Of course." She curtsied respectfully. The moment her father's back was turned she gripped Whitney's arm. "Take Auntie and go."

Whitney nodded and fled up the stairs to retrieve their aunt. Gillian took several deep breaths to calm her rolling stomach, then started toward her father's study. Behind her, she could hear Whitney talking to her aunt, the door to the house being opened by the footman, and then silence filling the air. She sighed in relief. At least she need not worry about her aunt and her sister now. That left Father and Westonburt. She prayed she would face them one at a time.

As she entered her father's study, she cursed inwardly. In the corner, in her father's favorite overstuffed chair, sat Lord Westonburt with a drink in his hand and a cigar in his mouth. A fire roared in the grate, sending a sliver of smoke curling through the air and casting an oppressive heat over the room.

Choosing to ignore Lord Westonburt's presence, she faced her father. "May I speak to you in private?"

"No," he clipped and waved a hand to a chintz chair.

Left with little choice, she strode toward the chair and sat back against the uncomfortable cushion. Sweat trickled down her back from the heat of the room, as well as her nerves. Her father poured himself a drink, swirling the liquid in the glass as if the situation were not at all odd. The ice clanked in the silence until the grating noise drove Gillian to her feet. Tension coiled through her as she glanced between the two men. Whom should she face first? Lord Westonburt was the obvious choice, since she wanted him long gone before she talked to Father.

He rose as if sensing her thoughts, which bothered her. She backed away from him, but he stepped forward and in two long strides closed the distance between them. His fingers curled around her arms, pinching her skin. His face came inches from hers. "You have been a diligent little debutante lately."

She forced her fingernails under his fingers and pried his hand away. "I don't know what you mean."

"Let me enlighten you, sweeting." He hauled her to the settee where he dragged her down to sit beside him. "It's come to my attention that you've been dallying with two other men. I hear the poor American fell into your web, and you ate him up and cast him aside like a spider getting rid of unwanted food."

Her stomach turned at his description, and her breathing, despite her best efforts, increased. Lord Westonburt's gaze lingered on the rise and fall of her chest. His lips curved into a smile. "Lionhurst only wants you because you're mine."

"That's not true," she retorted. Maybe it had been true in the beginning, but it was not now. Alex loved her.

"Did he tell you he loved you? Pour his heart out to you?"

She did not say a word, but heat flooded her cheeks.

Lord Westonburt smirked at her. "Silly fool. He's a rake. How many women do you think have fallen for the same act?"

"You're lying," she insisted, though doubt crept in. Was he still there waiting in the cabin? Did he really love her? She gritted her teeth. He did love her. She knew he did.

"I see you doubt me. Shall I tell you what he said to me at the ball?"

Her heat banged in her ears. "No. You'll just spew

lies." She wrenched her arm free of him, stood and faced her father. "I'll not marry Lord Westonburt, and nothing you can do or say will change my mind."

Her father slammed his glass onto the table sloshing liquor over the side. "You'll marry him."

"I won't."

Her father stood, his face mottled red. "You stupid girl. Westonburt knows about Whitney. If you don't marry him, he'll tell everyone that your sister murdered your mother, and he'll make sure Whitney's life is ruined. Will you do that to your sister? Will you cast her to the wolves?"

Forty-One

GOD. IT WAS WORSE than she had ever imagined. She stumbled to the settee and sat.

Lord Westonburt dropped down beside her, slapping his hand over one of her knees. "Don't be angry at your father, sweeting."

She knocked his hand off her knee. "Do not touch me," she spat, sliding away from him. She turned accusing eyes on her father. "How could he possibly know about Whitney?"

"Sweeting, I can answer that. My father was shagging your mother."

Gillian jerked away from Lord Westonburt. She was going to be sick. She breathed deeply and swallowed until she felt under control.

The sadness in her father's eyes left little doubt to the truth of Lord Westonburt's claim. "The man you saw with your mother was Lord Westonburt's father."

"Why did you never tell me?"

"I can answer that, sweeting. He hates you. You're not even his daughter."

"I'm going to be sick," she mumbled, snatching Lord Westonburt's drink out of his hands. She threw back the contents of the glass, the caramel liquor burning a fiery path down her throat and igniting a flame inside her belly. "Is it true?" She met her father's eyes.

"It's true. But I don't hate you." Her father cast a glare at Lord Westonburt. "I did. For years. Your mother told me the day she died you were not mine. I'd always suspected, but to hear her say it..." He shuddered.

Gillian clutched at her dress. "If you're not my father, then who is?" Her eyes trailed to Lord Westonburt, who was smirking at her. "You don't mean...? That is to say, we—" she motioned a hand between herself and Lord Westonburt.

"Rest easy, sweeting. You're not related to me. Your dear old dad is dead. Been dead for years, according to my dying father's confession. Your mother shagged her father's coachman. The poor sap ended up dead in a carriage accident. She married your father out of *need*, not love."

Gillian's heart wrenched at Lord Westonburt's words and the way her father flinched. The truth explained so much, though. The way Father had always treated her coldly. The way he had done everything in his power to protect Whitney.

"I'm sorry," her father said.

She shook her head. She didn't blame him. How could she? He'd been duped into marriage, then cuckolded and left to care for a child who was not even his. He could have turned her out to the streets, named her illegitimate, but he'd kept her here and done the best he could. She owed him, and she owed Whitney.

"Now you know almost everything, sweeting." Lord Westonburt smiled then as if it were all a game, as if ruining her life gave him pleasure, which it likely did.

She glared at him until his smile faltered. "What else can there possibly be?"

"Don't you want to know how I know about your sweet little sister pushing your wanton mother to her death?"

Gillian nodded wearily.

"Seems my mother had a suspicion my father was shagging another woman. She followed him the night your mother died. Mum saw everything and used it to her advantage."

"How could she possibly have used that night to her advantage?"

"My father was a weak man, God rest his pathetic soul. He told Mummy dearest everything, right down to the gritty details of your illegitimacy. Mum may be a black-hearted wench, but she's a rather smart woman. She used her newly acquired information to blackmail your father."

"Blackmail?" Gillian glanced at her father.

He nodded. "She threatened to tell the *ton* you were illegitimate and that Whitney was a murderer. So I bought her silence."

"For how long?" Gillian whispered, her head reeling from the truth.

"Since the year your mother died."

"You protected me?" She swallowed away a lump of emotion. She had told herself it didn't matter if he didn't love her, but it did. Knowing he had protected her mattered a great deal.

"Of course. As best I could. Until she demanded I betroth you to him." Her father jerked his thumb at Lord Westonburt.

Lord Westonburt smiled. "I suppose this is where I come back in. Father confessed everything on his deathbed to me. Naturally, I took up the reins of blackmail as is my duty and right. So you have a choice, my lady. You can marry me or I'll destroy you and your sister."

"I don't give a damn about myself," she snapped.

Lord Westonburt's eyebrows rose. "Such nasty language from such a lovely lady. You may not care about your own reputation, but can you say the same for you sister?"

He had her. He knew he did. She hated him. Her fingers twitched with the desire to claw out his beady eyes. But she could not do that. What she had to do was worse than maiming. Worse than murder. She would rather be dead. But she was not.

She was going to have to betray Alex to save her sister.

Fourty-Two

ALEX POUNDED THE door until it swung open. He had expected to have to push past a footman, possibly Gillian's father and hopefully Westonburt. Instead, Alex reached toward Gillian.

She flinched backward. Ice filled his veins. "What's wrong?"

"You shouldn't have come."

Westonburt appeared behind her. "It's pathetic of you to chase my fiancée."

"Your fiancée?" Alex didn't care for those words or what they implied.

"But of course," Westonburt replied. "Did you expect something different? Tomorrow she'll be my wife. Perhaps you thought we'd already married?"

He had no idea why Gillian had not broken the engagement yet, but he would sure as hell do it for her. "She's not going to marry you."

"Are you calling me a liar?" Westonburt demanded, coming face-to-face with Alex.

"Gillian, tell him."

"Alex." She stepped toward him, then stopped. Tears streamed down her face. "He knows everything. He's the blackmailer, and he'll destroy my sister."

Alex would kill Westonburt, but first he had to calm Gillian. He reached for her, but she shoved against his chest. Fear curled in his belly. “Gillian, listen to me.”

She shook her head. “I can’t sacrifice my sister to have you. I’d never be happy knowing what I’d done.” She pushed him back until he stumbled out of the open door and into the dark night. “Forget you ever loved me.”

Before he could protest, the door closed with a bang and the lock clicked with finality. He stood for a moment, fuming. He could break a window and get inside, but what good would it do? She was terrified for her sister and would sacrifice herself to protect Lady Whitney.

Alex needed a plan, and he needed one fast. There was no way he could live without her. He jumped on his horse, unsure where he was going to go. And then an idea came to him. She may end up hating him for what he was about to do, but he was betting eventually she would get over it. He prayed he was right.

Forty-Three

ALEX POUNDED ON LADY Davenport's door. When it swung open, he was surprised to see the entrance hall flooded with light. At such a late hour, he had assumed everyone would be sleeping, and his appearance would be the thing to wake them. But he distinctly heard several women speaking, and by the sound of it, they were all trying to talk at the same time.

"Might I help you, my lord?" The butler, if Alex was not mistaken, looked amused.

What the hell was going on in there? "I'm here to see Lady Davenport."

"Yes, indeed. She has quite the turnout of company at this late hour. I'm afraid it may be a while."

Alex shoved past the butler, giving the man a reassuring pat on the shoulder as he stepped into the receiving hall. "I've got to see her now."

He strode toward the voices with the butler on his heels. When he rounded the corner, he came to a stop, dumfounded for the second time in the space of an hour.

"Peter," Alex bellowed, "I assume you have an excellent explanation as to why you're here with Miss Mills."

"Don't be surly with me, Lion." Peter glared. "Miss Mills showed up at my home but an hour ago looking for you."

"For me?" Alex glanced at Caprice. "How in the world

did you end up here in the country and at the Primwittys' to boot?"

Breaking away from Peter, Caprice rushed past Lady Davenport and Whitney to fling herself into Alex's arms and hug him fiercely. "I don't mean ta cause trouble for no one, but I had ta find ye. It took me two days ta track ye here. You've got a right snooty butler. He didn't want ta tell me where he thought ye might be."

Alex glanced at Lady Davenport and was met with a cold gaze. It was nothing compared to the frigid glare Gillian's sister bestowed on him. He set Caprice away from him and faced the women. "I can explain."

Lady Davenport cocked her head. "That's good to know. I would hate to think I wasted my time scheming to get you and my niece together only to find you're a scoundrel."

He laughed at her admission. "I thank you for your help."

Whitney stepped toward him, her hands on her hips. "Not so fast, Lord Lionhurst. What are you doing here? And where is my sister?"

He cast a glance at Caprice, then back to Whitney. "If you'll give me a moment to speak with Miss Mills, I'll explain everything to you shortly."

Whitney and Lady Davenport nodded their agreement. Alex faced Caprice. "Why are you here? Is something wrong with Bess?" He might have ended his arrangement with his former mistress, but he still cared for her welfare. She was a good woman.

"Nothing's wrong with her. She's the one that set me on the path of where ta find ye. I'm leaving London and this life."

The chit had trekked across the countryside and dragged his best friend into his personal affairs to say goodbye. Alex wanted to growl with frustration. "Caprice, I don't have time for long goodbyes. I'm sorry. God speed to you."

"No, silly." Caprice slapped his arm lightly. "I want ta pay ye back for being so nice ta me."

Alex rubbed the back of his aching neck. Women would never make sense to him. "You want to give me money?"

"No, information. Listen ta me, Lord Lionhurst. I've come ta warn ye. Harrison"—Caprice glanced at the ladies and flushed crimson. "Beg pardon, my ladies. I meant ta say Lord Westonburt. He came ta visit me. Banged me up, he did." She pointed to her cut lip and held up a bandaged hand.

Alex curled his hands into fists. He should have killed Westonburt when he had the chance. "What does your visit have to do with Westonburt?"

"If ye'll remember, I told ye he's quite the talker when he's um, er, ye know?"

"Go on." Alex nodded.

"As ye wish. Seems Lord Westonburt knows a secret that he's using to marry Lady Gillian. He's blackmailing her father. I know you've a special interest in the lady. Bess let it slip."

Alex grabbed Caprice's elbow. "Perhaps we should retire to another room after all." If Caprice knew what he thought she did, he did not want her to be the one to spill the secret to Whitney. That was what he was here to do. Better him than a perfect stranger.

Before he could take one step with Caprice, Whitney and Lady Davenport moved in front of him. "Don't even think of taking this woman from this room," Whitney commanded, surprising him with the strength of her voice. "Miss Mills, why was Lord Westonburt blackmailing the Duke of Kingsley?"

"'Cause he knew that the duke didn't kill his wife. The daughter did, and the duke paid dearly ta keep his secret and protect his daughter."

"Do you mean to say that Lady Gillian killed her mother?" Gillian's aunt demanded.

"Gawds, no." Caprice turned to Alex and patted his arm. "Don't worry. 'Twasn't her. I mean ta say the other one did. What's her name?"

"Whitney?" Whitney whispered through bloodless lips.

"Yep." Caprice snapped her fingers and pointed one at Whitney. "That's her. Pushed her, she did. Right into the river and the woman drowned."

Forty-Four

EARLY THE NEXT MORNING, Gillian dressed carefully in black for her wedding. Her clothing fit her mood. With a glance in the looking glass, she grabbed her brush off her dresser.

Her maid frowned at her. “Will you not even let me dress your hair?”

“No,” Gillian replied, gleaning a certain pleasure from the ghastly picture she presented. She patted her hair, smiling at the severe chignon. She turned to Clara and held up the folds of the silk dress. “How do I look?”

“Like you’re in mourning.”

“Perfect.” Gillian nodded with satisfaction.

“What are you mourning on your wedding day, my lady?”

Walking to her bed, Gillian picked up the gown that she had worn yesterday. Clara had tried to take it earlier to wash it, but Gillian had refused to let her. She pressed the gown to her nose, inhaling the scent lingering on the fabric. She could still smell Alex on the material. She would never forget their day or what they had shared. Setting down the dress, she met Clara’s inquiring gaze.

“My wedding.”

Her maid raised her eyebrows. “Wedding nerves.” She nodded as if nerves explained everything.

Gillian sighed. “Go on, Clara. Come to fetch me when

the vicar is here or my aunt and sister arrive."

Before Clara could bob a proper curtsy, a knock resounded on Gillian's door. "My lady," the butler called. "I think perhaps you're needed downstairs now."

So soon? Her stomach clenched in fear. She wanted to run away, find Alex and beg him to forgive her. Instead, she stuck her feet in her slippers, clutched Clara for support and made her way down the hall to the stairs. She could not abandon Whitney or her father.

Midway down the stairs, Auntie's agitated voice reached her ears. Gillian hurried her step toward the library, her brow furrowing at the jumble of raised voices coming from within. What could possibly be going wrong now? She burst through the door and stopped, stunned by the scene before her.

In the far corner, Father and Whitney huddled with their heads together. Father patted Whitney, who spoke between hiccupping sobs. And on the other side of the room, a bald giant of a man struggled to subdue Lord Westonburt, who twisted until Gillian thought his arm might tear from the socket. Alex—Alex was here? She blinked, but he was indeed still here and yanking Lord Westonburt's other arm back behind his back.

"What's happening?" Gillian cried out, afraid to hope, but the possibility was there.

"I'll be back," Lord Westonburt growled, gazing wildly at her. "They can't keep me forever. You can't prove I ravaged that bar wench."

Gillian gasped and looked at Alex. He pointed to the Duke of Primwitty. "He saw the whole thing. Didn't you, Primwitty?"

The duke nodded. "Certainly. But the woman fled when I struggled with you. Didn't see her again until last night when I talked her into pressing charges."

"You filthy liar," Lord Westonburt roared.

He was right on one account. They were lying. The duke had no more seen Lord Westonburt ravish the woman than Gillian had. But there was nothing filthy about the men. They were quite impeccably dressed and ravishing. She smiled with the beauty of fate.

Lord Westonburt lunged for her, but his captor jerked

him back. "You're my fiancée, do you hear me? *Mine.* If you forsake me, I'll ruin your sister. I swear I will."

Alex's fist flew through the air. Lord Westonburt howled with pain as he grabbed at his nose. Blood seeped from between his fingers. "Take him, Constable Stevenson," Alex demanded. "The Duke of Primwitty will accompany you, and Kingsley and I will be down later to verify the whole story."

"Gillian," Lord Westonburt cried as the constable dragged him toward the door.

She met his gaze and prayed he could see just how much she detested him. "I told you I wouldn't marry you."

He gripped the side of the door as the men tried to tug him from the room. "I need you, Gillian. You can't forsake me. Without you, I'll never belong. I'll never be someone."

"But you are someone," Whitney said, stomping past her. Gillian watched in stunned disbelief as her sister marched up to the man who was the greatest threat to her future happiness. "You're a cruel devil and a black-hearted scoundrel. That's why you'll never belong. May you rot in hell." Whitney reached out just as Lord Westonburt's fingers popped away from the door ledge and slammed it in his face.

Shaking with relief and concern, Gillian rushed to her sister's side. "Whit, you don't know what you've just done."

"I know *everything.*" Whitney crushed Gillian to her. "Miss. Mills told me about Mother."

Gillian pulled back with a frown. "Who is Miss Mills?"

"It doesn't matter." Whitney waved a hand in Alex's direction. "He'll explain everything to you later."

Gillian swept her gaze around the room until she found Alex. Walking towards her, he shrugged, a seductive smile pulling at his lips. "It's complicated, my love. But remember, you trust me completely as you asked me to trust you."

"Oh, Alex." She threw herself into his arms. "I'm sorry."

"Shh." He brought her hand to his lips. "I understand.

But I must say you're lucky."

"Am I?"

He nodded. "I've never been good at following dictates."

"Thank God," she replied and pressed her head to his shoulder.

His lips came to her ear. "You can make it up to me later. I'll think of something."

"I've no doubt you will," she whispered in his ear.

A throat cleared beside her, and Gillian released Alex and met her sister's eyes. "I'm so sorry you and Father felt you had to hide the truth from me all these years. Do you hate me?"

"Hate you?" Gillian hugged her sister fiercely. "I love you."

Whitney drew away and looked down at her hands. "But I pushed her. Funny, I still don't remember a thing. I killed our mother."

"No, darling." Gillian reached for her sister and petted her head as she'd often done when they were children. "You ran to help her. You were a child. Don't blame yourself because if you do then I'll have to keep blaming myself for not stopping you when you ran from me. If I had stopped you, Mother would be alive."

She glanced at her sister, wanting to hold her and protect her, but in Whit's eyes she did not see fear, only sadness. "You're not afraid of Lord Westonburt?"

"No. Anyone worth my time won't hold such a thing against me. Give me the chance to take care of myself, Gillie. I'm stronger than you think."

Dear heavens. Whitney knew everything and did not seem to be crumbling under the truth. Gillian was free. She was actually free to think of her own future. She turned back to Alex, wanting to run to him, but she paused at the sight of her aunt and the vicar standing side by side.

"Reverend," she called. "I'm sorry for your troubles, but there will be no wedding today." She shivered at the thought that she might have been married to Lord Westonburt in a few short minutes.

The vicar nodded. "I'll be on my way, then." He did not get a step before Alex grabbed the man's arm.

"Reverend, can you be persuaded to come back to this house in three days to actually perform a wedding this time?"

The vicar's eyebrows rose into a bushy arch as he regarded Alex with curiosity. "And who'll be the happy couple?"

Gillian dropped her sister's hand and reached for Alex. His fingers enclosed her hand, and he squeezed gently. "We will, Reverend," Alex said, his words filling her heart with joy and love.

About the Author

Julie Johnstone is a bestselling author of Regency Romance. She has been a voracious reader of books since she was a young girl. Her mother would tell you that as a child Julie had a rich fantasy life made up of many different make believe friends. As an adult, Julie is one of the lucky few who can say she is living the dream by working with her passion of creating worlds from her imagination.

When Julie is not writing she is chasing her two precocious children around, cooking, reading or exercising. Julie loves to hear from her readers. You can send her an email at juliejohnstoneauthor@gmail.com.

Made in the
USA
Monee, IL

14143493R00169